T·H·E
FEARLESS
RISE

ANI'A MELANIE DUTTON

ISBN: 1490912533
ISBN 13: 9781490912530
Library of Congress Control Number: 2013912746
CreateSpace Independent Publishing Platform,
North Charleston, South Carolina

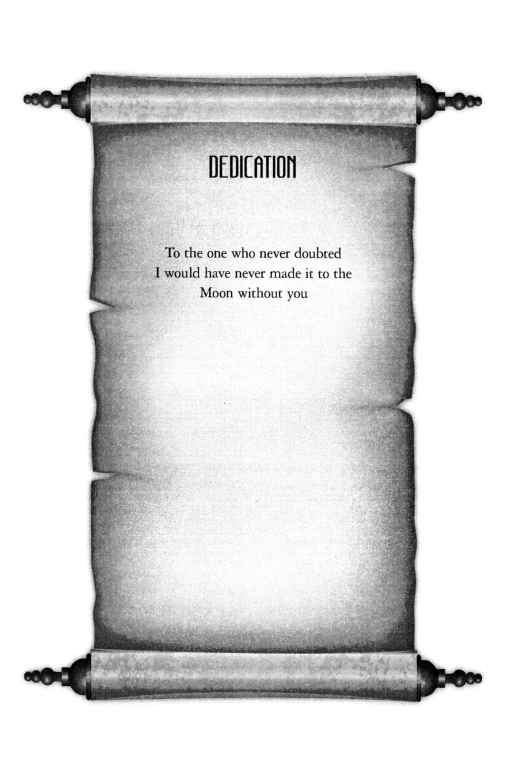

DEDICATION

To the one who never doubted
I would have never made it to the
Moon without you

CHAPTER 1

If you had told me three months ago that I would be the rebel leader of a small group of misfits, I would have laughed in your face. If you had told me that in two more months I would be leading an army of a thousand against five thousand, I would have scoffed. But, as it turns out, fate can be unpredictably peculiar. As the youngest child of four, *and* the only girl, I had a unique childhood. At first we were a land in peace, and swords were carried around more for bragging rights than anything else.

It started out simple enough, as most stories do: with revenge.

Because . . . you see, they took my family from me. And I'd go to hell and beyond to get them back.

Or die on the road . . .

When I was but a little girl running around the house in my underwear, my mother used to force me to sit in front of her so she could brush my deep crimson hair. As she hummed and gently stroked, she would whisper softly to me: "Ariel, someday you will be a person that the earth itself will have to reckon with."

At the time, I considered nothing of it. Having to sit still for more than a minute took all the self-control I possessed. All mothers think their daughters are exceptional and meant for something great.

But my mother wasn't an average woman. I used to hear whispers that she was gifted with the "sight," but I was too young to fully understand what that could possibly mean. Looking back, I realize my mother had seen something in me that I did not. I wonder, now, if she had been aware of the dark cloud hovering over our humble home. I wonder if she had seen the shadowed, twisty journey I would be forced to take in order to claim what would eventually be stolen from me. I lay awake many nights while I fled from certain death, wondering what precisely she had seen while brushing my hair.

Trouble was bound to darken our doorstep sooner or later. Beside the fact that my mother was gifted with the sight, my father was a highly respected, influential man. Not only that, but he was a man who was known to stand his ground and be true to his beliefs. The day he stood up and proclaimed he would not obey the newest proclamations the king had issued was the day he should have dug our graves himself.

I had been proud of him as he stood on the stage and bellowed for all to hear that he would fight for our freedom. My heart had swelled in awe as I elbowed my best friend Logan and whispered, "That's *my* father!"

None of us could have known how word would spread to the bloodthirsty king that my father had been speaking treasonous words. I certainly didn't expect the events that followed.

But, unlike me, my mother had foreseen it.

That's likely why she sent my brother Bryne and me into town early that morning with a long list of errands that would keep us busy well until night-fall. The crystal blue sky and brisk breeze didn't indicate this was anything other than an ordinary autumn day. However, as it progressed, it would soon be seared into my memory as the day that changed the course of my entire life.

It had been a long, exhausting afternoon of running around town try-ing to get everything done for my mother. Finally finishing up, Bryne and I shoved each other up the winding path that would take us home. He had a habit of thinking I would suffer his bullying, but what he didn't understand was that I always got even. You would think my brothers could learn that lesson already.

We lived high up on the mountain, nestled right against the border of the Shade. We were blessed with sprawling acres full of lush green grass, too many horses to count, and bountiful crops. It was a peaceful and breathtak-ingly beautiful land. No fences were needed because the townspeople were too afraid to be so close to the "haunted" forest. The solitude had never been a nuisance; if anything, it was a welcome gift.

We were just about home when we saw the plume of smoke rising through the trees and into the heavens.

Our eyes collided in dread.

Bryne bolted up the hill.

"Bryne!" Panic swelling in my chest, I sprinted after him. "Wait!" Cresting the hill, I was just in time to see our house devoured in flames— and Bryne charging right through the front door.

Not giving myself time to feel the fear hammering at my heart, I plunged right in after him. Holding my arms up to protect my face, I took a lungful of air and instantly regretted it. Flames licked at my face, taunting me with their insurmountable power. The ferocity of the heat almost drove me to my knees. Dense, choking smoke brought tears streaming from my eyes.

"Bryne!" I cried hoarsely, searching desperately for any signs of life within the house. "MOTHER!! FATHER!!!"

I collapsed to my hands and knees and began to crawl forward. Darkness veiled my surroundings. I had to locate my family. I wouldn't leave without them. Smoke filtered into my nose and mouth, wrapping an iron fist around my throat.

I couldn't breathe.

A pair of rugged boots appeared in my vision. Lunging forward, I wrapped tight arms around Bryne's legs. He fell to his knees with a relieved shout. Muffling my cough in his chest, I held on for all I was worth. "Did you find them?" Please let it be that the rest of my family was safe! I couldn't contemplate the thought of losing those most precious to me.

Bryne motioned for me to stay silent. What was going on? Had he found them?

Tears nearly blinding my vision, I uncharacteristically obeyed and followed his lead. Pulling me to my feet, he felt his way towards the outer wall. Coming to a stop in front of a busted up window, he looked over at me apologetically. Hoisting me up, he shoved me through it with little ceremony. I felt glass shred my skin before I landed in a heap on the wet grass. Struggling upright, I rubbed at my burning eyes, trying to clear my vision as Bryne crashed down beside me.

"Ariel. Move." The harshness of his voice and the blatant terror in his eyes sent fire through my veins.

What had Bryne seen in the house?

"I think it is too late for that. I was beginning to worry that my little show wouldn't bring you scurrying back to the nest." The voice was slick with amusement at our expense.

I lifted my eyes slowly.

An Imperial assassin stood in the clearing a few feet away from us.

The markings on his chest plate sent fear raging through me. It was the blood sun gripped in the talons of a dragon—the markings of King Titus. The assassin was part of an elite force that was nearly unstoppable. They shed blood for the king and never asked questions. They were known for their lack of mercy and cold-blooded torture techniques. The man's eyes were pitch black as he observed us. A thick, jagged scar zigzagged down the left side of his face, and I felt pleasure at the fact that someone had managed to land a strike.

Bryne rose to his feet, blocking me from view. "What do you want from us?" My brother's voice didn't waver, and pride shot through me. He had always been the courageous one of us all.

"This isn't your problem, boy. Hand over the girl, and I'll let you live . . ." he paused for effect, "this time."

What did an Imperialist want with me? I was a nobody living out in the middle of nowhere. The only challenge in my life had been to prove to my parents that I was just as strong and brave as the boys were.

Struggling to my feet, I placed one hand on Bryne's back and, with the other, reached for the dagger hidden within my tunic. The dagger had been a gift from Logan on my fourteenth birthday, and it had been a prized possession ever since.

Bryne slowly reached for his sword. "You want her, you'll have to go through me."

The assassin laughed mockingly. "Are you a fool? Do you think you can possibly defeat me?"

"Bryne—" I pleaded.

His head tilted towards me ever so slightly. "Go! Get help. I'll hold him off for as long as I can."

"No!" I screamed, as Bryne dived forward, aiming for the man's heart. I tried to grab the back of his tunic but grasped nothing but air. Bryne and the Imperialist collided with staggering force; the man looked slightly surprised at the skill Bryne so obviously possessed.

Fury and terror raged within me. It wasn't my style to stand by helplessly, but, at this point, my charging into the fray would only distract Bryne. Clutching my dagger with white-knuckled intensity, I watched diligently for my opening. Bouncing impatiently on my toes, I groaned internally. If only I had my quarterstaff, or even my throwing knives . . .

The wait was agonizing. The Imperialist obviously held the upper hand, and Bryne was visibly starting to wear down.

I was quick, I was small, and it was time to make my dent in the fight. "Bryne, DUCK!"

Listening, he ducked and I raced forward. Using him as a springboard, I flipped mid-air and my foot landed a hard kick to the Imperialist's face. Twisting mid-flight, I landed in a ready crouch. Lessons with Logan's father had finally proven themselves useful.

Bryne took the opportunity to slash at the man's chest.

The assassin roared. "Enough of this!"

Screaming, I tried to push Bryne out of harm's way, but the man's sword was quicker.

Bryne fell with a low moan, clutching his stomach. His hazel eyes dimmed as he looked up at me, horror splashing across his face. "Ariel—"

Dragging my eyes back to the Imperialist, I fought the despair that threatened to debilitate me. "I'll kill you!" I shrieked, red splashing my vision.

Bryne fumbled with his sword. With every last bit of his strength, he sunk it into the assassin's thigh. Shock and anger twisted the man's face as he staggered backwards, holding his leg.

"I'll come back for you, girl. Next time you won't be so lucky," he warned.

Sinking next to Bryne, my hands shook over his wound. "Oh, Wehjaeel, no! Don't let him die," I pleaded. "Please, not like this!" I pulled him into my arms and rocked him gently. Watching as the man disappeared into the dark smoke, I choked back tears. "Bryne, please. Just hold on!" Burying my head in his chest, I begged softly for him to live. As if the heavens sensed my sadness, water began to pour from above.

"So much . . ." he struggled to breathe, "so much we haven't told you." His voice began to fade. "You are . . . ready. Be . . . strong." His eyes flashed with pain. "Ariel, don't stop . . . fighting . . . Don't . . . stop . . ."

"No! Don't you dare die on me! Do you hear me? You can't die!" I pulled him against me tighter. His words of caution and instruction failed to hit my ears. "You can't . . ."

His hand wound weakly in my dark hair. "Be . . . strong . . ." With a last, shuddering breath, he went limp in my arms, his hand still tangled in my hair.

"NO! You can't die!" Shaking him roughly, a scream ripped from my throat, shattering the air with my anguish. Ignoring the oozing blood, I rested my cheek against his heart. "I swear to you, brother, I'll kill him."

I don't know how long I sat there holding Bryne, but a frantic voice jerked me out of my trance. "Ariel! We must move—"

Opening my eyes, I peered into the dark brown eyes of Logan. He was kneeling in front of me, cupping my cheek, disregarding the blood and grime that was getting on his skin.

Dazed, I peered over the sooty remains that used to be my home. The frigid rain pelted through my clothes and froze me to the core. Perhaps it wasn't the rain that was freezing me; perhaps it was the numb shock that had settled into my bones.

At that moment I could only see crimson blood, taste bitter sorrow, and smell putrid death.

"Don't touch me, Logan." My voice was lethally quiet.

My parents would be proud when they heard of their son's heroic deeds. That is, if they were still alive. What had Bryne seen in the house before I had arrived? Had he discovered the others?

Bryne had sacrificed himself to save me. It was a debt I would never be able to repay.

Logan leaned forward until his forehead was nearly touching mine. "Ariel, if we don't leave, Bryne's sacrifice will be wasted. The assassin will be back . . ." He didn't need to finish his sentence. I knew the murderer was hiding around here somewhere, dressing his wound. And if I found him, I would not have mercy. "We must go, NOW."

I ignored his pleading. Logan had been my closest friend from before I could walk, but this time he wasn't going to be able to convince me to see reason. I didn't want to fight. I didn't even want to survive.

Most of all, I didn't want to feel the gut-wrenching anguish that was tearing at my heart. If only death had taken me and not Bryne.

Logan's hand wrapped around mine as he gently peeled my fingers off Bryne. Hooking an arm around my waist, he hauled me to my feet. Screaming in rage, I fought him off, but I was no match for Logan's strength.

"Forgive me, Ariel," he whispered desperately in my ear as he threw my kicking and clawing body over his muscular shoulder.

White-hot rage burned through me. How had life turned into this? In a mere hour my home had been burned to the ground, Bryne had been murdered, and the remainder of my family had gone missing. I refused to believe they were dead; my heart couldn't handle that knowledge. Yet Bryne's distressed face flashed in my mind. He had seen something terrible, but what? My life had suddenly turned into bloody chaos, and I wasn't prepared.

Going limp, I sagged in Logan's arms. "Put me down; I'll walk." He hesitated but must have sensed I was done fighting because he let me slide back onto my own two feet.

Intertwining his fingers with mine, he met my sorrowful gaze. "I won't let anyone touch you, Ariel."

I cocked my head sideways and gazed up at him. Promises meant nothing to me at this point. It was almost impossible to push down the waves of anger and pain that threatened to debilitate me. But, if I was to survive, I was going to have to be strong. I was going to have to be like my fierce and spirited mother and my tough and righteous father. "Don't make promises you can't keep," I said quietly, turning around to stare vacantly at where Bryne lay.

He pulled me closer to him and, with a hand on my chin, forced my eyes back to his. "It's a promise I intend to keep. Now, come on." With my hand in his, he propelled me towards the eerie trees of the Shade.

The towering oaks stood like sentinels to an ancient, majestic kingdom. I had heard horrific and wonderful stories of what lie past the protective border of trees, but I had never been ignorant enough to test my mortality by venturing in.

I grimaced and held on tighter to Logan's hand. Fear clawed at my throat. "Logan! Where are you going? We can't go in there!" My words fell on deaf ears.

He didn't glance back at me, just kept yanking me along behind him. "I know someone who can hide you for a while. He owes me a favor," he said tersely. "He won't be able to refuse."

For the past few months, I knew Logan had started keeping secrets from me. Like where he disappeared to for days on end, and why he had such deep shadows in his eyes when he returned. At first I thought perhaps a girl had struck his fancy, but it didn't explain why he had begun to be so overprotective. He had become withdrawn, and none of my incessant badgering had caused him to open up to me. I had taken it all in stride, knowing our friendship wasn't in jeopardy. Logan was the one thing in my life I could count on above all else.

It was obvious, now, that I should have pushed harder to find out what Logan had been getting into. For nothing explained why he was plunging into the land of the Shade without even a tremble. He seemed comfortable with the terrain and didn't pause to look around in confusion at our whereabouts. It was forbidden to step foot on these grounds, a rule even my father didn't disobey. It seemed Logan was deeply involved in a mysterious world I knew nothing about. What had he gotten mixed up in? I knew all of Logan's friends and family, and I knew of no one who owed him a favor. So where was he taking me?

CHAPTER II

The wind shrieked through the trees, the sound chilling. The trees flailed at us, grasping for blood. Terror squeezed my windpipe. What was Logan thinking, bringing us into these woods? We had to be deep in the sacred Shade forest by now. Horror stories were told to us from a young age of the beasts that lived in these trees—of the blood-thirsty tribes that lived in the shadows.

Others whispered that it wasn't beasts that hid in the trees, but creatures of the Olden Times: elves, fairies, and the like. I didn't believe any of the tall tales that were spread, but I did know there was a reason we weren't meant to cross the border.

"Logan—" I started, ready to beg him to take me back. There had to be some other place we could escape to.

He rounded on me and grabbed my shoulders with enough force to leave a mark. "Ariel, you've known me longer than anyone. You're one of the only things I have left in this world that I care about, and if I don't get you to safety soon, I'll be forced to lose you too. I need you to stop fighting this and trust me for the time being. We have a limited amount of time to get where we need to go. Once night hits, it will be too late. So please, *please* just follow me and stop asking questions."

Startled, I swallowed my protests and nodded mutely. Allowing him to pull me forward again, I lost myself in dark thoughts. Minutes slipped by; I became unsure of how much time passed as I followed doggedly after Logan. I felt like I was trudging through quick-sand, each step becoming harder than the last. My eyes burned, and my body ached from being shoved through a window and then leaping into a fight. Could I keep up with his long-legged strides? Logan must have sensed I was lagging, because not seconds later he swung around and scooped me into his arms.

"I can walk—"

He ignored me.

It didn't take long for exhaustion to steal me away into oblivion. But, as sleep claimed me, blood splashed my vision. I saw Bryne's lifeless gaze—felt the terror of watching him fight the man with the scar and relived the feeling of fire against my face.

A scream gurgled in my throat as I jerked into consciousness.

Logan's arms tightened around me. "We're almost there," he whispered. "Then you'll be safe."

Safe? What was the point of safe? My brother was dead. The rest of my family was missing. My entire life had been shattered in hours. I shouldn't be safe. I should be fighting to find the remnant of my family at this very moment . . .

Logan, once again, interrupted my black thoughts. "We're here," he said, tucking me closer to his chest. "He'll take care of you until—"

My chance to argue was taken from me.

"You're playing a dangerous game bringing her here, Logan Gallagher."

I jerked to attention, my hand slipping inside my tunic to reach for my dagger. I was glad I hadn't forgotten it when Logan had dragged me away. What new danger had Logan led me into? Logan shifted me to my feet and kept a muscled arm around my waist.

"I'm here to collect a debt, Fairchild." Logan's voice was cool and crisp. He sounded every bit the man he had become, a man I had not previously seen with my jaded eyes. Where had time gone? When had the young rascal I grew up with melt into this rock-solid man?

An irritated growl sounded from the shadows. "You know not what you ask, boy. Bringing her here was a mistake."

Logan bristled beside me. "You don't have a choice."

I was getting tired of being talked about when I was clearly standing right there. A firm hand still on my dagger, I reached for Logan's hand and tugged. "Logan, let's just go—"

The man in the shadows spoke again. "You go back to your home, and you're as good as dead—just as dead as the rest of your family is."

My family was *not* dead! I simply wouldn't accept it. I turned with a snarl, ready to rip the man's throat out. Logan must have sensed my deadly intentions, because he latched onto my arm and jerked me to a standstill. "You don't want to get into a fight with him, Ariel."

Fury blackened my gaze. "With a coward hiding in the shadows, I don't have time to sit here and argue!" I ripped myself from his grasp. "I'm going to Midas."

A harsh chuckle sounded from behind me. I whipped around to meet a pair of shocking, gold-flecked, sapphire eyes. The stranger had soundlessly moved, standing inches away from me. A scowl coated his features. "You are a foolish child to think you could survive a trip to Midas. I told you . . ." he paused, his gaze searching mine, "your family is dead."

My hands shaking with rage, I gripped my dagger tighter, tempted to strike at him for his heartless words. "They. Are. Still. Alive," I gritted between clenched teeth. "Until I see proof of their passing."

"Ariel—" Logan's voice dripped with warning. Ignoring his desperate outstretched hand, I met the imposter's eyes, steel for steel.

"You are impetuous and foolish. You go stomping into Midas, and you're as good as signing your life away. You will *never* make it out alive."

Condescending. Arrogant. Mule-headed. If I never accomplished anything else in my life, I would enjoy smacking the smug look right off of his face.

Logan tried once again to gain my attention. "Ariel—"

I was exhausted, infuriated, bruised, and quickly losing my common sense. Sitting here arguing was solving nothing. I had an Imperialist to kill—and my family to find. With or without help, I would go to Midas. If I had to go to the throne of the king himself, I would find out what had become of my family.

Logan eased around me, facing off with the man. "Fairchild, I need you to keep an eye on her. I could care less if she *wants* to stay—"

Scoffing, I turned on my heel and began to stalk off the way we had come, not caring to hear anymore. Pig-headed chauvinists. No one was going to *keep an eye* on me! I could take care of myself.

An unfamiliar calloused hand latched onto my forearm and jerked me to a standstill. "Where do you think you're going, Wildcat?"

I was going to regret this later, but the supposed overseer had stepped too far by calling me Wildcat. Lashing out, I slammed my fist into his jaw as hard as I could. I'm pretty sure it hurt my hand more than it hurt his iron jaw.

He didn't even budge; his only reaction was a flash in his eyes.

Refusing to flinch, I glared up into the depthless eyes of the forest dweller. "Fairchild," I spat. Not knowing his first name, all my animosity would have to fit within that one word. I would kill Logan later for trying to hand me over to this behemoth. "Get your hands off of me," I demanded.

Instead of loosening, his fingers tightened and the corners of his lips tipped up in mirth. "Unfortunately, I do owe your friend a favor. So, until he says differently, you're staying with me whether you like it or not."

I went on my tip-toes to peer over his shoulder, but Logan was nowhere in sight.

"That coward." I mentally cursed him.

"Look, I don't need, nor want, your charity. I especially don't need to be looked after. Just point me towards Midas, and we'll call it good," I said, peeved. I was losing daylight, and I needed to get going before I lost all my courage.

An image of Bryne's lifeless eyes flashed in my mind, and I realized I would never lack the will to finish what had been started. I would get justice.

His eye's narrowed dangerously; bending at the waist, he came nose to nose with me before smiling tightly. "I thought you didn't want charity?"

How could one man be so exasperating? I forced myself to take a deep breath while I sized up my opponent.

He had a military shave and clean face, hinting at Imperialist ties. His deep blue eyes proved he had been born somewhere in the mountain provinces. Standing easily over six feet, with broad shoulders and muscular arms, he was obviously no stranger to hard work. A thick scar slashing through his left eyebrow showed he had seen some conflict somewhere. His clothes were nondescript. A sword hung around his hips, and it looked like a weight he was used to carrying. A hilt of a knife poked out of his right boot, and, if I had to wager, I'm sure he had more weapons hidden on his person. He must have intense skills with a blade.

If I didn't loathe him so much, he would be extraordinarily handsome.

As it was, I didn't have a prayer at beating him physically. I was quick and agile, but anyone who walked these woods was bound to be danger- ous beyond all reckoning. Which meant I would have to outsmart him to escape.

"Have I finally managed to shut you up?" Fairchild smirked down at me; he must feel pleased at the thought of gaining the upper hand.

Who *was* this guy? And why would Logan trust him enough to leave me? Tensing, I leaned as far away from him as his iron grip would allow.

I felt more than saw Logan reappear behind me. "Let me talk to her alone for a minute."

"With pleasure." Giving a smug sneer, he shoved me towards Logan and moved noiselessly a couple yards away, leaving us in relative peace.

I whirled around to scowl at Logan, my temper getting the best of me. "What exactly are you trying to do to me here? You're ditching me, like I'm some incompetent child, with a guy who must have been raised by a pack of wolves!"

Logan swept his hand through his hair, looking utterly vulnerable. "Ariel, have I ever led you astray?"

"Yes," I snapped, not feeling a need to be generous. "For example, the time you told me Elves stole young girls at night to eat, and the only way to keep them away was to rub butter over my face before going to bed. Or that time you were *supposed* to be on look-out and said I was all clear . . . I believe I received ten lashings from Madam Thistle for attempting to sneak away with her horse. Not to mention the time—"

"Okay, okay!" He threw up his hands in defeat. "I mean on things that really mattered."

Crossing my arms, I stood my ground defiantly. "I won't stay here and hide like a coward. It's *my* family's lives that are at stake."

Striding forward, he took my hands and squeezed them gently. "I'll do everything I can to find your family, Ariel. I promise you that." He sighed heavily. "*But* I can't go after them towing you along. I'll travel slower because I'll constantly be worried about you. Breaking into the borders of Midas is no small thing. It's never been done before."

I jerked my hands from his. "Logan! You know as well as I do that I can pull my own weight and protect myself. *Your own* father saw to that. I didn't train all those years with him for nothing."

Logan's face hardened at the reminder. It had always been a sore spot between us that his father had spent so much time training me to fight and survive in the wilderness. Logan had been under the impression that I would never need those skills.

My mother had been the one to set her foot down and demand my father send me to train. Another one of those things she failed to mention why I would need to know so badly.

"Please, there is more to this than you'll ever understand. Let me do what I'm best at and find them."

"I'm the better tracker, and you know it," I said stonily. "But go ahead and leave me. As soon as he looks away, I'm gone."

"Ariel! For once in your life don't be so mule-headed and listen to me! You *have* to stay in hiding for the time being, and Fairchild is the only one equipped to keep you safe."

Seething, I took a couple of deep breaths, preparing carefully the best response so he understood once and forever where I stood on this matter.

We were interrupted by a tense Fairchild.

"I hate to intrude on this little soiree, but we are about to have some unwanted company. Logan, if you want to leave, you have to go now."

Fairchild turned to me with an impregnable glint in his eyes. "Let's go, Wildcat." Grabbing my wrist, he yanked me to his side.

"Please, Ariel," Logan whispered before he disappeared into the thick shadows.

Grimacing at my predicament, I allowed Fairchild to drag me behind him. He was silent as a panther drifting through the trees, without even a murmur declaring his presence. I was an accomplished hunter and tracker, so I attempted to use my size and expertise to be just as quiet. However, I still felt like a clumsy child next to his prowess.

I wasn't sure what had spooked him into action, but I felt a deep unease in the air. It was the deadly silence that spoke of foreboding events to come. Fairchild released my hand, probably fairly certain I wouldn't bolt with something chasing us. I carefully inspected the area around me, so that I would recognize the land if I came back through.

As we continued to walk, the land began to change. The trees Logan and I had walked through were gnarled and thick. They had an ancient air about them, almost as if they had seen all there was of the world and intended to see the end of it as well. The forest floor was covered in spongy moss and crackling leaves while no sunlight filtered through the canopy of foliage above.

A trail of iridescent mushrooms became my first clue that everything I knew about the world was about to change. Everything was beginning to come alive with vibrant colors. I blinked when I saw the trees. There was a group of trees that looked like they were made out of pure gold. Smooth and shining, the leaves swayed, creating a quiet song that warmed my heart. From there we passed red, green, and even purple trees, each more magnificent than the last. Honey gold, crimson red, and emerald green were splashed all around, making it a royal feast of color.

Flowers sprang everywhere. I had never seen flowers like these in my life. They were so achingly beautiful, I was afraid to step on a single one. What was this place? Purple and green trees? I was delirious. A place like this couldn't possibly exist.

I quickened my pace to follow closer behind Fairchild. What precisely was hidden within these trees?

A light mist began to drift over us. Hearing a familiar whistle in the air, I managed to dodge seconds before a crudely-crafted knife landed in a tree inches beside me. Fairchild shoved me hard to the side of his invisible path, pushing me directly behind a tree that was large enough to hide ten men comfortably. Blinking, I had to smirk at the fact that he and I were already crouched next to each other, weapons drawn.

I felt woefully under-armed with only a solo dagger to my name. I was relieved when Fairchild shoved one of his extra blades into my free hand. The blades were like extensions to my arms. Instinct took over my fearful mind. I knew these weapons, and I knew how to handle them. With clinical precision, I spun them a few times between my fingers as I forced my breathing to even and my body to relax.

I could do what was needed. This took me one more step closer to Bryne's murderer. I could do this.

Fairchild leaned forward to speak softly in my ear. "I was hoping to avoid this fight altogether, but since I've failed in that aspect, give 'em hell."

Peeking around the corner to scope out what we were up against, my breathing jerked to a halt.

A trio of unearthly pale men with violent red eyes stood in a loose group just waiting for us to poke our heads out like trapped rabbits. Rotting clothes splattered with dried blood hung limply on their skeletal frames. The smell of rot and decay drifted to my nose, and I cringed backwards.

I looked at Fairchild with wide eyes. "Wha—"

"Go for the hearts," was all he said before launching out of hiding with a blood-curdling war cry.

It didn't escape my notice that he hadn't demanded I stay protected behind the tree. A cold sweat broke out on my forehead as I proceeded from hiding. Fairchild was locked into battle with all three of the beings, but as soon as I broke from hiding, one of them skittered my way.

Kill or be killed. The phrase didn't really put my heart at ease. I felt the bore of red eyes through my skull before snapping out of my reverie. Knives at the ready, I waited for the thing to get closer before throwing myself forward. Diving between its gangly legs, I sliced at the backs of its knees. With a screech, it brought its razor-sharp sword down, nicking at my left leg. Hurling myself to my feet, I took advantage of its momentary lapse of balance and dove straight for the heart.

I earned a thin slice through my leg, but I hit my target. Hot blood sprayed my face, and I winced at the contact. Blank surprise flashed across the creature's face as it fell to its knees. Yanking my dagger from its chest, I forced my mind to detach and then slit its throat for good measure.

Stepping over the crumpled heap, my eyes narrowed in on the battle before me. Fairchild had already dispatched one creature, then quickly disposed of the other with a flick of his wrist.

I closed my eyes as the head detached and fell with a thunk.

Turning away from the carnage, I stumbled a few paces away. I could faintly hear the sound of running water, and I blindly ran in the direction of the noise.

Chaos reigned in my head as tree limbs whipped at my face and snagged my clothing, attempting to slow me down. I ran straight into the creek the second it came into view. It was deeper than I would have imagined.

Falling to my knees in the icy water, I started scrubbing at the blood on my hands and arms. It was splattered on my clothing, clumped in my hair, and clotted under my fingernails. I couldn't scrub at it hard enough. Raking my nails over my skin, I shook with the need to get all traces of blood off my body. Dunking my head under water, my tears mingled with the crystal water droplets.

I had been trained at an early age how to take care of myself. I had been trained to live out in the wilderness and survive for days without food and water. I had never been trained to see so much blood and death.

Death I caused by my own hands.

"You stay in that water much longer and you'll die."

I just couldn't seem to get away from the man.

"Come on. Get out. I don't want to explain to Logan that I let you die of hypothermia."

I hated him. It was the only explanation for the rage that burned through my veins. I would beat the tar out of Logan for handing me off to this monster.

Fairchild splashed into the water with a growl. Grabbing me by the nape of my neck like a wayward kitten, he tugged me upright and directed me out of the stream. I was torn between fighting him, screaming, or just breaking down and crying until numbness overtook me. Weariness won. I collapsed on the bank and curled up in a tight ball. I hated feeling weak, but what I hated more was the fact that he was a witness to my complete breakdown.

Wrapping tight arms around my knees, I shook with bone-wrenching shivers. How had my life turned so upside down? My family missing. Bryne dead. Logan's bizarre behavior. Killing creatures I didn't even have a name for. I choked down my rising hysteria and hid my face from the perceptive gaze of the man staring down at me. I watched from the corner of my eye as he turned around and paced away, affording me a small amount of privacy.

It was time to grow up, to stop acting like a child who couldn't handle the world. I had my family to find. After they were safe . . . *then* I could fall apart. My fingers dug into the mud as I pushed myself to my feet. Wringing out my clothes as much as I could, I walked over to where Fairchild leaned insolently against a crimson tree.

"I'm ready," I said.

He nodded curtly, straightened his tall frame, and without a word began another trek deeper into the mysterious forest.

CHAPTER III

"Another couple miles and you can rest," Fairchild informed me softly.

I didn't look up to meet the gaze that I knew was burning into me. Trudging after him, I kept my eyes on the uneven ground. For the past hour we had walked without talking, and the silence was grating on my nerves. "What's your name?" I needed a distraction from my dark thoughts, and if bothering him was my only option, so be it.

"Not important."

I flicked my gaze up to stare at the back of his head. How hard was it to give a person your name? "Must be something embarrassing." I paused to snicker. "A girl's name, is it?"

The growl deep in his throat was rewarding. "No."

"Then why won't you tell me?" I needled, probably enjoying his discomfort a little too much.

"Why does it matter?" he asked.

"Marian? Francine?" I swallowed down my smile when he glared at me over his shoulder. "Come on, it truly can't be that bad?"

"If I tell you, will you promise to shut up?" he bargained.

I grinned. He failed to specify how long I needed to remain quiet. "Yes."

"Samuel."

Samuel Fairchild. It had a nice ring to it. Which really was a shame. It would have been so much better if it had been something humiliating.

I waited a good five minutes before I spoke again. "You always so charming?"

He shot me a dark glance. "I thought we had an agreement."

"I gave you five minutes of pure, uninterrupted silence. What more could you need?" I asked. I strayed into silence as I struggled to climb over a fallen tree. Who knew the earth could grow trees this massive? Skidding down the other side, I landed with an oomph. Pain lanced through my leg. Biting down hard on my lip, I pressed a palm against the gouge on my thigh.

My hand gleamed scarlet when I pulled it away. Grimacing, I swiped it off on my grimy shirt.

I must look like a crazy person.

Bloodied, torn, and singed clothing. My hair a riot of snarls and curls. Soot and scratches covered my entire face. With my fair coloring, I probably looked like a bloody ghost.

"You coming, Wildcat?" Fairchild questioned, pausing mid-stride.

Was it possible to hate a man more by the minute? Throwing him a haughty stare, I impatiently motioned him to move on. Chuckling under his breath, he continued walking.

A vibrant, sapphire, heart-shaped flower caught my attention. In a trance I paused and reached for it longingly. My eyes had to be playing tricks on me; it looked deceptively like the heart bloom was *beating*.

A tanned hand whipped out and snatched my wrist mere millimeters from grazing the silky exterior of the flower.

"If you value your life," Fairchild breathed, "back up. Now."

Trembling slightly, I allowed him to guide me backwards. What was the big deal anyway? But the way he held me cautiously against him, and the purposeful calmness of his voice, told me this was no joke.

Once we were safely a few feet away, he released me like I was on fire. Catching my balance, I looked at him warily.

He didn't waste any time in explaining. "One touch is all it takes to drop a 300-pound man. After the worst twenty-four hours of your life, you just stop breathing." He turned and began walking again. "There is no cure."

Casting a fearful glance at the seemingly innocent flower, I winced. Make that the third time I was almost killed today. Jogging to catch up, I fell back into step, following his broad shoulders. We shared an uneasy silence until he abruptly stopped.

"We're here," he announced.

After five hours of incessant walking, you would think *here* would be a little more spectacular. There was absolutely nothing here, not even a fire pit to claim his pathetic excuse of a hideaway. He gave a slight smile and pointed upwards, waiting for me to follow his gaze. Tilting my head back, I felt my jaw drop in astonishment. A miniature castle had been built between three goliath trees. No matter how far up I looked, I couldn't see the top of this ostentatious tree house. How had he managed to build such a unique masterpiece? "How—"

He cut me off with a lazy shrug. "It was a gift." He started towards the tree and shot me a serious look. "Stay here." He paused and added as an after-thought, "And whatever you do, *don't* touch anything."

Sticking my tongue out at him, I crossed my arms and tapped my toe impatiently. I watched as he climbed. His muscles flexed as he pulled him-self upwards with confidence. Getting into a tangle with him would prove to be deadly; I was going to have to get creative to get away.

He flipped himself gracefully over the railing and threw a rope ladder back over the side. What a show off.

Taking a firm hold of the flimsy ladder, I hauled myself up with a groan. I had never been so battered in my life, and the aches were starting to scream their protests at me. Taking a firm hold of the railing, I pulled myself over, hiding a wince of pain.

Samuel's eyes narrowed, but he didn't say anything. I watched as he rolled up the ladder and tied it to the railing.

"You can never be too careful in these trees. What we encountered back there is the least of our worries," he said.

I shivered at his foreboding tone. How in the world could those creatures be the *least* of our worries? They had been gruesome and terrifying, and I would never forget that smell . . . "What in the world is this place?" I asked, wrapping my arms around myself. "The trees are multicolor, the flowers are killers, and the inhabitants—"

Fairchild turned and walked around the balcony to a door that led inside the tree castle. "There is a reason few dare to venture past the old forest. The Shade is forbidden with good cause." Opening the door, he ushered me inside. "Without a guide, you are as good as dead."

My eyes swept over his abode. The first thing I noticed was how pristine everything was. The room we walked into must be where he spent a good amount of time. A brick fireplace took nearly one entire wall, and in front sat two rocking chairs. Odd choice for the type of man Fairchild seemed to be. A desk sat nestled in one corner, with papers and maps spread all across it. Papers were tacked on the walls and sprawled across the floor. What was he searching for?

He didn't give me a chance to keep looking; with a firm hand on my back, he propelled me forward towards a spiral staircase. Climbing the stairs, we walked down a long hallway with at least half a dozen different doorways. What did one man need with all of these rooms? And was that another staircase leading to yet another level?

Pushing open a door, he led me inside. The room was larger than a miniature cottage. An intricately carved, wood-framed bed was the focal point of the room. A plush quilt and several plump pillows were already calling my name. A wash-basin and full-length mirror rested in one corner of the room. An oak armoire, which matched the bed, took up the other wall.

"I hope this will be okay for the night. I'll bring you some water if you want to wash up."

I smiled at him, my eyes lighting up with pleasure. "Yes, please."

He nodded, a distant look entering his eyes before he disappeared. Wandering further into the room, I resisted the urge to sit down. Once I did, I wouldn't move again for the rest of the night. I wandered over to the mirror and stared at my reflection in distress. My eyes were sunken yet restless—skittish to the tiniest movement. My hair had collected twigs, leaves, and clumps of dried mud. My shirt was stiff with dried blood, and from there I shied away from further inspection.

Fairchild returned, carting water and an armload of clothes. He dropped the clothes on the bed in a careless heap. "These should be close to your size. Get cleaned up, and I'll make us something to eat."

And with that he was gone.

Gingerly peeling off my clothes, I bit back a groan. Teeth clenched, I dipped the rag in water and tried to clean up some of the dried blood. I was going to need to ask for some bandages and salve. The cut on my leg looked sickening.

I cleaned up as best as I could before inspecting the clothes he had delivered. They were unlike anything I had ever seen before: a pair of soft leather pants that fit like a glove, and a silky white dress that went over the top with two slits in the side. The dress and pants allowed my legs room to move for the next time I found myself in a fight. Where had he come across such exquisite clothing? Next, I pulled on thick socks and knee-high boots.

Slipping a dagger in each boot, I grinned at my expression. I looked like a warrior—someone who was ready to fight to the end and reclaim all that had been stolen. I finally looked like I felt.

Ready for war.

I tip-toed down the stairs as quietly as if I was hunting elk. My intention was to make it to the maps I had seen earlier before Fairchild discovered my absence. Peeking around the corner, I breathed a sigh of relief at the sight of an empty room. Luck was on my side tonight.

Sneaking forward, I began a quick search. The maps were composed of ancient, thin parchment that threatened to crumble under the lightest touch. The markings were in a language I couldn't decipher, and the areas they depicted were places I had never even heard of. Were these maps of areas within the ten realms? I knew the Shade spread its way through all the kingdoms; could these possibly be maps of the Shade itself? Where had he acquired all these maps, and for what reason did he need them? Questions boiled in my mind.

Those endless questions were going to prove useless, though, for nothing looked as if it would lead me to Midas.

"Find anything useful?"

Well, it looked as though my exploration mission was over. Face devoid of expression, I dropped the maps in my hand with fake confidence and turned to face him. "Not particularly."

Smirking, he glanced at me before his eyes wandered over the mess I had made of his desk.

"You try running off, Wildcat, and you're as good as dead. So get that idea right out of your head," he said, a dangerous glint sparking in his eyes.

He obviously wasn't used to being disobeyed. Too bad reality was about to come crashing down on his arrogant head, because I was leaving tonight whether he liked it or not.

"Whatever you say, Captain," I replied, sarcasm dripping off my words. I only had to deal with the bossy man a couple more hours before I was free.

His eyes squinted in agitation, but, before he could provide a snarky comeback, he was interrupted.

"SAMUEL!" A frantic male voice roared from outside.

Hand reaching out for my arm, Fairchild froze into a granite statue. His eyes swung to the reinforced door.

"SA-MU-ELLL!" The man yelled, louder this time while his fists pummeled the door. "They're coming! Get out! Get out now!" Silence reigned for a tense few seconds before a raspy whisper slithered under the door. "Run, Samuel . . . run! And don't look back."

Wide-eyed, I gaped at Fairchild. What in the world was going on now? A slight tremor rippled through him before he vaulted into action. Absolute silence pounded from outside while Fairchild fled from the room. Who? Who was coming? The incessant questions and constant unknowns were starting to get on my nerves.

Fairchild came bursting back in with two fully-loaded packs. He flung one at me, and I caught it by reflex and slung it over my shoulders. The weight was familiar and comforting. It reminded me of Logan's dad handing me a pack and telling me I had five days on my own and had better make good use of it. I missed those simple days. Now it was a sheer fight for my life, and I hated the fear that clawed at me.

I gasped in surprise when Fairchild yanked me forward by my forearms. "Whatever happens, however you feel about me, when we step out that door, you have to do exactly what I say when I say." I tried pulling back a little, but he lifted me into the air and shook me like a rag doll. "I'm serious! I can't guarantee your life unless you follow me step for step."

"What's out there?" I shrieked, my feet kicking for solid ground.

"A squadron of Eagles has been deployed from Midas."

Ice flooded my veins. Eagles were the deadliest soldiers that the ten realms had ever seen. Worse even than Imperialist assassins. You wouldn't know they were there until you were looking up at them from the ground. Entire armies had fallen to the strength of the Eagles. Composed of brute men who enjoyed nothing more than seeing blood on their swords, they knew only death and how to inflict it. "How—"

"Move," Fairchild hissed, dropping me back to my feet.

With steely eyes and steady hands, he threw the ladder over the edge of the balcony. Allowing him to assist me, I took a shaky hold on the ropes and climbed down as fast as my trembling body would allow. Sliding the last five feet, I landed with a thud. Fairchild was already beside me by the time I caught my balance. I watched with impassive eyes as he yanked the ladder down and hid it under the foliage.

Nimbly, he pulled out a piece of rope from his back and tied it around me tight enough to break my ribs. Then he looped it around his wrist. I didn't try to resist. At this point I was past trying to fight. If we made it through the night, I would owe him a lot more than just my life.

"Ariel." His voice drove my eyes to his.

"Yes?" Was that my voice? I sounded like I was being strangled.

"Whatever happens in the next few hours, don't stop running. If I don't get you to Airis, I know they'll find you. I'm sure Mace has already sent out scouts looking for us."

Nothing he had just said made any sense whatsoever. However, before I had a chance to ask who he was talking about, he took off sprinting. My only choice was to keep pace or be dragged.

After half an hour at steady breakneck speed, my lungs were on fire. Wheezing for air, I struggled to follow him through the dense trees. Purple, green, and gold blurred together until I wasn't sure what was what anymore. The only sure thing I knew was that, at any second, I was going to be sick, and it wasn't going to be a pretty picture.

"You're doing great, Wildcat," Samuel called back, not even looking to see if I was still alive or not.

The rope pulled taunt as I lagged behind. He showed no signs of strain; obviously I wasn't in as good as shape as I had once believed. "Fairchild . . ." I puffed, "I can't—"

He looped around until he was running right next to me. "You have to, Ariel." He wrapped an arm around my waist and swung me left to avoid a low hanging branch. "You have to stay alive to find your family."

Bryne. I had to avenge Bryne. I had to get to Midas. My brothers and my parents needed me to stay alive.

And for now, Samuel Fairchild was my only chance.

Breathless, I nodded my head at him, signaling I would march on for as long as I could. With a wild grin, he took off in front of me again.

"I knew you had it in you, Wildcat!"

I'd better have some sort of endurance in me, or an Eagle was going to catch up and gut me.

As night began to descend, the forest slowly transformed into a glimmering wonderland. Lightning bugs zipped by in a merry frenzy, buzzing joyfully at each other. The trees were starting to emit a soft glow, lighting our path perfectly. Flowers sparked as we brushed past, and the moss whistled with each step we took. How could this land be so breathtakingly beautiful and dangerous at the same time? If someone had told me this place existed, I would have scoffed.

But seeing it with my own eyes . . .

It was a dream-world come to life.

I slammed into Samuel hard. I hadn't even seen him stop, I had been so consumed with the night life around me. "What—"

He cut me off with a warning look. Yanking out a wicked-looking curved blade, he sliced the rope binding us together and pressed the knife into my hand. "Run, Ariel, and don't stop until Mace finds you."

"I don't understand," I whispered. "Why are you not coming?"

He shoved me hard, nearly knocking me over. "We don't have time for this; they've almost caught up to us. Get moving. Now."

It seemed cowardly to just leave him standing there. He didn't have a chance against an entire squadron. How could I live with myself, knowing I was leaving a man to die while he was trying to protect me? His eyes softened a tiny bit, almost as if he could sense the war raging inside of me. It was uncomfortable, the way his eyes slowly ran across my face. He looked like he was picking my thoughts straight out of my head. No one in my life had ever looked at me the way he was now, reading me all the way to the shadowed part of my soul.

"Please go, Ariel." He pushed me again, gently this time. "Find your family."

I nodded slowly. It's what everything came down to, wasn't it? My need to find my family. I wouldn't abandon them to death, not even if there was little chance for them. And if that meant leaving Samuel behind, it would be something I would have to live with. Decisions. Always so many decisions.

He sighed heavily as he pulled his sword free. "I've lived a dark life, a life that has gone on for too long already. This is almost mercy, Ariel. I'm asking you to let me do this."

I had always hated goodbyes, but this would be a moment I would never have the luxury of forgetting. Blinking away moisture, I took a slow step backwards. Thank you was so inadequate; he was giving his blood for me, and I was running away.

"Please . . . go . . . before it's too late."

And so I ran.

Each step more agonizing than the last, I held the knife like it was my last link to sanity as I ran blindly. How could I have just left him there? What kind of person did that make me? Sure, I thought he was arrogant and bossy. But did that give me the right to allow him to forfeit his life?

I skidded to a halt, fighting for air. Leaning over, I braced my hands on my knees and tried to ignore my whirling thoughts. Bryne wouldn't have left anybody when a battle was about to spark to life. My father had taught us courage, not self-preservation.

Courage. Whatever the sacrifice it required, no matter the consequences, always choose courage.

Stomping in frustration, I loosened my grip on the knife in resignation. The decision had been made long before the occasion arrived. I wouldn't let my family down by being a coward.

I was going to need some supernatural help on this one, for Eagles weren't known to leave survivors. "Give me wings, Wehjaeel," I pleaded, as I took off back the way I had come. "Please."

I heard the clang of steel and smelled the sharp tang of blood long before the men came into view. Skirting around the trees, I pulled another knife from my boot and assessed my opponents.

Samuel fought valiantly, and, by the two dead men at his feet, I would say he was holding his own just fine. I heaved a sigh of relief seeing he was still standing. Mesmerized by his powerful fighting style, I pressed tightly against the tree I was hiding behind. He was splattered in blood, but, from my vantage point, it didn't appear he had any mortal wounds. Just who exactly *was* this man? The way he parried and landed blows, it was almost as if he knew their exact training.

It couldn't be.

I shook my head roughly to clear the vile idea from my thoughts. I had bigger problems to deal with than figuring out his sordid past. Three men remained alive, and, because they were all focused on Fairchild, it gave me the perfect opportunity.

A beast of a man kept making wide circles around the fray. If I could just injure him enough to stop him from joining the other two soldiers against Fairchild, it might turn the tide . . . I would probably be killed instantly if I just rushed him. I looked up and studied the tree I hid behind; it had enough low-hanging limbs I could probably climb up without detection, and then drop down . . .

It was stupid. Reckless. And it might just work.

It was my only chance of not being sliced open right away. Dropping my pack, I returned one knife to my boot. Clamping the other between my teeth, I hauled myself up the first limb. Inching to my feet, I grabbed the next branch and swung upwards. Sliding out to its end, I fought for balance. I was now directly above where the man continued to pass, a manic smile plastered to his face. I only hoped I didn't miss, face-plant on the ground, and earn a sword in the back for my efforts.

With Samuel's knife in my hand, I clenched my teeth and waited as the man came closer and closer. Twelve feet. Six feet. Four feet. A few inches. A mere breath.

He reached my target point too soon, and, before I could think twice, I swan-dived out of the tree and crashed into the oaf with a loud screech. For a second it was like the world froze. I ceased to breathe as the scene came into perfect clarity. I was sprawled on top of a man whose eyes alone looked like they could murder.

Samuel's head snapped up to stare at me in wide-eyed terror. I could his hear his furious and terrified thoughts miles away with just one look into his bottomless eyes. The two men fighting him paused in astonishment that some wild-looking female dared to intervene in what was obviously none of my business.

The air slammed back into my lungs painfully.

"ARIEL!" How could there be so much pain and anxiety packed into one screamed name? I forced myself to focus and not meet his eyes; I had created a problem that I needed to solve—fast.

The soldier recovered in a blink of an eye. I pulled my hand back to land a deadly blow, but, before I was even close to his heart, he bucked me off and recovered his sword. Out of the corner of my eye, I saw Samuel fighting his way in my direction, but his opponents sensed his desperation and flagging focus. Flying to my feet, I deflected a bone-crunching blow. Digging my feet into the ground, I met the eyes of my would-be murderer.

He grabbed my raised arm, nearly wrenching it off. "You're out of your league, little girl," he rasped, revealing a row of crooked and chipped teeth.

I should have stabbed him when I had the chance. Twisting my arm free, I threw a hard elbow to his jugular and scrambled backwards. My arm spiked with pain. Holding it close to my body, I prayed that it wasn't dislocated. Reaching for the other knife in my boot, I twirled it in my hand as I tried to predict his next move.

The man was a walking zombie. Scars and burns spread across his face and down his arms. His nose was crooked and deformed. How many times had someone broken it? His hair looked like someone had taken garden shears to it. I guess appearances didn't matter when all you lived for was to kill innocent people.

"You really should have your mother stop cutting your hair," I called lightly, hoping to spark his fury. I heard Samuel choke back laughter somewhere to the left of me, but I didn't dare glance his way.

The man's eyes narrowed dangerously as he advanced towards me, tossing his sword up and down like an apple. Taking a chance, I drew back my arm and let one of my blades fly. While he was dodging, I charged forward and jumped, barely managing to grab hold of the branch I had spied out.

Using my momentum, I kicked him hard in the chest before swinging up into the tree. I may be small, but I had never been more proud of my speed. Clenching my teeth, I ignored the searing burn in my shoulder and climbed higher in the tree.

The man circled under the tree, his curses drifting up to me, causing a grim smile on my part. Straddling the limb I was sitting on, I rested against the trunk for a split second. Samuel had killed another one of the soldiers, and, by the looks of it, he was about to dispatch the other one.

"You gonna hide up there like a coward?"

My eyes drifted back to the pacing Eagle below. Hiding seemed like a really good idea at this point. That was, until he decided to start climbing up after me. "Now would be a really good time to show up, Samuel," I muttered, scurrying up another couple of branches. Maybe climbing the tree hadn't been such a wonderful idea after all; I had effectively trapped myself.

"Ariel!" I looked down and winced at the alarm on his face. My eyes danced around, trying to find some sort of escape. The closest tree would still be quite a leap. I was out of options; the soldier had just about reached my precarious location.

Vaulting forward, I caught a handful of leaves as I began to plummet down. Screaming, I clawed at air as I fell. I slammed hard into a thick branch. Catching it with one hand, I swung limply in the air.

"ARIEL!!" Samuel was standing beneath me, breathing hard. "Grab the branch with your other hand, Wildcat, and pull yourself up," he coaxed.

I nodded weakly. I didn't bother to explain that the arm just hanging there was refusing to cooperate. Moving it an inch felt like someone taking a branding iron to me. My eyes caught sight of the Eagle who had stalked me in the tree now sneaking up behind Fairchild. "Sa—"

Samuel slammed his sword backwards into the man's chest without ever looking behind him. Bewilderment flitted across the man's face as he fell to the ground. Fairchild's eyes never left mine. "Come on, Ariel," he pleaded.

I dug my nails into the bark, flaking gold glitter onto my skin as I began to slip.

Fairchild didn't waste another second. Scaling the tree, he was beside me in an instant. Balancing on the branch below me, he held out his arms. "Drop." It was an order to be obeyed.

He didn't need to worry; I couldn't have disobeyed if I had wanted to. Plummeting like a rock, I smashed into him with a low groan. He held me tightly to his chest for a long moment. "Why in the world did you come back?" he hissed, pulling back to read my face.

"Don't let it get to your head," I said, not meeting his burning gaze. "Now, let go."

Immediately his arms disappeared, and I hated myself for the regret that twisted through me. I shouldn't be feeling safety in his arms. I shouldn't be feeling content. The only thing I should be feeling was irritation. Cradling my arm to my chest, I slid down the tree, carefully refusing his help. I had had enough of depending on him. If I couldn't take care of myself, I would never make it to Midas.

When I reached the ground, I looked myself over. I was coated in gold and green glitter. The trees shed glitter? Seriously? Could this place get any stranger? I was now a walking beacon for anything else that felt like killing me tonight. "Wonderful."

Fairchild landed next to me with an envious amount of agility. "It might be dislocated."

"You think?" I snapped, turning away from him.

I felt him move closer to where I stood. "We need to get moving, so sit down and let me look at it."

"You have such an impressive bed-side manner," I said, slumping to the ground. Bracing my back against the tree, I watched him warily. He crouched next to me and, with a gentleness I didn't believe possible of him, examined my shoulder.

"It's not dislocated, and it doesn't look broken. If I'm correct, he just twisted it nearly to the point of breaking. I'll make you a sling until we get to Airis. Once there, Mace can take a better look at it."

As he moved away to create a sling, my eyes took in the carnage around us. How had he managed to kill all six Eagles? I watched Samuel with a new awareness. What had Logan known about him that I didn't?

There wasn't a man in this world that should be able to do what he just accomplished.

"Stop looking at me like that," he demanded as he knelt next to me.

"Like what?" I asked. He didn't meet my eyes as he tucked my arm carefully into his makeshift sling. His hand lingered on my shoulder until I repeated my question. "Like what?"

Rising to his feet, he stomped over to where he had hastily dropped his pack. Fiddling with the straps, he kept his electric eyes away from mine. "Like I've suddenly grown horns."

I couldn't prevent the laughter that bubbled past my lips. "Are you kidding me?" I struggled to my feet and retrieved my own pack. I smiled briefly. "Fairchild, I *always* thought you had horns."

His head jerked up in astonishment, and for a split second he half grinned. In a blink the smile was replaced by his usual stoicism. "Come on, Wildcat, let's get out of here."

"No arguments here," I said, avoiding the puddles of blood. I was so tired of seeing dead bodies.

"That'll be a first," he called over his shoulder.

Rolling my eyes, I followed after him. At least we weren't running.

CHAPTER IV

M ace wasn't a thing like I expected him to be.

I expected a burly old guy, with scars to spare and suspicious squinty eyes—his best friend a bottle of whiskey. In fact, to be quite honest, I expected a human.

He found us sprawled out at the edge of a viscous-looking river taking a much-needed breather. I was sitting on a boulder, my feet kicking to a silent beat while throwing twigs at Fairchild when he appeared.

And when I say appeared, I mean appeared.

I blinked, and within the next instant there was someone standing next to Samuel.

"She isn't exactly what I expected," the person mused, taking me in before turning to Samuel. "Hello, brother. Master Cyrus said you would need to be fetched."

Closing my eyes, I counted to five before peeking. Sure enough, the "man" still watched me, his expression looking like I had some mental issues.

Samuel and the newcomer whispered while I just gawked. It was the ears I noticed first. Pointy. They were, without a doubt, no matter how many times I blinked in dumbstruck awe, pointy. Silver-blonde hair spilled over his shoulders and down his back. A pair of lavender eyes shifted my way occasionally as he spoke to Samuel. Willowy and slender, he was impeccably dressed in pearlescent white. He had an otherworldly beauty about him. With one look, he could trap any girl he wanted under a spell she wouldn't be able to understand but wouldn't bother questioning.

"Hey, Wildcat, you all right?" Fairchild asked, a wicked gleam flashing in his eyes.

Slamming my mouth shut, I tried to stutter out a semi-intelligent answer. "Uhm . . ."

Samuel gestured to his new companion. "This is Mace. He has come to travel with us to Airis," he announced, as if this were an everyday event.

"He's a—" I started, swallowing hard, trying to clear the cotton out of my mouth. Since the moment I had stepped into these enchanted woods, my entire world had been shook up and torn to pieces. Then it had been handed back to me with a dare to try to make sense of it now.

A smile lit up Mace's face; it was so brilliantly breathtaking I was forced to squint from the power of it. "I am an elf, Ariel. When Master Cyrus spoke of you to me, I assumed you knew more of our world. Obviously, he left out some key details." His voice was soft and melodic, but each syllable rang with music.

My eyes drifted to Samuel. "Master Cyrus?"

Fairchild nudged Mace aside so he could stand next to me. "If there is one thing you should know is that when you're in the Shade, myths and legends are all that exist. Nothing is impossible. This is a world that has not caved to the changing of times." He touched my knee reassuringly. "When we get to Airis, I promise everything will be explained."

I cast another long look at Mace, my eyes lingering on his ears. "I miss the world I used to know," I said softly. Avoiding both of their eyes, I slid off my perch and jerked up my pack with my good arm. "I'm ready."

Or at least I desperately hoped I was.

We traveled for three days, stopping for no more than a few minutes at a time. Mace would disappear for hours at a time, but Samuel never seemed to lose his bearings. He also never asked Mace where he took off to for such lengthy amounts of time. I couldn't help but be curious about the relationship between the two and the unwavering trust they shared. How had Fairchild ever come into contact with elves, and why was he even living in the Shade in the first place?

"You're awfully quiet, Wildcat," Samuel remarked, dropping back to walk next to me.

"I'm sure that just devastates you," I quipped.

He shrugged. "Silence doesn't suit you well."

I glanced at him out of the corner of my eye, stifling exasperation. I was weary to the core. Since the moment I had arrived to see my burning home,

I'd been running, and days later I was left with more questions than answers. As fun as annoying him was, I just wasn't up to the task. Give me a day of uninterrupted sleep, and it might be a different story.

Mace did his maddening appearing thing next to me. "Grab a hold of her," he instructed Samuel. "We're at the gate."

He was joking, right? We were standing in the middle of a clearing of trees. Everywhere I looked was trees, trees, and *more* trees. No gate in view. No sign of any type of civilization.

Samuel hooked his hand under my elbow obediently. Mace stepped forward. Brushing his hand across thin air, he mumbled something under his breath. Mace reached back and yanked us forward.

It felt as if I were falling through sheets of ice water. My world was shoved into abrupt darkness. Screaming for air, I latched onto what I hoped was Samuel as we continued to plummet through nothingness. We slammed hard into emerald grass. Forcing open my terrorized eyes, I looked into the merry eyes of Samuel.

The man was *laughing*.

Fury coiled through me. Yanking myself to my feet, I made sure to accidentally kick him on my way up. "You couldn't have given me some kind of warning?!"

Samuel climbed to his feet, picking up both of our packs. "And where would the fun have been in that?"

Mace stood a ways off, unsuccessfully trying to hide his smile. Hissing, I whirled around only to jerk to a dead stop. We stood at the base of a massive mountain, and built into the sides of it stood a gleaming white city. Colossal pavilions and towers stretched high into the air, smooth as white pearl. Crashing over the edge were thundering waterfalls, the water spilling into sapphire pools not ten yards from where we stood. It was the most majestic, breathtaking sight I had ever beheld, and I was looking at it from down below.

"Wha—" I began, my eyes soaking in every little detail.

"Welcome to Airis, my lady. A part of the old world that has not yet crumbled." Mace touched my arm lightly. "Let's go get that arm looked at."

We hiked around the brilliant water, water that beckoned me with every step I took. At the base of the mountain was a hidden stone stairway. We climbed around and around until I felt like I could lift my fingers and graze the white clouds that floated above. The craftsmanship was surreal.

Samuel had a tight hold on my elbow, although I'm not quite sure where he expected me to run off to. It's not like I had a whole lot of options for escape routes, or that I had even tried to escape . . . yet.

His grip remained firm until we came face to face with the gate that protected the city. I thought my first brief glimpse of the city had been awe-inspiring, but the gate alone was magnificent. Built into the rock of the mountain itself were two black marble doors inlaid with millions of blinking diamonds. It stretched upwards for what seemed like miles, and standing next to its giant ruby handles was an elderly elf at least seven feet tall.

The only sign of his age were strands of glittering white streaked through his ebony hair and slight wrinkles under his eyes. He stood tall, his vivid green eyes piercing straight through me. I shifted uncomfortably. It was like he was peeling at the shadows that wrapped around my heart, and he could sense my deep hunger for revenge. Those eyes gripped me in a vice; deep wisdom and an uncanny perception observed me as I inched closer to Samuel.

"Samuel. Mace." He nodded, his voice low and soothing, and I instantly began to relax. "We were beginning to worry."

Samuel dipped his head respectfully. "It's good to see you again too, Master Cyrus." And there it was; his voice carried a slight sarcastic edge to even someone I assumed he held in high esteem. Samuel was coiled tight, ready to spring into action at the slightest provocation. "Can you protect her?"

Out of all the things I expected him to say, that question hadn't even crossed my mind. Jerking from his side, I kept my face blank and my eyes focused on the door. Had he brought me here just to drop me off? As enchanting as the city may be, I wasn't staying. I had one purpose and one purpose only.

To get to Midas.

"Ariel?"

I snapped back to attention, my face growing warm to find all three of them staring at me. It must not have been the first time Mace had called my name. "Ariel, this is Cyrus Drenuellon, one of our five elders. Master, this is—"

Mace was gently cut off. "I know quite well who she is, son. I've been waiting to see her fair face for many years now." Cyrus reached for my hand and brushed a light kiss across my knuckles. "It's an honor to finally make your acquaintance, my dear."

I smiled cheekily, hiding my wariness. Was he gifted with the sight as my mother was? "It's a pleasure to finally meet the mysterious Master Cyrus. I haven't heard much about you, I'm afraid. I was told all my questions needed to wait." I looked sideways at Samuel. "Actually, I think it was more along the lines of, 'Be quiet. I'm tired of your thousands of questions.'"

Cyrus laughed softly. "You have grit. Good." His eyes dimmed a bit as his voice lowered. "You'll need plenty." Before I could question him, he tucked my good arm in the crook of his. "Let's go get you to the healer."

We walked into a city I couldn't have dreamed up in a million years. Even my crazy, overly active imagination could never have created what was before me.

A road made of jade twisted leisurely up to what must be the main castle. We passed by monstrous houses. Some were made of brick, others of glass and marble. The only common theme was that they were covered in swirling patterns of precious stones. Silver trees grew along the road, their limbs tangling together over the pathway, creating a glimmering tunnel. I had to peak through the cracks in order to gawk at the houses.

I couldn't soak in my surroundings fast enough.

"After I've gotten you to the healer, and you've had sufficient rest, I will show you the city. Few humans have ever had the privilege to pass the gate, and it will give me great pleasure to give you a tour of our fair city."

My head swiveled back and forth. "How have you remained hidden so long?"

"We have been long forgotten by the human race. What was once history is now just outlandish tales told to small children. The Shade seemed the perfect place to hide and live in relative peace." He paused for a moment, his grip on my arm tightening a bit. "Until we are going to be needed again, that is."

I had a feeling that being around Cyrus was going to be a lot like living around my mother had been: annoying cryptic statements meant to warn, and eyes perpetually on the horizon to a time I couldn't hope to see.

"And here we are!" Cyrus exclaimed cheerfully, guiding me to a small cottage nestled among silver and sapphire trees.

It was modest compared to the other luxurious homes I had spied out, and perhaps that's why I suddenly felt comforted. It was homey, a safe haven amidst a strange world.

"The lady Carressa will fix you right up, and then I'll take you back to your protector."

I hadn't even noticed Samuel and Mace slip away. I didn't inspect the pang in my heart too closely. "He's not—" I hesitated, scrambling to find the right words. "Samuel isn't my anything."

Cyrus patted my hand gently. "My dear, whether either of you like it, Samuel is one of the few things standing between you and a very painful death." His eyes gleamed with something I couldn't decipher. "You two have an interesting journey ahead. Don't make the grave mistake of taking him at face value. Beyond his purposely rough exterior is a man worth knowing."

"Cyrus Drenuellon, you get that girl in here this instant! She looks about ready to fall over!"

Cyrus turned sharply, his eyes filling with laughter, and I could see why. The elf throwing around the demands was a dainty creature that looked as if the wind would steal her away at any moment. Silky, ebony curls framed her flawless face. Warm hazel eyes, rosebud lips, and luminescent skin made her absurdly beautiful. I felt pale and washed out next to her. Even my wild crimson hair, which I had always felt was my most beautiful trait, felt limp in her vivid presence.

Her smile was warm and her touch cool as she drew me away from Cyrus. "I will bring her to you when I am done, Cyrus, and not a minute sooner. So no sulking outside my door."

Cyrus bowed deeply. "Whatever your wishes, milady."

This healer must have some guts to order him around as she did. I had to stifle a grin; I liked her already. She shooed him away with her hands and then slammed the door in his face without even a hint of apology.

She circled around me and appraised me silently. Lifting my hair between her fingers and lightly grazing my bad arm, she muttered under her breath, "Well, I have some work ahead of me."

I didn't take offence at her words. I knew exactly the picture I presented, and it wasn't a pretty one. She scooted me over to a large bronze basin that was already full of steamy warm water. I swear I started drooling in anticipation.

"First, we get rid of the twenty layers of dirt, and then I'll take care of your wounds." Before I could react, she had stripped me and thrown me into the water.

Ten minutes later I was scrubbed red, and my hair had been washed three times. She was ruthless in her pursuit of cleanliness. I swear I had never been so immaculate in my entire life. It felt strange to be attended to; usually a quick dip in the nearby stream with a bar of soap was all I needed. I squelched my feelings of embarrassment and tried to remind myself that she was the healer. Whatever she used smelled like lemon and honeysuckle, and I decided I liked the light feminine scent—although I would never confess that to a single soul. If Logan had been here, he would have been bent over double, howling with laughter.

Just thinking about Logan chased away any of my happiness at a warm bath. Where was he? Was he okay? I had only experienced a slight taste of the Shade, and I knew enough to know it would be hard to survive on your own when you didn't know its dangers.

Carressa assisted me out of the water and sat me down on a small stool. With a determined look, she drifted her hand over the gash in my leg. Fiery warmth spiked through my leg, and I gasped in astonishment as the wound knitted together and disappeared. All that was left was a thin white scar to prove it had ever been there in the first place. I looked up at her wide-eyed. "What—"

She smiled widely. "I have a rather strong gifting in healing; this is the first I've had to use it to a major extent in a thousand years. Usually I get the occasional broken bone or a multitude of bee stings." Her fingers drifted over the scratches across my face and the abrasions on my hands.

I had never heard of such a gifting in my life. I knew of the gift of sight, but I thought that was a rare fluke my mother happened to get.

She grazed her hand over my arm, and I moved it pain-free in wonder. Her eyes narrowed in on me. "You look as if you never thought this could be possible."

I forced my eyes away from my arm to look at her as she wrapped a blanket around me. "I am in an elf city—"

She waved her hand dismissively. "I'm not talking about the many wonders of Airis. I am talking about giftings. You do have knowledge of giftings, do you not?" Her eyes widened in shock when I didn't answer. "Where have they been hiding you, dear child?"

She didn't wait for an answer. Mumbling under her breath, she stormed over to a chest and pulled out some clothes. "Cyrus had these delivered a couple days ago, and it's a good thing because what you were wearing I already burned."

I dressed quickly in fitted ivory trousers and a tunic trimmed in gold. Pulling on butter-soft brown leather boots, I sighed in comfort. However, it nagged at the corner of my mind how Cyrus guessed my size perfectly and why he knew to have a set of clothes delivered to Carressa. What was going on in this place, and was I the only one not to have a clue?

Samuel asked Cyrus if he would be able to protect me. Who exactly was after me? If the Eagles being dispatched were any indicator, I would say the king. However, I couldn't dream up a single reason why Titus would expend such resources on hunting me down. There were too many puzzle pieces missing, and I had a feeling that a lot of those pieces Cyrus held tightly in his hand. He was probably waiting for just the right moment to drop them into my lap and destroy my world all over again.

I wanted answers, and tonight I planned to get them.

I was ushered into what Carressa explained to me was the Great Hall. Chandeliers dripped light into every corner of the elegant room. White pillars lined a path to where five thrones sat, and seated on the middle throne was Cyrus Drenuellon. Just exactly how important was Cyrus in Airis? The other thrones were empty at the moment, and I breathed a sigh of relief. The only ones who were in the hall were Samuel, Mace, Cyrus, and one other elf I did not recognize.

The elf I didn't know turned around, his glare of hatred slicing through me. I was jerked back, and, within the blink of an eye, Carressa was protectively shielding me from view. Stunned, I sought out Samuel, but his gaze remained unflinching on the newcomer.

"I thought you were going to take care of this, Cyrus," Carressa snarled, backing us up towards the door.

"You dare protect that human?!" the angry elf roared. "Turn against your own kind for a mindless girl that will be dead within days? You turn the king's wrath on us, and soon he will search us all out and kill every last one until he has *her*!" The meaning of his words smashed into my mind with brutal force. Did everyone know what was going on besides me? It seems I had been correct in my hunch that the king was the one after me. I had been hoping to be wrong. If he was the force behind all this chaos, the lives of my family swung on a thin thread. The king wasn't known for leaving survivors.

Samuel took a menacing step forward, his knuckles white on the hilt of his sword. "You had best take care of your next words, Zorack."

Cyrus stood and walked between the two, his eyes sweeping over to me. "That is quite enough. Zorack, you are dismissed."

Fury emanated from him as he glowered at Samuel. "You will regret this, Cyrus Drenuellon. You will forever regret the moment you let that she-devil step foot into Airis."

Cyrus's face darkened. "I believe I said you were dismissed."

Zorack hissed in displeasure as he vanished into thin air. I blinked slowly a couple of times, trying to forget the looks of hatred he had directed my way. Carressa grasped my wrist and tugged me forward against my will.

She deposited me next to Samuel before going toe to toe with Cyrus. "You promised me, Cyrus. You promised this would be dealt with before she arrived." Rigid as a bow, she stared up at him, her anger spiking.

Cyrus looked down at her in weariness. "What would you have me do, Carressa? Throw him into the dungeons? Banish him? If I don't keep a close eye on him, he could go rogue, dishing out disaster wherever he stepped."

"You know as well as I do that he has grown dark. I expected you to do what needed to be done. If anything happens to her—" Carressa looked back at me, her eyes turning into such a well of sorrow that I strove to catch my breath. "I'll blame you, Cyrus Drenuellon." With those last forbidding words, she swept out of the hall.

Cyrus sighed heavily. "Let's all get some rest, and we'll pick this up in the morning." He motioned us to follow him. "I will show you where you shall be staying."

As Mace and Samuel started to follow him, I stood firmly planted. Samuel turned around to look at me questioningly. "Wildcat?"

I ignored him, my eyes boring into Cyrus. "I would like some answers tonight."

Samuel answered for him. "Come on, Wildcat. It's been a long day. Let's go get some much-needed sleep. Questions can wait until tomorrow."

I shook my head slowly. If I had to hear it could wait until tomorrow one more time I might scream. "No!" I paced a few steps, clenching and unclenching my fingers. Forcing air into my lungs, I whipped around. "No. I've waited long enough for someone to start telling me what's going on. I want some answers *tonight.*"

No one answered; they looked everywhere but into my eyes. Was it really all so terrible that they had to keep shoving the truth into another day? I felt something within me finally snap, relinquishing all the control I had managed to have thus far. "Enough! My home has been burned to ashes, I've been threatened by an Imperial assassin, abandoned by my best friend," I swallowed hard, my hand attempting to hold my raging heart within my chest. "I've been chased by skeleton-looking men, almost killed by a flower, hunted by a squadron of Eagles, and thrown into an elf world I never even knew existed!" I looked hard at Cyrus, blinking back the tears that threatened to appear. "I held my brother while he died," I breathed in anguish, hiding my shaking hands behind me. "And I want to know why! Why is all this happening? Why can't *anyone* give me a straight answer?"

"Mace, Samuel will stay with you as usual. I will see you both in the morning as we arranged." Mace and Samuel left without another word, but my eyes remained on Cyrus.

"Please tell me why this is happening to me," I begged. I felt like a small child trapped in a thunderstorm. Everyone else knew where to hide and ride out the storm, but I was being tossed around, unsure of where to go next.

Cyrus tucked my arm under his and escorted me to a small garden adjoining the building. It was as magical as the Shade was at night, everything glowing in the moonlight. We settled on a small bench next to a sapphire pond. My eyes watched the neon bodies of fish dart back and forth while Cyrus gathered his thoughts.

"I knew your mother once, a long time ago. We who are gifted with the sight always manage to cross each other's path at some point. We both knew, with that one small happenstance meeting, that one day our paths were going to cross again . . . and it was going to be for a much darker reason."

Drawing my knees up to my chest, I wrapped my arms around myself. I wasn't going to like this at all; his voice was too soft, his eyes too distant.

"She had just found out she was pregnant with you, and she knew who you were long before you started to grow within her womb. She knew how important you were going to be, and how the evil in this world would seek your death. King Titus had not yet pulled off his bloody coup and taken over all ten realms, and she feared for the daughter she would soon birth into the world. I sensed her seeking for me, and so I concealed my identity and met her in the city where she sat waiting for me." He smiled. "You are a lot like her, you know. Fiery, determined, not letting anyone push you around. We made a plan that day that, when the events we both foresaw would unfold, I would protect you. I would be your guide until you could fulfill your destiny. That is why I made sure your friend Logan met Samuel. I knew when the time came he would take you to Samuel, and Samuel—not knowing what else to do—would bring you to me." Cyrus leaned over me and cupped my chin. "You have no idea of the dangerous world you were just thrust into. But I promise you, for as long as I breathe, I will protect you to the best of my ability."

I knew this was no small promise, but what I didn't know was why he felt the need to make it. "I don't mean to be difficult, but you haven't really given me any answers. Just a lot more questions."

He leaned back, pressing his fingers together. His face was a perfect mask of peace, but I could see the storm in his eyes. "How much do you understand of giftings?"

I sighed and rubbed my temples. What did giftings have to do with anything?

"Ariel?" he prodded.

"I know my mother was gifted with the sight. Most people were afraid of her; they said what she did was unnatural. Lady Carressa can heal with her hands, and I suspect you possess a gift a lot like my mother's . . . " I shrugged miserably. "Other than that, not a whole lot."

He surged to his feet, his face wreathed in distress. "I assumed your mother would have prepared you better. I thought she and I—" His eyes flashed to my face in agitation. "You were supposed to have been warned! What did she expect, that she could avoid all of this coming to fruition? That she could keep you hidden in the shadows?"

"I don't—" How many times could I possibly say I didn't understand?

He grabbed my hand tightly. "You aren't ready yet, Ariel." He pulled me closer to him, his eyes compelling me to try to understand. "I could sit here all night trying to explain every little facet of what you will need to survive in the coming months, but, when I'm done, you will still look at me with those blank eyes. You have come to Airis far, *far* too soon. You must learn some things first; you must discover the answers on your own."

He didn't give me a chance to reply. Dropping my hand, he muttered a few words under his breath and disappeared. The next second, he reappeared by my elbow, his arms laden with supplies. I stood dumbstruck while he fastened a cloak around my shoulders, hoisted a pack onto my back, and handed me a bulky sealed envelope.

"I'm sorry, Ariel."

"Cyrus?" I whispered, fear streaking through me at the pity in his eyes.

"You have much left to do, and you won't be able to accomplish any of it here." Beckoning for me to dip my head, he dropped a chain over it. On the chain was a small pendent of two crisscrossing swords. Two crimson stars were on either side of the swords, resting delicately on my collarbone. The stars were sending out cerise sparks, and the swords were glowing a steady crystal white. "This will guide you—and warn you when danger is near. It will not dim even when darkness takes over your entire world." He next handed me two wicked- looking daggers that were inlaid with silver and had a strange language inscribed on them. "These will protect you." He stroked my hair. "Never give up, Ariel. No matter what you do . . . never give up."

He touched my forehead gently, setting the world into a whirlwind around me. I snapped out of my bewildered trance with a vengeance. "What are you doing?" I screamed, latching onto his wrist before he could pull away. "I want some real answers. Not more puzzles!"

He pried my fingers loose, mouthing words to me I couldn't hope to hear within the vortex. I ceased to be able to see Cyrus anymore. Black and gold spun around me in sickening circles. My stomach dropped to my toes when I felt myself lifted off the ground. Icy coldness sucked my breath away and left me coated within a wintry shell.

And then . . . nothing.

CHAPTER V

I woke up alone.

With a groan, I sat up and threw off a pack that felt full of rocks. Furious, I ripped open the envelope. There had better be some spectacular explanation for dumping me in the middle of nowhere by myself.

A thick, folded piece of vellum fell out, along with a leathery map. Opening the letter first, I stared down at it, fighting past my choking hysteria.

Dearest Ariel,

You will not understand what is going on, and you won't for a very long time. I know how you hate to be out of control, but understand this . . . no matter the cost, or how difficult the task, you must never give up. Survive. You must stay alive! I would ask you not to come after us, but I know you too well for that. You will go on the war-path, and you won't stop until you find us. However, I have to ask you to stay away.

My guess is that the king will hide us deep within Midas, and he will expect you to come looking. You must not step foot into Midas. Stay hidden. Stay away from the king. Because, you see, your death has the power to destroy the world!

I am sorry I do not have more answers, but Cyrus is right. You need to find the answers by yourself. I will tell you this:

trust Samuel. No matter what rises to the surface, no matter how bad it looks, never lose your faith in him.

I love you so much, my daughter.

You can do what will be asked of you in the coming days. You have more strength in you than you realize. I am so proud of the young woman you have become. Keep the fire within you burning; don't let them break you.

Your spirit, your tenacity, your deep love, your grace . . . these qualities are what are keeping us all alive. Don't lose sight of who you are. The entire ten realms are depending on you. Keep the faith.

Forever in your heart,

Mom

Gripping the paper tightly, I bowed my head. More cryptic nonsense. Did this mean she was alive? Or was it something she had written when she was pregnant? Why, when it came to those gifted with the sight, did everything have to be muddled? As for Samuel, well, Cyrus had taken care of that all by himself. Samuel was nowhere to be found. I was on my own. Grabbing the leather map, I spread it out over my legs. It was momentarily blank. As I stared at it in frustration, black lines spiraled onto the page. Holding my breath, I waited in anticipation. I smiled widely at the map that now lay before me; it was a map straight into the heart of Midas, and in the far corner was a small sparkling star that I assumed represented where I was standing.

I grinned wickedly. A letter that said to stay hidden and survive at all costs and a map that led me straight to my family—well, it wasn't really a question, was it? Tucking the letter into the inside pouch of my tunic, I stood with new resolve. Hoisting up my pack, I smiled down at the map. I would find them.

And I would bring them all home alive.

I stood on the edge of a sheer cliff with the map held tightly in one hand. I had been here at least fifteen minutes, deciding if I really wanted to attempt to cross to the other side. The bridge, if it really could be called that, looked more like it had been built for an easy suicide attempt. It swayed haphazardly in the wind, its creaking sound sending chills down my spine. Some of the rope dangled uselessly in the air, and the wood planks were already bowed, looking ready to break at the slightest touch.

"You have got to be kidding me," I mumbled, more to prove to myself that at least at this moment I was still alive. I looked down at the map again, and still the answer remained the same.

This was the only way to get across.

Grimacing at the inevitable, I tucked the map safely into my pack. Clenching my teeth, I inched forward, feverishly praying that I would make it across alive. I had never been afraid of heights before, but with one peek downwards, my heart dropped to my toes.

I paused when I felt the pendent Cyrus had given me warm against my skin. Pulling it out of my tunic, I stared at it. The stars were sparking like crazy, and the swords continued to grow hotter. Was this my warning? If so, I planned to ignore it. I needed to cross the river.

"I wouldn't go any further than that if you value your life."

Whirling around, my dagger already clutched in my hand, I blinked at the man who stood behind me. Had I really been that lost in concentration I hadn't heard him approach? I stepped off the bridge slowly, watching as he took a step back in response. I felt my pendent begin to cool against my skin, and I wasn't sure how to feel about it. Did this man not pose any danger? Or was the necklace just a pretty trinket Cyrus had handed over to make me feel better about being alone?

I eyed the man cautiously, trying to size him up. He was older, and, from the shadows in his eyes, I could see he was weary of life. However, he presented a menacing picture. He had to be from far into the fifth realm if his dark skin was any indication. Snarled dreads snaked down his back, and bulging muscles proved that, no matter his age, he was still very much in shape.

"There is another way across the river if that's what you are attempting. Unless," he paused, sizing me up, "unless it isn't across the river that you wanted."

He hadn't made any move for the scimitar on his hip, so I slowly lowered my hand to my side. "According to my map, this is the only place to cross." I glanced back over at the bridge and added quietly, "And I have to get across."

He eyed me curiously. "You realize that going across means you are headed into the deepest part of the Shade?" His head tilted questioningly. "Few make it through alive."

"I don't have a choice," I said. "My only path lies on the other side of that bridge."

He nodded slowly. "Your map is correct; this is the spot to cross, but not by that bridge. You have to walk north about a mile. There is a hidden path down the cliff that you need to take. Once down, you walk back to this spot. You will see a secluded cove. Inside is a raft which you take across, then send back by the rope."

It didn't make sense why a perfect stranger would stop me from going across the bridge and then tell me the precise way to get across. "Why are you helping me?"

He smiled tightly. "I'm good at reading people, kiddo. Nothing was going to stop you from getting across, so I might as well keep you from getting yourself killed."

I sensed nothing but sincerity from him, and I couldn't help but be intrigued. He was unlike anyone I had ever come across. Our small town hadn't seen a lot of travelers, and, being from the seventh realm, I hadn't seen a whole lot of the rest of the world. I smiled at him, inexplicably feeling like I had just found a long-lost friend. Putting my dagger away, I offered my hand. "Ariel Deverell. It's good to meet you." He stared at my hand for the longest time, but I refused to take it back. "It's either a handshake or a hug; you can decide." I smiled a little wider at him when he reached forward and clasped my hand in his. My little hand looked dwarfed in his, but I didn't feel any fear. Instead, I felt drawn to this man who looked like life had broken him years ago.

"Colter Grey." He held my hand gently before letting it go. He sighed heavily. "Where are you headed?"

Here it came, the point at which I really had to choose whether to trust him or not. However, I couldn't ignore the feeling that he was exactly the person I was supposed to meet. "I'm not sure you'll believe me if I tell you."

He shrugged, pretending he didn't much care, but I knew it had to plague him as to why I was traveling by myself through the most dangerous territory known to man. "Nothing really surprises me these days," he said.

"I'm going to Midas." I waited for his reaction. Disbelief? Amusement? Shock? What I wasn't expecting was the slow smile that spread across his face, transforming him into a much younger man. Maybe he wasn't as old as I had previously thought; could life have really treated him that badly?

"There isn't a man alive who has made it past the borders of Midas; King Titus stays hidden there for a reason. They think the Shade is dangerous; it is *nothing* compared to Midas." He chuckled softly. "Why would you risk your pretty little neck trying something as crazy as that?"

I tried to hide the bit of joy that leapt in my chest; he was talking about Midas as though he had actually been there. His disheveled appearance, being so far from his realm, and his spiritless eyes meant only one thing . . . "How long have you been a deserter from the Imperial army, Colter?" I questioned, watching closely for his response.

The smile slid from his face, and he looked at me with a new awareness. "You know nothing of the hells I have been through, girl. Nothing."

"No, but I'm about to enter some of them. Titus has my family, and I aim to get them back." Turning to where he had previously pointed, I started walking. If I wanted to get across the river by nightfall, I needed to pick up the pace. As much as I wanted to unfold the mystery that was Colter Grey, I didn't have the time.

"You won't make it."

I shifted my head and saw that he was keeping pace right beside me, his chocolate eyes dark with memories.

"I will, actually," I rebutted, turning my eyes back to the ground. "I have to."

I heard another long sigh come from him. "I'm coming with you."

I stopped mid-stride to stare up at him. "Why? You've already helped me. Why do you feel you have to tag along?"

His gaze shied away from mine as he inspected a swaying red tree for the longest time. "Because, for the first time in a long time, I feel like I could have a purpose again." He looked down at me, his eyes pleading for me to understand. "I've only known you for five minutes, and already I feel like . . . " He struggled for words. "It doesn't matter why; I'm coming with you."

We traveled for days in near silence, getting used to being around each other. I found, when he actually talked, that he had a dry sense of humor that was refreshing. I purposely ignored his nightmares, and he diligently hunted and kept a close eye on my safety. I pretended to myself that, when darkness hit our camp, I didn't miss Samuel and his crankiness, but the truth was, I did. As much as he drove me crazy, I kind of missed being able to tease him.

"You can stop looking at that map every thirty seconds; I know where I'm going."

I grinned at Colter over the campfire. He had three rabbits in his hand, and I shook my head slowly in awe. "You have a downright unnatural tracking skill."

"Always been good at it. I grew up in a large family; hunting was the only way to survive. Didn't take long before I was better than my pops, and he sent me out by myself."

"Do you miss them?" I asked.

"They're dead," he replied flatly, getting to work on skinning the rabbits.

I watched him, wanting to say something comforting, but not sure words could make much difference. To lose your whole family? I knew how that could twist your insides and leave you debilitated. I stood up slowly and went to sit next to him. He paused what he was doing to look over at me.

"Ariel?"

"An Imperial assassin killed my brother, and I swore as he died in my arms that I would get revenge."

He moved to sit on the rock next to me, which was unusual. Normally he tried to keep wide distance between us.

I continued. "The only thing I have left to hold onto is the hope that the rest of my family is still alive. I can't imagine losing them all. So, I just want you to know how sorry I am that you lost yours. And—" I swallowed hard past the lump in my throat, "and to thank you for helping me try to find mine."

I leaned my head against his shoulder and felt him wrap an arm tightly around my waist. "I promise, Ariel, I'll help you to my last breath."

Yet another person promising to help me until they were forever incapable; I could only hope I really deserved such devotion.

A hand clamped over my mouth and jerked my body into the air. Fighting for air, I grappled, trying to reach one of my blades. "Shh . . ."

I stopped fighting and allowed my body to hang limp when Colter whispered into my ear. What in the world was going on? He moved me deeper into the shadow of the trees we had made camp under and stood in front of me, his sword held menacingly in front of him. I watched in horror as black-hooded creatures began to spill into our camp and converge on us. Pale, claw-like hands were all I could see from my vantage point.

"You thinks youss hass a chance 'round uss, big man?" The voice shrieked through the clearing, causing my ears to pound with pain.

Whipping out my two elven blades, I waited for Colter's directions. Wincing at the scalding heat from my necklace, I was glad it was hidden under my tunic, concealing its sparks.

"What are they?" I whispered.

Colter leaned back and grasped my wrist tightly. "You run, do you understand me, Ariel?" His eyes never left the dozen creatures that had taken over our camp. "You run and don't stop until the sun rises."

I'd been through this once before. I knew better this time. I wasn't leaving him.

Right as I was about to tell him to kiss grits, fire-arrows started to rain down. With an oath, Colter pulled me to the ground; wrapping himself around me, he shielded me while the assault continued.

The screams coming from the creatures were enough to make me want to rip my ears off. I felt something warm begin to spill from my nose and ears, and I prayed that the screams would stop.

Finally, the world went silent.

I felt myself lifted and tucked under Colter's arm. The world spun in dizzying circles around me as I tried to regain my balance. What was wrong with me?

Fire was flickering dangerously around the camp, but no bodies littered the ground. What had just happened?

"Ariel? Ariel!!" I tried to focus on Colter's face as he shook me. "Ariel? Can you walk?" It felt like he was yelling to me from miles away. Wait a second. Why was blood all over him? Where did the blood come from?

"Are you—" I swallowed, and tried swallowing again. What had happened to me? "Hit . . ." I trailed off, staring at the flickering fire, so caught up in the beauty of it, I ceased listening to Colter as he yelled at me.

"Ariel! We have to move! ARIEL! Look at me!" I felt like I had been drugged, and I just didn't care what was going on anymore.

Colter started dragging me from the clearing, his eyes narrowed dangerously.

"Stuff . . . our stuff . . ." Was that slurred voice really coming from me?

"Put. Her. Down."

The command came from the darkness ahead of us; the only thing visible was a sword that was lit on fire. Entranced, I didn't protest when Colter pulled me tighter to his side. The faint voice had sounded familiar . . .

"Not likely," Colter hissed, baring his teeth.

I needed to throw up. "C-c-col—" I didn't want to throw up on him; that would be just too humiliating. He wasn't paying any attention to me. He was yelling again—not at me, though. Groaning, I buried my head against him, wanting the noise to stop.

"You won't leave here alive if you don't hand her to me."

And then my memory clicked. I shoved against Colter feebly. "S-sam-mm-uel. Is s—"

Colter looked down at me, trying to figure out what I was saying. "Ariel?"

I watched as Samuel stepped closer to us, his features becoming discernible. Did he look . . . relieved? I reached for him and managed to grab the front of his tunic. Everything around me was still hazy and muted, but I felt my head clear the littlest bit. I'm not sure how things all got worked out, but the next thing I knew I was sitting next to a newly blazing fire. Samuel was crouching next to me, wiping a cold cloth across my face. I flinched, but he continued cleaning my face.

"I'm just trying to clean up the blood, Ariel," he soothed.

"What happened?" I saw Colter standing just a few paces away, his hand protectively on his sword. His eyes never left Samuel.

"I've been trying to catch up with you since the moment Cyrus sent you out of Airis. I don't think he expected you to get so far so fast. I finally came across you tonight just as the Critadayas entered the camp."

I pushed his hand away and shakily sat up. "Why am I bleeding?"

"It was their screams; you were to close to them when the fire hit their skin. Fire and water are their only weaknesses, but most of the time their victims don't have time to get to water or start a fire. First, the screams will just incapacitate you." He reached forward with the cloth and wiped at the dried blood on my collar. "When you are so hazy with pain, that's when they begin to torture you. If you were trapped listening to the screams long enough, it would kill you."

I tried to ignore the feeling that flared into my chest as I stared into his absorbing eyes. Why had he come after me? I thought he would have been thrilled that I was out of his hair. "Why are you here, Samuel?"

"Cyrus sent me."

I flicked his hand away from where it lingered against my neck. Figures.

"You can go back to your tree kingdom, Fairchild. Colter will see me to Midas, and you can go tell Cyrus your mission has been completed. You've found me." I inched back from him, feeling vulnerable. How had I actually missed the man? "Now go away."

"Ariel—"

"Please be gone by morning." Grabbing my pack, I planted myself beside Colter without sparing another look towards Samuel. Resituating my bedding, I feel into an uneasy sleep.

Samuel wasn't gone that morning. In fact, I had the joy of waking up to him and Colter arguing about who got to stay.

"I swore to protect her! Besides that, she asked you to leave, not me!"

"She was put into my protection long before you entered the scene," Samuel responded, his voice whipping through the air.

"Yes, and where were you when she was about to cross skeleton ridge?" Colter asked.

If my splitting headache was any indication, this was going to be one really long day. "Enough!" Glaring at them, I reluctantly pulled myself out from under my blanket. It was too early in the morning for this. Plus, it was an argument I had planned to avoid—*if* Samuel had left last night like he was supposed to. For a man who was only here because Cyrus had ordered him to be, he sure wasn't easy to get rid of. "Fairchild, I thought I told you to leave."

"You really want to travel with a Saerdothian from the fifth realm? And you actually think he'll take you to Midas?" Samuel glared at me. "Have you lost your ever-lovin' mind?"

Furious, I chucked a rock at him, hoping to wipe that arrogant look right off his face. He managed to dodge the rock, but I wasn't through with him yet. He was just lucky I maintained enough of my patience not to throw my dagger. "Colter isn't some piece of trash!" Colter's eyes darted in my direction, surprised at my fierce protection of him. Did he really think I wouldn't defend him?

"He's a—" Samuel began, rising to his feet in agitation.

Stomping over to him, I shoved him hard, not budging him an inch. "I know *exactly* who Colter Grey is; *don't* pretend you do. As for trusting him, at least he isn't staying with me out of some misguided sense of duty! If anyone can get me to Midas," I jabbed a finger in Colter's direction, "it'll be him!"

"You're being a fool, Wildcat," Samuel spat. "His kind can't be trusted."

I looked at him in disbelief. "His kind?" I looked over at Colter in compassion. His native tattoos, his dark coloring, his eyes . . . How could Samuel think he was inferior? I stared at Samuel, willing him to stop before he went too far. My voice lowered as Colter looked down at the ground in shame. "How is he any different than us, Samuel? Because he is from a different realm? Because he has a different coloring? He's looked out for me for the past week with no concern for his well-being, with no gain to himself. How can you ask me to treat him any differently than I would anyone else?"

"Ariel—" Colter touched my arm hesitantly. "You don't have to defend me to him."

Samuel cleared his throat and looked away. I kicked him in the shin to get his attention.

"Ow! Ariel—"

"You sound like a pompous pig, so knock it off," I ordered. "If you insist on staying with us, you'll keep your opinions to yourself—or you can get lost."

White-lipped, he stared down at me with restrained frustration. "Fine," he growled.

I smiled at Colter. "That's as close to an apology as you're going to get, but he means well. Now, let's get moving."

CHAPTER VI

The unusual beauty of the Shade was beginning to taper back into the protective line of ordinary maples and hawthorns. "Where are we, Colter?" I asked, carefully making my way down a steep incline.

"In a few minutes, we will be at the border of Gabriel, the crown city of the eighth realm." He paused, his eyes sad. "It's one of the few cities that is attempting to fight against the crippling tentacles of Midas." He chuckled darkly. "However, they have only so much fight left in them. Soon, they'll be like everyone else. Honest men will become thieves and killers. Women will fall to the street corners to make an extra coin just to survive. Children will die in ditches and be ignored." He looked over at me, his gaze burning a path of sorrow straight into my heart. "It won't be long before they will fall and live in despair like all the other realms."

Samuel remained quiet where he stood, waiting for us to catch up, his toe tapping the ground impatiently. "What?" I asked. "No snide remarks?"

His lips thinned into a tight smile. "Whether I like to admit it or not, he—" he gritted his teeth as if his next words were going to pain him considerably, "is right." Grunting, he kept moving, still uttering words of despair. "Gabriel, Airis, and any other city that dare stand tall will be torn down and mocked. Titus will not rest until this world is shadows and ash."

I felt like rocks had dropped into my heart; each beat hurt worse than the last. Why was it that I cared so much that the land itself was surrendering to Titus's death-inducing reign? Was there no other option than caving to the waves of helplessness?

Colter looked at me knowingly as we wove our way through the rest of the Shade. "Your family needs to be your only concern. You can't save the rest of the world too."

I stopped and stared at the two men. In some ways they were vastly different, and yet they were so very alike. Both of them thought the fight was long over. When I rescued my family, then what? We would still be stuck in the madness of Titus's newly-made world. Was there even anything past the ten realms? Anywhere else to escape to?

Samuel grabbed my arm, clamping down painfully. "Get that look off your face, Ariel," he said through gritted teeth, his eyes bursting into flames. "Now."

I pulled against him futilely. "What look?" I muttered, resenting him more by the second.

"Get it out of your pretty little head that *you* could actually do anything," he growled, his face inches from mine.

Peeling his fingers back, I began walking again. "As long as one person continues to stand and to hope, then nothing is ever over."

I didn't bother to look at their skeptical faces. What was the point? They'd lost their will to struggle against Titus's unyielding rule. They figured that what was now was what would be forever. But why did that have to be the case?

I missed my mom and her tenacity; I could really use some of that right now. I missed my father and his unique way of looking at everything. He had a way of making people see beyond the tips of their noses. Oh, and my brothers! Their unrelenting joy for life was something I sorely lacked at the moment.

How was I ever going to tell them about Bryne? Juliet, his betrothed, was going to be devastated. Against my will, I imagined her face as she crested the hill—the horror of a hollow house and a lifeless Bryne would destroy her.

"Ariel?" Colter touched my shoulder gently.

Cartwheeling back into reality, I realized I stood on the thin line between the Shade and the city of Gabriel. I didn't answer him. I stared vacantly at the one city that dared to stand against a tyrant. I didn't have to step foot into it to know that I loved it already.

"Wonderful. The city of fools," Samuel muttered, his eyes sweeping disdainfully over the city.

"Wrong," I snapped. "A city full of the most courageous people you will ever have the pleasure of getting to meet." Cyrus had shoved a sack of gold into the bottom of my pack. If I was lucky, I could purchase a horse, provisions, and even a weapon. I should buy a sword, but the long bow Samuel was carting around spiked my jealousy. It was a beautiful weapon, and one I was more than proficient in. However, what would be the smarter choice?

"You are an idyllic simpleton sometimes, Ariel," Samuel said, his eyes hard.

Colter glared at Fairchild for me, which made me secretly smile. "And you are an asinine, arrogant, mule-headed, pathetic excuse for a man." My smile was full of acid as I strolled forward.

Gabriel was a well-kept city, with a subtle beauty that made it charming. Everywhere I looked were white-washed houses with extraordinary gardens. Most of the houses had flowers sprawling up the walls, but, instead of looking abandoned, the overgrowth gave them a cheery quality. The city was alive with people. There were no pinched, worried faces; everyone was laughing and smiling. It reminded me of home, and an intense longing rose in my heart. How I missed home!

Ambling down the road with Colter and Samuel on my tail, we received more than a few strange looks. It didn't surprise me; I was traveling with two behemoths who were armed to the tenth degree. I needed to ask somebody where I could find a horse. Gabriel resided in the eighth realm, and I had heard legendary tales of the realm's magnificent horses. It shouldn't be too difficult to come by a good mount. However, before I could stop someone, my eyes landed on a wanted poster.

Dread pooled in my stomach. I curled my hands into fists, fighting the urge to tear it off the wall and shred it to bits. Each detail of the carefully-drawn face made me cringe.

It was a perfect replica of me, down to the light sprinkling of freckles across my nose. I traced my fingers across it in horrified shock. Bold letters proclaimed I was wanted, preferably dead. My head would bring 100,000 gold coins. That was a fortune to even the wealthy.

"You don't need to worry." A warm voice spoke from right behind me.

I spun around, my hand clenching compulsively around my dagger. A stocky man with jovial eyes beamed at me. Half of the city's population stood behind him. Colter and Samuel moved closer to my side, muttering up a blue streak.

"Pardon me?" I flung a hand back at the poster. "I think that causes a bit of a reason to worry." I kept my voice level, but panic was burning the air from my throat.

The entire city had turned eerily quiet while all eyes centered on me. The man remained smiling, but I saw his eyes light with understanding. "Yes, anywhere else that would be cause for great concern. However, you are not anywhere else. . . .You are in Gabriel." He spread his arms wide. "For as long as you are here, you are safe."

I felt the idiotic urge to cry, but I had made an oath to myself in the Shade that I aimed to keep. There would be a time, later, to cry. I wanted to know why he offered a safe haven so easily, but I had a feeling the only answer I would get was that I was in Gabriel now. "When did this appear?"

He clasped his hands behind his back, his eyes going from the poster to my face. "A little more than a week ago. I must admit I saw it and laughed. The messenger dropped it on the border, spouting off about how dangerous you were and that we were to kill you on sight, no questions asked." His head tilted as he observed me. "The only reason I put it up was so we knew to protect you if you wandered through—and here you are."

An elderly lady made her way to stand next to the man who was talking to me. The crowd parted in silence, allowing her to slowly make her way to the front. Piercing eyes struck my heart as she tapped her cane on the ground a few times. "Interesting . . ." She continued to tap her cane, her face expressionless. "Very interesting, that King Titus is afraid of such a slip of a girl. You must be extremely cunning and all sorts of evil to stir up his righteous wrath."

I gulped for air like a fish out of water. "Uh—"

She broke into a rich, throaty laugh and winked at me. "I don't know why he is so desperate for your death, but whatever you did, it's a job well done." She waved her hands dismissively at the people milling around, staring. Tapping her cane, she impatiently ordered briskly, "Back to work, all of you." Instantly, every last person drifted away, going back to whatever business he or she was attending to before we walked into town. The man who had first spoken to us—and the woman—was all that were left. Samuel and Colter remained strangely silent, but I could feel their tension thicken the air.

"Come, lass; let us speak over a warm meal."

CHAPTER VII

Within an hour of being in Gabriel, I had gained enough knowledge to make me seriously reconsider my sanity. I wasn't just on a rescue mission anymore. Now I had a rather steep price on my head—which was going to make traveling difficult. I was going to have to avoid all settlements and cities. In every single realm, the monarchs were either deep in hiding or lay dead in their beds. My new protector's names were Maven and Henry. It didn't take too long for me to figure out they were mother and son. And Maven's cane was purely to annoy people with its incessant tapping.

I touched my necklace unconsciously, feeling for that searing heat. There were no sparks snapping at my skin, and no heat scalding me. According to the necklace, I was, for the moment, in no harm. Still, my eyes sought out every possible exit and found every conceivable weapon.

"Lass, I can hear the hum of your thoughts all the way across the table," Maven said, "and it's giving me a headache."

I twirled a fork between my fingers, testing its weight, deciding how good of a dent it would make in an enemy. I had to lean past Colter to meet her gaze. "So is the ceaseless tapping of that useless cane," I retorted. "I know the only reason you carry it is to drive people around you mad, and whack them with it when they hesitate to obey."

Her lips curved into a small smile before they disintegrated back into a hard line. "Nonsense." She smoothed a hand over her immaculately coifed hair. "My balance isn't what it once was."

I was tempted to mimic her, but my mother had instilled too many manners in me. No, that wasn't true. My mother had *attempted* to, when I was younger, and for some reason they were choosing now to take a foothold. Leaning back into my seat, I nudged my food around my plate.

My mouth watered from the scrumptious aroma, but every time I swallowed, I felt like I was choking on ash. Ever since I had seen my own wide eyes staring back at me from that poster, my stomach had been in knots. Colter and Samuel shared no such feelings; they were inhaling everything in sight.

"You shouldn't play with your food," Maven remarked, her cane once again tapping.

I leaned back around Colter to stare at her. "That's nonsense. Your eyes must be going with your balance."

Another wicked smile lighted upon her face before flying away. "You must have been quite a handful growing up."

"Probably just as much as you were," I said, daring her to disagree. Samuel covered his laughter with coughing, but I didn't spare him a glance.

"You got a mouth on you." She finally set down her cane on the floor. "And a perceptiveness I find irritating." This time the smile stayed on her lips. "I feel as if I am looking at a ghost of my younger self."

I pushed my dinner plate away from me. "I think," I said, "I'll take that as a compliment."

Her laughter filled the room with warmth. "Come, lass; let us leave these barbarians to their food." She stood, winked at me, and left her cane where it lay. "I have something you must see."

She led me to the royal lodgings—a luxurious stone castle covered in sapphire and violet roses. Idly, I wondered how they got roses to grow up a wall. She continued to direct me around the castle to the invisible border of Gabriel.

The acid building in the pit of my stomach told me this was a moment I wasn't going to have the pleasure of forgetting. The velvet darkness was interrupted by hundreds of blazing torches. Each torch stood sentinel at an unmarked grave. I swallowed thickly against the bile that rose in my throat. Clenching my trembling hands into fists, my eyes zeroed in on a small child who was methodically lighting more torches.

Tears streamed down his face, and he had to pause every so often to wipe them away so he could see. He was so careful at every grave it made my heart clench. Soon, I lost sight of him, but as torches continued to burst to life, I could track his progress. Glassy-eyed, I flinched when Maven wrapped her hand around mine.

"You walk another mile and you'll see where the actual battle occurred." Her voice was hushed, but it reverberated like a scream in my head.

Breaking away from her light grip, I walked woodenly past the graves. War cries, the clash of steel against steel, and screams of pain had to be just pure imagination. I passed the small boy huddling by a grave, clawing at the dirt. I tried to block his pleas for whomever it was to come back, but I couldn't escape his grief.

Is that what I was soon to become? A specter in the night, tearing at my family's graves while I begged them to come back? The problem was that I could see it too clearly. My life was on a precipice, and one wrong move could bring everything crashing down around me. What was Maven's motive in bringing me to this catastrophically huge gravesite? What was she trying to show me? The tangible sorrow and suffering in the air ate at me. How could a man live, knowing he had caused such horrors?

A king was not a king when his reign was secured by fear and innocent blood.

I left the grieving boy behind, but his inhuman wails of pain hunted my footsteps. The terrain began to dip down into a wide valley, and I paused briefly. Breathing deeply, I allowed my eyes to flutter shut. The crispness of the air attacking my skin did little to take me away from the nightmare I had been shoved into. The coppery smell of blood filled my mouth, and I choked against the pressure in my heart. Straightening my spine, my eyes flicked open with resolve. It didn't matter what I was about to walk into, this knowledge would make me stronger. You had to know your enemy to beat him, and Titus seemed to know a lot more about me than I felt comfortable with. It was time to even the playing field and, to do that, I needed to know what he was capable of.

Sliding my way down into the valley, I allowed my gaze to stroke over the land and take in every ghastly detail. After my intense perusal, I promptly fell to my knees and retched. Heaving in air, I wiped the backside of my hand against my mouth and begged my whirling stomach to calm. My shoulders sagged as I climbed to my feet.

The soil had turned black with dried blood, and the smell of decay brought moisture to my eyes. On either side of the valley was a row of spears jutting out of the earth, and displayed prominently on each was a head. Broken lances, forgotten swords, and rotting bodies littered every inch of the ground. Horses lay where they fell.

"Every time we manage to clean the valley up, they come back." Maven's voice barely disturbed the stagnant air. "We gave up long ago trying to match bodies to heads, and we're left with the dishonor of just burying the heads of our loved ones." Her strong voice wavered as tears spilled down her weathered cheeks. "We collect the weapons, knowing we'll need them for the next wave of soldiers. We burn their dead. Yet, no matter how we try to purge the day's events, this valley is scarred with it." Her eyes pinned me to the ground. "We have enough citizens left to put up one last fight. The ones left alive will be forced to live as slaves. We accepted our fate long ago, but then . . . everything changed."

I looked at her, begging her silently to tell me that there was hope—that Titus could be stopped. Because if Gabriel was doomed to fall . . . If Gabriel was to fall, no one else had a chance. "How?" I whispered.

"The wanted poster of you was dropped on our border and, with one look at it, I knew." She smiled grimly, her eyes hardening to emeralds as she stared at the wreckage. "I touched the paper and felt vicious triumph, because it was obvious then."

What? What had been so obvious? When I had brushed my fingers over the poster, I had felt nothing but distress. What had she seen that I had not? "*What* was?"

Her eyes snapped to mine, and I felt myself step back from the waves of strength that were pouring off her. Here was a woman who had nothing but pain and loss to call her own, and yet she stood tall. What did she know with such certainty that I did not?

Her smile was brittle. "I touched where he marked the poster with his insignia, and I felt his emotions like he was standing right next to me. Touching things and feeling the emotions behind them has always been a strange gift of mine, but what I felt I was not prepared for."

I wanted to scream at her. I was so tired of all the riddles and half answers! "What," I managed to ask through clenched teeth, "did you feel?"

"Fear." Her eyes raked over me before they settled on my face. "He's *afraid*, Ariel. He's afraid of *you*."

I stumbled away from her. She was a crazy old lady, that's all. She was a crazy old lady who thought she could feel someone's emotions by touching an insignia, for goodness sake. Of course, not a week ago, I had an elf heal me with her bare hands. What had Maven said? Touching things and feeling emotions had always been a strange gift? Could it even be possible? Could there be such giftings in this world? Was I so blinded by ignorance that I thought the gift of sight was the only gift that could exist? Why had my mother never told me of the world around us? I was a like a newborn colt sent out to wonder aimlessly—and maybe by sheer luck survive.

Why would King Titus be afraid of me? What did I possess that threatened him?

"I brought you here for a specific reason, Ariel."

I looked over the valley again. Her reason had better be phenomenal, for this image would be the source of my nightmares for years.

Maven grabbed my chin, forcing my eyes to hers. "I want you to know what it looks like. I want you to witness what Titus's greed for power will do. I want you to know the smell of death miles before you reach it. I want you to know the feeling of your comrade's blood against your skin." Her hand forced me to look back at the valley. "I want you to know the sight of an ocean of blood miles around. I want you to familiarize yourself with what is left in the wake of a violent man's quest to destroy all freedom, all hope." Her hand dropped to her side. "I want you to know, Ariel Deverell, because from now on this is your life. Until somebody dares to stop him, you will live in a red world. Get used to death now. You'll be an angel of death, and you'll watch in despair as everyone you love falls beside you."

"I just want my family back!" I yelled, the frustration I had been trying to hold back rising to the surface.

"Get out of your own little world," she demanded, her eyes sparking. "This isn't just about you and your family anymore. It's so much bigger than that."

She had the wrong person. "I'm just one person," I said. What could I possibly do that could make any difference? If all the monarchs had already been beaten, what did I have to offer?

"If not you, then who? Get rid of your feelings of inadequacy; there just isn't time for them. Your people need you—someone who will find a spot worthy to defend and will take a stand. Someone who isn't afraid to take on Titus."

But that was just the problem, wasn't it? I *was* afraid. I had no means to take down someone like him. "But I don't know how." I felt as if I were drowning, and the more I screamed for help, the further I sunk. What was Maven expecting me to do, start a rebellion?

"One day at a time."

What kind of answer was that? "You're asking me to commit treason." I was really grasping at straws now, but she had to realize I wasn't the person she thought I was.

"Ariel, you're already wanted dead. He's taken your world away from you; why are you so afraid? What more can he possibly do to you?" she asked.

What of my family? If I were killed before all this was over, who would rescue them? However, to be honest, that wasn't the fear that was eating at me. "What if I fail?" I whispered. What if I failed and more valleys like this appeared?

"What if you never tried?"

What if I never tried? It was an excellent question. If I didn't try, Titus would continue to kill by the hundreds, and places like Gabriel would continue to be destroyed. No one else had stepped up to do anything about it. The monarchs seemed to be completely out of the picture. So, if not me . . . then who? I bit down on my lip. I wasn't a little girl any longer; I couldn't depend on my parents forever. Somebody had to take a stand. My father would, if he was here. My mother would already be knocking on Titus's door.

So it was to be me, then.

Maven seemed to know something had shifted within my heart. Her arms wrapped around me in a tight hug. "You are beyond a special individual, and one day, Ariel, you will see it."

I wrapped my arms around her, inhaling her lavender scent. We stayed that way for a long moment. I soaked in as much comfort as I possibly could, because from here on out it was bound to get a lot worse.

She pulled back and smiled up at me before dropping a small silver key into my hand. "When the world has gone completely dark, and the very land is screaming, remember . . . to hope. At the right moment, you'll know what to do with this. Safeguard it with your life." She closed my fingers over the small key. "And one more thing. Find the monarchs and you'll find your way." Her hand tightened around mine. "The monarchs will be your way to take down Titus. Find them, and find them fast."

CHAPTER VIII

M y desire to tear up my wanted poster was nothing compared to the raging need to shred Cyrus's map. My hands shook violently as I glared at what lay before me. I had unrolled the map expecting to still see a detailed depiction of how to get to Midas. I knew, for at least the immediate moment, I was going to have to put my rescue on hold. Yet, the map was my one reassurance that I could still get there at any time. Now, though, it no longer showed Midas. No. Now, it was a map of all ten realms, with twenty blinking markers on it. If I had to wager a guess, and it really wasn't much of a leap, it was the exact location of all the monarchs.

The scream that ripped from my throat shattered the peaceful stillness of Gabriel and sent my companions running to my side. Maven was to blame for this. Not only had she altered my course, now my map was completely rewriting itself. Seriously, what map changed locations overnight?

"Ariel!" Colter's frantic voice lashed through my daze, whipping me back to reality. "What happened?"

I wasn't given a chance to answer.

Samuel's hand latched around my wrist with enough force to break bones. "How did you get Isidora's map?" he asked, his voice deadly calm. I vastly preferred his constant yelling; his quietness meant something else entirely.

I glanced over at Colter, who was choosing to studiously ignore the exchange. His hand still rested dangerously on his sword as he paced away.

"Whose map?" I asked, my attention swinging back to Samuel. As far as I knew, I had never heard the name Isidora before, but of course I also had never heard of giftings, or of the massacres Titus had been responsible for.

"Where did you get the map, Ariel?" Samuel asked, avoiding my question—which was really no surprise; he excelled in dodging every question I ever asked of him.

What he didn't realize was that two could play that game. "Let go of my arm," I demanded, covering my confusion with bravado. "Who is Isidora?" And why did it bear such significance to him?

His jaw started to spasm in agitation, but he dropped his hold on me to jab a finger towards the map. "Answer my question, Ariel Deverell. Where did you get it?"

I rolled the map up slowly, the leather supple in my hands. With wary eyes trained on him, I tucked it in my pack carefully. "Cyrus." I snapped. "Before he oh-so-kindly dropped me in the middle of nowhere."

Colter stalked back to where we stood. "Are you saying she has in her possession the map of Isidora Emaggen? You had better be mistaken, Fairchild."

"No one asked you, Saerdothian," Samuel said, not even bothering to look at him.

I flinched at the way his lips curled around the word Saerdothian. Colter didn't deserve that type of degradation; calling him a Saerdothian was worse than calling him a rabid dog.

Murder flashed in Colter's eyes. "Rather a Saerdothian than an Imperialist pig, and if that truly is what you say it is, keep your voice down." With that, he paced a few feet away and took up vigilance at the edge of the town square.

Samuel rubbed his chin in irritation. "I can't believe you don't even realize what you have in your possession."

Did he realize he still hadn't told me who Isidora was? "Yes," I snapped. "I do. A very irritating map."

He ground his teeth together, his way of trying to swallow the insults before they spilled out. Ironic, since he usually didn't worry about having self-control. "Why Cyrus gave that to you, without properly explaining it, is a mystery I intend to solve. Unfortunately, I can't deal with him until later," he said, anger underlying his words. "For now, don't let that map out of your sight for a mere second. Do you understand me?"

He had to be the bossiest person alive. The only pleasure I could find in any of this was that I could give him absolute fits, considering I had to be the most stubborn person alive. "Are you going to explain what is so special about this map?"

He sighed heavily, a sign of defeat. "There are three maps that exist in the ten realms that are . . . well, special in nature: Isidora's, Kieran's, and Oddisan's. The maps are said to lead you to your greatest desire, with the exception of Isidora's. Hers is rumored to lead you to your greatest need. Not only that, but since her death it has remained invisible." He peered down at me, speculating. "Cyrus is, well was, in possession of two of the three. Oddisan's was lost generations ago. If any of the maps got into the wrong hands, well, I shouldn't have to spell it out for you."

Dread tugged at me. Why had Cyrus handed me something so powerful? If someone like Titus got his hands on one of these maps, no one would be safe. There would be no hiding; the entire ten realms would be an open book for him and his bloodlust. The thought sent shivers through me.

The next thought was just as disturbing. Why was the map visible to me? If it had been invisible since Isidora's death, why did it choose now to suddenly work again? Also, if Samuel was correct in his history and Isidora's map led you to your greatest need . . . that meant Midas was no longer where I was meant to go. Now it wanted me to find the monarchs. I could ignore it, of course. I knew Colter could still get me to Midas; he had been telling me for days he didn't need the help of a map. I reached up and touched the necklace hidden under my tunic. Cyrus had sent me out with a warning device *and* a map that led me to my greatest need. The least I could do was attempt to track down the monarchs. If I had to stumble around in the dark for a little while longer, trying to figure out the puzzle, then so be it. Cyrus had entrusted me with two invaluable objects, and I had made a promise to Maven.

I couldn't let Gabriel down.

I wasn't lucky enough to get rid of Samuel. I had to try to cut loose Colter, though; he shouldn't have to risk his neck any more than he already had. Ignoring Samuel, I walked over to where Colter stood guard. I touched his arm gently and pasted a confident smile on my face. "Colter, you've given up so much for me already. Saved my life twice, and I'll never be able to thank you enough for it. But I have to do some things before I can go to Midas, and you shouldn't have to protect me any longer."

His eyes darkened as he stared down at me. "What of your family?"

My fingers tightened on his arm. "If I don't accomplish what I need to before I go get them, it'll all be a moot point anyway. They'll never be truly safe."

"You mean to take down Titus," he said, his voice grim.

He had lost his entire family to Titus, and now it looked like I was abandoning mine to attempt the impossible. He would never understand any reason I gave him, and the thought of him leaving, thinking I was a coward and fool, hurt. "I—"

He reached up and clasped my hand gently. "Ariel, wherever you go, so do I. I can't pretend to understand why you are choosing to not go to Midas, but whatever the reason is, I know it's a good one." His eyes filled with resolve. "And I'll be right behind you the whole way."

I couldn't help myself; I threw my arms around him, giving him a tight hug. I only held on for a split second, knowing his embarrassment would make his dark skin light up like a candle.

"What fool-headed plan have you concocted this time?" Samuel asked, his voice ringing with dismay.

If only it were possible to get rid of him! Turning my head slowly, I met his gaze. "You're not invited."

He growled under his breath before stalking over to me. "For days I've been forced to hear how you have to get to Midas." He leaned forward, going nose to nose with me. "Midas this, and Midas that," he mocked, his eyes sparking. "And now, *now* you're saying we aren't going?"

My toes curled in my boots. How I would like to kick him right now. "I don't believe I stuttered. I said I wasn't going at this precise moment. You, however, can do whatever you want." I saw his eyes narrow in victory, so I added hastily, "As long as it takes you far away from me."

"Logan—" he began, before I cut him off.

"Logan isn't here," I said, filtering the emotion out of my voice. "I don't know if you've noticed, but he left. So any debt you had with him is null and void."

"I'm not going anywhere," he stated, crossing his arms with such determination that, for a mere second, I thought his motives were more than a debt to be repaid. "Not until Logan releases me from service."

Tapping my foot impatiently, I glared up at him. "Unbelievable," I muttered. I was a helpless fool. The fluttering feeling I had experienced in the bottom of my stomach when he had first appeared was replaced with reality.

An ear-shattering trumpet pierced the air, interrupting what was going to become an unending argument. The horn blows following set my teeth on edge and the ground trembling. It was the sound of Midas, created for the sole purpose of inspiring fear. Colter's sword was already arcing through the air as he prepared to meet whatever obstacle came rushing his way. Samuel drew his sword and stood with its blade pointed downwards. He froze into utter stillness, eyes searching for any incoming danger.

Henry burst into the square with three horses in tow. He handed reins to each of us silently, his movements calm and precise. "King Titus has sent another battalion; it won't take long until they break through our border. You must leave immediately; they can't discover that you've been here."

Words were inadequate. "I will never be able to thank you enough," I said. Gabriel would forever hold a special place in my heart, and I only wished I could take them all with me.

Henry beamed at me. "No matter what happens today, it'll all be well worth it as long as you survive to see the next sunrise." He pushed me towards my mount. "Now go. Go!"

The eighth realm was famous for its horseflesh. I only hoped the wildly outrageous rumors proved to be somewhat true. We were going to need every ounce of speed we could get. Considering he had handed me a beautiful bay Meshkaret, I held high hopes. Colter and Samuel had both received Storphians and were already mounted. Following suit, I reached down to clasp Henry's hand. "You tell Maven I'll keep my promise."

He nodded tightly, his eyes darting to something behind us. His hand flew out and smacked the back of my mount. Wrapping my hands tightly around the reins, I leaned forward and prayed we had a chance of getting out of Gabriel alive.

"Colter!" Samuel hollered, keeping even pace with me. "Get us back into the Shade, NOW!"

Colter signaled that he understood, and with a sharp turn he headed us straight back from where we had come from. The necklace beat against my skin as we rode, its scalding heat a reminder we had a ways to go before we were safe.

The booming of Midas's horns sunk claws into my skin with vicious precision. Titus didn't strike me as the type to allow survivors. Henry and Maven, what would happen to them? What would happen to the town that dared protect me? My heart stuttered and gasped to the pounding of my mount's hooves.

Would we ever be able to stop running?

We rode hard for most of the night, attempting to put as much distance between ourselves and Gabriel as possible. When dawn began to streak across the gray sky, Colter was the one to break our strained silence. After wincing at the sound of every broken branch and would-be pursuer, we were shocked at the sound of his voice: "We should rest for a while."

For once, I didn't bother to argue. My poor horse had to be exhausted, and yet she hadn't wavered once. Colter found us a small glen, and with a weary sigh, I slid out of my saddle. Would I ever be able to walk normally again?

"I wish I had a treat for you, girl," I murmured, unbuckling the saddle and pulling it off. "The rumors of the eighth realm don't even come close to the truth about you." She nuzzled against me, eliciting a dim smile. My lips cracked painfully. When was the last time I had bothered to smile? The revelation was not a welcome one; indeed, who exactly was I becoming?

Focusing back on the spirited mare, my attention was caught by her eyes. They were a brilliant emerald green—and filled with an unusual amount of understanding. "Odd," I said, feeling as if I were missing something blatantly obvious. Leading her over to a nearby stream, I let her drink her fill before settling her in for the night.

"Hey, Wildcat! You done yet?" Samuel called from where he was building a fire.

Rolling my eyes, I tossed him a dirty look. "What? Need someone to hold your hand and tell you what a good job you're doing?"

He ignored my remark. "Talking to animals is the first step towards insanity."

I laughed, but the sound was hollow and foreign. "No, traveling with you was my first step," I retorted, kicking a rock his way.

Colter smirked, but quickly hid his grin from Samuel's glare. "I'll take first watch." He wandered away, and I listened as he climbed into a nearby tree and made himself comfortable.

As usual, Samuel flopped down next to the fire, his breathing deepening within minutes. I envied his ability to fall asleep anywhere at any time. Drawing my blanket around my shoulders, I hunched down next to his still form.

Fatigue weighed me down, but my mind refused to quiet. Pulling out Isidora's map, I carefully unrolled it and spread it over my lap. Never had I seen such an intricate and detailed map. Everything was labeled: roads, towns, rivers, crown cities. I trailed my finger to where a pulsating star glowed. It wasn't until then that I noticed two smaller stars had joined my marker. Why stars? Sighing, I turned my attention to the other pinpricks of light on the page.

Maven had said that Titus killed a good portion of the monarchs during the coup. If that was the case, why in the world did I have twenty markers? Without even realizing it, I bit my lip so hard I tasted a trickle of blood while trying to quell my frustration. Pulling the key out of my pack, I twisted it between my fingers. What was so stinking special about it?

It was so light it felt like I was holding air, and it whistled softly every time I moved it. If it was so important, why did Maven have it in her possession? One would think a monarch would keep control of it. A stray thought tickled my mind. "Samuel?"

He rolled over to scowl at me. "What?"

"What happens when a monarch dies?" I inquired, still toying with the key.

"A keeper is named until the next monarch is crowned," he grunted, before burying his head under his arms again.

"A keeper of what?"

He didn't immediately answer, so I nudged him with my foot. "Samuel! A keeper of what?"

"Ariel! For ten seconds stop thinking and get some sleep!" he sighed, refusing to move.

"Answer me first. A keeper of what?" I demanded, my eyes scouring the map. What was it trying to tell me? I had never considered myself dimwitted, but this map had me doubting my ability to deduce anything.

"Nobody knows. Very few keepers have ever had to be named. Usually the surviving spouse will just hold onto it."

I knew I wasn't going to get any more answers from him; his breathing was already slowing and deepening again. Seriously, how did he do that? I looked back to the key in my hand. What if the key was what was passed on from monarch to monarch? Did every monarch in the realms have one? Had Maven been named a keeper after Titus's initial attack? Did that mean a monarch of the eighth realm survived somewhere? Or was the key completely unrelated to my search for the realms' dethroned royalty?

It was an unending circle in my head.

There was a marker not far from our current location, balanced between the eighth and sixth realm. That would be our first destination then, and maybe when we reached whomever it was, I would find some much-needed answers.

"You're going to give yourself permanent wrinkles," Samuel said, "if you glare at that map any longer."

Okay, so maybe he wasn't as asleep as I had thought. I opened my mouth to tell him to go jump off a cliff, but the words died in my throat.

Sitting up, he reached over to take the map out of my hands. Methodically, he rolled it up and placed it by my knee. I watched in confusion as he then yanked the key from my fingers and placed it on the map. Unsure of what he was up to, I was caught off guard when he gathered up my hands in his, causing me to stare at our joined hands in a stupor. My hands were dwarfed by his, and pale against his deeply tanned skin. Yet, it wasn't the startling differences between them that wholly captured me. No, what was disturbing was the small jump my heart made at the contact.

What was the deal with me? It was Samuel freakin' Fairchild, the man who excelled at being arrogant and annoying on a daily basis.

"Ariel, everything will work itself out, you'll see." He let go with one hand long enough to reach up and gently pull on a wayward strand of my hair which he then tucked neatly behind my ear. "You may drag us all over the realms for some perceived noble quest, but I'll make sure to be right next to you until the moment you're standing within the borders of Midas."

His words shouldn't have mattered so much, but they did.

CHAPTER IX

"Y ou sure that map is correct?" Colter asked, his skeptical eyes sliding to mine.

I hated to admit it, but I was beginning to wonder the same thing. We stood in a clearing, staring at a dilapidated shack that looked ready to cave in on itself any second. As far as hiding places went, it left a lot to be desired. "According to Isidora's wonder map, this is the place." My horse, whom I had affectionately named Aaleyah, stamped her hooves in protest when I handed her reins to Samuel. Pulling out my blade, I stared at it a long moment before stowing it back in my boot.

"Ariel Deverell, what are you doing?" Fairchild hissed, his eyes narrowing to dangerous slits.

"Whoever is in there is not our enemy," I said, forcing my expression into one of utter calm. "And you aren't exactly the picture of friendliness, so I'm going in first." I didn't really want to tell them they had no worries because my magical necklace wasn't burning me.

"I don't think so," Colter growled, grabbing my sleeve.

Sighing, I pried his fingers loose, one by one. "Just stay here," I muttered. Was everything going to turn into fights between the three of us? He started to grab for me again, but I danced away from his hands and raced across the field to the door of the shack.

"Hello?" I didn't really expect an answer, but the shuffling inside was the only indicator I needed. We were definitely in the right spot.

Colter and Samuel were breathing down my neck, but I didn't spare them any attention. With a brush of my fingers, the door opened, revealing inky darkness.

"Go ahead. Kill me."

Swinging my head to the left, I allowed my eyes to adjust. A man was huddled in the corner; he was wringing his hands and rocking back and forth like his next breath depended on it.

"I've nothing left," he moaned, grabbing at his head and yanking at his disheveled hair. "My beloved, gone . . . forever gone . . ."

Motioning for the guys to stay put, I crept forward. "Sir?" The tattered tunic he wore had the mark of the eighth realm, which would make him King Slade. Maven must have been named keeper, for it sounded like Queen Rosalind was dead.

His hand snaked out to grab my tunic, bringing me nose to nose with him. He reeked of decay and sorrow. "Don't play with me; just do it already!"

Out of the corner of my eye, I saw Samuel inch forward and Colter draw his sword. Wiggling my fingers at them to signal they shouldn't move, I willed the right words to come. "I'm not here to kill you," I said, striving to keep my voice soothing.

He ground his teeth together, his eyes whirling in a frenzy. He began shaking me to the point that I thought my neck was going to snap. "Why not!" he cried, his voice breaking.

I felt myself wrenched from his hands. "Ariel, are you okay?" I nodded mutely at Samuel, waiting for my vision to clear. King Slade began rocking again, mumbling to himself about lousy Imperialists.

"What are we doing here, Ariel?" Colter asked. "He's lost his mind."

Who could blame him? His kingdom had been torn from him, his wife was dead, and he was hiding in a hovel. Stepping away from Samuel, I moved back to Slade's side. The pendent under my tunic turned so frigid I yanked it out with a startled gasp.

The second Slade saw the crisscrossing swords he stopped rocking. With wide eyes he reached forward to hesitantly touch it.

"The mark of Emaggen." Pulling back sharply, his face lit up. "You're the one."

I looked at the glowing necklace in my hand and then back to the astonished Slade. "I'm the one?"

Fumbling in his tunic, he pulled out a small silk pouch and withdrew a silver key identical to the one Maven had given me. "Take it," he ordered quietly, some of his regal bearing slipping back into place.

I had been expecting a lot of things. However, being nearly shaken to death, declared that I was the one, and then thrown a key had not exactly been my first thoughts. I kept my hands clenched, refusing to take the key. "What do you mean, I'm the one?"

He cocked his head sideways like I had spoken another language. "You carry the mark around your neck, and yet you do not know?"

If I knew what nonsense he was spouting, I wouldn't have asked. "Please explain."

His eyes cast nervously from me to the men standing behind me. "At the summit, he told us to watch for the one with the mark . . . we were so foolish . . ." He grimaced. "Rosalind, my Rosalind paid for it. If we had only listened to his warnings . . ." He offered the key to me again. "You'll need this."

I took it hesitantly, along with the pouch. "Who warned you, and what did he warn you about?"

Slade slumped against the wall, his eyes filling with tears. "He told us one would rise and secure his position by blood. He said he knew it was useless to warn us, for we would do nothing to stop it, but that we must know to watch for the one with the mark." Shoving the key at me, he ignored the tears dribbling down into his beard.

"Why was the mark so important?" I had to know why, to finally have some concrete answers.

The king smiled sadly and patted my knee. "Because the one bearing the mark will be the one to save us all, and I know better than to disbelieve Cyrus Drenuellon."

Stealing Samuel's longbow, I left the men in order to track us down something to eat. So far we hadn't experienced any problems with finding wild game, but soon we were going to need to stock up on rations. Slade would be the first to join our merry little band, but what happened when we found more royalty? What were we going to do with them all? We couldn't be traveling around the realms with an entourage; stealth was our only ally at the moment.

After taking down a couple of rabbits, I headed back to the campsite. We had hidden ourselves back inside the borders of the Shade, hoping no Imperialists would come around. I felt for the silk pouch in my boot and sighed in relief when my fingers brushed against it. I had hidden both keys within the pouch, and I was beginning to doubt the wisdom of that decision. I was going to drive myself crazy by checking on it every few minutes, but the thought of losing it set my heart racing.

We ate in weary silence, and it wasn't until Samuel left to take over as lookout that I moved closer to Slade. "Sire?"

His eyes moved sluggishly to mine. "Slade, please. I'm not a king, not anymore."

It felt wrong not to use his title when addressing him, but if that was what he insisted, then fine.

"Slade, I was hoping you could answer just a few questions—"

"I'm not sure I'm the best one to be asking anything," he said, picking at his pant legs.

He was going to be worse to draw answers out of than Samuel. "Please, if you could just answer a couple of questions."

He nodded slowly, focusing all his attention on his pants. "Okay."

"The keys, what are they for?" I asked.

"Don't know."

He didn't know? Who *would* know, then? "Who would know?" Maybe I just needed to be a little more specific with my answers.

"Don't know."

Clenching my teeth, I reined in my temper. My mother had admonished me more times than I care to admit about my lack of restraint. "Do you know the fates of the other monarchs, who lives and who has been murdered?"

"No."

Clamping my fingers together, I forced a smile. "Can you tell me about the summit Cyrus called?"

"Already told you all I know."

This was pointless. I was dragging around a man who was so lost in self-pity he didn't want anything to do with anybody. "Okay, thank you."

Exhaling slowly, I stood and walked a few feet away. If Slade didn't know of the key's use, why were they so important?

Colter patted the spot beside him, so I dropped down next to him with a heavy sigh. "Will anything ever make sense?" I asked, keeping my voice low so Slade wouldn't overhear.

Colter shrugged before adding another branch onto the fire. "Nothing in this world worth doing is ever easy, and you're attempting the impossible."

Why did it have to be impossible? How had Titus managed to do so much damage in so little time? "How did Titus rise to power?"

"Brutality. Most say he's been bestowed with the dark gifting. Although, he didn't take over the realms by himself; his warrior did most of his dirty work."

Pulling my knees up to my chest, I wrapped my arms around them. "His warrior?"

"Most call the man the devil's champion. He always wears a dark hood cloaking his features, which is why there are so many wild stories about him—such as he breathes fire and has eyes as red as hell. Nonsense, all of it."

"But you said Titus had help." I was a little lost by his explanation, and more than a little worried that Titus might actually be gifted with brutality. At this point, giftings were starting to become an annoying pattern in my life.

"Oh, the warrior exists, all right," Colter said. "But he isn't from the fires of hell. Worse, actually."

There was something worse? "How so?"

"He can't be beaten. Whether he has a soul or not, it doesn't really matter. There doesn't exist a person in this world who can best him."

Pieces began clicking together in my head. With a sick feeling in my stomach, I looked at Colter. "You're saying Titus has control of a man who can never be beaten?"

"Titus has many resources at hand, and he's not afraid to kill to get his way. Fear is how he got control, and it's how he'll turn everyone into hopeless slaves. He started his coup by taking out the monarchs. In the ensuing chaos, he took out crops and all food sources. He sent armies to bully towns into submission. He built Midas in secret and spent years gathering an unconquerable army to keep himself protected. There are few who are still actively fighting against him, Gabriel being one of the remaining places." He paused, his eyes drifting to the fire. "And we know how that turned out."

"How did they let this happen? The monarchs did nothing—" I said, my anger slicing into the air.

"We were a world in peace."

My head snapped up to see Slade standing by the fire, staring at me blankly. How much of the conversation had he just overheard?

"We were at peace, and then the next morning we wake up to find men in our rooms trying to kill us. We didn't know."

"If Cyrus warned you—"

He laughed, the sound frenzied and broken. "An *elf* appears out of nowhere saying the old world has not yet fallen. He says that soon we will be attacked, something which has not happened in hundreds of years. He says that, in our arrogance, we forgot our history, and we shall pay for it. He was a laughingstock—" Slade choked on his words and batted at the moisture on his cheeks. "We laughed and laughed, called him a fool and a liar."

I felt pity for Slade but agreed with Cyrus. The monarchs had been arrogant; did they think the realms of Algernon were the only lands that existed? Worse, it wasn't outsiders who attacked; it was one of their own. "Do you really not know what the keys are for?"

He fell in a heap, his sorrowful eyes finally meeting mine. "They were passed down from generation to generation. They were made in the olden times, when elves, dwarves, and humans lived amongst each other. Then the Great War broke out, and the land was attacked by outsiders. Chaos reigned for at least a hundred years, and the old world crumbled. Once the outsiders were beaten, new territories were marked, and we fell into a peaceful lull. The legend is that they open a gate, a gate to a new land that was long closed off for our own safety. I do not know if it is true; we were just told to protect them." He shrugged. "I do not know what is truth anymore. A few months ago I would have told you I didn't even believe in elves."

A gate to a new land. Could it be possible?

"It's a legend, Ariel," Colter said, cutting into the conversation. "One you would do well not to put too much faith into."

You had to put faith into something, and so far an old legend was all I had. Wehjaeel help me, I only had so many options left.

CHAPTER X

When I was younger, I had always awakened before dawn dared touch the sky. It had been the time of day I spent with my brother Fallon. We were the closest in age, and nearly inseparable. We spent our entire childhood terrorizing our older siblings, and we loved every minute of it. When first meeting us, most people assumed we were twins, and since we were only a year apart, we basically were. Fallon had been the gravity to my reckless flights—and probably the sole reason I was still alive. If he had been with us now, perhaps I would've awakened to greet the day in the fashion I was used to.

This morning, though, something went horribly wrong. I didn't wake up because of my body tugging me into the real world out of instinct; I woke up because steel was scraping across my throat.

Wheezing, I wrenched myself into reality and fought madly against the soldier hauling me to my feet. "Let me go!"

"Now, now, now, what do we have here?" the man drawled as he hauled me up against his chest, entrapping me with his sword to my neck.

My panicked eyes sought out Slade first, but he was nowhere to be seen. Where had the man gone? Colter was being held down by a half dozen soldiers, and Samuel was trying to fight his way to my side.

"I suggest, men, you stop your fighting before I'm forced to detach her pretty head from her body."

I winced at the sound of my captor's voice. How had they come upon us? Obviously, my sleeping habits needed to change.

Colter immediately went still and earned a bloody nose in payment. Samuel hesitated, his eyes gauging his chances before falling to mine. The man holding me was already slackening his grip, thinking I wasn't worth much in a fight. Throwing my head back, I heard bone smash, but I didn't let it deter me. Slamming my elbow into his kidneys, I slipped out from his arms and went for the daggers in my boots.

Samuel and Colter took that as their signal to continue fighting.

"You will pay for that, girl," the man roared, swiping the blood from his face with the back of his hand. It was a useless gesture; his nose was smashed to the side in sickening fashion.

Circling each other, I kept a wary eye on the sword he kept slicing through the air. He was over six feet, with enough muscle to cause some serious damage. I was going to have to depend on my speed to win this fight. Roaring, he charged, looking more like my neighbor's prize bull than a man.

Standing my ground, I deflected his first blow, but the impact jarred my slight frame. We wove in and out of a sick dance, both drawing blood frequently. I could tell he thought he had the upper hand with his oversized sword, but I was holding my own with the blades Cyrus had given me. I began to favor my left leg in hopes he would sense weakness. Sure enough, he kicked my right leg out from under me, but instead of crumbling, I dove forward, plowing my dagger through his heart.

Shock flashed in his eyes as blood gurgled from his mouth. "Y-you'll join me s-s-soon," he gasped, before crashing to the ground. Yanking my blade free, I looked up to see that Colter had gotten free, and Samuel had almost made it to my location.

Where was Slade?

Narrowly dodging a sword to my stomach, I let one of my daggers fly. It landed in the soldier's jugular, spraying me with his lifeblood. He was just a boy sent to do a man's job. Fighting past my rising nausea, I collected my blade and cut down the soldier engaged in a deadly duel with Samuel.

Samuel reached out to clasp my forearm and tug me close; his eyes searched our surroundings as he moved me to the side, away from the bloodshed. "Are you alright?" he asked, meeting my eyes briefly before continuing to scan the area around us.

"No," I answered simply, letting my hands dangle at my sides. It had been one thing killing creatures that hardly seemed human; this was entirely different. I had just killed soldiers who were only fighting us because of orders from a demented man. I had killed a boy who wasn't even old enough to shave, and I was supposed to be okay with it?

Those three men had been somebody's father, son, or husband. They had been somebody's Bryne.

"Ariel!"

The chaos around me deadened at the sound of that one voice. Samuel dropped his hold on my arm and moved to assist Colter, his eyes on someone behind me. I wasn't aware of what was going on, but I knew that voice as well as I knew my own face.

Logan.

Swinging around, I blindly launched myself forward, knowing that wherever he was he would catch me. Caught in a bear hug, I buried my head in his familiar woodsy smell and breathed a sigh of relief. "Logan, where have you been?" I cried, holding on for dear life.

His arms tightened around me. "Hey, Ari. Long time no see."

He sounded old, worn out, no longer the boy he had been when he had dropped me off in the Shade. I tilted my head back to look at him, and, with one look in those brown eyes, I felt like I had managed to reclaim a small piece of home. "How did you find us?"

His lips widened into a welcoming smile. "Been trying to catch up to you for days now. Ran across the Imperialist squad and decided to follow them. Sure enough, they led me right to you."

Remembering we weren't alone, I broke from his grasp to check on Samuel and Colter. The squad of soldiers lay dead where they had fallen. Samuel was checking out Colter's nose, and Slade was still nowhere to be seen. I could catch up with Logan in a minute; first things first.

"Where's Slade?" I inquired.

Colter shrugged. "As soon as the first boot of an Imperialist landed in our camp, he was running. I imagine it's second nature to him; he's been running for his life for almost a year."

He couldn't have gone far. Keeping my blades in my hands, I stamped my way into the woods, looking for any sign of his flight. "SLADE!" Granted, I had the key. I could let him find his own way around. There was a part of me, though, that felt responsible to keep him alive, and he wasn't going to live much longer if he took off on his own.

"Just let him go, Ariel." I hadn't realized Logan had followed me.

"I can't do that, Logan," I said, my eyes catching sight of a partial boot print. "SLADE!"

It didn't take long before a head poked around a tree. "They gone?" Slade asked, his eyes sliding to Logan.

I smiled tightly. "Yes," I answered. "Now come help us so we can get out of here."

He followed us back to camp like a whipped dog, and it wasn't hard to understand why. Colter and Samuel were glaring a hole through the man. "Don't even start with him," I ordered, sheathing my weapons.

The dead soldiers deserved individual graves; unfortunately, we did not have time to bestow that dignity. Walking up to the first body, I dragged him to the side of the camp. Panting with the effort, I followed suit with two more of the corpses.

"Ariel, you're bleeding," Colter pointed out, softly stopping me mid-stride.

I looked down at myself, taking inventory. I wasn't seriously injured, just a little scratched up. To be honest, I didn't want to take the time to think about it. If I started thinking, I would be forced to come to grips with the fact that I had killed three men. So, since I didn't want to go down that path, I concentrated instead on piling up the bodies. There had to be a couple dozen men here; we were lucky to all be walking away alive.

"Ariel." Samuel's strained voice coerced my blank stare toward his eyes. "We don't have time for this. We need to leave before another squad comes running to avenge their buddies."

Logan spoke before I could gather my scattered thoughts. "Fairchild, I don't actually know why you are still here. Consider your debt paid in full."

I watched carefully for Samuel's response. To me, this moment was going to make all the difference in the world. Would he leave now that Logan had released him? Had his words last night just been uttered to make me feel better about life?

Samuel didn't flinch from my questioning gaze; it must have been a trick of my mind because it looked as if his left eye dropped in a leisurely wink.

He strolled to my side with slow, precise movements. Relaxed, he pulled out a handkerchief and dabbed it in his canteen. What was he doing?

He smiled lightly at me before gingerly wiping at the blood that had sprayed my face. His gaze stayed connected with mine as he answered Logan. "Sorry, Gallagher. I made a promise I aim to keep." He pressed the handkerchief into my hand, his natural look of superiority slipping back on his face. "You've got ten minutes, Ariel."

Stunned, I clutched the handkerchief. He was staying. In fact, he hadn't even hesitated for a second. On top of that, for a brief murderous moment, Logan looked ready to tear him to bits.

Was I going to be forced to completely reevaluate Samuel Fairchild?

We piled up the bodies and, after a brief prayer, burned the remains. It was the best I could do for them, and I hoped their families would understand. I juggled the small pieces of wood in my hand that I had found on each body. Little rectangles of wood imprinted with a name, rank, and squad number. Somehow, when this nightmare was all over, I would find the families and apologize.

It was the least I could do for them.

We were lucky that several of the Imperialists' horses were still ambling around. Snatching one for Slade and an extra for our packs, we set off. Logan found his way to my side, and though I knew I should wait for him to voluntarily share with me, I wanted answers too badly. "Where did you go when you left me, Logan? What have you been up to for the past couple of weeks?"

He kept his eyes forward, staring a hole into Samuel's back. "I've been working on a plan to get into Midas and rescue your parents." He finally looked over at me, his eyes dark. "The better question is what have *you* been up to? You and Samuel were supposed to stay hidden. Low and behold, I find you traveling around, towing a Saerdothian and former king. What have you gotten yourself mixed up in this time?"

I opened my mouth to defend myself, but he obviously wasn't done ranting because he cut me off before I even began. "Ariel, when will you learn to leave well enough alone? Why couldn't you have trusted me and just stayed put?"

Irritated, my hands involuntarily tightened on the reins. Aaleyah shifted under me in response to my agitation. "First of all, don't talk to me like I'm three, Logan Michael Gallagher. I can still whip your butt in any fight." He rolled his eyes, but I was just getting started. "Secondly, don't refer to Colter as a Saerdothian; he's a man just like you. Therefore he deserves your utmost respect. He's saved my life twice now."

"What of your family? Have you forgotten them so easily?"

I whipped my head around to glare at him. "We've been friends since before we could walk. What do you think?"

He had sense enough to look ashamed. "I just don't understand why you are traveling away from Midas."

I attempted to tell him the story of how I had ended up on my quest for the monarchs—and about Isidora's map. I told him about the keys and the legend of the gate. I left out the bit about Cyrus and Airis; that wasn't my secret to share. I also left out how Samuel had so easily dispatched of the Eagles; some things Logan didn't need to be made aware of.

He whistled softly. "You sure have been busy, haven't you? You want to tell me why all of a sudden there are wanted posters of you showing up in every city?"

I shrugged, trying to look nonchalant. "He's starting a harem?" I laughed softly at his expression. "Don't give me that look. You look as if you've been sucking lemons."

"You're not taking this at all seriously. Titus Ephraim is not a man to mess around with. He'll kill you for looking sideways at him. With your mouth, you're likely to get into all sorts of trouble; you need to keep your head low." He reached over to clasp my hand. "I don't want to see anything happen to you."

I tried to smile at him. "What sorts of trouble could I possibly get myself into within the next couple of days? All I'm doing is rousting monarchs who've been in hiding because a monster is out for their blood."

CHAPTER XI

I f there was anything I would hate for the rest of my life it would be snow. Fat, white flakes stuck to my clothing and face, soaking through my thin clothes and freezing my skin.

"Here—"

I looked up to see Samuel dangling his gloves in front of my face. "Take them."

"No." Tucking my chin against my chest, I let Aaleyah take the lead. All I wanted was a blazing fire and some dry socks. Okay, that was a lie. I also wanted a warmer cloak and some hot food.

Samuel leaned over and yanked my hands out of my cloak. Fighting for balance in the saddle, I glared at him. "Are you trying to get me killed?"

Shoving his gloves on my hands, he released his hold on me. "No, I'm trying to keep you from losing your fingers."

They were nice gloves, a little big but extraordinarily warm. "Thank you," I whispered, braving another look at him.

He nodded mutely and moved back to the front of the line of miserable riders. We were headed to a small outskirt town in the sixth realm. Isidora's map showed three blinking lights clustered together. What I hadn't counted on was the first snow-fall of the year. We were woefully unprepared; poor Slade couldn't stop shivering, causing Samuel to toss his cloak at him hours ago. If we didn't find some shelter soon, Samuel was going to be throwing the remainder of his clothes at us and then dying from exposure.

"Colter!" I immediately regretted yelling; I felt like I had inhaled icicles.

He wheeled around to trot next to me. "Yes?"

"You know this land better than all of us combined; we can't stay out here much longer." I hoped he had some wild idea up his sleeve because I had run out of them a while ago. "Please, tell me you know somewhere we can go?"

He stared at me for a couple of seconds, deliberating. "I know of a place a few miles south of here, but they won't be happy to see us. I can't promise what they'll do." He sighed heavily. "We'll be lucky if they just shoot us on sight."

Logan appeared at my elbow. "You can't seriously be thinking—"

I smoothly cut him off. "Take us there. We have no other options left."

Colter ended up leading us to the Cliffs of Desdomna. I hadn't realized we had been so close to them, but I knew instantly why he had been hesitant to lead us there. "Your idea of shelter is the slave mines?"

Colter nodded slowly. "I did tell you it was a bad idea, didn't I?"

Samuel lurched to a stop. "You *are* joking aren't you? This is some sick joke?"

I pointed back at Slade, who was beginning to turn blue. "We are out of choices. This snow will kill us." Aaleyah was already struggling with the snow-drifts; soon I was going to have to climb off and lead her.

"Doesn't matter anyway," Colter interjected. "We're here."

The cliffs rose up around us, gray monstrosities that blocked the sky from view. A narrow opening marked the passage inside, the cages of dead men and women being the silent warning. Were the mines even in operation anymore? They had been the creation of a dark time, and the home to criminals and slaves alike.

Suddenly, an arrow sliced through the air, landing a few feet to the left of me. I lifted my head up slowly to see a thick line of men. Some held clubs and axes; others held shoddy bows and arrows. A robust, swarthy man stepped forward. "Imperialists or refugees?" he boomed, smacking his club against his hand.

With open hands so he could see I meant no harm, I slid from my saddle. "Neither," I yelled back.

Colter dismounted and took up position next to me, comforting me with his large presence. With a hand on my arm, he leaned down to whisper in my ear: "Let me take this." When he saw my small nod, he yelled back at the man. "I demand to see Blessing Aysi!"

I turned slightly to see that Samuel had come up on the other side of me. Logan was holding onto Slade's reins—for one of two reasons: either because he was afraid he would fall off his horse dead, or because he was afraid he would bolt.

The man who was blocking the entrance looked at Colter in shock. "And how you be knowing Blessing?"

Colter shifted so he was standing in front of me. "None of your business. You tell her Colter Grey is here. She'll see me."

The man pulled a young kid to his side, whispering something in his ear. The kid took off running, supposedly to find Blessing Aysi. Had Colter at one point been kept in the mines? A couple minutes later, a young woman came hurtling out of the mines and straight into Colter's arms. I moved closer to Samuel, who seemed just as shocked as I was.

From what I could tell, she was a beautiful girl and currently sobbing into Colter's chest. He held her tightly, as if the wind was a threat and going to steal her away at any moment. Finally, Colter pulled back to wipe the tears from her face. "Please, Blessing, we need shelter for the night."

Her big brown eyes found mine and widened in recognition. I guess wanted posters had made it to the mines as well. "You shouldn't have come here, Colter. It isn't safe."

Colter looked back at me for a mere second, then returned his gaze to her. "Please."

She nodded slowly, her eyes still on me. "Let's get you all inside."

It turned out that "inside" was stretching it a bit. Small huts lined the walls of the cliffs, but they couldn't have possibly been enough shelter for the hundreds milling about. I spotted a crackling fire and, without permission, dragged Slade over and planted him in front of it. "Stay put, or so help me." He reminded me more of a lost child than a former king. What life does to people is cruel.

Returning to Logan's side, I waited for an explanation from Colter. He had his arm wrapped tightly around Blessing's waist, and she was leaning her head on his shoulder. There was definitely something more than friendship between the two of them.

"Ariel, I would like you to meet my betrothed, Blessing Aysi." Colter's voice was soft, like he couldn't believe he could claim her.

I smiled widely and offered my hand. "The pleasure is all mine."

With one look at her dazzling smile, I knew we were going to be instant friends. Her laughter was infectious and her smile genuine, so why hadn't Colter fetched her sooner?

We settled around the fire with warm bowls of stew. Blessing talked while we inhaled the food. "Titus has left us mostly alone, but each day more refugees come flooding in. He's destroying everything. All of a sudden the mines aren't a prison . . . they're the only safe haven to go to."

Logan spoke up first. "When he finds out how many are gathering here, do you think he'll come?"

Her dainty shoulders shrugged. "Our hope is that he doesn't find out how many we've taken in. Imperialists don't tend to make it back to their squads alive."

I looked around at the gaunt and weary faces staring at us. What happened if a squad tracking me came across the truth? The spoon I had been holding clattered down into the bowl. I couldn't stay here; too many lives were at risk. Snow or no snow, I had to leave.

"Ariel?" Slade patted my knee, trying to get my attention.

"Yes?" I answered automatically.

"Are you okay?" he asked, keeping his voice low. But we were already catching the others' attention.

Blessing pried herself from Colter's side to sit next to me. Long rippling waves of black silk swayed around her as she moved; I would kill to have hair like that. She took my hands in hers and smiled so wide that all I saw were teeth. "You mustn't think of leaving. We'll hide you for as long as is needed."

"I'm putting you all in danger," I said.

"No. You being alive offers hope to us all." She spoke softly, but her words were causing the people to congregate closer. "You are the very symbol of courage. Titus has unleashed all his forces to take your life . . . and yet you have remained one step ahead. You're our hope that one day we will be free of his reign of fear and death."

I squeezed her hands lightly, debating my response. Maven had told me to get out of my own little world—to stop pitying myself and my circumstances. I suppose I should put her advice to good use. "I'll do everything I can."

She laughed, the sound bouncing off the walls in ripples of joy. "Oh, I know you will." She winked and walked back over to Colter. "Not only that; you'll succeed."

I refused to take over one of the huts and instead bunked between Logan and Slade. My necklace wasn't sparking or doing anything else crazy, but I still slept with one hand wrapped around my dagger. I wasn't going to take any chances. These people were former slaves and refugees, but a spy could be hiding anywhere. Curling into a ball, I pulled the blanket Blessing had provided closer.

It seemed that everywhere I stopped the decision had already been made to make me some kind of symbol of hope—all because Titus had sent out some posters demanding my death. Did he realize the only thing he had done was cause people to rally around me? His plan had backfired horribly; it was ironic, really.

"Ariel, you awake?" Logan asked, interrupting my thoughts.

I kept my eyes shut but moved my head in Logan's direction. "Mmhm."

"Do you miss home?" That sounded more like the Logan I knew.

Opening my eyes slowly, I took my time answering. "No," I said, "because I have no home to return to."

"But—"

"All I have left, Logan, is my family. If it's the last thing I do, I will get them back." I had lost Bryne and, so help me, I wouldn't lose the others.

My heart stuttered in my chest. How I missed them! If my three brothers had been with me, this would have been an entirely different journey. I wouldn't have to feel like the world was riding on my shoulders. Bryne would have taken control; he had been a natural leader to the core. Levi would have kept us from fighting, and Fallon would have kept us laughing until our sides hurt. I would have been with them just to drive them all crazy.

Logan remained quiet, and I didn't draw him back into conversation. Enough was going on in my own head at the moment. I fell into a restless sleep that, thankfully, Blessing woke me out of. She nudged me lightly, and I had to snap my body back under control. My arm flinched with the instinct to whip my dagger up to her neck. Easing my breathing, I purposely relaxed the muscles in my body. I smiled up at her. "Blessing?"

"Ariel, would you take a walk with me?" she asked, keeping her voice low so she didn't wake the boys.

Logan had been my best friend growing up, and I had been raised with three older brothers. I wasn't so good at the girly heart-to-hearts, and I only hoped I didn't come off as cold or distant. Nodding my head yes, I reluctantly slipped out from under my warm blanket. Tucking my dagger back into my boot, I motioned for her to lead the way. She chose to intertwine our arms as we picked our way through the sleeping bodies. Her path led us deeper into the cliffs towards the entrances of the deepest mines in the realms. There were no loitering inhabitants to be seen; she had actually managed to find us a place to ourselves.

"The people won't come near the mines anymore now that we've conquered the overseers." Her soft voice bounced off the walls.

I settled against a post marking the mine entrance as number three. I might as well get comfortable; she had brought me here for a specific reason—a reason she clearly wasn't going to come out and just announce. "What happened here?" I inquired.

She sat next to me, her fingers dancing to an invisible tune. "When Titus sent his armies through our realm, it was chaos. They stopped by the mines, but only briefly. They cut down a couple dozen just to prove who was now in charge." Her eyes glazed over, her mind traveling to a place I wasn't sure I wanted to follow.

"When they left, the overseers went absolutely berserk; half ran away, trying to get back home to their families before the Imperialists hit the crown city. Others decided to prove their loyalty to Titus . . ." She looked down at her hands, and the gesture told me more than her words ever could have.

After I had killed the soldiers, I had looked at my hands the same way; the blood staining them never seemed to disappear. Leaning over, I took her hand in mine. "Sometimes, to protect the ones you love, you're forced to do things you never thought you could. I think Wehjaeel will forgive me in the end."

Tears slid from her hazel eyes. "He was going after the children. I begged his soldiers to stop . . ."

"You saved the future generation; you gave them a chance to live another day. I fought for my life and the lives of my travel companions. If that means I'm forced to live with the ghosts of the lives I took . . . well, I'll take that punishment." It didn't ease the guilt, knowing I had killed out of necessity. But I did recognize I had no other choice. She would realize that truth one day herself.

She bobbed her head in silent agreement while she wiped away the moisture trailing down her cheeks. "The Imperialists haven't been back— probably because they don't view us as much of a threat at the moment. We consist of the bitter, the elderly, and the young. Not exactly an opposition to them."

"Keep it that way," I said. "Titus doesn't need an excuse to send more men."

She shook her head in disagreement. "You see, that's one of the reasons I wanted to talk to you. We had a council meeting, and we unanimously agreed that when you called we'd come. We may not be much of an army . . . but we're willing to help."

"Blessing—" I started, wanting to tell her to not make such crazy promises. She had no idea what she was signing up for. To be honest, I hadn't a clue what I was in for either. Gather the keys. Okay, I understood that part. Gather the monarchs. If I could deal with Slade, I could manage that too. Rescue my family. That was nonnegotiable. Kill Titus. Well . . . that was a harder goal to achieve. The thought of amassing an army stole my breath away. Who did these people think I was? They really wanted a twenty-three-year-old to lead them into a war that would probably kill the majority of them? Titus had been preparing his take-over for years; his army was unparalleled.

She tore me out of my thoughts with a few well-placed words. "One day soon, Ariel, you will believe in yourself as much as I do. For now, just know we're waiting on your call." She nudged me with her shoulder and gave a girlish grin. "Don't worry; you aren't alone, and you never will be. Just you wait; you're going to see how many people have fight left in them."

Colter had found himself a keeper. Not only was she gorgeous in rags, she had a massive heart. I nudged her back. "Okay, what's the other reason you dragged me out here?"

Her smile dimmed a little bit, but she looked determined. "I made a promise to you; do you think you could make one to me?"

I knew what she wanted me to promise her, and I only hoped I could fulfill it. "Does it have to do with one Colter Grey?"

She nodded solemnly. "I would never ask him to stay. For the time being, you need him more than I do. I already owe you a debt; a little while in your presence and he is almost restored to the man he was before he lost his family. But I can't—"

I wasn't going to force her to finish the statement. "Blessing Aysi, I promise you that I will do everything in my power to bring him home to you alive." It was a promise I was determined to keep. Blessing deserved her happily ever after.

Tears once again trickled down her face. Throwing her arms around my neck, she sobbed into my shoulder. "Oh thank you! Thank you!" She pulled back with a vibrant smile. "You understand; he is all I have left in this world. I could ask him to stay, and he would, but that is not right. He must go with you. I could force him to take me along, and he would reluctantly agree, but that I also cannot do. My duty," she said, raking her fingers through the dirt while peering up at me, "is here to my people. I must protect them while I wait for your summons."

Gathering her hands, I squeezed them gently. "We are bound to succeed when I have people like you behind me."

Her laugh was music to my ears. If it were possible, I would bottle the sound and listen to it in my darkest moments. "We can't fail; with you fighting for us, we've got something to believe in."

"I'm not invincible," I whispered, uncomfortable with her rock-solid faith in me.

"No one thinks that you are; however, with you not giving up, you've given us something very important: hope. And with hope, you can do anything."

I silently watched astride Aaleyah as Colter and Blessing said their good-byes. It was a heartbreakingly sweet picture, the way he gathered her up against his chest and just held her. He was lucky to have found her; she was exceedingly rare. Of course, the same could be said for her.

"We're going to lose a lot of ground if it keeps snowing," Samuel commented, pulling up beside me.

"We don't have time to wait out the snow," I said. "But we do need to stop somewhere and purchase some warmer clothes." A few minutes in the whipping wind and I was already frozen to the bone. Dressed as I was, I would freeze within minutes—and Slade barely had anything on.

"You can't be seen in town. We've gotten lucky so far, but we can't be foolish enough to believe that luck will continue. "

Was it really just luck? Or something more than that? My attention shifted back to Colter and Blessing. It had never bothered me before that I wasn't married and didn't have children. Although it was unusual I didn't at least have a prospective mate at my age, I had too many other things in life to concern my time with. Yet, watching Colter and Blessing, I couldn't help want that kind of love. What would it be like to have someone know you better than you know yourself? To have someone to talk to who would also wipe away your tears? To have someone never leave you?

"Ariel, maybe Fairchild is right . . . we should keep away from main cities," Logan piped up, coming up on the other side of Samuel.

Any sentence that started with the possibility of Samuel being right was sure to be absolutely wrong. My eyes stayed trained on the parting couple. "People aren't inherently bad, gentlemen. As of right now, they're scared and persecuted. I won't hide like a scared rabbit." Finally, tearing my eyes away from the sight that had so bewitched me, I focused on my companions. "I'm not going to cower from the very people I'm trying to help."

Samuel's eyes flashed, his hands clenching the reins. "You're making a mistake. No one can be—"

"I'm not making a mistake," I snapped. "I'm trusting that the realms are still filled with good people, and if I have to deal with an occasional tracker, so be it."

Logan pounded his fist against his leg. "You just don't get it, Ariel! Do you realize how much gold Titus has offered for your head on a silver platter?"

"There won't be any good people; right now everyone is desperate . . . and that amount of gold will guarantee their survival," Samuel said, his quiet voice impacting me more than a scream ever could have. "To walk into any town is to sign your death warrant. So do yourself a favor and keep your head down."

Colter walked our way, leading his horse, but my eyes traveled to where Blessing stood watching. She would probably stand there long after we were little black dots on the horizon. And, if I knew her at all, she would probably come out every day and watch for some sign of our return or summoning. "You're wrong." I whispered.

I would prove to all of them that there was something left to fight for, that everything we were doing was not just a futile attempt. Gabriel had shown me that people were still good and honest; Blessing had demonstrated bravery and honor. I wasn't naïve enough to think that everyone we met would show kindness, but I wasn't cold enough not to expect the best out of them.

"Ariel—" Logan began, ready to launch into another argument.

I wasn't in the mood to bicker. "Let's just get going, okay? We all know we need supplies, so let's get them."

CHAPTER XII

Keeping to the cover of the Shade, we followed parallel to Brickfield road. Since Brickfield was the road all merchants and army squads used, we were taking our chances with whatever we might encounter in the Shade. The group had drifted into a tense silence after the argument of me venturing into town—except for, of course, Slade, who had been singing nonstop since our departure from the cliffs. He had a rich baritone voice and, as irritating as his incessant singing was, I much preferred it to his moodiness.

Aaleyah shifted in agitation, and my ears immediately perked up. Straightening in the saddle, I searched for some sign of danger. What had her upset? Slade paused a brief second before drifting into another song, but it was long enough to hear a gurgled scream. The men didn't seem to notice, or perhaps they just didn't care that someone nearby was in trouble.

I faintly heard another scream, and that was enough for me. "Find her, Aaleyah," I pleaded, giving her free rein to chase after what she had sensed. With a snort, she broke out from the cover of the trees and raced straight for Brickfield road.

"ARIEL!" It was Samuel's voice that cut out the others' cries, but I didn't dare stop long enough to explain. Besides, he would probably stop me, and that wasn't an option; someone needed help.

It didn't take long for Aaleyah to find where the screams originated. Two men held down a girl while a third fumbled with her dress. The second we were in range, I slid a dagger free and flung it with deadly accuracy. It speared through the third man's hand like butter, and the snarl that darkened my face had nothing to do with pride. These men needed to learn what fear was.

Within the next blink of an eye, I had my other dagger in my hand, and Aaleyah was slamming her head into the first attacker. The man stumbled and, with the aid of my boot smashing into his face, fell to the ground unconscious. The girl had managed to wrestle free and go after the man who had been attempting to undress her.

One last attacker stood standing. I wanted nothing more than to teach him a lesson he would never forget.

"You—" The man's shout was cut off from the arrow that impaled his heart. Trust Samuel to steal my vengeance and instead issue justice. At the moment, I despised him for it.

The girl was straddling her attacker, her fists pounding into his face. As much as I wanted to let her continue, I knew I had to stop her. The man's face was nothing but blood, and I could swear I heard bones crunching. She packed a nasty punch.

Flying from the saddle, I hauled her off him. "Stop it," I ordered.

Kicking and screaming like a banshee, she was out of control, and her head narrowly avoided smashing into my own face.

"It's okay!" I cried, finally depositing her on the ground away from the men. "It's going to be okay!"

She was exceptionally beautiful, although she bore the scars of abuse. Her nose had once been broken, and scars marred her arms. Seeing Logan binding up the two living men out of the corner of my eye, I crouched next to her.

Soft gray eyes stared up at me in shock. "You saved me," she whispered. "Why would you do that?"

I felt Samuel's presence at my back. "Ariel, you've done your good deed for the day. Now, let's go," he commanded. I could only imagine the murderous expression on his face.

The girl, not as young as I might have first predicted, reached forward to snag my tunic. "Please—"

She was obviously upset and spouting nonsense, so I wasn't going to leave her to wander around by herself. "Samuel—"

He reached down to grip my arm. "That's Liv Tara, the most famous companion in the realms, and she can take care of herself," he hissed. "We need to get off the roads before we are spotted."

"We're not just leaving her!" I exploded. What did I care that she was a companion? She was obviously in need, and no one deserved to be left behind in this state.

She jerked upright at my outburst, but her grip on me didn't slacken. Shaking off Samuel's hand, I pulled off my cloak. I tucked it around her shivering form, less to give her warmth and more to cover her torn dress.

"Ariel! We don't have time!" he growled, pacing back to his horse.

"Then we'll make time," I said, forcing my jaw to relax. The worst part was that I couldn't understand his motivations. Was he truly worried that standing here was putting us in danger? Or did adding another to our party not fit into his perfect little world?

As if just talking about the possibility of Imperialist troops was enough, the familiar sound of Midas's horn blew in the distance. For a second, we stared at each other in blank shock as the sound registered. We were sitting ducks right in the middle of Brickfield road, and, before this was all over, Samuel was surely going to remind me that he had told me so.

We would never make it out of here as a group. There were too many of us, and we would be way too easy to track down and capture. Our only hope was to split up and divide the incoming soldiers; perhaps, if we were creative enough, we could all just fade into the Shade.

"Colter, you take Slade. Logan and Samuel, you need to go the opposite direction," I instructed, slipping into the authority role I never wanted.

Assisting Liv to her feet, I watched as she climbed into my saddle without being asked. I was thankful she had a clear head and wasn't screaming we were all going to die. She wanted to live, and it made my job all that much easier. "We'll meet in Archercrest tomorrow."

Adrenaline coursed through my veins, helping me fight past the metallic fear that was pooling in my mouth. Collecting my dagger, I tucked it back into my boot, all the while purposely ignoring Fairchild, who was following my every move.

Samuel stepped in front of me, halting my movement; his eyes were filled with an emotion I didn't have time to decipher. "Ariel, we are not splitting up."

"Samuel, it's the only way," I whispered. He knew that. I knew that. Life didn't give us the luxury of going the way we wanted it to; it was how we adapted to its punches that defined who we were. "Please see that." He would forgive me for this; eventually he would see that my way had been the only feasible option . . . Pushing past him, I sprinted to mount Aaleyah and saw soldiers round the bend. Another horn-blow later, and the boys were scrambling to their mounts as well. The Imperialists could figure out what to do with the men we were leaving hogtied; perhaps they would distract them long enough so we could escape.

"Tomorrow!" I yelled, refusing to read the horror that played on everyone's faces.

Liv clutched the back of my tunic as Aaleyah leapt into a gallop that made my eyes water. Guiding us back into the Shade, she whipped through trees with enough force to create a tornado in our wake, but I wasn't breaking our speed for anything. I didn't hear any signs of pursuit, but that didn't matter much.

I only hoped I had paired everyone correctly. Colter had shown an affinity for knowing every trail and hiding hole, which would give him the advantage he needed to protect Slade. Samuel knew the land almost equally well; he would be able to disappear with Logan. As for Liv and I . . . Hopefully, with the aid of Isidora, we could get some distance between ourselves and the Imperialists.

The trees blurred together to create a mirage of anxiety and unease. The necklace wasn't pulsating with heat, so I figured we were relatively safe. But I was hesitant to slow down. Liv made the decision for me; her grip on me began to slacken, and I worried she would let go and fall from exhaustion. Slowing Aaleyah to a walk, I breathed deeply to steady my cart-wheeling heart.

"Why?" Her question was so soft I almost didn't catch it. I wished I could see her face and gauge her emotions, but I didn't have that privilege.

"You needed help, so I helped," I said. "Simple as that."

She didn't interrogate me further, so I turned my attention to finding us somewhere to catch our breath and some sleep. Locating a small, tucked-away glen, I settled her down with my bedroll. Lighting a fire would be too risky, so I dug into my reserve rations and, after forcing her to eat, announced I would take first watch.

Adapting Colter's technique, I had gotten used to finding my perch in the trees, but I had to admit I missed the vibrant trees from deeper within the Shade—regardless that I had always come away drenched in glitter.

Cyrus's necklace was my first warning that something was off. Pinpricks of heat bit my skin as I silently shimmied to my feet to balance on the branch. Dusk had descended, painting everything in shadows, but the world had grown too calm. Something, or someone, was out there. Pulling both my daggers free, I painstakingly surveyed every inch of the area around us, but nothing seemed out of place.

Liv had curled herself into a ball and was peacefully sleeping, completely unaware we were about to have some unwanted company. Leaving my spot in the tree would be a mistake, but time was steadily ticking by, and Liv was defenseless against whatever was watching us.

Stilling my racing heart and regulating my breathing, I inspected the darkness more closely. My senses weren't off; the necklace proved that much. So whoever it was seemed content to stand by and just watch. It was unnerving. If they would just make a move, I could deal with the danger and be done with it.

Blonde hair appeared first, right along with a pair of eyes I wouldn't have the pleasure of forgetting any time soon.

Zorack.

He was creeping to Liv's side, his sword winking in the encroaching night. Hissing, I launched myself out of the tree and smashed into him with bone-crunching intensity. I wasn't about to let him touch a hair on her head. After I sliced my blade against his cheek, he responded with a punch to the kidneys and a dizzying blow to the head. Liv awoke somewhere in the middle of the struggle, a scream ripping from her lips.

"Stay out of this!" I yelled, trying to clear my vision of the double Zorack. I had to find leverage; it wasn't like I had ever been trained to fight an elf. His movements were smooth and lightning fast. I was playing games with a cobra and I knew it.

She scrambled to the side, and for her sake I hoped she stayed far away.

I tried to aim for his heart, but he broke free and jumped to his feet before I could land my strike. Rolling to my feet, we circled each other. He was favoring his right leg, but odds were it was nothing but a decoy.

"You will die, girl, and it won't be a peaceful end. He'll torture you slowly, until he has the pleasure of draining every last drop of blood from your body." His smile dripped malice, his words slithering through the air, trying to find cracks in my defense.

Cyrus had a serious breech in defense if Zorack was running around loose. Pulling my lips into a feral smile, I bounced on the balls of my feet in anticipation. "Try it," I dared, shoving my dread so far back into my mind I only displayed cold confidence.

His eyes lit up with greed. "With pleasure."

We collided in a flurry of blades and fists.

My arms screamed in protest as I protected myself from his onslaught. I was so busy trying to defend myself that I failed to notice one very important thing. We were no longer alone.

"That is quite ENOUGH!" The order stopped Zorack cold. He froze, his sword inches from my neck. If I were a dirty fighter, I would seize the opportunity for the kill strike. Perhaps it would have been the wisest decision, but it wasn't in me to attack when my opponent was stalled.

Cyrus Drenuellon stood next to Liv, a comforting arm around her quivering shoulders. "You will stand down, Zorack Frostguild, or you will die."

I didn't doubt the power pulsing off Cyrus, and apparently neither did Zorack. "You will regret this, old man," he spat, before disappearing into the wind.

Muscles tense, I let my arms dangle uselessly by my side. "Cyrus." I wasn't sure if I should be irritated he had interrupted the fight, or relieved. I was still mad at him for dumping me in the middle of nowhere with no warning and a dozen more unanswered questions.

"Ariel, I do hope you will forgive me for this. Carressa will have my head when I return home, I am sure."

It would serve him right. It seemed my pity was at an all-time low. My temper was starting to rear its ugly head; my mother would be ashamed. Certain that my displeasure was flashing across my face, I allowed myself to focus on Liv instead. She was white as a ghost and swaying unsteadily. If she didn't sit down soon, she was going to collapse. Reluctantly tucking my daggers back into my boots, I tugged Liv away from Cyrus and sat her down.

Her eyes were wide and confused. "Just who exactly are you?" she asked, her eyes skipping from Cyrus to me.

I was saved from answering by the elf I was trying desperately to ignore. "Ariel? I will find him and punish him. You need not worry about him coming back for you."

Leaping to my feet, I was in front of him in two short strides. "And why didn't you deal with him *before* he nearly took off both our heads? Is this another one of those 'you must figure it out for yourself to truly appreciate it' lessons?"

"Ariel—"

I cut him off, tired of placating smiles and assurances that everything would be okay. "You left me in the middle of nowhere, Cyrus!"

His expression was remarkably closed off. You would think he would be irritated that I was in his face, screaming at him. "I did what I thought to be right; you seemed to have come along just fine."

My fingers curled into tight fists. "I'm tired of your riddles. Would you care to explain the necklace? Or the map that seems to only show itself to me? Or why King Slade is telling me you had a summit, warning them I was coming? You couldn't mention *any* of this before?"

Catching my breath, I stepped back and saw incredulity etched on Liv's face. Apparently, she had never seen anyone yell at an elf before.

"Having all the answers would serve no purpose to you. You'll find out when you are meant to, and not a minute before."

Anger burned in my throat and blinded my vision. "Is there a reason you've decided to show up now, or were you just hoping for a nice chat and some tea? If so, I'm sorry to disappoint. I'm all out of tea, and I would really rather not waste my time trying to work out the puzzles of everything you decide to say."

His smile was brittle at best. "Regroup as quickly as you can with your traveling companions. You shouldn't be so far away from Samuel."

And with that, he was gone—leaving me with yet another riddle. Why was it so important I be with Samuel?

CHAPTER XIII

"You should probably leave me behind now."

Liv's voice interrupted my perusal of Isidora's map. I had been reluctant to pull it out at first, but I was relatively sure she didn't know its origins. Besides that, my blade would be at her neck before her fingers even brushed its soft leather. According to Isidora, we were on the right track; we would reach Archercrest by afternoon, and the three beacons had stayed stationary.

I mulled over her words as I stowed the map away. "Should I?" After my temper-tantrum with Cyrus, Liv had remained painfully quiet. I had decided not to push, and chose to ride out her silence. I enjoyed talking and all, but some peace and quiet seemed long overdue.

"I'm not someone worth saving." Her fingers picked at her silk dress. It was tattered and muddy. If she was going to keep traveling with us, I was going to have to get her something suitable to wear. There was no way she would fit in my clothes; she was five inches too tall, and her curves were a lot more defined. She wasn't a small woman, but her features had a rare delicacy about them. She was a woman who knew she was achingly beautiful—and had grown to hate every feature that made her that way. "I've given you nothing but trouble."

Pretending I was only half listening, I methodically checked the pouch in my boot and the accessibility of my daggers. Allowing the tenseness in my muscles to drain away, I answered, "You think so?" The woman needed to break down and cry. She needed to come to grips with her assault so she could move forward from the nightmare. I would keep her safe for as long as I was physically able, but first I needed her to face the shadows that haunted her. If forcing her to be angry at me was the way to get an emotional reaction, then so be it. If there was anything I had learned in the last couple of weeks, it had been that I had toughness in me yet.

"I'm not clean—" She struggled with her words in an effort to explain to me why she wasn't worth my time.

"I see." I kept my responses curt as I went to check on Aaleyah.

"Would you listen to me!" Liv screamed, jumping to her feet. With a quick look out of the corner of my eye, I saw her chest heaving and angry tears spilling down her cheeks.

About time. I hated acting calloused when someone was in desperate need of a smile and some comforting words. Wheeling around, I stared her down. "You think because of your occupation that you're trash. The problem with your theory is that I just don't care." She recoiled as if slapped, but I didn't stop my verbal assault. "I don't care what you've done or who you've been with." Saying that made my cheeks heat up the tiniest bit, but I plowed on. "We've all done something we're ashamed of to survive; I don't care about your secrets or your mistakes."

Sweeping my pack onto my back, I pointed towards the patient Aaleyah. "All I care about is what you choose to do now. Choose to become someone different; choose to make a difference"

Squaring her shoulders, she wiped her tears away. "You are like no one I've ever met before. What could you have ever done to be ashamed of?"

Coldness seeped into my veins as I let my arm drop and dangle uselessly. "I'm a murderer." The words didn't come easy; I had pieces of wood weighing down my pack with names on them I would never be able to forget. "Not only that, but I will continue to kill anyone who gets in my way until I save my family."

Her eyes widened a fraction. "I was sold when I was six. I didn't choose this life for my own, but I never tried to break away. I was scared."

Her confession eased the pounding in my head; here was someone who would be able to understand me. Someone, perhaps, to whom I could confide my dark desires for revenge. She clearly knew what it meant to be thrown into situations you never expected. Just as she had survived, so would I.

"Even as the old world once crumbled, Titus has destroyed all that the realms used to stand for," I admitted. I wondered if this was how the people had felt a hundred years ago during the Great War: lost and uncertain as to what to do while the fire raged around them. The kingdoms had fallen; the magical creatures had fled. Of course, the Realms of Algernon had surfaced from the ashes, so perhaps there was a chance for us humans yet again. "You have a fresh start now; be a new Liv Tara."

"Is that even a possibility?" she asked. "When people see me, I'll still be nothing more than a companion."

My mouth managed that unfamiliar smile again. "So give them something else to talk about when they see you. Make a stand."

She pondered my words a while before changing the subject. "Titus can't be beaten, not with the devil's champion as his lapdog."

"Titus Ephraim is only a man. One day soon everyone will realize that." I smiled bitterly. "And all men bleed."

"This can't be the place," I breathed, staring at what was supposed to be Archercrest. Liv and I walked side by side into the town, my disbelief apparent.

"Welcome to the reign of Titus." Her voice was emotionless, but I saw the sadness flicker in her eyes.

Most of the houses had been burned to the ground, their charred frames grisly in the sunlight. The streets had turned to mud—though, by the smell, I was sure a large portion of it wasn't mud at all. People milled around aimlessly, their hungry eyes stalking our every step. A tendril of fear crept down my spine. Obviously, entering the small town hadn't been the best of my ideas, but I needed to know if anyone else had arrived. The inhabitants were stirring from their restless state as Liv and I came to a stop.

"Maybe we should wait on the border," Liv whispered, grabbing for my hand.

I nodded silently, holding tight to Aaleyah's reins. These people looked past the point of starved, and, if they made a move for my horse, it wasn't going to end well. I had grown attached to Aaleyah, and they didn't want to pick a fight with me once I formed a bond. "Liv, get on Aaleyah. Now." If this turned into a fight, I wanted Liv as far away from it as possible. She was another thing I wasn't going to let any harm come to. She obeyed without question.

A group of half a dozen men sauntered up to where we stood. One man with a sooty face and missing teeth stepped forward to leer at Liv. "We haven't had comfort in a long time, darlin'. Your price dropped any?"

Pulling my blades free, I glared at him. "I'll give you one warning to watch your mouth, or I'll knock out your remaining teeth for you."

He grinned at me, his posse cackling behind him. "I like spirit in my women. Makes it all the more enjoyable. How much are ye?"

Nausea rolled through my stomach. "You're a—"

"Dead man if you lay one finger on her."

I turned slightly to see Logan with his sword drawn. The man didn't start to inch away until Colter appeared on the other side of me. I had never been so thankful to see the pair of them. Colter pulled loose his battle-axe, and it was enough to send the rats scurrying. We slipped into a side alley between a caved-in livery and a boarded-up bakery. "Colter, where is Slade?"

He patted my shoulder reassuringly. "Don't worry about him. We arrived last night and already located who we were searching for. You can thank Slade for that later; he's waiting with them right now."

Nodding in relief, I turned to Logan. "And Samuel?" Samuel wouldn't have stayed behind when a fight was brewing.

He shrugged nonchalantly, his eyes sweeping the alley for any source of incoming trouble. "I couldn't tell you."

Anxiety sliced through me. With Logan and Colter already here, Samuel should have arrived safely long ago. If anyone had trouble arriving, it should have been Logan—which is exactly why I paired him with Samuel. "What do you mean, you can't tell me?"

His eyes settled on mine. "We got split up on the way. I found this place by dumb luck."

Panic bloomed in my chest. Logan had left him? "You were supposed to stay together!"

Logan rolled his eyes in exasperation. "Ari, I'm sure he's fine. Fairchild is known for being able to take care of himself."

Colter gripped my shoulder, exacting my attention. "We need to get out of the open. We can continue this conversation when we are safely inside."

Liv materialized next to me and took my hand again, squeezing it reassuringly. I had to admit, there was something about her presence that calmed my racing heart. I followed Colter woodenly, my hand clutching Liv's. We ducked through more alleys and trudged through more scorched buildings than I cared to count. Each person we passed broke my heart a little more; everyone seemed so helpless and shattered.

My pulse shot to my throat when I saw a group of children fighting over a dog-bone. Wrenching away from Liv, I dug through my pack and pulled out every last crumb of rations I could find. They flinched when I drew near, but they didn't run. I suppose the food lured them to stay. "It's all I have—" I whispered, handing some food to each child.

A small girl with tangled brown braids wrapped atrophied arms around my legs. Her hot tears soaked into my pants as yet another child, and another, wrapped their arms around me. Sinking to me knees, I gathered them in my arms, kissing each on the cheek. I wiped their tears away, none shying from my gentle touch. Nine pairs of eyes blinked at me, and I wanted to bring every last one along with me.

"Ariel—"

Sighing at Logan's intrusion, I hugged them all one last time. "Take care of each other, and never give up." Reluctantly breaking away, I forced myself after the others. Was this what all the realms looked like now?

We came to the back entrance of a tavern that had seen better days. Colter led Aaleyah to the adjoining barn. "Don't worry, Ariel, no one in this town messes with anything of Big Pete's."

I still twitched, watching her disappear from my sight; it was the furthest I'd been from her, and I didn't like the separation. We waited for Colter to come back before ducking into the small tavern. An eight-foot giant, who must be Big Pete, promptly nodded us toward a flight of stairs leading under the building.

Logan stepped between Liv and me before we started to pick our way down the narrow steps. "You shouldn't have given your food away," he muttered, reaching out a hand to help me.

Brushing past him, I kept my eyes trained on Colter's broad shoulders. Logan had left Samuel behind and, when I confronted him, he better have an extremely good reason why. And if Samuel was lying somewhere injured, Logan would pay for his cowardice.

My thoughts caused me to stumble. Missing a step, I clipped the wall before slamming hard against Colter. "I'm sorry," I whispered, embarrassment flooding my face.

Why was I so convinced that Logan had done something dishonorable? He had been my best friend my entire life, and here I was, possessing zero faith in him. The realization scared me. You would think I actually *liked* the asinine Samuel by my behavior. I'm sure Samuel Fairchild was perfectly fine.

"Ariel, are you okay?" Colter asked, his eyes inspecting me for injury. My head bobbed mutely. He didn't look convinced, but he didn't push the issue.

We wound our way downwards until we reached a faded blue door. "Slade!" Colter kicked the door a couple of times, causing dust to rain on our heads. I squirmed in discomfort. Being underground was something I usually didn't have a problem with, but this place seemed ready to collapse at any moment. "Open up!"

The door creaked open to reveal an exuberant Slade. "You found them!"

The room we entered was large enough to fit a small house inside. The floor was dirt and straw and there were few furnishings. On the left side of the room was a table large enough to fit twelve men comfortably. On the other side of the room was a mound of ratty blankets that I was going to be hard-pressed to go near. Rats and I didn't get along well, and if I had to wager a guess, one or more rats still dwelled inside them. I didn't question why a tavern would have a secret room hidden underground; I only thanked Wehjaeel that it existed.

Two young women and a handsome middle-aged man sat around the table with weary eyes. We piled into the room, claiming our seats at the table in silence. Chocking back an unaccustomed twinge of claustrophobia, I watched as Liv scooted her chair next to mine. I didn't mind the intrusion; my heart stopped pounding when she came near. My eyes narrowed. This was the second timed she had calmed me with her presence. Was she gifted? This was something I was going to have to ask her about later.

Slade was the first to speak. "Ariel, let me introduce you. These two ladies are Eliza and Marie, keepers of the fifth realm." Which meant King Trey and Queen Ionia were two more victims in this senseless war. "And this is King Rowan of the sixth realm." He turned to us newcomers. "This is her, the one I've been telling you about."

Eliza and Marie were undoubtedly sisters; they had the same mousy brown hair and green eyes. The gentleman looked just like a king should, stately even amidst the dirt.

It bothered me that no one introduced Liv, so I spoke up. "This is my friend, Liv. She's been helping us."

Rowan ignored my introduction, causing me to bristle. I'm sure in his esteemed position he knew all about Liv Tara. But it didn't matter if he was a king or court jester; Liv had done nothing to earn such blatant disrespect. "I would like to see the proof before I talk openly. No offense, Slade," Rowan said, his amber eyes watching me curiously. "That she is the one seems a little preposterous."

Ah, so he was not only rude, he also harbored a sharp tongue. I pulled the necklace out with a thumb and bored expression.

"It seems I am mistaken," he murmured, a speculative light flaring in his eyes. "How is it possible that a mere girl is destined to save us?"

"How is it possible that one man defeated the militias of ten realms and the ruling of twenty monarchs?" And there went my temper again. "I guess the world is full of unexplainable mysteries." I really needed to get better control of my emotions. You would think I was talking to one of my brothers, not a king.

His eyebrows arched in fascination. "You've got a temper on you, girl."

My teeth ground in frustration, and although it felt as if someone was dumping waves of calmness over me, my anger wouldn't melt. I cut my eyes to Liv briefly; she had been holding out on me. Planting my hands on the table, I leaned towards Rowan with a snarl. "I'm past the point of exhaustion, and permanently frozen from this blasted snow. I've got a whole bunch of you to find and collect like souvenirs, and along the way must somehow figure out how to transport and hide you all safely. And each time I find another one of you, I'm going to have to go through this all over again. There's a madman on the loose killing thousands, and I'm sent on a quest to find keys that I don't even know the purpose of! My family is being held captive, and I'm missing a member of my expedition. Explain to me, *sire*, how I'm supposed to retain my cheery disposition the entire time."

A slow grin crept across his face. "I take back my previous assumptions. You are perfectly suited for the job."

I felt Liv's hand on my back, and I unconsciously sat back in my chair. Resentment seized me, but, before I could say something I would regret, Rowan was dropping a key made of stone into my hand.

"Let us hope that entrusting you with this is not a grave mistake."

He could hold his breath and hope until he was blue for all I cared. I thought Slade's loony behavior had been hard to deal with; a pompous king was by far worse. Eliza and Marie had stayed quiet thus far, watching me with suspicious eyes. Eliza was the first to speak. "You truly think you can help us?"

My fingers tapped restlessly against my knee. "I think it's time somebody tried."

"He killed my king and queen, nearly killed my sister and me. I need more than a try. I need you to guarantee me revenge."

Marie touched her sister's arm comfortingly. "We've been through a great deal, as you can see." Her voice was light and airy, nothing like her sister's bitter words. "Queen Ionia held my hand as she died and made me swear that I would find the one bearing the mark. We just want to know that it wasn't all for nothing—that we have a reason to put such hope in you."

My fingers stilled. "I won't sit here and make promises I'm not sure I can keep." I had already made so many promises . . . "But know this: Titus has captured my family, had my bother killed, and now seeks my death. No one is more motivated to see justice than I am, and I will fight to my last breath to see him pay for the blood he has spilled."

Eliza and Marie simultaneously produced two birch keys and placed them on the table. "Good enough," Eliza said, the anger and bitterness in her eyes beginning to dissipate.

Conversation flowed for a while, with Logan and Colter finally jumping in. Liv sat silently next to me, but she showed no signs of hurt feelings.

I hoped she wasn't used to this treatment, because I wasn't going to accept it when I was around. I listened intently while Eliza and Marie shared their story of how they ended up traveling with Rowan. Rowan had been in search of his spouse when he came across them, and they had been together ever since.

Big Pete brought down dinner a few hours later but didn't stay to chat. After we ate our fill, and more, I waited impatiently for everyone to bed down for the night. I lay with my eyes wide open until everyone's breathing deepened and their fidgeting stopped. Samuel still hadn't shown up, and there was no way I was going to allow myself to sleep while he was missing.

Fallon had taught me stealth when I was a toddler, and I now used that skill-set to tip-toe past the prone bodies and slip out the door. I must be getting rusty, though, because Logan caught up with me when I was halfway up the stairs. "What is it you think you're doing?" he asked, keeping his voice low.

"You try to stop me, Logan, and I swear you'll regret it," I hissed, turning to face him.

His eyes begged me to reconsider. "Ari, your life isn't worth his black heart."

"I owe him, Logan." That, of course, wasn't the full story, but it would do. Cyrus's warning was still bouncing around in the back of my head. Besides that, I had gotten used to his surly presence. "Now, go back down and watch out for the others until I get back."

His eyes hardened. "I never thought it would be possible for you to grow even more reckless as you aged, but apparently I was wrong."

Refusing to acknowledge his accusation, I turned my back on him and took the stairs two at a time. Bursting out into the night air, I breathed deeply; fresh air had never tasted so wonderful. Of course, the air in Archercrest really couldn't be considered fresh . . . Freeing Aaleyah from the slanted barn, I hugged her around the neck before walking her to the edge of town.

Moonlight pooled on the ground, illuminating the melting snow. Few things had been working in my favor lately, but tonight I wasn't going to be forced to ride blind. Snatching Isidora's map from my pack, I unrolled it with bated breath. I wasn't sure what the deal with the map was, but it hadn't failed me so far. I smiled when I saw the map now only depicted one shining beacon. "Thank you, Isidora," I exhaled.

Samuel was a good hour past Archercrest. Why had he gone north of Archercrest? He had known exactly where he was supposed to go; it couldn't be as simple as he got lost. Samuel didn't get lost. Was he hurt and disoriented? Something serious had happened; he wouldn't simply bypass his destination. Something deep in my heart stirred. He wouldn't just leave me behind, and I knew it.

Swinging into my saddle, I stowed the map away and nudged Aaleyah with my knee. "Let's go save the arrogant mule."

She took off at a run. It was uncanny how well she understood me. I gave her slight direction with my knees and she responded with ease. I had never seen another horse like her. "You know, Aaleyah, you're spoiling me," I yelled, leaning close to her ear. Her ears twitched in response, and her chest rumbled as if she were laughing. I knew at that point I was going insane. I actually thought a horse was laughing at me?

We rode hard in the general direction I had seen the beacon, and I used the time to chatter at Aaleyah. I told her stories of my brothers, and I admitted how scared I was that I was going to fail all the people depending on me. She was the best listener I had ever encountered; of course, that was probably because she couldn't talk back.

Pulling out the map again, I nudged her to a stop. According to Isidora, we were right next to Samuel's location. I didn't want to just start screaming his name. Who knew who was about? I saw no signs of civilization, but it wasn't humans I was afraid of. Scanning the area around me, I searched for any sign of his passing, but the darkness obstructed too much.

Putting the map away, I started to circle the area wider and wider. Where was he?

"Wildcat, please tell me that you aren't out here all by yourself."

I froze, trying to find the origin of his voice. There was a soft whistle, and I tipped my head back to see him resting in a tree. He looked intact, but he was also too far way for me to see him clearly.

"What do you think you are doing?" he inquired, his voice staying remarkably level.

"I'm rescuing you, of course," I quipped, relaxing the slightest bit.

I heard him sigh from all the way up in his perch. He climbed down a few branches before dropping in front of me with an annoyed expression. "And what made you think I needed rescuing?"

"You're Samuel freakin' Fairchild. You should have been in Archercrest long before any of us arrived." Here came the hard part. Did I actually admit how worried I had been when he hadn't been there? No, he would just scoff and say I had been acting foolishly.

His hand reached up to rest on Aaleyah, next to my leg. "That doesn't explain why you took off by yourself."

He wasn't going to make this easy. I shifted in my saddle, uncomfortable with his intense scrutiny. Why had I come after him again? "I was afraid you were hurt."

In the next blink of an eye, his face softened. "I had a tracker on my tail, and I didn't want to lead him to you. I wandered in the Shade for a while until he lost my trail. I was going to loop around to Archercrest in the morning when I was positive I had lost him."

So he wasn't bleeding to death, and he hadn't abandoned me. The fierce relief that poured through me was disturbing. When had he started to matter so much anyway? "Oh."

He grinned wolfishly. "Where is your ever-present shadow, Logan?"

"He told me not to risk my neck for your black heart," I responded, without truly thinking about my words. Something dark flashed in Samuel's eyes, and it bothered me I couldn't pinpoint the emotion. "How did you two get separated?" I asked.

He shrugged much the same way Logan had, but this time I knew Samuel was lying. "Couldn't tell you. One minute he was there, the next he wasn't."

It wasn't coincidence that Logan had made it into town fine and Samuel had ended up with a tracker following him. Something niggled at the corners of my mind, but I couldn't quite figure out what was bothering me about the whole thing.

His hand gripped my ankle. "As much as I appreciate the sentiment of you riding to my rescue," his fingers tightened slightly, "don't ever ride off by yourself again."

I saluted him with two fingers, knowing that if the situation ever arose again, I would do the same exact thing.

CHAPTER XIV

My nightmare was haunting me again. Would the flames ever stop aching to burn me? They dogged my steps and licked at the air, trying to tangle me in their deadly embrace. Raising my arms to protect my face, I launched into the inferno that was beckoning me.

"ARIEL! STOP!" A band of steel wrapped around my waist and hauled me backwards, just as the door of Pete's Tavern caved in with a crackling intensity.

Samuel protected me from a flurry of sparks as he continued to drag me away from the people I had sworn to protect. "You wouldn't survive a minute in there," he breathed into my ear, his voice hoarse with regret.

Tears filmed my vision as I watched the tavern crumble to the ground. I couldn't just stand here and watch everything turn to ashes; it went against every fiber of my being. I had to try to save them, regardless of the consequences. They were my responsibility. Maybe so far underground they were temporarily safe from the flames, but trapped with no escape . . . I couldn't let them down. I fought to break loose from Samuel, my hysteria blinding me to the damage I was inflicting. "I left them!" I screeched, clawing to get free from his impenetrable grip. "I left them all defenseless . . . I didn't . . . I just . . ." My knees buckled slightly as I heaved for air.

Samuel twisted me around so I was facing him and, after I sent a left hook to his unbreakable jaw, he captured my wrists with a grunt. "Calm down. You don't know they were in there—"

Sagging against him in defeat, I looked up. "What if they were?"

A familiar, cackling laugh floated our way, and my head whipped around to see the same group of men who had welcomed us to town. Rotten teeth grinned at me as the men approached. "I can just imagine how sweet you're going to taste before we deliver your head to the king."

Samuel growled low in his throat, his body tensing against my hands. Pinning me to his side, he inclined his head ever so slightly towards me. "Stay out of this fight, or so help me." Fury contorted his face as he simultaneously threw me behind him and charged the men.

Catching my balance, I watched in horror as Samuel took on a dozen men single-handedly. Granted, they weren't by any means soldiers, but a desperate man could do a lot of damage. Stay out of the fight? He was joking, right? By now, he should be well aware that I wasn't helpless and his chauvinism wasn't appreciated. Snarling, I drew my blades and launched into the skirmish. These men had burned my friends in their sleep, and they would pay for their crimes.

I ducked and weaved, causing as much harm as I could without staying in one spot for more than a few seconds. In less than five minutes, Samuel had already succeeded in dropping half the men. His agility and skill with his sword was so inhuman it stole my breath. Once again I was forced to wonder who exactly Samuel Fairchild was.

An arm latched around my neck, but, before I instinctively buried my blade in his belly, I smelled the familiar scent of my irritating protector. His other arm slipped around my waist as he inched me away from the battle. "I told you to stay out of this, Ariel Deverell." He dropped a quick kiss on the crown of my head, winked impishly, and then hurled me through the air.

I landed on my butt and skidded another five feet before I came to a bruising stop. Slowly my hand reached up to touch the spot where his lips had touched. Had I just imagined that entire encounter? Pulling my hand down, I stared at my fingers wonderingly. It had been a trick of my mind, right? I glanced up to see him just finishing off the last man and sauntering my way.

I was hallucinating; my mind had finally turned against me. That was the only plausible explanation. It had to be the only explanation because I would accept no other one. I had too many other things to deal with than the betraying pounding of my heart every time he stepped near.

My hands went into spasms when a small child clutched my sleeve. Relaxing my fingers on the hilts of my daggers, I looked into the eyes of the little girl I had fed yesterday. She was on her hands and knees, and her eyes were frozen in fear as she watched Samuel advance. "Miss?"

She shouldn't have been subjected to the violence that had just been displayed. Of course, she also shouldn't be fighting over a dog-bone as she slowly starved to death. Slipping my blades back into my boots, I touched her arm gently. "Yes?"

Her eyes turned to me, so full of sorrow and weariness. No child should ever look the way she did at that moment: innocence torn from her before she even had a chance to be a kid. "Your friends . . . they are alive."

My world slowed as it zoned in on her. Hope bloomed in my chest, making it hard to breathe. "Where are they?" I had promised Blessing I would bring Colter home, I had sworn to myself to protect Liv, and I owed Maven protection of the monarchs. If they were still alive . . .

She scrambled to her feet and tugged on my hand. "Come!"

"Wehjaeel, please," I whispered. I wondered if he got tired of me asking for things all the time. Please save my family, please keep them alive, please keep me alive.

Please don't let me fail.

The girl kept a tight grip on my hand as she led me outside of Archercrest and straight into the Shade. Samuel was a step behind me the entire way, his steady silence more assuring than anything else ever could be. I knew without asking when we were close to the others; a heavy peace blanketed me. Liv was trying to calm everybody down.

She hurried through the trees with a joyous shout. Catching her, I wrapped her in a tight hug and pretended ignorance when she discretely wiped her tears away. Everyone sat in solemn silence, their eyes lighting with relief when they saw Samuel and me approach.

Colter sat with two of the orphans from yesterday, Slade had two little girls asleep in his lap, both Eliza and Marie held little boys, and Rowan held the last two. Logan sat a ways off, his eyes locked on Samuel.

I grinned when I realized it was the orphans from yesterday. One of the boys next to Colter stood to his feet and marched my way. Liv pulled back as he stomped to a stop in front of me. "My name is Cadell, and I be the one in charge."

"You saved them?" I asked, relief uncoiling the tension in my stomach.

He nodded with a pleased expression. "I heard old Fergus talkin' 'bout torchin' the joint, so I sent me lads over real quick like. The girls found us a spot to hide, and we snuck away to wait fer ya. Big Pete is out of town; I 'magine he's going to be a sight upset when he returns."

I crouched down to meet his strong gaze. In a way, he reminded me of a young Bryne, full of life and more courage than was good for him. "I don't know that I will ever be able to thank you."

"Well, ya see . . . ." he shuffled his feet nervously, "we wanna come with ya. We won't be no trouble, I be promisn' ya that. We can help—"

Everyone was listening in rapt attention as Cadell pleaded his case to me. Taking on nine kids would be an impossible task; we were too big of a group as it was. How would we feed them all? Not only that, but our traveling speed would be greatly reduced. But how did I say no? They had lost their parents, and they lived in a town that was decaying from the inside out.

"Cadell, where we are headed . . . it isn't safe. I can't knowingly drag you into danger like that. You have to understand—" I began, striving to find the right words to make them all understand they just couldn't come with us.

He stopped me with a raised hand. "No, *you* have to understand. Hedia said our best chance to live was to follow you. I've learned over the years that she never be wrong. So, ya see, you gotta let us come with you."

Most of them didn't even have shoes! It was winter, and even with Aaleyah I had a difficult time traveling through the snow.

"Wehjaeel told me that we needed to go with you."

The words stopped me cold. I looked down at the little girl who had led us here, the child who had first captured my attention in Archercrest. Her hand reached out to grab mine, and I clutched it to my heart. "Wehjaeel told you?"

"Ariel—" Logan warned, appearing at my side. "You can't possibly be thinking . . ." He didn't finish the sentence; his eyes said it all.

Hedia moved closer to me. "We are to go with you. We must."

Rubbing the heel of my hand against my eyes, I took a deep breath. I needed some space and time to think; I needed to be away from everybody's expectant eyes. "Why don't we all get some sleep? We'll talk about this in the morning. I'll take first watch."

But with one look into Hedia's eyes, I already knew my answer. If Wehjaeel told her that they were to go with us, then I would find a way to make it possible.

Pacing didn't seem to be helping. The only thing it accomplished was wearing a permanent path in the ground and stroking up a pounding headache. Scattered thoughts and half-formed ideas tumbled around my head with bewildering intensity. So many misplaced people, and this was only the beginning. How could I help everyone?

"Wehjaeel, I could really some help right about now," I whispered, stopping to lean up against a gnarled tree in defeat. "I'm running around the realms like that proverbial chicken with its head cut off. I need . . . " my head dropped in defeat, "guidance."

"Not a lot of people pray to Wehjaeel anymore."

I looked dully over to Cyrus. His appearing-out-of-thin-air tricks were ceasing to fascinate me anymore. In fact, they were really starting to aggravate me. "I bet that percentage increased after Titus took over."

"And it will only continue to rise," he agreed, moving closer to where I stood, his robes whispering over the ground. "Titus Ephraim has only begun to spread his darkness over our land. As things continue to worsen, the people will start crying out to Wehjaeel to help and beg for someone to lead them."

"I'm not afraid to lead," I said, straightening when I realized how true my words rang. I wanted to help more than I feared failure. "I just don't know where to lead them *to*, Cyrus."

His lips lifted in a practiced smile. "My advice? Learn from history. This is not the first time we have encountered such a darkness."

"This is going to get a lot worse before it gets better, isn't it?" I asked, the truth turning to lead in my stomach.

Cyrus reluctantly gave a tight, affirmative nod. "This is just the beginning, Ariel."

The Great War had reaped the lives of thousands upon thousands. How many lives would be lost by the end of this war? How many homes destroyed and families splintered? What would the Realms of Algernon consist of after Titus Ephraim was done?

"Why can't you ever just tell me to 'go here, do this, and then you'll be traveling down the right road'?" I inquired.

Laughter bubbled from his lips, the sound so enchanting it bewildered my mind for a moment. "If only life could be solved that easily!"

Yes, if only. No more riddles or quests, just straight answers and clear direction. "So that's the only clue you are going to give me?" I questioned, prodding for at least a little more information.

"You're a clever girl, Ariel. If you remember your roots, and you remember our land's past, that is all you need to know for the answers you seek."

I sighed when he vanished; his hint was not enough to work with. The Realms of Algernon were steeped in history. What part, exactly, was I supposed to be remembering? The Great War spanned nearly years. As for my roots, I had spent nearly my entire life nestled into a peaceful mountainside. Nearly.

My hand reached up to trace the tattoo that snaked from behind my left ear, down my neck, and sprawled across my shoulder blades. The feel of the jeweled eyes of the phoenix captured my throat in a vice. How could I have been so utterly foolish! I had spent too many years hiding my heritage. I had completely forgotten the sole reason I had managed to stay alive thus far.

"*Fool,*" I breathed. Cyrus must have thought me truly thick-headed not to have figured it out sooner. I had been sitting on the answer the entire time.

The Hollow Hills.

Relief poured through me, releasing the tension in my shoulders. It wouldn't be easy to gain entrance, but it was feasible.

Shrugging off my pack, I withdrew Isidora's map and studied it carefully. I would need to move us in the direction I wanted without causing too much suspicion. No one needed to know what I was up to; the existence of the Hollow Hills was a closely-guarded secret—a secret that was punishable by death if shared, something I was determined to avoid. If I could just get us close enough so that I could disappear for a day and make my case to the council . . . They wouldn't be able to refuse, for it was the very people they swore to protect who needed sanctuary.

My finger trailed the edge of the third realm. There was a flashing beacon just past the crown city of Etherdayle. Even traveling slowly, we should still be able to arrive within three days, and if I insisted we camp near Etherdayle, I could vanish before anyone expected a thing. Liv might be a problem, of course, depending on how extensive her gift was. Which reminded me: I needed to have a talk with her long before we arrived.

At the very least, I now had a plan to work with. Not an easy one, but a plan.

I would be moving into familiar territory when we hit the third realm, and it would be nice to see land I was acquainted with. Home of the scholars of Abisai, it was heavy with history and knowledge. Most importantly, it was the entrance to the Hollow Hills, where I had been trained to be a warrior for five long years.

"Ariel?" Samuel's voice was soft as he approached where I knelt gazing vacantly at the map.

I stopped my fingers from drawing out the route I wanted to take. No one needed to know my motives on this one; it was essential I kept my agenda hidden. "I think we should head to this marker next." I tapped my finger against the light that beamed on the edge of the third realm.

He crouched next to me, inspecting the map. "Wouldn't it be closer to head for the markers clustered over here?" he asked, nudging my finger a little to the left of us. His logic was infallible, of course; but I didn't have time to take the windy journey to the third realm. I needed to get our ever-increasing band to a safe location—not to mention the mass of people waiting with Blessing.

I pointed back towards the first marker. "I really think we should head this direction. Going that way will take us through the passes, and with this snow . . ."

He planted his hands on his knees to stare steadily at me. "You plan on taking the children, then?"

"Was there ever really a choice?" I asked, rocking back on my heels. "We can't leave them—"

He cut me off as he rolled up the map. "Anybody else would."

"I'm not anybody else." And I wasn't leaving anyone behind. I would secure them a safe haven, and then it was back to business as usual. "I won't leave them."

His half smiled as he took my wrist in his free hand. "I wasn't asking you to leave anyone behind."

Paralyzed, I stared at him, expecting him to spout off about what a fool I was being. "I expected . . . "

He placed the map in my hand and released my wrist. "I'm not a complete monster, Ariel, just mostly." His eyes melted with sadness. "I know I don't always agree with you—"

"Try never," I butted in with a scoff.

"I'm not—" He visibly struggled with his words as his eyes swept the trees around us. "It's not that I don't want to do the right thing, like you seem propelled to do every time we turn a corner. I'm just used to doing what it takes to survive." His depthless eyes found mine, stealing my words from my lips. "You really are quite incredible. I've never before come across anyone like you."

Heat rose to my cheeks under his intense scrutiny. "Samuel—" It was the most he had ever spoken to me. Unconsciously, my hand moved up to the spot where he had kissed me. I still felt the heat from his breath, and the feelings knotting in my stomach were unwelcome. "I'm really not all that special. I only want two things out of life: my family back and the death of the assassin that killed my brother."

He lifted his hand to brush his knuckles across my cheek, and I had to refrain from leaning my face into his touch. "You, Ariel Deverell, are a gift that the world will never truly appreciate."

Boots crunched loudly next to me before Logan appeared with a scowl. "Ari?"

I jerked away from Samuel's hand and then flinched when I saw the hurt flash in his eyes before they settled back to the coldness I was familiar with. I busied myself with my pack and avoided Logan's poker-hot stare. "Yes?"

"I thought you were on watch. I came to relieve you," Logan muttered, crossing his arms.

Samuel rose to his feet and strode away without so much as a backwards look. The man was a walking contradiction, and it was irritating that I felt drawn to him like a moth to flame. He was heartbreak ready to happen.

"Ari?"

I shook myself when I realized I had been staring at the void Fairchild had disappeared into. "Logan, answer me a question truthfully."

"Anything," he responded, a small hitch in his voice.

There were so many answers I wanted from him. Where had he been after he ditched me with Samuel? How had he and Samuel become separated? However, there was a very important answer I needed to know first. "How did you ever meet him?" Samuel wasn't a person you met in our small town of Boadicea, and Logan had never been further than our crown city.

"When I went to go try to find my father," he responded woodenly, his eyes staring stoically at the ground.

Horror crashed through me at his admission. "I told you to never—"

"And you think that was going to stop me!" he spat, fists clenching at his side "He was MY father, Ariel! A man I lost when I was five, and for some reason *you* got to spend *years* with!"

I reached up to rub my neck wearily. "We've been over this a thousand times before, and I thought you understood."

He lurched forward, grabbing me by the shoulders. "You have been my best friend since before we could talk, and when you came back—" He laughed acidly, his eyes edged with a wildness I had never seen before. "I begged you to give me even a general direction of where he was hiding. You were hardly even you anymore, the way you watched everything . . . It's like you're now constantly waiting for something to attack you! You were a small town girl. What could you have possibly been doing all those years!"

"Logan—" I began, trying to wiggle out of his bruising grip.

"You are always so stubborn! *Still* you won't utter a word of what they did to you!"

"Let her go, Logan." Samuel's voice whipped through the air, shattering the crazed state Logan had fallen into.

He stiffened at the sound. "This doesn't involve you, Fairchild," he gritted through his teeth, his eyes never wavering from mine.

"It's about to, unless you get your hands off her," Samuel said, his words razor sharp.

Slamming my boot down hard on Logan's instep, I elbowed out of his grip and shoved him back. "What has gotten into you?"

Remorse streaked across his face as he stumbled away. "Ari, I'm sorry." He hesitated for a moment, his eyes swinging from Samuel back to me. "I—"

Logan would never understand why I had been sent away and he hadn't. No matter if I were able to tell him where I went and what I had been doing, he wouldn't understand. To him, I had betrayed him by stealing coveted years with his father. I couldn't explain to him that his father was a secret hero, not a family-abandoning coward. No words would make a difference to a man who, inside, was still a hurt little boy.

So I didn't try. I left him stuttering and apologizing to thin air as I made my way back to camp. I didn't hear Samuel following, and I didn't have the energy to care what was going on between the two men. Liv, Eliza, and Marie were settling all the children in for the night—a reminder we needed supplies, and fast: blankets, warmer clothes, and, most importantly, shoes. Archercrest was out, so hopefully we would pass another small settlement soon.

Colter was sitting next to the fire, a pensive look on his face, so I settled next to him silently. Leaning against him, I rested my head on his arm. "Colter?"

He looked down at me, his dreads swooshing over his shoulder. "Yes?"

"Thank you for sticking with me," I whispered, keeping my eyes on the crackling fire.

"I promised you, Ariel, until the end . . . I'll be here until the very end." He wrapped his muscular arm around me and squeezed tightly. "Keep your chin up, kiddo. We'll make it through this yet."

CHAPTER XV

We were a solemn traveling party as we ambled our way through the outskirts of the Shade. What a rag-tag group of individuals. Logan had taken pains to avoid me since the scene from yesterday, and Samuel was back to his taciturn self. I walked slowly, leading Aaleyah, who was presently carrying two children.

Liv walked next to me, softly humming a lullaby, and it reminded me I had some information I needed from her. I was never really one to beat around the bush, so I asked her flat out: "You're gifted, aren't you?"

Her steps faltered as her head whipped up. "Why would you think that?"

Keeping my gaze level with hers, I smiled tightly. "Let me rephrase," I said. Why people tried to lie to me when I so obviously knew the truth was something I would never understand. "You are gifted."

Her face blanched and her hands trembled as she shoved them under her cloak. "I've never considered it a gift. It's only ever been a curse to me."

After all the people I had encountered and whose gifts I recognized, I had yet to meet a person who considered her blessing to be a curse. I was intrigued by her reaction. "Why?"

She didn't answer for a while, her lips tight with distress as she fumbled for a reply. Finally she sighed heavily and let her shoulders droop in resignation. "It's why I was part of the reaping of my home village. They heard I could heighten emotions—though at the time I was mostly only able to calm." Bitterness was etched in her movements as she continued to spit out valuable information. "I wasn't a famous companion because of my fair face. My gifting threw me into a life I never wanted, and I've never been able to forget that." Her eyes drifted into recollections of her sordid past.

I immediately regretted dragging her back into the memories she was trying so hard to erase. I had told her she could have a fresh start, and yet here I was, slamming her back into her darkest times. Perhaps, though, she needed to realize her gifting wasn't a curse. It was something infinitely special—a special gift for a very special person. "To what point can you calm someone?"

Her voice was raw when she answered. "I can calm a person into a coma, or I can excite someone until his or her heart bursts. I was bestowed with a dark gifting."

I stopped walking and grasped her thin shoulders. "Your gift is what you make it, Liv. You've used your gifting on me, and it has done nothing but sooth and help me make clear-headed decisions. You've helped the children to not give way to their fears. It's only a curse if you allow it to be."

"I've never thought of it in those terms. I just got so tired of feeling other people's emotions . . ." Tears built in the corners of her eyes. "How did I calm the other girls who were being trained to be companions when I was so scared I couldn't breathe myself?"

I pulled her into a tight hug. "Liv, it won't be easy to change your life around, but you've been given a unique opportunity to try. Each day you wake up, you'll have to make the decision to do everything differently than you used to. It's not an easy task, but I can promise you it'll be worth it. A good starting point would be your perspective on your gifting. You truly have been blessed with an unusual gift."

We continued to walk again, keeping our voices hushed as we talked. "Do you ever get tired of always being so hopeful?" she inquired, her eyes trailing the group of children and men in front of us.

I laughed. "Rarely." I paused to mull over her question and why it was I never seemed to give up hoping. "But when I do, Wehjaeel tends to give me another dose."

"Please don't take this wrong, but your faith in someone who can't be seen is staggering."

Chuckling, I nudged her with my shoulder playfully. "If that's the worst you have to say about me, then I'm doing all right."

A small grin appeared on her face. "There really isn't a person in this world like you, you know that?"

It wasn't the first time someone had said that, and I didn't know what people found so fascinating about me. I beamed up at her. "I hope not. I'm not sure the realms could handle two of me. Fallon and I together were enough to make nuns swear—" I stumbled over my words at the reminder of the havoc Fallon and I used to create. I missed his infectious grin and dare-devil attitude.

"If there's any pair of people who can accomplish the impossible, it would be you and Samuel. The king doesn't stand a chance of keeping your family from you."

It was interesting that she thought Samuel was the one who would help me accomplish my goals . . . I pulled myself from my musings. "Why are you so sure Titus can be beaten?" I was clutching onto the fact that every man had a weakness. What was motivating *her* faith?

Abruptly she stopped, causing me to almost trip over her. "I guess your stubborn faith is contagious—and your unyielding hope, though impractical, is awe-inspiring."

She resumed walking and I followed, a bit dumbfounded by her announcement. Was I really that idealistic?

We ended up traveling straight through the night so we could reach Etherdayle by morning. I reluctantly let Liv take Aaleyah's reins so I could walk next to her and keep a close eye on the children who were fast asleep. Thankfully, Aaleyah was keeping her gait steady and smooth. Every once in a while I had to push a sliding child back into the saddle, but it was a small price to pay to get to Etherdayle faster.

It was a dangerous idea to travel at night in the Shade, so we kept our talking to an absolute minimum. We were all tense, waiting for the moment when the next monster chose to attack us. So I was surprised when Samuel made a point to loop around and talk to me. Although I shouldn't have been. He, as always, was too observant for his own good.

"I would like to know what is so important about Etherdayle." If there was anyone who could beat me in directness, it would be Samuel. Straight to the point and demanding—how typical of him.

I kept a sharp eye on my charges as I dropped back to quietly converse with my shadow. "It's home to the priests and scholars of Abisai, and it'll be a safe place to buy supplies. They are notoriously staunch supporters of peace." I was rather proud of how my voice remained unaffected by the spike in my pulse.

"If anything, they're obstinate and unhelpful in times of warfare," he retorted, his eyes rolling at my weak cover story.

I was going to have to become a better liar around him. "At least they won't be screaming for my head the second I step within their borders," I groused, thinking back on the disastrous visit to Archercrest.

"That is, if their borders still exist. Who knows what Titus has done to the pacifists."

He was always trying to poke holes in my carefully-laid plans. "Well, I guess we'll find out."

"You haven't answered my question, Wildcat." His eyes speared through me, digging for the information I was trying so hard to withhold from him.

"I told you," I snapped, feeling the weight of his scrutiny. "Supplies."

"Liar," he whispered with a scowl. "Whatever it is that you're so desperate to get to Etherdayle for, don't think for a mere second that I'll be letting you out of my sight." His face was tight with something akin to worry.

I grinned up at him. Game on.

Much to Samuel's chagrin, Etherdayle was very much intact. Leaving our merry band huddled at the border, Colter, Samuel, and I ventured into the crown city, weapons ready. Samuel tucked himself close to my side, and I had to smile to myself. Did he really think he could stop me from disappearing if I was determined? Not likely.

"Far from home, are you not?"

I flexed my fingers around the hilt of my blade and adjusted my stance into false relaxation. The priest who had addressed us looked harmless, but I knew this realm. Looks here were highly deceiving.

The man stood in the middle of the street, his amethyst ropes sweeping the ground every time he breathed. Silvery hair and intelligent brown eyes peered at us, speculatively.

Colter bowed his head, showing deference to the elderly man. If there was any group of people who received more respect than even the monarchs, it would be the priests and scholars of Abisai. "We're just travelers looking for a place to restock our dwindling supplies."

It was the first time I'd witnessed Colter take the lead, and the sight was a welcome one. He needed to realize he wasn't inferior to any of us, and he was meant for a lot more than just guard duty.

The priest's eyes swung to gaze at Samuel before they landed on me. "Wehjaeel has blessed whatever journey it is that you have embarked on," he remarked, clasping his hands together.

Colter faltered on a response, so I stepped into the conversation. "Thank you for your kind words," I said, forcing myself to lose the tension that wrapped through me. I was so close to my destination, I just wanted to shake my company and head out already. I didn't want to sit for an hour and make small talk with a priest, having to remain polite the whole time. "Would it be possible for you to point us in the right direction to your mercantile?" I had to watch my words carefully; the priests of Abisai weren't just any priests. They were hand-picked and trained from the age of three to spend their entire lives in meditation and pursuit of knowledge. If you weren't approved to be a priest, you could stay in the third realm as a scholar.

The priest didn't respond to my request. Instead he stood still, soaking in our appearance. I knew we looked ragged from traveling, but truly we couldn't look that horrible. His eyes snapped to mine. "Do you even realize?"

I realized I was impatient and desperately wanted to be somewhere else. I realized I was tired of riddles and, if he introduced another one, was going to be less than pleased. It was possible the priest was just a little off; his occupation and life's pursuit, though noble, was not an easy one. His shoulders were slumped with age and his wrinkles abundant. Had age addled him? "Sir?"

He shook himself out of his reverie and offered me a jovial smile. "Pardon me and my rude behavior! My name is Father Ira." At least he didn't launch into his position in the hierarchy of priests. It was complicated, and the one time my father tried to explain it to me left me with a splitting headache. I did know his white cuffs meant he was somewhere in the middle of importance. "It would honor me greatly if you would come with me and allow me to introduce you to Father Eli. He would be very disappointed if he didn't get a chance to meet you."

He motioned for us to follow him, but I kept my feet firmly planted where I was standing. Father Eli would be the one priest who was bound to recognize me, and that was exactly what I didn't want to happen. "At another time, please? We have individuals waiting for our return, and we really must purchase our supplies quickly and return to them." I was pleased with myself: not even the slightest hitch in my voice to betray my distress.

Father Ira eyed me with a pensive expression. "It will only take a moment, and then I can help you—"

I gave him a polite but resolved smile. "No, thank you."

Colter leaned close to my ear. "You're denying a priest of your faith?"

Yes, I must be absolutely sacrilegious refusing a priest's request—a priest who was about to blow my carefully laid plans. Samuel didn't need more reasons to doubt my motives, and when Father Eli recognized me, it would bring forth a lot of unwanted questions. As soon as Samuel had proof that I had ulterior reasons for heading us in this direction, he would be all over me.

"You're right," I said, taking a step backwards. "Colter, Samuel—you go ahead. I'll go tell the others we'll be longer than expected, then catch up."

Samuel reached back and grasped my fingers. "Ariel?"

His eyes darkened in uncertainty. "I don't think the others will mind if we are gone a little longer than we told them."

I slipped from his grip. "Really, Samuel, I'll only be a couple of moments behind you. Go with Father Ira. You've got nothing to worry about."

He sighed and rubbed the back of his neck. "When it comes to you, Ariel, I've got a multitude of things to worry about."

Father Ira courteously interrupted our whispered exchange. "We could wait here for your return if you would like."

The priest was making my escape exceedingly difficult. "No, really, go ahead, please . . . I'll be right behind you." And before any of them could argue, I turned on my heel and sped away.

I knew Samuel was watching, so I slowed down my walk to a stroll, heading back the way we had come. The third realm could seriously be considered a museum. It was a maze of ruins, graveyards, old battlefields, massive libraries, and halls of knowledge. History was so thick, here, you could cut it with a knife. Just about every corner had a monument or memorial. It wouldn't be possible for anyone to journey through and not remember the Great War and the repercussions it had. Thankfully, everything was oversized, allowing me the perfect opportunity to vanish. Rounding the corner, I cut through a side street boasting a bakery that made my mouth water. Ignoring my gurgling stomach, I aimed for a path that led a ways out of Etherdayle to Mount Algernon. I had to take the long way around to not only avoid Samuel and Colter, but also everyone else we left on the border. A brisk twenty-minute walk and I was at the base of the mountain. It was steep, its narrow path built more for a mountain goat than a human.

The mountain was aptly named, for it had been a key battlefield in the Great War. King Algernon had forced his troops to the top during one of the harshest winters in recorded history. After relocating all his men on the mountain, the king and his soldiers waited patiently for the armies that pursued them and then picked them off, one by one. The pass only allowed one man at a time to travel up it, and the trek was so difficult you were unable to climb and fight at the same time. This insane decision, however, had allowed Algernon to face an army triple his size and lay devastating waste to his foes. It had cost the lives of a couple dozen of his men and, instead of leaving his deceased men where they lay, Algernon dug graves for each one—despite the frozen ground.

When the war finally concluded, Algernon came back to the mountain and had a proper graveyard erected. Few visited, of course, since the journey was incredibly difficult and the weather challenging, even in the summer months. But, if you did dare the passage up, it was a sight you would never forget.

It took me three solid hours to reach the top. In some places I had to scramble over fallen boulders; in other places I had to scale the mountainside and find finger-holds in the rock. Luckily, it was a pass I had traveled regularly, and I knew all the tricky spots. By now the boys would realize I had ditched them. They would either be furious at my duplicity or worried I had been harmed on my trip back.

If I came back successful, they would be forced to understand why I had to take such actions.

Stomping my boots on the ground, I attempted to knock off some of the clumped-up snow. I braced myself for the confrontation I was about to face. I was about to ask Algernon's hidden warriors to share the secret they had faithfully kept since the Great War—because not only had Algernon come back to the mountain to place a graveyard, he had also formed an order of warriors to be called upon in the next time of duress.

The original response wasn't going to be pretty, I already knew. I could be exiled from the order for even having the audacity to make such a request. Desperate times called for desperate measures, though. This was where I needed to take my stand and, Wehjaeel help me, hopefully my position wasn't stripped from me.

Swiping my sweating palms across my pants, I forced a couple of deep breaths. This encounter was about to change everything I set out to accomplish. I only hoped it changed in the way I wanted it to.

The entrance to the cemetery was an ornate brass gate inlaid with a quote written in the old language. It read, "The brave, the strong—they march only to Algernon's song. Here they rest, forever to be remembered as the heroes who won the war." I traced my fingers over the words in respect. My mother had forced me to learn the dead language when I was a girl, and I still didn't understand why. No one spoke it anymore, and it was rare to find anything written in it.

I was delaying, and I knew it. Odds were, they already knew of my arrival at the gate and were waiting for my next move. Pushing the gate open with the palms of my hands, I strode into the cemetery with as much false bravado as I could muster. Winding around the graves of the soldiers, I walked to the mausoleum of General Caedmon Deverell.

My great-great-great grandfather, a man I never got to meet, but he had managed to influence the path my life had taken. He was the sole soldier who had been graced with such a memorial to his name. That might have to do with him sacrificing himself to save Algernon from a battle-axe that would have cost him his life. Saving the high king was no little thing, and so Algernon had built the entire graveyard around the mausoleum of my ancestor.

However, the mausoleum was more than just a building to memorialize a great man. I walked around the lavish, marble structure to its back corner. Crouching, I slid my hand down the wall until I uncovered the *fleur-de-lis* near its base. Dragging my finger over the design, I felt for the groove.

"Come on," I whispered impatiently. I was freezing, and I wanted to have my word with the council before the knot in my stomach got any worse.

Finally, my nail caught on the niche and, with a whoop of delight, I pressed down simultaneously, tilting the stone scrollwork to the left. Holding my breath in anticipation, I listened for the click of the mechanism to signal the release of the lock. Hearing the telltale sign, I traced out the block of marble that should now be loose. Smiling in victory, I pressed hard against the marble, forcing the door to give way. A stale whoosh of my air slapped me in the face as I peered into the darkness. It was an infinitesimal opening to reach the inside of the mausoleum, but it was the only entrance that had been shared with me. The council was going to have to be willing to share the other doorways so that I could transfer large groups in quickly.

Dropping to the ground, I painstakingly wiggled my way through the opening. Cautiously, I used my hands to feel for any obstructions as I dragged myself the rest of the way inside. Balancing on my haunches, I replaced the wall to its rightful position, reluctantly dousing any light I had to work with. It was spacious inside the building, but the darkness was so intense it was enough to suffocate me. Mercifully, I knew every inch of this building, and I didn't necessarily need any light to guide my way. Aligning myself next to the wall, I counted six steps before moving to the right another five steps.

Bracing myself, I felt the floor slide out from under me before I was skidding downwards. My arms flapped uselessly for a brief second before I balanced myself and took a flying leap to clear the edge of the stone slope. It was a nasty fall for someone who didn't know to avoid the edge of the incline. Dusting my hands off, I beamed at the young kid who was gawking at me in wide-eyed silence. Knowing he wasn't going to get me anywhere, I decided to play nice anyway. Twisting around, I pulled my hair out of the way, bearing the phoenix to his view. "I seek a meeting with the council."

The kid looked like a fish out of water as his mouth flopped open and then closed in shock. "Uhm . . ."

The boy was barely twelve and obviously just learning the ropes about sentry duty. His medosta was probably hanging close by, but I didn't have the time to sit here and wait. "Look, kid, you've seen my marking." I moved to shuffle him out of the way. "Now, let me pass."

"Hey lady—" He attempted to shove me back while pulling himself to his puny height. "I have to wait for the proper permission to let you any farther . . . and I certainly can't be calling the council for you—"

"Ivan? Do you know who it is you are talking to so capriciously? That's Lieutenant Colonel Deverell, and you address her by her title and nothing less. She is your superior, not an imposter."

The poor boy went ashen white as he scampered away from me. "My d-deepest apologies, L-Lieutenant Colonel."

I flinched at the title. I had been the youngest in generations to reach the rank in the few short years I had been here, and I still didn't feel I deserved it. Liam Glass melted out of the shadows with a wide grin. "It's been too long, Ari girl."

Home. That was the word that kept echoing through my head. Finally, I had returned to the one place in the world where I felt I perfectly fit. My mother had refused to let me join the order and move to the Hollow Hills permanently, and it had been the only point of contention in our relationship. After the five and a half years I had spent here, I had never wanted to leave the place I had so deeply connected with.

Joy flooded through me as I launched myself into Liam's arms. "Liam!"

His arms latched around me as he swung me through the air. "Oh, Ari girl, you stayed away for far too long!"

Liam had been in training when my father had first dropped me off. Few girls got sent to join the order, and my gender had caused me a lot of hassles. Liam had taken me under his wing from the second I spilled my dinner all over him. He had become as close as a brother and, behind Logan, was my closest friend and confidant.

The desire to sit and talk for hours tugged at me, but each second that ticked by counted. "You have no idea how much I would like to catch up with you, but first I must meet with the council," I explained, pulling myself out of his arms.

His brows furrowed in confusion. "Ariel, you can't just demand the council to gather. There are protocols and—"

"I know, Liam. I know what I'm requesting and the consequences of such actions. There is no other choice, though; the council must meet immediately." Not only that, but they must act just as swiftly. Algernon created the order to protect the people of the realms, not to hide in secrecy for all time.

We were needed. If the council didn't choose to step in and help, then they had forgotten the purpose for which they had been created. If that were the case, I would remove every mark that I used to bear proudly, for I wanted no association with cowards.

"Ariel, you can't!" he exclaimed, dragging an agitated hand through his thick hair.

We had an audience, and I didn't want to get into this argument at the moment. "There is no choice." Maybe if I repeated the words enough, somebody would start understanding. Titus had stolen the choice from us, and now it was time for us to take back our land.

I didn't need him to call the council for me; I was quite capable of sounding the alarm myself. It was a long tunnel to the main grounds, but enough torches decorated the path that I would be okay without my own light. Clutching his arm, I spoke softly, "You will come to understand, Liam, why I must do this."

Leaving him behind with his charge, I strode down the tunnel with a newfound purpose. Being here filled me with a fire I had forgotten. I had been called for such a destiny as this. It felt right to be home and, if the council refused my request, I would find our people sanctuary elsewhere. I would do whatever was needed to reclaim the realms from tyranny.

"Ariel, wait!" Liam's voice boomed after me, and I hesitated slightly until he caught up. "I will call them for you. Don't yet raise the alarm; I'll get them together."

I nodded my agreement and didn't break the tense silence that had fallen. I was going to need all my wits and persuasive tactics for the upcoming battle, and I refused to wear myself out arguing with Liam.

"You realize they could strip you of your rank?" he asked, sorrowful gray eyes meeting mine. "Worse, they could banish you from the order altogether."

"My rank is a mere title," I replied dryly, "and if they deny my request, then banishing me will be a gift."

He cringed but didn't stop walking. "Does this have to do with the reports we've been hearing about the coup?"

The tunnel began to widen into a whole new world, and my attention was caught by a pair of monstrous stone soldiers guarding the entrance. "It has everything to do with it."

CHAPTER XVI

The Hollow Hills was an entire world in itself. It was a massive network of rooms and tunnels that ran underneath the entire ten realms. The order only inhabited a part of the land the dwarves had originally called their home. Barracks and homes spread out for miles, all centered around the building I was now standing in front of. It was ostentatious, but it was where the council gathered and made all decisions. I loved the marble pillars and stone buildings that were left by the dwarves, but I missed the sun when I was underground for any length of time.

I paced in front of the doors, my hands clasped behind my back. I was going to be dealing with a disgruntled crowd since I had pulled most of them from meals or their beds. Liam was taking a massive risk himself, being my messenger, and I hoped he wouldn't be punished for my actions.

"Ariel?" I turned to see Liam standing in the doorway, his shoulders hunched. "They're ready for you now."

I smiled at him and patted his arm as I walked by. "Cheer up, Liam. I'll be okay. I always am."

He didn't respond; he just followed me as I twisted through the empty halls to the main chamber. He moved around me and opened the door with a warning look. "Watch your tongue in there, Ariel. I'd like to see you come out with your head still attached."

Biting back words had never been my forte, and I doubted I was going to start now. Liam ushered me inside, and I rolled my eyes when I saw it was pitch black. So they were going to start by playing games? I stopped at what seemed an appropriate distance from where I knew the platform to be. I had to assume they were already seated, and so I waited patiently for them to address me. I'm not sure why they continued with the charades. I knew each of them personally and was no longer an impatient novice. I would stand here all day in silence until they spoke, if I had to. Was this my punishment for forcing them to gather? Were they treating me as a novice to prove their point?

I waited for a solid ten minutes before General Burns spoke. "What is the meaning for this gathering, Lieutenant Colonel?"

"I apologize for my break in protocol, General, and for forcing you to gather on such short notice." I kept my voice respectful as I uttered all the right words. "But unfortunately I had no other options."

General Wallace spoke up. "And why is that?"

"I am not sure you are completely aware of what is happening above ground, or the—"

Burns interrupted. "Are you implying we don't know what is going on in our own land?"

I never liked Burns, and it took effort not to tell him to shut up until I was done speaking. Out of all the council members, he was the most arrogant—and downright rude. "That was not what I meant, General. I am simply trying to explain—"

"If your purpose is to tell us that Titus has taken over, then you are wasting your breath and our time," Burns exclaimed, the sound of a fist hitting wood reaching my ears.

Anger began to spike in my blood and force my pulse to pound. "First of all, why don't we stop with the childish games and light the torches."

"You are not the one calling the shots here, Deverell," Burns retorted, his smug voice oozing across the distance between us.

However, a torch suddenly flared to life on my left, and it wasn't a surprise that Logan's father was the one who had lit it. Slowly he went around the room, lighting all the torches before he returned to his seat. "Now, please proceed." General Wallace motioned for me to continue, his face a study in boredom.

Five men held the power to destroy my hopes, and it looked like General Burns was going to be my biggest adversary. They had to understand what Titus was doing. "He is destroying everything he can get his hands on, and more and more refugees are being made every day. I would like permission to open the Hollow Hills to the people." I could spout a lot of pretty words, but it was best to get straight to the point.

Burns jumped to his feet, knocking his throne back a few inches. "You dare suggest we reveal the greatest secret—"

"I suggest," I ground out through clenched teeth, "that we do what we were created for: protect the people."

"Things have not yet reached the point where we are needed to step in!" Burns boomed, his face turning purple. "And yet you suggest such a—"

My control snapped, and I knew this was not going to go well from here on out. "How bad must things get before we do something? He—"

"You are out of line, Lieutenant Colonel!"

All the other members seemed content to watch in silence, and that only infuriated me more. "Stop. Cutting. Me. Off." His eyes bulged, and I could almost swear he wanted to leap off the platform and murder me. "Titus has taken my family and laid waste to everything we hold dear. High King Algernon created us for the sole purpose of watching out for the people—"

"So this has nothing to do with the people; it has everything to do with your quest for vengeance!"

"Titus Ephraim has murdered most of the monarchs and is killing thousands just because he can. When does this start becoming a problem to you? Or are you so content to sit on your throne and cower in your secrecy that you bury your head in the sand?" My hands trembled in rage. "How do you live with yourself knowing that everything is going to hell above your very head?"

Burns launched off the podium, and, before Wallace or Gallagher could stop him, closed his hands around my throat. "I should snap your neck for such words."

I stayed perfectly still, my eyes spitting out enough fire to burn him where he stood. "And Wehjaeel should strike you dead for being such a coward."

His fingers tightened to the point that I started gasping for air. My hand drifted down for my dagger but, before I could act, he was ripped off of me. Wallace and General Spartz forced him back to his seat in poorly disguised disgust. Nolan Gallagher rose to head my way, but I motioned for him to stay seated. If he showed me any sign of favoritism, his vote would be considered forfeit.

Refusing to rub my throbbing neck, I faced the council confidently. "Is this what we have turned into? We have strayed so far from our history that we can't even remember why we exist? Our ancestors died on this very mountain to defend a land and people they loved above all else. Algernon created the order to stand in the gap and protect the people against any foe that threatened our livelihood. Titus Ephraim is an evil we can't allow to keep spreading. I need a place to hide the people while I chase a lead I have of beating him."

General Spartz shook his head slowly. "You do not know what you ask. You are not only asking us to join the fight, you are also asking us to give up our stronghold, and hundreds of years—"

"Hundreds of years of preparation for a time we may be needed again." I stared at them in astonishment. They were really just going to sit there and tell me the secret of our existence was more important than helping to stop Titus? "And now, we are needed."

General Burns sneered at me. "You think you know and understand so much. How about we step down and *you* take over."

Well, that comment was going to backfire on him. "So be it, but you tell me what I need to know first."

Shock flared in his eyes. "Just who is it you think you are?"

"I am Ariel Callan Deverell, daughter of Caius and Eleanor Deverell, great grandchild of Sargent Caedmon Deverell. I've been appointed by Cyrus Drenuellon, King of Airis, chosen by the monarchs, and called by Wehjaeel. I'm meant to lead, and so I shall. So either you help me or you get out of my way."

I felt a strength and courage flow through me that I had never known I possessed. I wasn't a little girl searching for her identity anymore. No, I had a purpose and a destiny. The council was not going to lend me any assistance, I could see that clearly now. They were going to stay hidden in their cozy hidey-hole and pretend they were doing the right thing by retaining their secrecy.

So be it.

Burns leaned back in his chair, relaxing his hands on the arms. "When you were first initiated into the order and climbed the ranks so swiftly . . . well, I would have never guessed you would fall so far so fast." He smirked, his face twisting into a grotesque mask of greed and deception. "You really have made a grave mistake, and, instead of begging for leniency, you act as if you have some special calling and can walk on water."

I felt my pendent pulse a wave of heat, and I swallowed my revulsion. What had happened in the short time I was gone? What kind of man was Burns to be leading the order?

I kept my face a study of indifference. "When this is over, I won't be the one with blood on my hands. When the mass graves start appearing, I just want you to know it was in your power to prevent it."

General Wallace leaned forward, his face pinched with distaste. "Regimes and leaders fall all the time. Who are we to decide who calls himself king? We just—"

I scoffed, failing to hide my rising amusement at his sense of logic. "You just what? I haven't *seen* you do *anything*."

Burns motioned Wallace to stay silent. "I've had enough of her insolence. Obviously, we are in agreement to let the situation above remain the same for the time being. The question now is the fit punishment for her actions."

At least someone was acting, and even if I was to be punished for it, it was worth it. How had our leaders fallen so far? Burns wouldn't be so smug if Algernon's heir was in attendance. Puzzle pieces clicked in my head; the latest son of Algernon's bloodline—and current king—had not taken up residence in the order because he had gone missing seven years ago. What if Isidora's map could locate him? Because, no matter how many decisions the council made in his absence, he still had the power to overrule them.

Hope flickered in my heart at the thought. Maybe this fight wasn't over quite yet; maybe I could still secure the Hollow Hills as a sanctuary. I gazed at Burns in pity as he sneered at me—and I wasn't surprised when another wave of heat shot off Isidora's necklace. This wasn't going to be the last day I dealt with Burns; I had a feeling he was going to become a chronic problem in my life. "Well, can you decide already so that I may be on my way?" I was getting a little snarky, but at this point I had nothing to lose. I had already torched my bridges . . .

Nolan visibly flinched, his eyes begging me to get on my knees and grovel for forgiveness. I wasn't going to stoop to that level, and I wasn't particularly sorry for anything I had done today.

Burns stood to his feet, shaking with barely restrained fury. "You are hereby sentenced to thirty lashings and stripped of your position. If you enter the premises again, the cost will be your life."

Spartz, Nolan, and Wallace sprang to their feet, mouths gaping. "Perhaps," Spartz started, "we should discuss the severity of her punishment. To completely disavow her—"

Nolan's hands slammed down on the table. "This has always been your agenda, Burns! You can't—"

Burns fingers scrunched into fists. "You dare protect her? Careful, Gallagher, you're treading on dangerous ground."

Wallace shoved his way between the two men. "Nolan, she has done this to herself!"

My eyes sought out the remaining council member who stayed seated as the other men argued. General Kai had always been a silent, formidable force in the order. On more than one occasion I had finished a sparring session to find him watching me, and then, without a word, turn and leave. I've heard countless stories of how heroic and courageous he was on a battlefield. At his speculative expression, I knew how the end of this argument was going to turn out, and it would not be in my favor. A pang of agony speared through me, and I reached into my pocket to touch Samuel's handkerchief. I was going to lose my home again, and, when they tossed me out, I could only pray Samuel found me in time. After thirty lashings, I would never be able to make the trip back to Etherdayle. Bringing my hand out of my pocket, I kept a tight grip on the small piece of fabric; maybe a slice of Samuel would give me the strength I needed to lose another home.

The generals continued to bicker as I watched impassively. I wouldn't give them the satisfaction of seeing my pain. If I gave any indication, they would be like sharks that smelled blood. I had expected a demotion in rank, even earn lashings for my impudence. But Burns had reached new levels in making it impossible for me to ever return.

"Tate! Liam!" Burns hollered for the men who had kept vigil behind the council, just in case any trouble arose. They moved close to where I stood and turned to face the council, distress evident on their faces.

Burns regarded me, his glee apparent as he issued his next order. "My punishment for her insubordinate behavior stands. You will escort her to the lower arena."

Nolan bounded down the stairs, but I waved him off before he got any closer. He didn't deserve any repercussions on my account, and at this point he needed to put as much distance between us as possible. Liam looked ready to pull his sword and start a fight, and I needed him to calm down. He was another individual who needed to step away from me. I didn't want to see any harm come to him.

Curling my fingers protectively around the handkerchief, I watched as Tate gripped my arm and handed Liam a rope to bind my wrists. The precaution wasn't needed, for I had no intentions of fighting them or trying to escape. Liam hesitated before loosely wrapping the rope around me. His hands lingered and I forced a smile to my lips. "I'll be okay, Liam," I whispered reassuringly.

"None of this is right," he breathed, his eyes flicking to Tate.

"What is the delay?" Burns inquired, appearing behind Liam.

Liam shifted to grab my other arm. "Nothing, sir. We're ready, sir." His words snapped with anger, but Burns didn't seem to notice.

"Get her out of here," he spat.

Burns led the procession from the room, his head held high and his stride that of a man who had tasted the sweetest of victories. I heard the other council members move to follow us, but I didn't allow myself to look back and read their expressions. News had traveled fast, for when I stepped out of the doors, a massive group of solemn people watched me. Burns faltered on the steps, his shrewd eyes scouring the mass of people.

I recognized many and felt my heart splinter, knowing this would be my farewell to them all. Nolan had been my medosta, and our bond was as deep as if he were my father. Liam had been my fiercest protector and comforting shoulder for the tearful nights I didn't think I could survive another day. Most were good friends—comrades I had gone out into the field with. And they were all staring at me like I could somehow fix what had already been done.

"Ariel Deverell has committed grave crimes against the order and therefore will be punished to the fullest extent," Burns informed the confused people. "Now, move aside."

Grave crimes? I had called a council meeting that was unheard of when you didn't go through the right channels and hoops. I had asked for help and stood my ground when they accused me of only wanting vengeance. The man was obviously stretching it a bit to call my actions grave crimes. Of course, I had called him a coward, but I was never one to lie about something that was true. Thinking about it now, I should have called him a weasel-faced, corrupted coward. That would have been more accurate.

Shocked gasps and grumblings rippled through the crowd. I wondered what Burns thought he was accomplishing with this display. Was he just trying to flex his muscles and prove who was in charge? Or was I to serve as an example for others to not stand against him? Both, most likely. Yawning loudly, I captured his attention. "Are you done making a spectacle of yourself?"

His fist smashed into my face and, under normal circumstances, the blow would have driven me to my knees. Luckily, Liam held me upright as I blinked the stars from my vision. I felt blood slide down my face but offered Burns a brilliant smile. Making sure my voice carried, I spoke: "You'll never be able to hide the truth from them. You're choosing to let a man kill thousands, and you insist it isn't our duty to interfere. And if that is what we Phoenixes stand for, then go ahead and throw me to the wolves. You'll be doing me a great service."

Dissent sparked through the observers as they pressed closer to where we stood. My words may not shove them into action at the moment, but this encounter would stick in their minds. The order really was full of good and noble people, and hopefully my banishment would open their eyes and propel them into doing something. Contrary to Burn's belief, the council was not going to have the final say; when this was all over, I would not be the only one opposing them.

Burns's eyes hardened and, if it were at all possible, he would be spewing fire. I was lucky he was human and not a dragon. That idiotic image drew a smile to my lips, which only enraged him further. Tilting forward, he clenched his fingers around my face, bruising the tender skin. "You'll regret the day you crossed me, Deverell. You show your face around here again, and I will take intense pleasure in killing you slowly."

My eyes flickered up to his hatred-filled ones. "We'll see." He was past the point of reason. It was either madness or the craze for power that drove him. Whatever it was, before this was all over, I would see him stopped.

His hand dropped like it was on fire before he spun around to the crowd. "I want you to remember this moment clearly. This is the punishment for anarchy." Burns marched down the stairs, shoving people aside when they didn't move fast enough.

Liam and Tate followed him a little more slowly as hands reached out to touch me in comfort and support. I offered them smiles and nods of encouragement, but what could be said? I was ushered to the arena where the young ones spent most of their time training. Liam froze when Burns pointed to the rowan post that I could remember spending hours whacking. It had provided a great surface for pounding out my frustrations and anger.

Nudging Liam, I motioned for him to bend down. "Watch your back, Liam. Do you understand me? This is just the beginning. As soon as I can . . . I'll be back."

He nodded slowly before releasing his hold on me. "Stay strong, Ari girl."

Burns ripped me away from Tate, slamming me against the post. My head crashed into the wood with a deafening crack. Reeling against the pain, I mutely allowed him to bind me against it. Struggling would only aid the belief that I had committed a crime and this was fair and just punishment.

Nolan materialized next to my elbow and reached forward to wipe some of the blood off my face. "Burns, you could create a mutiny with your decision and public demonstration."

I could no longer see those gathered, so I couldn't judge their reaction to the happenings. I heard Burns crack a whip to the left of me, and I had to control the shudder that wracked my body. I refused to give him an ounce of satisfaction.

"The council has been in command for over a hundred years. We have decided when to step in and when to wait dozens of times throughout history, and we will continue to do so for years to come." The whip snapped again, closer to me this time. "No mere girl is going to tip the balance of power."

Nolan's eyes pierced through me in agony. He was powerless, and we both knew it. If he persisted to raise a ruckus, he would be sentenced to the same fate. However, he couldn't resist speaking. "She isn't a Lieutenant Colonel for nothing, you know. Your unrelenting pride is blinding you to the fact that everything is about to change."

"Get out of my way, Gallagher, before I string you up next to her," Burns snarled, the whip cracking the air mere inches from me now.

Sorrow had a vice-grip on my windpipe as Nolan pressed a soft kiss to my forehead and faded back into the crowd behind me. The council would regret letting Burns make this decision for them; Nolan had been correct when he said everything was about to change. I knew what I was going to be forced to do, and I loathed the fact that I was going to be tearing apart an organization that had been put together so lovingly.

My head drooped as the first slash of the whip tore into my skin. I clutched the handkerchief tighter and tried to breathe through the pain. If only I had brought Samuel with me; he would never have let me get myself into this predicament. I should have trusted him. My secret had been worthless, for here I was, still being stripped of my honor. A blessed numbness overcame me as lash after lash ripped into me. I lost count of the vicious strokes; my only focus was to remain conscious through the attack. I was going to need my wits to find my way back to the boys. The length of time I'd been gone had to be driving them crazy.

"That's enough, Burns."

I felt like I was fighting against pounds of sand as I raised my head to stare at General Kai, who had finally decided it was time to speak.

However, Burns's whip didn't cease at Kai's words. Blood-curdling screaming was the last thing my mind registered before I skyrocketed into blackness.

CHAPTER XVII

Awareness dripped into my mind slowly.

I was afraid to open my eyes and meet the leering gaze of Burns. I had tried so hard to stay strong and not succumb to the pain, but, by the evidence of my burning throat, the horrific screaming had come from me. How long had I screamed before I fell into the comforting waves of oblivion? Chills coursed through me, and it was at that point my eyes sprang open to see that I was surrounded by snow.

"I hate snow," I mumbled in disgust. They had pitched me out the door, then, and left me for dead. Nausea tumbled through me as I attempted to bring my arms under me and rise to my knees. I plummeted back to the ground with a loud oomph. How was I ever going to make it down the mountain?

I curled my arms around my body, and it was then I saw that my hand still gripped the handkerchief. A soft smile lit my face as I brought it close to my heart and closed my eyes. I could do this; I knew I was strong enough to at least get to my feet. I had to get back down to Samuel to tell him I was all right. I would deal with everyone's anger and disappointment if only I could be close to him again.

"ARIEL!!"

Joy lit my heart as I heard the hoarse yell. He never failed, did he? I wasn't sure how he had found me, and so quickly, but gratitude was the least of my emotions. Gentle arms wrapped around me and tucked me close to a warm chest. "Ariel? Please answer me . . . Ariel, are you okay?"

Dazed, I blinked up at a face that was slowly worming its way deeper into my heart. "Samuel," I breathed, letting my head rest against him. "You found me."

He brushed the hair away from my temple, his expression hidden. "Did you expect anything different?" His voice was so soft and soothing it made me melt into him.

I heard footsteps approach, but my eyes were focused on the man who clutched onto me as though the air might carry me away. I unclenched my fingers to show him the handkerchief that had given me courage solely because it had been a tangible piece of him. His eyes shot to the gift I was holding out to him. "Ariel." His voice was a whisper as he leaned his forehead down to meet mine. "Please tell me you are okay."

I was surprised he wasn't yelling and that his face was pale, not a violent purple. No, he looked absolutely panicked and somewhat relieved. I continued to offer him the handkerchief. I was having a hard time focusing on his question or my surroundings. My mind was too wrapped around the fact that he had found me.

He reached down to take the handkerchief and then promptly tucked it back into my pocket. "Ariel?"

I had never noticed before that, when he wasn't screaming, my name rolled off his tongue like music. His face was so close I could feel his breath fan across my lips, and it was making my mind positively dizzy. Or maybe it was just the blood leaking from me that was messing with my head.

A hand landed on Samuel's shoulder. "Perhaps now would be an excellent time to take her to a healer. It appears as if she is still bleeding heavily."

Father Eli peered down at me, but I didn't bother to acknowledge him. His presence explained how Samuel had known to climb up Mount Algernon to find me. Curling my fingers around Samuel's tunic, I let myself drown in his bottomless eyes. It didn't matter who Samuel used to be or the demons that plagued his steps. To me, he was so much more than a haunted man looking for redemption. And I had a feeling that was precisely what he was searching so desperately for. "Don't leave," I begged, my voice hitching in anxiety.

He seemed shaken when he noticed blood all over his tunic and pooling under me, but he managed a crooked smile. "You aren't that lucky, Wildcat."

After so many attempts to get rid of him, it felt strange pleading for him to stay. Curling tight against him, I couldn't swallow the whimper that fell from my lips. Moving an inch felt like I was tearing open my skin with my bare hands.

Fear raced across Samuel's face and he remained frozen. "Ariel, why would anyone do this to you?" His words were so soft I had to strain to hear.

It was a complicated question. Unfortunately, it wasn't what they had done to my body that hurt the most. It was the damage they had done to my heart that made me ache down to my toes.

"Samuel—" Colter knelt next to us, his hand wavering over me. "If we don't get her to a healer—" His face was strained as his eyes searched mine. He didn't need to voice what was going through his head for me to understand. If they didn't get me off this mountain soon, I would die.

And I had so much left to do . . .

I had people to protect, revenge to enact, a family to rescue, an order of warriors to put to rights, and a tyrannical ruler to destroy. It was a little much for one person to handle, but until my dying breath I would accomplish as much as I could. Which meant that I couldn't die up here. Not yet. Too much was left undone.

Gritting my teeth, I wound my arms around Samuel's neck and nodded to him tightly. "I'm ready." I wouldn't ever be ready, but he didn't seem to detect the outright lie. The sight of my blood seemed to unhinge him in a peculiar way.

He rose to his feet with me securely in his arms and grimaced when a yelp escaped. "This is going to take a miracle," he muttered, his feet sure and his gait steady as he descended the mountain.

Someone was suffocating me.

With a banshee scream, I rushed to life and lashed out wildly. Nails clawing and teeth biting, I reared against whatever dared to hold me down.

"ARIEL!" Samuel boomed, his blurry face somewhere to my right.

A shriek, not quite human, tore from me as I battled harder to get free. I was *burning*. Couldn't he see that someone was trying to murder me right in front of his eyes? My back arched in agony as someone shoved me hard against the mattress I had been placed on.

"Hold her down!" The voice was unfamiliar and panicked. "FOOLS! Hold her down or she is as good as dead!"

Samuel came into focus, but he didn't try to help, no. No. His hands joined those constricting me. Tears spilled from the corners of my eyes at his betrayal. Did everyone want me dead? It wouldn't take long; the fire licked at me . . . "NO!" A fierce desire to live spurred me into another struggle.

Samuel's hands clenched my face between his palms. "You have to calm down—" he beseeched, his eyes boring into mine.

Couldn't he see I was on fire? Throwing my body against the mattress, I tried ripping from his grip, but he latched onto me. "He's trying to save you!"

"I hate you!" I spat before another scream was wrenched from me. "STOP BURNING ME!" I implored, my hands flailing across my skin in an attempt to stop the fire.

"Keep her *still*," someone instructed tensely, right as another wave of heat burst over my skin.

Samuel's hands moved to pin my shoulders down, but, no matter how much I bucked, he was too strong. "Hate you . . ." I mumbled, causing him to flinch.

"He's saving you," he whispered, his eyes spearing into mine. "Don't leave me, Ariel . . . please, not yet."

"Stop the f-fire . . ." I wheezed, my chest heaving. "Please . . ." My head lolled to the side, and I heard a desperate cry. But the darkness was too welcoming.

For as long as I could remember I had been landlocked between grassy hills and a boundary of forbidden trees. So, as far as my judgment was concerned, I could be mistaken. But I had seen pictures, and I could swear that somehow, someway . . . I was standing on the ocean shore of the realms of Algernon.

My toes buried themselves in the sand as I watched indigo and amethyst waves crash onto pearl-white dunes of sand. Pictures didn't do the roaring pulses of water justice. Silk brushed across my calves, and it was with a sinking heart I realized I was clothed in an emerald- green summer dress that flowed with the wind.

I was dead, then.

My fingers crunched into fists. Who would stand against Titus now? Who would rescue my family?

"Ariel."

The voice was so soft I almost missed it. Spinning around, I reached for the blade that I no longer had. I froze when my eyes fell upon the man who stared at me. "Bryne?"

His eyes sparked with concern. "What have you done, Ariel?" he asked, stepping towards me gingerly. "Why are you here?"

I had been a fool and had demanded the impossible. "I need you," I whispered. How I had missed him! He pulled me into his arms and tucked me against his chest like I was a small child. I yearned to be young again, to reclaim the innocence I had lost.

Leaning his head down, he met my eyes before speaking. "You are strong enough to do what needs to be done."

"I'm sorry I failed you." If I had been swifter on my feet, my arm a little stronger, perhaps I could have made the needed difference.

"You only fail when you cease to try, and I've never known my sister to stop at anything until she has succeeded."

The girl he was talking about had long ago vanished. I pulled from his embrace and walked to the edge of the water. The water spit and hissed at me, but the frigid droplets were a reminder that I could still feel. "I feel like I am doing everything wrong and have yet to accomplish one thing."

Bryne nudged me with his shoulder. "Protect the people. That is the only mission you need to focus on. No matter the consequences, or the cost, protect the people."

I looked down at the dress and back out to the waves. "A little hard to do when I'm dead."

Bryne's expression turned serious. "Not yet, you aren't." His hand gripped mine. "I hope it is a good many years before I am to see you again. Wehjael's land will still be here when you are an old woman . . . Now, go back!"

Confusion overwhelmed me. How did one simply go back? Did he think I could just poof myself back to the world of the living?

"Ariel!"

"No need to yell," I muttered, looking over at Bryne. But the look on his face told me clearly he wasn't the one who had yelled my name.

He placed a soft kiss on my forehead. "I would have died a thousand times over to protect you. Don't waste the life you've been given. Go back, Ariel."

"Ariel!"

I whipped around, but there was no one in sight except Bryne. "But—"

His look was tender. "You've nothing to fear."

"Ariel! Please!"

I knew that frantic voice, if only I could remember its source. I felt fingers dig into my

arms and someone thrashing me back and forth.

"Ariel . . . I need you . . . "

Samuel.

I knew it was him calling me back, and although it was ideal on this peaceful beach with Bryne, I needed to go back to him. Something hard slammed against my chest, and I felt my heart thunder in response. I instinctively reached out to Bryne, but he was moving away from me. "They need you, Ariel," he said, his face serene. "He needs you."

The waves I had been watching in fascination built in height and crashed around me, showering me in shimmering sprays. Inching back, I held my arms out in front of me protectively. Could you drown when you were already dead? Those waves didn't look friendly, and I certainly didn't want to find out by trial and error. Sensing my fear, a massive wave leapt out and encompassed me.

Throwing my hands up, I began to scream and inhaled the poisonous water as it dragged me out deeper to its bottomless depths. Gagging against the assault, I kicked and thrashed, attempting to get back to air. Nothing but darkness surrounded me as I clawed for leverage against the waves that continued to shove me around.

"ARIEL!"

The name was roared in my ears, and it renewed me just enough to keep me striving for the surface. Hands yanked, tearing me out of the water and—

Choking for air, I leaned over the side of the bed and convulsed in an attempt to clear my lungs. Samuel's hand thumped my back, helping me expel the last of the water I had so stupidly swallowed. His mind had to be working overtime after watching me roar alive with a vengeance, expectorating water everywhere.

Clinging to him, I let my head hang over the bed, my hair hiding my face. It was a bit mortifying to find I had draped myself over his knees and was now literally lying in his lap. Gently, he shifted me so he was cradling my limp body. Reaching back, he pulled free the blanket that was tangled around my feet and cocooned me inside its warm folds.

"Hey," I croaked, wincing at how the word scraped across my tender throat.

His hand swept away damp ringlets of hair from my dazed face. "I thought I had lost you," he mumbled, before staring at the water all over the floor. "How—"

How indeed? I would have chalked it all up to being nothing but a crazy dream in my head—except the water pooling on the ground mocked me.

"The healer said—" He stopped, a shield falling across his face. But his eyes were alive with such intensity it stole my breath.

"I'm too stubborn to die," I whispered, allowing my head to drop against his chest in exhaustion.

His arms tightened around me. "Do that to me again, and I'll wring your neck. You understand me?"

Despite myself, I laughed. "Noted." I blinked drowsily, feeling myself start to slip into a much-needed sleep. Trying to keep my eyes open, I caught the tender look that suffused Samuel's face.

"Go to sleep, Ariel," he whispered, smoothing a finger over my eyebrow. "I'll be right here." With the promise of his parting words, I fell into a dreamless sleep, knowing he wasn't far way and would be ready to pull me back into this mortal world if I started to slip again.

CHAPTER XVIII

hree days passed in a sad, slow march as I reconciled the fact that I was indeed alive. I wasn't sure what to feel or how to act. How could I explain to anyone what I had encountered in the time I had been . . . dead? I knew it wasn't a figment of my imagination, for Samuel had confirmed that I had ceased breathing for some time. Not only that, but the water all over the floor told its own story. I didn't tell anyone what had occurred in the time I had slipped from this world, but Samuel's long looks asked the questions his lips didn't.

My strength started to return by the fourth day, but I still found myself listless and unwilling to engage in the world around me. The healer had managed to patch up my physical wounds, but my energy and willpower were completely zapped. Samuel hadn't left my side once, but he stayed silent, allowing me to reside in my mind without interruption. Curled up in a chair by the small window in my room, I watched the bustle of Etherdayle. I gazed out the window as dawn painted the morning and dusk stole the color of day. I don't know how long I sat and just stared at the small square of the world the window afforded me.

I was alive.

Each time I closed my eyes, I worried I would be dragged back to the beach and told that this time I wasn't going to receive a second chance.

A second chance.

My hands gripped the sides of the chair as the words settled in my mind. What was I doing, losing myself in dark thoughts? Bryne had told me that my only concern needed to be protecting the people. I couldn't guard anyone when I was sitting in a chair, drowning in memories and regrets. Death no longer scared me, and in fact, in some ways, the idea was welcoming. No more stress or worries. No pain. No fear. But that lack of fear for death could be crippling, for if I went into a fight wanting death, that's exactly what I would receive.

My lukewarm attitude about defeating Titus also needed to be changed. The only thing I found myself crazed to do was rescue my family. My perspective had been so skewed it was laughable. What did I think I could do? Rush Midas, rescue them, and get out without a scratch or care in the world? I really was horribly idealistic.

I took a deep breath and pushed myself to my feet. I heard Samuel shift and stand to the side of me to offer aid, but I didn't take his outstretched arm. My legs were a bit wobbly, but the longer I stood the better it got.

I wasn't the same person anymore. I couldn't be that naïve girl any longer. I had to be stronger, braver, and less concerned with my piddling problems. I had to stay focused on one goal and one goal alone.

I had to protect the people.

If that meant destroying Titus, then so be it. If that meant I got my family back, then so be it. If I got my revenge against the assassin, then so be it. But I couldn't scatter my attention to all the different tasks and hope to accomplish anything. Protecting Algernon's inheritance came first. He had given us a peaceful, prosperous land where we could live free. And soon it would be time to take back that land. First, I had to relocate and hide as many people as I could.

I wanted the Hollow Hills, and I planned on getting them.

I looked over to where Samuel stood quietly watching. A slow ache began to build in my chest, and the knowledge that filled my mind hurt. I wasn't even going to get a chance to think of a future with Samuel in it. He may care for me, and he may not. If I was forced to be honest with myself, I barely knew the man. I couldn't allow myself to dwell on what ifs. Maybe, after all was said and done, I could consider the possibility of Samuel staying in my world, but, with what I had to do, it wasn't fair to either of us to go any further. He had stayed thus far, but who was to say he would continue to do so? I had lost enough in life already, and I wasn't going to stand by idly and watch my heart shatter. How did I know this wasn't all just a game to him, that I wasn't just some passing diversion?

"Ariel?" It was the first word he had spoken for days, and it shouldn't sound so hauntingly wonderful.

"Where—" I cleared my throat and tried again. "Where is everyone?"

His eyes clouded. "Father Eli has set up a small campsite for them in the middle of the city since they refused to disband." He shook his head slowly in disbelief. "He offered warm beds and a roof over their heads, and they all refused, saying they would prefer to stick together." He eyed me wonderingly. "I guess you've started to wear off on them."

I gave a weak smile. "Oh." Using the furniture for balance, I made my way over to the small bundle Father Eli had left for me a few days ago. My eyes swept the room, concerned. "Fairchild, where is my pack?"

He grimaced, and his expression did little to settle my frayed nerves. His hand rubbed the back of his head as he peered at me in hopelessness. "We looked for it—"

"I'll throttle that man!" I snapped, stomping my foot like a petulant child. Burns had his hands on Isidora's map, and I could only pray the map remained invisible to him. Thankfully, I had been smart enough to keep the keys in my boot and not in my pack. Small blessings.

"I'll just—" Samuel stopped struggling for words, his eyes casting over the entire room. "Well, I'll be outside the door while you—" He gestured at me soundlessly before slipping out the door.

Father Eli had supplied me with new, badly-needed clothes. It felt great to wear something that wasn't torn, muddy, blood-stained, or smelly. I wasn't sure where he had come across tight-fitting black pants and a cobalt tunic, but I knew not to question the man. He was resourceful and highly competent. When Eli wanted something bad enough, he tended to get it. After quickly braiding my hair, I let a few tendrils fall loose. I wasn't really into being ordinary and reserved, and completely binding up my hair seemed like a real shame. Double-checking my boots for the keys and my blades, I let out a deep breath. Ready as ever.

Samuel stood guard outside the door, his legs spread and his hands loosely clasped behind his back. I sucked in a small, shocked breath; he looked so much the consummate soldier it was startling. Who was Samuel, and, when I found out, how hard would it be to accept it?

He turned at my little outburst with a cocked eyebrow. "Ready?"

I nodded dumbly. His eyes swept over me appreciatively, and I felt a light flush crawl up my neck in response. How in the world had he managed to get under my skin?

"Wildcat?" His eyes glimmered with devilish amusement, and it shook me out of my reverie.

I was going to have to get better at putting up a wall between him and my emotions. "Yes," I murmured, smoothing my hands down my pants. Maybe the clothes fit a little *too* well, because they didn't leave a whole lot to the imagination.

To my relief, he didn't linger and question my discomfort. He led me out of the small infirmary and towards Bellalinca square. Interesting that Father Eli had set up the camp in the dead center of Etherdayle . . .

Cadell and Hedia came running up when they saw us approaching. Catching up Hedia in my arms, I kissed her forehead lightly and hugged Cadell. "Hey, half-pints," I laughed, as they chattered excitedly. I answered as many questions as I could, but the other children were crowding close, and I couldn't hear what they were asking with all the noise they were making. Giving them all tight hugs, I kissed their heads and counted to make sure they were all there. Cadell, Hedia, Fagan, Sophia, Maddy, Emily, Noah, Ian, and . . . "Where is Brody?" I inquired, my eyes sweeping the gathering.

Slade shrugged his shoulders. "He's taken a shine to Father Ira, and since the Father didn't seem to mind, we let Brody follow him around for a while."

The tension leaked out of my shoulders to see that everyone was all right, and a genuine smile touched my lips.

Liv wriggled her way between the children to throw her arms around me and hug me tightly. "I was so worried about you," she said, hugging me tighter still. "No one would allow me to check on you. They said you needed your rest . . . "

Was it because they thought I actually needed my rest, or because she was an ex-companion? But with another quick glance at everybody, I saw they didn't seem to be tossing her any dirty looks. Nevertheless, it was something I would need to keep an eye on. "I'm okay, Liv," I soothed, letting her hang on for dear life. "No worse for the wear, actually; just a little tired."

Colter's eyes met mine, and, seeing the sharp look in them, I knew Samuel had told him the truth of what happened. He was keeping his mouth shut, though, and that's how I wanted it. No one else needed to worry about what had gone down. Liv stepped away, allowing Eliza and Marie to hug me as well. Slade tapped me on the back with a hearty howl of congratulations that I was moving again, and even Rowan offered me a smile. Colter kept his distance, but I could read his actions just fine. I was in for a lecture later, and I couldn't say that I didn't deserve it. Logan stood a ways off, his shoulders hunched, and I couldn't help but offer him a tentative smile. We hadn't talked since his blow up, but I missed my friend. I wasn't going to be the road-block to getting past what had happened.

After the group calmed a bit, and the children moved off to start a game of hide and seek, I sat down with the adults. It was time to get everyone on the same page so we could move on.

I debated on how to start the conversation, but Liv beat me to the punch. "Ariel, what are we going to do now? We can't continue to cart these children around with us. That's no life for them . . . "

Tapping my fingers against my knees, I met her worried gaze. "That is precisely the reason I had us travel into Etherdayle. I wanted to find us a safe—" I choked on the word safe when the image of Burns and his whip slammed into my mind. It was going to take a while to forget the feel of that whip searing into my skin, and the laughter that had spilled from him. Moistening my lips, I tried again. "Safe location. I know of a place that would be ideal, but I ran into some difficulties." I didn't want to give them too much information; spilling out the secret of the Hollow Hills and offering them hope only to rip it away would be cruel. "However, until we have a place to start hiding people, I can't be searching out more monarchs just to bring them into harm's way. Which brings me to the fact that I am going to have to leave most of you here while I track down someone I think can help."

Samuel and Colter jumped up in sync. Fury shot from Samuel, and Colter just look horrified. A tremor shook Samuel as he glared at me. "Can I talk to you," he paused, staring at everyone's shocked faces, "privately?" His teeth were clenched.

I shook my head no. "My mind is made up, Samuel." If I could find Algernon's heir and then convince him to help me reclaim the Hollow

Hills . . . It was the only place in the world right now that would provide a safe haven for everyone.

"Like hades it is!" he roared, stomping over to me. Scrambling away, I wasn't quick enough to avoid him snatching up my arm and dragging me away from the group. Colter followed us, his face as determined as Samuel's.

"I'm not a child, Fairchild!" Scrabbling against his hold, I managed to rip away from him.

"You could've fooled me," he hissed, bending down to meet me nose to nose. "What idiotic idea is lodged in your brain now?"

Colter smoothly stepped between us, his hands tight on our shoulders. "Ariel, you can't possibly think of going back there," he said, his eyes intense.

"If I can find who I'm looking for, Burns will have no choice but to step aside—"

Samuel lunged for me again, but Colter stopped him short. "They almost killed you!" Samuel's eyes glowed with rage. "I take that back. They *did* kill you . . . and you want to march back in there? Are you that much of a fool?"

"I'll do whatever I need to do to," I insisted. "If I have even the slightest chance of succeeding, I'll take it."

"Ariel, there has to be another way," Colter offered. "I'm sure there is somewhere else we can take everyone."

I turned to him. "Where, Colter? No place is safe from Titus's grasp, and I refuse to keep taking those children into the Shade. Pretty soon we are going to run out of dumb luck and face an attack we can't beat. The Hollow Hills offers us a unique chance to keep everyone safe *and* move around the realm undetected."

"I won't sit back and watch you die again," Samuel growled, his jaw tensing. "I *won't*! So don't ask me to."

My heart constricted at the raw panic radiating from him, but I had set my course and it was time to follow through. "I'm not talking about charging the gates with just my blades for backup. My plan has a little more finesse."

Samuel waved his hand impatiently. "Oh please, do tell."

I glared at him, but it was nothing compared to the blue lava that sparked at me in return. "I plan to find Algernon's heir."

Samuel looked at me and then at Colter, his confusion evident. Colter shrugged at him before staring down at me. "A little more information would be nice; we only received the highlights from Father Eli."

I should be intimidated by the two behemoths staring me down, but, knowing them as I did, they weren't all that scary. "The order was originally designed to always be led by an heir of Algernon. The council was created to balance out the power, but, when it comes right down to it, the heir—who also serves as our king—has the final say. If I could just get him—"

Samuel waved me into silence. "Where exactly is he?"

I shifted uneasily and peeked at Colter, but no help was coming from that corner. "I'm not entirely positive," I muttered. "He disappeared around seven years ago, shortly before I was summoned to the Hollow Hills." I flinched, waiting for the barrage of angry questions sure to come my way.

Colter crossed him arms, satisfied for the moment that Samuel and I weren't going to kill each other. "Disappeared?" he inquired, doubt coating his words.

They were not going to make this easy. "General Burns believes he is dead—" I talked louder when Samuel started to interrupt, "BUT, Nolan always had his suspicions that he ran away since there was never any evidence of foul play."

Samuel sighed in exasperation. "Ariel, you've officially gone off the deep end. Even if this guy is still alive, you don't have Isidora's map. How in the world are you expecting to find him?"

Someone needed to smack this obstinate man into reality and inform him that he wasn't all-knowing. In fact, I would love to be the one to do it. "That's why I need to consult with Father Eli. Not only does he have his fingers in all the pots, he has detailed maps of the realms. They send out expeditions every year to map the changes." They could ask all the questions they wanted, but I had thoroughly thought this plan through.

Colter looked pensive. "You actually think Father Eli would have an idea of where he went?"

Samuel's head whipped around, his eyes stabbing through Colter. "You're forgetting that the man is most likely dead."

"Fairchild—" I began, wanting nothing more than to bang his head against the wall a couple of times.

"Don't. Start. With. Me." His words were frigidly precise. "I watched you *die*, Ariel." His knuckles went white as he fought down his emotions. "And now, now you want to go on some fool's errand to find a man who is most likely dead and who may or may not even help us!"

"I know it's a long shot, but it's worth a try," I said quietly. "If we've got hope, then we are never truly defeated, and I've got enough hope for the both of us that the heir is alive and will help us."

He rubbed the back of his neck in a gesture that conveyed resigned long-suffering. "Colter?"

I watched curiously as Samuel asked Colter's opinion. Maybe there was a chance for friendship between the two of them after all. By the way Colter hesitated, I knew he was conflicted. Forcing my fingers to uncurl from my shirt, I hid my anxiety. I really needed him to side with me, because having them both against me would be impossible to deal with.

His attention focused on me. "I told you I would follow you until the end." He paused, searching for words. "I'll help you track down this heir, but unless you're positive we can take over your place without getting yourself killed, I will stop you."

I could live with those terms. I glanced over at Samuel, his seething a bad sign of what was to come. He opened his mouth to say something before snapping it shut again. His eyes closed in defeat. "I swear you are going to be the death of me."

I bounced on the balls of my feet in excitement. "So, that means—"

He pried opened his eyes reluctantly. "It means lead the way, milady. I am your ever-faithful lackey."

I beamed at the both of them. "Then let the adventure begin!"

They groaned in unison, but at least they weren't hollering about my stupidity.

Before filling in the group about our upcoming departure, I left the boys to go search out Father Eli. I wandered through the labyrinth of architectural amazements, taking my time to arrive at Hawksend. If I knew anything about Eli, it was where he would be mid-morning. He had a habit of praying amongst the ruins—although it was more than likely he would be telling Brody all about their historical roots.

Sure enough, I found him pointing out to Brody where yet another famous battle had occurred. It was said that a peasant boy named Gadiel had come into town one day to fetch supplies, only to find it under attack. A feared giant called Raidon was destroying the town, and no one dared stand up to him. So Gadiel had picked up his sword and bow and went after the giant. The astounding part was that he won. Of course, the giant, after being slain, had fallen and smashed Hawksend to pieces in the process. The Great War had raised so many heroes from the ashes of suffering it was astounding. Gadiel's story was just one among many.

I waited until the father was done showing Brody around and handed him off to a young pupil before I approached.

"Ariel, it is good to see you back on your feet!" he exclaimed, joy lighting up his face.

I smiled at him, remembering when he had blessed me at the ceremony of my acceptance into the order. "It's good to see you again, Father."

He offered his arm gallantly, and I wound mine through it. "Sad the circumstances that have brought you back to my doorstep."

I nodded in agreement, letting him lead me to his chosen destination. "When I left, I dreamed of nothing but coming back. But now that I have returned . . . "

"Yes," he sighed, "a great many things are different."

He drifted into silence, so I spoke up. "Father, I have some questions for you."

His eyes twinkled when he looked down at me. "Yes, I figured you might."

If he was going to try the whole ambiguous thing, I might have to tear out some of my hair. "Father—"

He patted my arm gently. "I'm not trying to be difficult, my dear. I just want to get us somewhere private."

Seclusion for the upcoming conversation was probably a very good idea, so I kept a tight rein on my patience. The order had ears all throughout

Etherdayle, and it would not be beneficial for them to know what I was up to. He ended up leading us to a small pond that glimmered an iridescent white.

Eli had once told me that the pond was created from angel's tears, but I still think he was pulling my leg. I wasn't sure what made the water white, but, with the weeping willows ensconcing the area, it was a nice hideaway. I settled on the lush grass and trailed my fingers through the shimmering liquid.

"Why don't you tell me how you ended up in Etherdayle with the group you did, and we'll proceed from there," Eli suggested.

My fingers were glowing softly now, and I pondered what had created the strange water. "Father, I'm not even sure where to begin." So much had happened in such little time, it made my head spin.

He sat down next to me, unconcerned about soiling his luxurious robe. "From the very first moment, of course."

My mind rewound to the first fire that had propelled me onto my current path, and, with that memory flickering in my head, I launched into my story. I left out bits and pieces, including the part where I died, but I told him most of what had occurred. After I wrung out everything I could remember, I sank back against the grass and stared up at the gold-tinged sky.

Eli sat in contemplative silence, mulling over what I had just confided. "Even without the gift of sight, I knew the minute I saw you that you were intended for something important. I just never realized you were going to be the one to save us all."

Snapping to attention, I gaped at him. "Pardon me, Father?"

He grimaced and stared long and hard at the pond. "Your blessing was significant, and so your destiny is phenomenal. I've never met another as gifted as you are in my entire life, Ariel. I've only heard of such a thing happening once before, and even then the gifting didn't match the caliber of yours."

Now, how did he know what I was gifted with? Answering my unspoken question, he gazed at me reprovingly for not being aware. "We are trained in the art of discerning gifts, and I am the High Priest. Children are brought from far and wide to be told what their gifting is. Of course I know what blessing is on you."

Pulling myself up into a sitting position, I looked at him longingly. I desperately wanted to know what was supposedly so special about me. "Father—"

His brows lowered in concentration. "I think it's high time you have a little lesson in giftings, no?" He shook his head in admonishment. "This is what happens when you live in a realm where everyone just wants to be left alone—and with a mother who wants to protect you from every little thing."

Surely he saw the yearning in my eyes. Was he really going to leave me with more unanswered questions? If they were trained in discernment, what was going to stop me from forcing the answer out of some other unsuspecting priest?

"When we are born, each of us is granted a gifting—a sort of identity, so to speak." His every word was enunciated and carefully chosen, meaning I was about to have a lecture.

Resting my chin on the palms of my hands, I soaked up as much knowledge as he would give me. Giftings were something I would really like to understand. It struck me as ironic, though, that he considered them one's identity yet was withholding mine from me. Maybe I was just a bit tired of fumbling around in the dark. So why did he refuse to hand me a light?

"Some giftings are small, like the ability to grow spectacular gardens. Others are considerably more substantial, such as the gift of sight. And then—" He stopped as if he was about to say too much. I cornered his silver eyes, but still he was stubbornly silent. Seeming to make up his mind, he continued, "And then there is that extremely rare person who comes along. One who is greatly gifted."

Granted, I didn't know much about gifts, but when did great gifts enter the picture? I rubbed at my temples, trying to ease the pounding in my head. "Greatly gifted?"

He nodded sagely, expecting me to grasp something he wasn't saying. "Father, please," I begged. "Lay this out in plain English." I wasn't sure how many more conundrums my mind could handle.

He patted my knee comfortingly with a grandfatherly smile. "You see, there are some among us born to be the guardians of mankind, and so Wehjaeel blesses them greatly." He gathered up my hands in his and lightly kissed my knuckles. "I wish I could tell you how significant you are, but alas, Wehjaeel has other plans. I will tell you this, though: never have I seen or heard throughout history of an individual being as gifted as you." A shadow crossed over his face. "I'm afraid you will face trials and obstacles that will take a special kind of strength to endure. Your upcoming days will not be easy."

Tell me something I didn't know. I knew not to press him for more details, but I wish I could understand why no one would tell me what I was gifted with. Another question was niggling at my mind: "What of dark giftings? How do those happen?"

He released my hands and sighed deep within. "Everyone is born with a good gift, but humankind is what it is. A good gift of hunting can turn into a dark gift of murder. A person's heart can go dark, and when that day happens, his or her blessing becomes a dark gifting."

It made sense in a horrible, forbidding way. If Titus was gifted with brutality and his champion gifted with victory, I was in some deep trouble. "Are there individuals who have great gifts turned dark?"

Eli winced. "I think you know the answer to that. Titus was once a good and honest man, I'm sure. Now . . . "

Now he was a murdering psychopath. My mind churned, making my stomach tilt nervously. "How do you beat someone gifted in victory?" Titus was a problem all in himself, but I would have to face his champion first.

Eli gazed out over the water and answered gravely. "You find something stronger."

Something stronger than victory . . . What precisely did he have in mind? I was mute a moment, not yet ready to raise the subject of Algernon's heir. "Will anyone ever tell me what my gift is?"

"One day very soon you will find all the answers you seek." He met my hungry stare. "I hope you will be prepared for them."

Unwilling to push him further, I pondered the issue of the champion. "During the Great War, was there someone greatly gifted?"

Eli's eyes twinkled with amusement and a secret begging to be spilled. "Two actually. Algernon himself, and the woman he loved: Isidora Emaggen."

There was something vitally important about what he just shared, another riddle I was meant to discover. "Who is this Isidora, and how come I am just now hearing of her existence?" Also, how angry at me was she going to be for losing her map?

Father Eli rose to his feet and offered his hand. "Come with me, Ariel. I've something to show you."

CHAPTER XIX

obblestone paths delivered us outside the borders of Etherdayle. I felt exposed, crossing under the stone arch that declared its entrance. "Father—" I started to dissuade him from going further as I cast a wary eye around us.

"No need to fret; we haven't far to go." His steps didn't even slow down at my balking.

The road turned to dirt as we wound around the tipsy edge of the Shade. Pines and oaks sprang up, blocking all sight of the crown city. Unease crawled through me, but I kept pace with Eli's sure steps.

"I want to show you our land's heritage," he said, his eyes signaling something I couldn't quite comprehend.

He hadn't changed much in the years I had been gone. His once rich, ebony hair was mostly white now, but his silver eyes had never been sharper. His face was lined with age and wisdom, but his years of service were evident in the bags under his eyes. Laughter creases surrounded his mouth, and they said more about him than anything else ever could. He took his trials and tribulations in stride, facing them all with joy. He was a handsome man, but time was beginning to weigh on him.

I was so focused on him I didn't immediately realize we had arrived. But there was no mistaking that what I was gaping at was what Eli intended for me to see: a limestone mansion nestled on the outskirts of the Shade. I should be concerned, of course; but really, I had seen stranger. The Shade hid all sorts of treasures.

It was a spectacular display, and I could only imagine how long it had taken to make such a majestic building. Four stories high, it scraped the canopy of trees with pride. The door was guarded by two ferocious, obsidian gryphons that were easily five times my height. Their eyes seemed to follow every movement I made, and the sensation of being watched was disturbing. The windows glowed with soft candlelight, and the cerise door beckoned me like the proverbial moth to a flame.

"What," I whispered, "*is* this place?"

"A dedication and preservation of a legacy," he answered, his eyes also entranced.

I licked my lips nervously when I saw one of the gryphon's tails flick. "Um, Father—"

Eli paused, but he didn't seem unnerved. "A high king deserves protection even in death, don't you agree?"

I felt the warrior in me rise to the surface, ready to fight. I was facing an unknown opponent, and it put me on edge. Everything was eerily still and utterly silent. Was the very wind afraid?

I jumped back at least ten feet when the doors suddenly flew open with a thundering whoosh of air and the gryphons started to . . . purr?

"Finally!" The voice that spoke was captivatingly lyrical, but it was nothing compared to the woman it came from. "I've waited a long time to meet you." She held her hands out in a gesture of peace, but I was too spellbound to move.

Lavender eyes watched me curiously while she addressed Father Eli. "I thank you for delivering her, but I think what is to happen next should be just between her and me."

He bowed respectfully, the action sending me for another loop. Who precisely was this woman? Rivers of sapphire silk flowed around her as she descended a couple of the steps. Her hair fell in raven waves around her shoulders to sail down her back. She was the epitome of elegance and ageless beauty, and it was the lack of ageing that arrested my attention. I was in the presence of yet another elf.

Father Eli bowed once more. "As you wish." Turning, I saw a secretive smile cross his lips. "Behave yourself, Ariel."

I was stunned speechless when he began to walk away. He really was going to leave me with a perfect stranger and two impossibly alive gryphon statues? Gaping, I stared at his fading back as he was enveloped in the encroaching dusk.

"Ariel?"

I spun around, my fingers itching for the familiar feel of my daggers. But I had a feeling that holding them would constitute a threat. And, to be honest, I didn't particularly want to be gobbled up by gryphons.

Her rose lips twitched in amusement, as if she were picking my thoughts right out of my head. "Would you come inside?"

The temptation to say no rested on my tongue. Why should I trust her? I didn't even know who she was or why Father Eli deemed it necessary to bow to her. A falling ray of sunshine slipped between the trees to catch on a pendent around her neck.

Crisscrossing swords and two stars pulsed with light, and, in a trance, I reached up to finger the necklace that was around my own neck. Odd. Heat wasn't radiating off of mine, and there was something about her steady presence that drew me near. Why would she have the same necklace that Cyrus had given me?

A knowing look crept into her eyes, but she stayed firmly planted on the bottom step, waiting for my next move. "He just . . . " I breathed deeply and forced my mind to stop spinning.

Her eyes shot a glance behind me and narrowed in concentration. When they returned to mine, they were flashing with urgency. "I hate to rush you, but it is time for you to come inside or it won't be good for either of us."

It was the way the gryphons tensed—in combination with their rumbling growls—that decided me. Flying across the distance between us, I leapt the stairs two at a time, following close on her heels. She slammed the doors shut and whispered something under her breath. I heard more growls, a high-pitched shriek, and then nothing.

I looked down at the daggers in my boots and back to her. "Father Eli is out there!" I wouldn't stay nestled in safety if his life was at risk.

"Your friends have already ushered him back into Etherdayle, so I'm afraid you have no excuse not to stay with me for the time being." She was matter-of-fact, and her comment almost got me to smile. But I was still uneasy.

We stood in an ostentatious entry room, and it perfectly fit the opulent exterior. My muddy boots sank into plush carpets, and I grimaced at the sight. I really wasn't making a very grand first impression. My gaze took in the ornate staircase winding upwards to my left and the palatial living room to my right. "How do you possibly know that?" I inquired.

A brilliant smile sparkled at me. "Your education of giftings for the past hour obviously wasn't extensive enough."

My eyes narrowed, but she just smiled innocently. "Who are you?" I asked.

She waved her hand dismissively. "My name hardly matters, but who am I? Well, that is a very interesting question indeed." She glided towards the stairs without a backwards glance. "To you, I might just be some desperately-desired answers. To others, I once was a lady of great importance. To me?" She laughed, the sound echoing around her. "I was once a woman in love, and now I am a forgotten memory guarding a legend from being lost." She twisted around, her eyebrow arching delicately. "Now, are you coming?"

Huffing slightly, I followed her up the mahogany staircase. It peeved me that not even her dress whispered against the wood, yet I was clomping behind her like a loutish child. "Do you enjoy being deliberately obtuse?"

"Yes," she answered simply, "because I know it annoys you, and that brings me great amusement."

"Well, at least I know you're honest," I mumbled, my legs tiring after the fifth flight of stairs.

She continued on as if she hadn't heard me. "Lately, amusement is a rarity, so when the opportunity arises . . . " She laughed again, and it struck me that perhaps in solitude she had lost her mind.

"I certainly have not," she shot back, coming to a landing and a solitary white door.

Embarrassment pulsed through me, causing my cheeks to flush, "I—"

She reached out a tentative hand to touch my shoulder. "I can't read your mind," she said reassuringly. "It just wasn't hard to guess what you were thinking."

I breathed a sigh of relief, but my cheeks still burned with shame, causing her smile to widen. My own smile was sheepish. "Sorry."

She tilted her head in acknowledgment, her expression turning solemn. "I asked Eli to bring you here for a very specific reason. It's time you truly understand what you are up against—and also the power you have in stopping an encroaching darkness." Her hand reached out to grasp the doorknob with care. "But, in order to do that, I need to show you a very important and pivotal part of our history."

My stomach knotted in apprehension. Was I going to regret passing the threshold of this door, regret what I saw on the other side?

She nudged the door open and stood framed in soft candlelight. Her entire expression softened as she stared into the room. "I want to tell you the story of High King Algernon. The full story."

Passing through the door, I followed her slowly.

"I want to tell you the *true* story."

The room we walked into spanned the entire length of the mansion. My eyes traveled the black marble floor to the dais at its end, holding a stone coffin engraved with gold lettering. All around the room were oil paintings. There had to be hundreds of them lining the walls. Some were no bigger than my hand; others were the size of six men.

"Oh my," I whispered, awestruck. "Are those . . . "

She nodded slowly, her eyes centered on the coffin. "It took many years to find the perfect person to depict what happened. I came across a young boy gifted with art, and in all my years I had never seen someone so talented. His paintings could make you weep with sorrow or shout for joy. I knew then he was perfect to forever capture the life of Algernon."

Floating forward, her hand swept over the tomb in tenderness. "So here we are. Are you willing to listen to what I have to say?"

"I would very much like to know." As is the case with all past events, the details tend to get muddy and the truth lost. I found myself genuinely yearning for the real story of the man I had dedicated my life to serving.

"I thought you might." Motioning for me to follow, she moved to the right corner of the room. "So, let us start at the beginning."

The first picture was done in brilliant reds and golds, with small tendrils of other colors entwined. A young boy was sitting on a hill overlooking the long-gone city of Riversbend. Looking at the picture, I felt like I could touch it and be transported into the scene.

She trailed her fingers over the gilded frame surrounding it. "Before the realms of Algernon were ever created, we were one land under the Quinn reign. Algernon was the youngest of six sons, and he had no illusions that the throne would ever be his. He was passionate, courageous, and somewhat reckless." Her eyes cut to me. "He was, in fact, a lot like you."

I swallowed my retort and let her continue. She pointed to the next picture of a young Algernon kneeling with a sword in front of his father's throne. "He wanted nothing more out of life than to serve in his father's armies, and, as the youngest, it didn't really matter what he chose as long as he didn't bring dishonor to the throne. So, with his father's blessing, he joined the army. With his quick wit and intelligence, it didn't take long for him to climb the ranks. He was charming and gregarious, no matter who he was dealing with. Compassionate to all, he served with a willing heart and a bravery few possess. He inspired loyalty with no aid of the crown."

She moved us to another painting, this one done in muted grays and blues with splashes of red trailing down stone walls. It was of the Quinn castle, and coming over the walls was a terror I felt from years away. "What are those?" I asked, gesturing with a shaking finger.

"An ancient terror. Soldiers so depraved and bloodthirsty they lost their souls long ago to become but shadows of men. They were the army of Chayse Andros, a man so evil it was said he was birthed from the fires of hell. They were called the Shara'han."

I shuddered as I stared at the painting. There was no resemblance to men in those faces; they were nothing but beasts thirsting for blood. My heart flipped in my chest. Was I to face such a force?

"Andros broke our land with his thirst for power. He turned brothers against each other, parents against their children. Families were splintered apart, and, as if that were not enough, enemies from beyond our borders joined Andros. Alliances were severed as Andros fought to destroy the Quinn kingdom, a feat that had never before been attempted." Her eyes were not really on the painting but focused instead on a time I couldn't hope to understand.

We passed by several more frames, each more horrific than the last. They depicted the beginning of a gruesome war that was to last for years and years. She started to speak again, her words startling me out of the sickness that was building in my stomach.

She stopped before a small frame with an agonized Algernon prostrate over a coffin. "Two years into the war, Algernon was promoted to General. The majority of his family had fled, hoping to be leagues away by the time Andros scaled the walls. All that was left in the Quinn castle were Algernon and his father." Her smile was feral when she looked down at me. "Algernon held back the attacks and stopped Andros from advancing for months on end. For a while, it looked like there was a chance at victory. Although Andros had a mighty army, he was no match for Algernon and his supporters." Her eyes darkened. "Until the assassination of King Quinn by his oldest son."

Her trembling hand reached up to brush at the tears on Algernon's face as if she could somehow rid him of the pain. "Our fragile kingdom crumbled with the news of his death. After all, who was to lead them now? The people were at a crossroads. The king was dead. One son had betrayed him, and the rest refused to come out of hiding. The only Quinn who stood undaunted was the youngest—Algernon. Never before in history had the youngest ever assumed the crown, especially if his brothers were still living. Yet, there was just something about Algernon that caused people to . . . hope." Her eyes flickered to the stone coffin, a fresh pain streaking her face.

Pulling herself together, she straightened and nodded to the next painting of a young Algernon being crowned. "It was a unanimous decision that Algernon be the one to lead them. Andros still was unable to breach the wall, but that was when he decided to tip the scales in his own favor. During the Quinn reign, most magical beings were relegated to the side—or to a life spent surviving the Shade. They lived in the shadow of man, and they were restless with their lot in life. So Andros offered them their own land if they would help him conquer Quinn lands."

Her eyes directed me to a painting that made my heart begin to pound. "It was at this time that the war broadened to something more than just a skirmish between men."

My eyes concentrated more on the painting than her words. A barren field stretched beyond one's imagination with a line of blood dividing it into two halves. At the line stood Algernon and Andros, toe to toe, each man's expression murderous. On Andros's side was, of course, the Shara'han, but it was what was *behind* them that captured me: ogres, giants, dwarves, elves, and every other magical being you could spend a lifetime imagining.

"The world of magic decided it was time to get involved in the affairs of man. Most joined Andros, but some sensed the evil in him and instead joined Algernon." She nudged me forward and tapped the next frame.

It was a piece done entirely in swirls of blacks and grays, and I could feel evil slinking from its bold strokes. It was Andros standing with his hand outstretched to a cloaked figure.

"Andros met with the most powerful being he could think of—a greatly-gifted elf who was not only a warrior but also second to the elf king Baldric. Even better, the elf was female, making it supremely easy to infiltrate Algernon's ranks. She agreed to help Andros and get close to Algernon so she could sabotage from within; in return, Andros would grant her a kingdom in the new regime." She stopped talking, but I figured she was just taking a short break after all the speaking she had been doing.

Leaving her to her silence, I moved to the next frame and came to a screeching halt. I took a shuddering breath as my mind tried to catch up with my eyes. It was the elf Andros had just enlisted to be a mole. She was dressed in full battle regalia, and several dead men lay at her feet. It wasn't the ghastly display of deaths that shell-shocked me. No, it was the face that stared forward stonily. "T-that is—" My head snapped back to look at the elf who stood next to me, her expression impenetrable.

"I could not keep the truth from you much longer; after all, I did promise you the true story." She laced her fingers together and met my wide eyes. "My name is Isidora Emaggen, and I've loved Algernon Quinn with every fiber of my being for all the years I've been graced on this earth."

CHAPTER XX

Leaning over, I braced my hands on my knees and tugged in a dozen deep breaths. She was going to be furious when she learned I had lost her map. I decided right then and there that I wasn't going to mention it until she outright asked. It just seemed safer that way.

"Ariel?"

"Just—" My voice came out shakier than I would have preferred, so I sucked in another lungful of air. "Give me a minute," I whispered. I knew that elves had unnaturally long lives, and that it wasn't implausible she was who she claimed she was. Of all the things I expected Eli to do, never could I have prepared myself to meet Isidora herself. Granted, I had just started to learn about the woman, but how come no one thought to mention to me that Algernon's great love was an elf? Not only that, but an elf who had been sent in with the sole purpose of destroying him?

Reining in my chaotic emotions, I straightened and met her worried gaze. "Well," I said, "that wasn't what I expected."

A grim smile appeared on her lips. "Sorry to spring that on you."

My retort felt stilted. "I highly doubt that."

Her eyes radiated unexpected warmth. "You're right. I'm really not that sorry." Her head inclined toward the next picture. "Should we get back to it?"

Gleaming white tents beckoned from the next frame. The young boy who painted was truly gifted to produce such works. The detail and care taken was phenomenal. I was only briefly looking at the masterpieces, yet I felt transported to each captured memory. So, as I stared at the ever-growing army milling around the base of what was now Mount Algernon, I could almost taste and smell the atmosphere.

Isidora's face softened as she looked at the next picture. Algernon was holding out his hand to a pale and bloodied Isidora. "Andros roughed me up a bit so I looked like the genuine deal when I crawled into Algernon's camp. As of yet, Algernon had only a handful of dwarves and centaurs in his ranks, so when I declared my loyalty to him, I wasn't too intensely questioned. He welcomed me like I was long-lost family and enfolded me in his protection. Never before had I been treated that way. At the time, I was in a dark world where my race was feared and persecuted. He made me believe I could lead a life outside that darkness and the bloody times I was used to."

How difficult it must have been for her. Andros had promised her land where she could seek refuge and escape oppression. It should have been a cakewalk assignment for her, and instead she was met with Algernon's unwavering kindness.

"At first I maintained the course; for years I had dreamed of a haven to escape to. It wasn't hard to weasel my way into Algernon's good graces. I had a pretty face, and I knew everything there was to know about war. I had already lived through so many. It was only a matter of days before the trusting fool that he was invited me to become part of his war council, thus providing me unfettered access to inside information."

I stared at the painting of her sitting in on a council meeting. She looked engaged and willing to make a difference—all the while plotting to betray them.

"For months I gathered information and passed it to Andros without hesitation. Things began to get complicated when Algernon decided he wanted to get to know me." A bitter laugh escaped her lips, and she looked at me cynically. "If only he knew what he was getting himself into! I was no innocent flower. I seemed to intrigue him in some way, and, no matter how hard I tried to avoid his advances, I was a fool for them. I did the unthinkable and fell for Algernon Quinn. I couldn't stop the love that grew in my heart for that stubborn man. Although such feelings were forbidden, my heart betrayed my mind. Against all odds, even knowing it was inevitable I would lose him, I loved him. And I never regretted a second of it."

A painting depicted them next to a lake, holding hands in the moonlight. My heart clenched with an unfamiliar desire. Would someone ever look at me the way Algernon was looking at Isidora? What would that type of steadfast love be like?

Her thin shoulders shrugged in astonishment. "I'm not even sure how it happened. One day I was doing my best to ignore his puppy-dog looks, and the next I was basically throwing myself into his arms. At this point I was faced with a difficult choice: stay loyal to Andros and receive the haven I craved, or have faith that Algernon's love would stay true after he learned the truth. Ultimately, it wasn't much of a choice. A home without Algernon wouldn't be much of a home at all. No one before him had ever offered me the unconditional love he did. No one had ever made me feel hope for a better tomorrow. Although I knew it was taboo to allow myself to love a human, I did so regardless.

"Feeling unusually noble, I wrote a letter to Algernon telling him the truth of who I was. I left out no dark details; I told him every last sordid bit of my past and intentions." Her haunted eyes swung to mine, revealing a pain she couldn't quite shake. "I never expected him to ride after me."

I could hear the horse hooves pounding in my head as I stared at the next picture. Isidora was bent low on her mount, speeding away from camp with a determined Algernon right behind her.

"I'll never understand why he didn't take my head off my shoulders, but all the man wanted was for me to stay with him—to give us a chance. To allow love to overcome all the obstacles in our way."

Soft laughter spilled from her. "I couldn't refuse his pleas, especially when I hadn't wanted to leave in the first place. He never held my past deeds over my head; he simply accepted me for who I was. Together, we concocted a plan. I went to Andros, giving him false information about where Algernon was moving his troops, and, while I was in his camp, I started covertly turning people to our side. It wasn't hard to do. Algernon had filled me with a kind of unquenchable hope that we could win."

The next picture showed an impassioned Isidora huddled with a group of elves, compelling them to change sides. "I got most of the elves, a large group of dwarves, and even some of the giants to defect. Algernon created a distraction at the edge of the camp as we fled the opposite way. Later that night, when we had all regrouped, Algernon held a meeting with the newcomers. Using only a few well-chosen words, he sparked a passion in them to do right—to strive for a better world. He gave them what they had so long been deprived of: hope."

The picture of everyone congregated around Algernon was breathtaking. How could one man be so inspiring?

"I expected resentment and quarrels throughout the camp, but nothing ever occurred. Algernon had united us in a way no king before or after him ever has. It was around that time that he made the brilliantly insane decision of forcing us to the top of the mountain—a battle I know you are intimately familiar with."

The picture of his army chugging up the side of Mount Algernon stole my focus for several long minutes. Isidora remained quiet as I traced the path to the top. Who would be crazy enough to force an entire army up to the harshest place in all the realms?

"That battle changed the tide of everything. It was the first time Andros realized he could indeed be beaten." She pointed to a picture of a raging Andros. "For a while things fell into routine. We were in a pausing period as both armies decided how to proceed. Algernon proposed to me, and we decided we weren't going to wait for the war to end—too many things could happen. Besides that, the camp was all too happy to take their minds off war and plan a wedding instead."

The next picture elicited a spontaneous smile on my heretofore serious face. An ecstatic Algernon was spinning a grinning Isidora while the entire camp scurried into action. The entire painting seemed suffused with joy. I felt an uncharacteristic urge to dance just looking at it. Before I could do so, however, a feeling of dread crept into my heart when I noticed the way Isidora was focusing on the picture beyond. She seemed afraid to move from the spot where she stood rooted, and I knew the story was about to take a drastic turn.

"We never made it to the wedding," she said, her voice curiously void.

It seemed unfair that a couple who had overcome so much would be denied the one thing they craved—to be bound to each other for eternity.

"On the morning of our would-be nuptials, Andros launched an attack. The day was to be remembered not as the day I got married but as the last battle of a war that had lasted far too long."

She was quiet for a good five minutes as she stared at the picture of dead bodies mingling with flowers and her wedding décor. Her eyes glazed over in familiar pain before she shook herself from her reverie and moved forward.

"Andros was severely weakened after the battle on the mountain, and his attack was more out of spite than superior planning. It was to be his last mistake." Her lips pursed as she pointed to the picture of Algernon and Andros circling each other, swords in hand. "I thought I was going to lose Algernon in that duel, but it was like I willed him my gift of victory. He had fearless hope that he could win—and he did."

The picture depicting the beheading was so gruesome I quickly shuffled past it. How did pictures become so lifelike?

"After Andros was killed, the remainder of his army scattered over the border, but I knew things weren't finished yet. They would never be over until his entire army was extinguished. So, we were left with a problem. I knew how to solve the dilemma, but it would cost me everything. When I shared my plan with Algernon, he threw an epic fit, but it was my only assurance that he and his land would be safe."

The intense picture of Algernon and Isidora fighting reminded me of Samuel and myself. We had been in countless arguments like the one depicted before me now.

"I created a gate at the border of what used to be the Quinn land. I used every last ounce of magic I had to create an impenetrable gate that would protect him against everything that tried to intrude. I gathered all who were not mankind and prepared them for the sacrifice we had to make."

I knew where this was going, and internally I cried for her. She was giving up the love of her life to protect him for all his days. How did one even go about giving that kind of sacrifice? A new respect arose in my heart for the elf standing in front of me. What she had done was truly remarkable and selfless. My fingers ached to tear the next picture off the wall. It was of the gate she had created, and all the magical beings were gathered in front. How had she ever done it?

"I also created a map that would show Algernon his greatest need so that, when the time was right, he would be able to find a way to locate me."

I grimaced at the picture of Isidora handing Algernon the map and bestowing him a desperate kiss. I was going to have to confess about that map.

"I took my army, along with all those who decided to retreat, back to the Shade. I didn't argue with the few, like Cyrus, who were meant to stay behind. With my supporters, I crossed the border to hunt down all of Andros's followers and free the world of a horrific evil. It was also a fresh start for those who had hidden so long."

I couldn't help interrupting her. "But you all fought together! Why could you not live together as well?"

"A war," she said, "brings the unlikeliest foes together. However, that camaraderie would not last forever. There was too much bad blood between humans and those of the magic realm. Algernon could never understand why I insisted it was the only way—but he couldn't see what I did: if I didn't create the gate, another war would soon occur, and this one would be far worse than the one Andros created. The only way to save him was to leave him."

The painting of their departing was gut-wrenching. I closed my eyes, trying to block out the intense sorrow emanating from it.

"Algernon ended up taking the Quinn kingdom and dividing it into ten realms to evenly distribute the power. He then created twenty interdependent keys to hand out so that he did not have the power to open it and come after me."

Puzzle pieces started clicking together in my head. She had just given me the answer to the keys, and confirmed there was indeed a gate to another land. We were about half way through the room when she stopped me in front of a distraught Algernon standing at the gate she had created.

"This is as far as you need to go for now," she said, shifting her weight to block the painting that came next. "I had you brought here so you could see firsthand how the realms came to be, and for you to better understand a truly great man. I also needed you to know the evil he fought—for you are fighting the same evil." Her eyes flinched away from me. "The reason Titus escaped into this land is my fault, and I am afraid I cannot fix my mistake." Reaching out, she grasped my chin gently. "You and your gifting are the only things that can save us now."

CHAPTER XXI

should have asked why Titus was her fault. Honestly, I opened my mouth to do just that—but it didn't come out how I had planned. "Who am I?" I whispered. I desperately needed to understand what I could offer these people. If she thought I was the one who could save them all, then she needed to give me the part I was missing. My mother had withheld something important from me. Perhaps her intentions had been noble—after all, her only desire had been to protect me. Yet, in the process of trying to do good, she had stolen the person I could have been.

Isidora's eyes narrowed in concentration before she dropped her hand and glided over to the dais. Resting her hand against the stone, she touched her forehead to the coffin and offered a quick prayer in the old language. What must it be like to know, every day, that your lover was at your fingertips and you would never see him alive again—all because you had given him up to protect him?

"You know who you are, Ariel Deverell. You always have." She lifted her head to stare at the far wall. "You don't need the name of your gift to understand who you are and what you are meant to do. Follow the lead of your heart, and you will never go wrong. However, I will tell you part of the answers you seek, for it is all you need to know for now."

I stumbled over my feet in my eagerness to stand opposite of her. "Yes?"

Her eyes captured mine with a knowing that sent prickles of uncertainty through me. "Sometimes, Ariel, knowledge is a burden." She sighed. "Are you positive you want this one?"

Crossing my arms, I didn't flinch from her intensity. "I've always preferred knowing the cards I held before getting myself into a fight."

Her head dipped in silent approval. "You are not only blessed with a great gift, you have been greatly gifted three times over. It is an occurrence

I have never seen or heard of in all my many years. Wehjaeel has created you for something truly extraordinary." She opened her mouth to say more but was cut off by a pounding that rattled the downstairs door.

I blinked and barely caught sight of Isidora skyrocketing down the stairs. Was everything destined to work against me? Palming my blades, I hurled myself after her. If it was something dangerous at the door, wouldn't the gryphons have ripped it apart by now? Leaping past the last six stairs, I skidded to a halt, my mouth dropping in shock.

Samuel was wrestling with a gryphon and had finally managed to get it in a headlock when Isidora jumped on his back, trying to tear him away. I should have stepped in to help—or at least offered an explanation to Samuel as to my disappearance. But the humor of the situation won out. Rocking back on my heels, I burst out laughing and nearly fell to the ground. The whole thing was so idiotically hilarious it brought tears to my eyes. "W-what are you g-guys doing?"

Everyone froze, their eyes shifting to me in disbelief.

Isidora's eyes narrowed dangerously. "He started it."

The statement seemed ridiculous, especially coming from a thousand-year-old elf. Rolling my eyes, I waded into the mess. Yanking Isidora off Samuel, I leaned over to meet him face to face. It was an uncomfortable position, considering a snarling gryphon was inches from my head. "Let him go, Fairchild," I ordered, my fingers working to disengage his grip.

The violence in his eyes seeped out when he looked up at me. "Ariel." My name was a harsh whisper from his lips as his arms fell limply to his sides.

Another growl rumbled from the gryphon as he leapt away to pace indignantly. Saliva pooled in his mouth every time he cast a heated look Samuel's way. I had a feeling that, if Isidora hadn't been nearby, the gryphon would go in for a retaliating bite.

Isidora stood next to the stairs, her displeasure radiating from her in murderous waves. "I should have known you would show up."

I watched as Samuel climbed to his feet, keeping his sword tight in his hand. He shifted in front of me to hide me from the gryphon's line of sight.

Her shoulders suddenly slumped. "It's really just as well, I suppose. Two birds with one stone and all."

He must have sensed that no immediate danger was forthcoming, because he moved to lean up against the wall. "Who," he asked, looking toward Isidora, "are you?"

She delivered a mock curtsey, a slight smile on her face. "Isidora Emaggen, at your service."

Oddly enough, he didn't look surprised. In fact, besides a slight narrowing of his eyes, he showed no outer reaction whatsoever. "Indeed," he murmured. "I was led to believe you resided on the other side of the gate."

My heart dropped to my toes. Not only did he know of her existence, he knew of the gate? I had flat out asked him about the keys. Why would he not tell me of the gate, then? Isidora was silent for a few beats, her eyes skipping between the two of us. I expected her to turn her attention to him, but she didn't.

Fisting my trembling fingers together, I hid them behind my back. His shadowed eyes met mine, but he remained stubbornly silent.

"Ariel." Isidora's voice was imploring. "I'm going to tell you something, and I need you to listen carefully."

Willing my eyes to hers, I stifled the anger and sense of betrayal rolling through me. I had trusted him. Trusted him more than any other person in my life. And he had purposely withheld information from me.

"Most importantly, I need you to trust what I'm about to say." She continued to speak, but my mind tuned her out. My gaze was too focused on the unflinching Samuel. Just who was he? Had I sorely misjudged the man I thought him to be?

Besides that, why should I trust her? She was almost a perfect stranger to me. Why should I allow myself the repercussions of her possibly leading me astray? Pressing my lips together, I turned away from them both and withheld the words burning in my throat. Why did everything have to turn into a snarled mess? Swallowing hard, I wheeled around to face them and was caught off guard. Isidora had moved to Samuel's side and was conversing with him. Stepping closer, I realized Samuel was answering her in the old language. Their words stopped the instant they saw me watching.

"What," I asked, my words clipped, "am I missing?"

Samuel sheathed his sword before crossing his arms and settling against the wall again. "Are you willing to listen to her, Wildcat?"

No, not really. "Yes." If they could smell the lie, they didn't comment. But I couldn't shake Samuel's gaze. Whatever he was silently trying to communicate was getting lost in translation—mostly because, at the moment, I wanted nothing to do with him. Besides that, why was he all of a sudden so cozy with her? My fingers spasmed with the need to hit something.

"Ariel?" Isidora reached out and grasped my wrist, forcing my attention to her. "Please. This is more important than you could imagine."

Everything these days was a matter of life and death. It didn't surprise me that the new knowledge she was sharing was going to be equally dangerous. Really, important had become relative.

My body coiled with tension when she removed her hand and the gryphon crept closer. A chill slithered down the back of my neck, and all my senses went on high alert. Darkness was crawling through the swinging front doors. The gryphon had stopped pacing, his head cocked towards something hiding in the night. Samuel's fingers kept brushing the hilt of his sword, and Isidora looked—terrified. "What—" I began, but was swiftly silenced.

"Go!" Isidora barked, causing the gryphon to bolt through the door with a vicious snarl.

Samuel straightened and was by my side instantly. "What's wrong?"

He really could go somewhere else. The last thing I needed was his macho-man routine. I was more than able to look out for myself.

Isidora looked quickly at me. "Unfortunately, we are not going to have as much time as I would have liked." Her words were rushed and laced with panic. "So you need to listen carefully. At all costs—" her eyes speared Samuel before returning to mine, "and I mean *all;* you must stay alive."

Well, that wasn't asking for much at all. "Why—" I started to interject, but she cut me off with a downward slash of her hand.

"For at least five minutes don't interrupt me; I don't have time for it. You will listen to what I have to say, and then Samuel will get you out of here." Her words were so forceful it took me back a step.

I nodded mutely.

"Titus seeks your death because you are the last person in all the realms who can destroy him. You are the only one who will be able to lead our people to victory—the only one who can protect us from the evil he is spreading."

How? How was I to do that? She must have sensed the screaming in my head because the fierceness in her expression eased.

"Your gift, Ariel. You have been gifted with hope—just as Algernon was all those years ago."

Her words thundered in my head. Besides what Isidora had just told me upstairs, I had heard stories of the gift Algernon wielded, and it had been no light thing. He had held the power to destroy kingdoms and bend anyone to his will if he so chose. I wasn't sure I wanted that kind of power residing in me.

Samuel reached over and interlaced his fingers with mine. I looked hard at him, begging him to save me from the horror clutching my heart. "She speaks the truth, Wildcat. I didn't need their special talents or discernment to tell. I knew what you were the first moment I was around you. You're hope to your core. Every second you're around, it fills every pore of our bodies. We now basically hum with the stuff. Why do you think people are drawn to you? People like Colter, who ran to the Shade to hide from the world?"

His words did nothing to quell the panic wheeling through me.

Isidora spoke up. "If you die, Titus wins. There is no getting around that. When I say you must stay alive, I absolutely mean it. You are literally the only thing that stands between us and the world he is trying to create. He will kill thousands unless you make a stand, and he will do everything in his power to make sure you never get the chance. He knows the danger you are to him, and he will spend all his resources to put your head on his wall."

Well, that was a wonderful image. How could one person make such a difference to so many? And why had Wehjaeel chosen me?

"You have a potent gift." A high-pitched scream erupted from the darkness, and Samuel tugged me closer to him. "Use it well. Samuel, get her out of here *now!*"

"Wait!" I screamed. "How do I beat him? Who is he?"

Isidora was moving towards the door but stopped dead still. Rushing back to me, she bent down to whisper in my ear: "Whatever happens from now on, you *never* stop trusting Samuel. You stay by his side at all costs."

If we didn't end up killing each other, it would be a miracle. "I understand."

She gripped my arm tightly. "Be fearless, and hopefully one day we will meet again." Her eyes met Samuel's above my head as she addressed him. "Remember what I told you, Samuel Fairchild."

He nodded sagely before ripping me away from her and dragging me towards the back of the house.

"Wait—" I pleaded, digging in my heels.

Isidora's eyes grew hooded as she stood in the doorway, her fierce beauty a terrifying image. "Be fearless, Ariel Callan Deverell. Be fearless."

Easier said than done.

She disappeared through the door at the same moment Samuel began propelling me forward again. "What about—"

With my heart in my throat, I allowed him to lead me a couple of steps further. My body jerked when I heard a woman's terrified scream. "No!" I cried, fearing the fate Isidora had willingly walked into. Spinning around, I aimed for the door but was cut short. Picking me up with one muscled arm, Samuel sped us through a maze of hallways.

"Isidora—"

"Would kill us both herself if we dared to go after her," he said, his eyes searching the area around us. There wasn't a lot to see. Vaulted ceilings, brown walls, and floor-to-ceiling windows. It was a sitting room, though one more elaborate and grandiose than most.

My futile kicks for freedom were ignored as Samuel grunted and lugged me up so I that I was now dangling over his shoulder. He was lucky I didn't take my blade and stab his butt. With a growl of frustration, he tossed me onto a nearby couch. My jaw dropped when he picked up a chair and flung it with a curse through the windows. Isidora was not going to be happy when she saw the destruction he had just caused. If she stayed alive long enough to see it, that is.

Sensing my yet unformed thought, Samuel reached back and grabbed my elbow. Dragging me to my feet, he towered over me dangerously. "Don't *even* think about it," he hissed, his eyes a raging storm.

I was already thinking about it. How did he expect to stop me? I opened my mouth a little, too delighted to tell him what he could do with his orders, but I never got the opportunity. A gryphon came thundering into the room, blood trailing behind him. He took one long look at us before huffing in exasperation and chomping down on the hem of my shirt.

"Hey!" I was more furious that he had just destroyed my new shirt than terrified he would continue to bite off something more important.

With a toss of his head, he had me out the window and skidding on my butt. Tasting blood in my mouth, I prayed my tongue was still in one piece. Grunting, I scrambled to my feet and spit out the vile stuff.

Samuel jumped across the broken glass with an envious amount of grace. "Let's go,

Wildcat."

The gryphon butted his head against the back of my legs, nudging me forward. "Great. You're coming too?" I muttered, shooting him a dirty look while dragging the back of my hand across my mouth.

His head shoved me a little more forcefully this time, and I could swear Samuel was laughing. "Why isn't he out helping Isidora?" I groused.

Samuel pointed deeper into the Shade. "Perhaps because he knows that at this moment you need him more. Now, get moving."

Casting a wary look at the both of them, I trudged in the direction he had gestured. The gryphon was right on my heels, and I was surprised that, for an obsidian statue, he wasn't louder when he walked.

We wound our way deeper into the Shade, allowing the darkness and soft trickle of rain to mask us. I wasn't sure what had dared to attack Isidora and her protectors, but whatever it was had managed to scare her. If Samuel knew what was after us, he didn't share; he just kept his sword at the ready and his body alert.

Abruptly, the gryphon growled and nearly tripped me in his haste to get in front of me. "Stupid cat," I growled, throwing my hands out to regain my balance.

He flicked his tail at me, the obsidian smashing into my skin and eliciting silence from me. He had better have truly sensed something threatening, or I would find a way to break that tail into a million pieces. Rubbing my leg, I scowled at him, but he paid me no attention as he stalked into the darkness.

Samuel paced back to my side. "I don't like this," he whispered.

"Speaking of which, that cat had better watch himself—" I threatened.

He gave me a dry look. "I wasn't talking about the gryphon, and you had better not call him a cat again."

The temptation to stick out my tongue won out and earned me another scathing look. I can't say that childish moment wasn't worth it, though. The irritating gryphon reappeared and jerked his head in an invitation to follow. He led us another three miles into the Shade before looping around and back-tracking us.

I peered behind me. "Samuel?" It was so dark I could only see the soft glow of Samuel's eyes.

"I think he's trying to get us back within the borders of Etherdayle," he said softly.

I wasn't sure how he always managed to read my mind, but he did a superb job of it. And, to be honest, I hated the fact that he could. If he had been a dimwitted male, perhaps it wouldn't be so difficult to keep my distance from him.

It took us another hour before we were on the edge of the Shade and staring at the bright, beckoning lights of Etherdayle. The gryphon moved to step out of the trees and, in a panic, I reached out to grab his tail in an attempt to stop him. "I don't think so, kitty!"

He lunged from my grip and nipped air too close to my hand for comfort.

Samuel grabbed my arm and yanked me behind him. "Ariel, what do you think you are doing?"

"He can't go into Etherdayle looking like that! He'll cause mass hysteria, No, he stays here," I explained, peering past his shoulder to look at the disgruntled gryphon.

With a low growl, he stared me down, just waiting for me to give in and save myself from the pain of his teeth. "What! Go back and help Isidora. I can't have a gigantic statue following me around!"

A large crack sounded and, in a daze, I felt Samuel whirl around and cover me protectively. We were surrounded by smoky greens and blues that choked out all sight of the gryphon. After hacking up a lung and clearing the tears from my eyes, I was greeted with the sight of a . . . dog. With a loll of his head, he bared his teeth and grinned at me. "You've got to be kidding me."

Samuel turned around slowly and then burst into laughter. "Guess you can't call him kitty anymore."

It served me right, I supposed, but at least he turned himself into a good-looking dog. Still enormous, he was a lovely shade of brown with a sleek black sheen on his back. With a long nose and pert ears, he sat obediently, waiting for me to gather my wits. I chose not to let myself dwell on how a gryphon statue had turned itself into a dog. His golden eyes laughed at me, and I hope he realized how much easier he was to harm now.

"Well, that solves that problem. Now," Samuel said, gesturing towards Etherdayle, "shall we?"

Eyeing the gryphon dog-thing, I elbowed Samuel. "You first, trigger."

Sighing, he scooted me in front of him. "I'll be right behind you; so please, get moving."

Grimacing, I shot the thing a dark look. "Don't bite me, please." He barked once and I was tempted to chuck a rock at his head. Slinking out of the protective trees, I gingerly made my way towards the stone arch. I was really hoping I didn't get an arrow in my back as we picked our way through what was sure to be the most dangerous part of our escape. There was too much land between the Shade and the arch, and absolutely no place to hide.

With bated breath we passed under the arch and sped to where our camp was.

CHAPTER XXII

MIDAS
Nails dug into wood as he cowered before his liege. He knew, with the news he bore, that his life was forfeit. Fear swirled through him as he planted his head against the marble. His liege preferred marble; everyone knew it was because the blood could be cleaned away easier. Although he blamed his tear-stained eyes, it *did* look as if the marble was tinged a permanent pinkish hue. Blood couldn't be erased completely, he supposed, especially not the amounts his liege dared spill. The devil himself must have fathered him from his loins, for no man not of Satan could be as evil as the man sitting before him. He lounged on his throne, an animal ready to attack at the slightest provocation. Unfortunately, he was about to be the next provocation.

His liege's nails scraped against his throne once more as he waited for his servant to speak.

"M-m-my L-l—" He swallowed thickly and tried to moisten his lips. He didn't want to die.

"Spit it out. I don't have time for your stuttering." The words were clipped. Precise. Edged with a desire to inflict pain.

His body convulsed the tiniest bit; this was not the end he would have dreamed for himself. "Many of our soldiers have returned—"

His liege flew to his feet and crossed to where he crouched in mere seconds. Tight fingers wound around his throat, jerking him to his feet. Gasping for air, he writhed a bit, toes struggling for solid ground.

"Her head? They've returned with the witch's head?"

Here it was. The moment he had dreaded with every fiber of his being. He wanted to live! "N-n-no, Sire . . . she has . . . " The fingers tightened and he felt his head lighten. His mouth floundered for air, but none could be found. In his last moments of life he prayed that, if Wehjaeel truly existed, the witch would manage to beat her adversary. He didn't care what his liege screamed about her. She had to be better than the dark eyes that stared at him now. They were full of such gleeful malice. How had he ever found himself serving such a monster? Oh, yes . . . he had wanted to live then, too.

"She has what?"

His liege drew him closer, so close he swore he saw hell frothing from his eyes. "M-manged to elude—" He wasn't allowed to finish. He felt the bones snap in his neck as his liege threw him to the floor with a roar. And before his head smashed into the ground, he had one last thought . . .

Wehjaeel strengthen the witch in dispatching Titus Ephraim.

CHAPTER XXIII

Colter greeted us at the arch, his face pinched with worry. Taking my arm, he drew me in for a tight hug. "I heard so much screaming, and these horrific sounds—" He shot a dark look behind him. "Father Eli stopped me from going after you."

Half pulling out of his hug, I gave him a lopsided grin. "We're all fine, Colter." But we weren't, not all of us. One had remained behind, and her death would forever be on my shoulders. I had run when I should have fought, and it was not a mistake I would make again.

Father Eli stood a ways off, his eyes glimmering with unshed tears. Was it regret for leaving me? Or regret that a friend of his was surely dead? "Father—" He shook his head numbly, his eyes trained on my chin. Grimacing, I wiped at the blood I guessed to be there. "Father Eli, I need you—"

"It was not supposed to happen this way. None of this was planned. You were supposed to . . . " He choked on his words and wiped vainly at the tears falling down his cheeks.

A lot of my life had gone off the tracks, and very few things had gone as planned. This realization no longer sent me into a tailspin. I would continue until the last drop of blood drained from my body, and I was content with that decision. Whether I had a few days to live or many years, I would make the most of every minute. More than that, I would stand for this land. The realms deserved so much more than the darkness it was being plunged into. "Life does not often go as we foresee it; however, it is our duty to make the most of what we are given." Resting my hand on his arm, I peered up at him. "Her death will not be in vain; I can promise you that." Colter started at my words, and I knew he would not rest until he had the entire story.

Eli nodded while trying to hide his tears, but his sorrow was palpable. He glanced towards my new companion. "Where did you acquire him?"

I looked over at the transformed gryphon with a new appreciation. "A gift, from a mutual friend." I wasn't sure how long he would stick around, but if Isidora had sent him, he would be a loyal companion. I winked at the gryphon. "His name is Kitty." My words elicited a feral growl, but I just smiled.

Eli's head tilted as he watched the massive guardian pace closer and plant himself at my feet. "What will you do now?"

My eyes shot up to his in deep concentration. "Whatever it takes, Father." Seeing that Samuel was busy filling in Colter, I lowered my voice. "I'm going to ask you a question, and I would appreciate it if you would honor me with a straight answer."

Father Eli rocked back on his feet, debating. "And that question is?"

I crossed my arms and watched him flinch under my stare. "Where is Algernon's heir, Father?"

The flash in his eyes betrayed his words. "A-ariel, he is surely dead."

My smile was strained. "And here I thought you would bestow me the dignity of the truth. I didn't ask you for your opinions or your half-truths. I would like to know where he was headed when he left."

Eli seemed to gain traction in his lie. "He did not leave, Ariel. He was attacked. The council is the power now."

"I do not know why you are lying to protect him, or why he ran away from what he is. And I am sorry I am requiring you to break an oath of trust, but there is no other choice for you. You will tell me where he went, Father."

Eli paced away and gained the attention of the boys. "I told you, he is dead!"

Gritting my teeth, I leaned close to him. "It is not becoming for a man of faith to lie, Father. So, when he left the Hollow Hills, where was he headed?"

"Blast it, Ariel! Why can you not leave things well enough alone?" Distress creased his face.

Some days I wished I could, but I needed the heir, and I would find him. Something in me knew he was alive somewhere, and that was why I refused to let Eli wiggle his way out of answering. "I will ask you one last time," I said slowly. "Where is Daniel Quinn, the heir of Algernon and the true leader of the order?" Eli's eyes beseeched the boys for help, but they watched him stonily. I should have known that, even without them knowing what was going on, they would have my back.

"Why do you need him anyway?" Eli inquired, his desperation evident.

"I need him, Father, because he is my key to reclaiming the Hollow Hills. I need him because, as of right now, the very people who are supposed to be keeping evil at bay are being lied to and misguided. I need him because he is the son of a king and meant to lead. I do not care why he left, or why he continues to hide. All I care is that I am able to find him and bring him back." I pinned him with a dark look. "Where is he?"

Eli's eyes sunk to the ground as he shuffled his feet like a disobedient three-year-old. "I swore to him I wouldn't tell a soul he was still alive."

"You didn't tell me he was alive. I already knew that piece of information." I bit down on my lip to slow down the impatient words that burned my tongue. I appreciated the fact that Eli could keep a confidence, but I was afraid this was one he was going to break. "Father?"

His broken eyes finally met mine. "The last I saw of Daniel, he was headed to the Port of Tullaryn to leave the shores of Algernon's realms forever."

Well then, I was just going to have to hope that something had prevented him from leaving, for I was years late in stopping that ship. At least now I had a starting point, though. Inclining my head in thanks, I left him to his growing despair. Father Eli was a strong man, but today would have taxed any individual.

"Colter, I need you to gather the adults and meet me here in ten minutes. Samuel, I need you to prepare three horses for travel and get back here as soon as possible." I turned to Eli. "Father, I need you to go with Colter and stay with the children. I don't want them to know or worry about what's going on while I fill everyone in."

Colter grabbed Eli's arm and began to lead him away. "Come on, Father."

Samuel's eyes swept over my weary face. "Do you know what you're doing, Wildcat?"

I laughed harshly. "Unfortunately, Isidora didn't deem it fit to leave me with step-by-step instructions. I'm doing what it will take to protect our people, and Wehjaeel help the man who gets in my way."

A small smile appeared. "I knew you were the one." Nodding his head in my direction, he sped off toward the livery.

I was sure I wouldn't soon forget the strained faces that stared at me when I explained why I was leaving. I hated to leave behind those who were in my protection, but speed and stealth were a necessity. Besides, if I *was* successful, which I planned to be, it would offer them long-term sanctuary.

I offered Aaleyah an apple as Logan stood next to me, seething. "You mean to just leave me here *babysitting?*"

Sliding him a hard look, I didn't soften my words. "I can't trust you to watch my back, Logan. So you'll stay here, and you will take excellent care of my people until I return." I then turned fully to him, my voice lowering. "And if a single hair on any of their heads is harmed, you will answer to me."

"What has happened to you? Who is it you think you are? *Your* people? Give me a break!" Bitterness spilled from his eyes as his fingers bunched into angry fists. "You are a selfish, reckless child who thinks that you actually have some meaning in this godforsaken land."

His words sliced through me, but I kept my expression void. I didn't have time for his temper tantrums. "There was a time, Logan, that I would have done anything for you," I said, my hand softly skimming down Aaleyah's neck. "Unfortunately, that feeling has expired. I think the better question to be asked is who, exactly, have you allowed yourself to become?" Hoisting myself into my saddle, I leaned over to go eye to eye with him. "Not a single misplaced hair, Logan Gallagher."

His eyes sunk to the ground. "When you get back, I'm gone."

I stared at him, willing his gaze to meet mine, but he refused to make eye contact. What had happened to my friend? "So be it," I whispered.

I trotted Aaleyah over to where Colter and Samuel patiently waited. "Let's go, Kitty," I called with a mischievous grin. I didn't want to constantly refer to the gryphon as the dog-like-thing, so Kitty he would be. Predictably, he growled—but it was half-hearted at best. Flashing him a dark grin, I turned my attention to the arch leading out of Etherdayle. I wished vainly for the map that was no longer in my possession, but wishes didn't seem to go far in this life.

"Ariel?" Liv appeared next to me, her hand reaching tentatively for my arm. "You'll be safe, right?"

My eyes caught on Logan, who was watching Liv with a little too much interest. He saw my scathing stare and quickly shuffled away. Clenching my teeth, I formed a beaming smile and patted her hand. "If there is one thing you can count on, it's me being safe."

A reluctant smile rose to her lips. "Oh, yes, you're definitely known for staying out of trouble."

I winked. "You know me so well."

Shaking her head in amusement, she stood back a few steps. "Don't be disappointing me, Ariel Deverell."

I nudged Aaleyah forward with my knees. "Wouldn't dream of it."

Colter took the lead and set a hard pace towards the Port of Tullaryn. It felt right, just being the three of us again. We were comfortable with each other and didn't need to fill the silence with useless chatter. We stopped a few times, but just briefly—only long enough to water the horses before moving on. After riding three days straight, exhausted seemed too mild a word to describe how my body was feeling.

"You really think we have a shot at finding this guy? He obviously wanted to leave these shores pretty badly," Samuel said as we trotted into the crown city of Tullaryn.

"He's a Quinn. He wouldn't have completely abandoned Algernon's lands," I answered, steering towards the livery.

"He was a coward. Why would his Quinn blood lead him to do anything?"

I silenced Samuel with a sharp look. "You don't know the first thing about the man, and even if he is a coward—" I slid off Aaleyah and handed her to a young boy, along with a silver coin. "He is still a Quinn."

The boy grinned and tipped his cap at me. "Thank you, milady! Much obliged, milady!"

I watched him lead Aaleyah away, and she tossed her head back like she wanted to wish me luck. She really was a strange horse, and I loved her for it. Kitty paced at my feet, and I had to push him out of my way with my foot. "Give me some space, will you?" He growled but obediently moved a few inches farther away.

Colter's eyes scanned the busy shore-front. "As a rule, I don't generally like to agree with Fairchild, but I have to admit that finding this guy is a long shot."

I half grinned. "I didn't say it wasn't going to be difficult. All I said was that no Quinn would willingly leave these lands." And of that, I was positively certain. He was hiding somewhere in these realms, and I would find him. If he came willingly or not would be his choice, but one way or another he would be going back to where he belonged.

"And so where are we going to look first, oh wise one?" Samuel inquired, eyebrows arching.

Rolling my eyes, I gestured behind me. "Tullaryn is known for its fine ales, so why don't we find out for ourselves?" Taverns were worse than women's knitting groups when it came to the gossip mill. It might help that the men's tongues were loosened when a drink was set in front of them. I may be looking for a needle in a haystack, but it was a good bet at least one of these seasoned sailors would have noticed someone of Daniel's bearing. From what I had heard, he was a hard guy to miss. Tullaryn, being one of the realm's richest cities, was nothing if not classy. Even its shore-front was above reproach. The sailors kept a tight lid on their mouths, and ships arrived and left like shadows in the night. The waters churned with activity; the area was busier than a bee's nest. If you wanted to trade with Tullaryn, you kept yourself presentable and your actions respectable. Taverns still filled the streets, of course, but even they were orderly. Any unruly drunks were promptly removed from the premises and escorted to the nearest holding cell. The buildings were freshly painted and the streets immaculate. Really, it was all a farce. Once you entered the buildings, they were just like any other place. Rich people were uncouth and rowdy just like the rest of us.

I tried to wipe the dust off my pants, but my efforts were in vain. I looked travel-worn, and no amount of primping would erase that. I'd hate to see myself in a mirror at the moment. Surely dark shadows haunted the areas under my eyes, and it would take an hour's worth of brushing to free my hair of its tangles.

"You sure you want to go into these places? Colter and I—"

I scoffed and headed towards the closest tavern. "Right, because I trust you guys to stay out of trouble."

Sidling past a man so large he looked like he had eaten a house, I found myself neck-deep in boisterous sailors. I ignored the baby-faced ones and the men who looked too drunk to know their own names.

"Hey, lady, ye in the right place?" A slobbering man grabbed my hand and jerked me to him. His foul breath beat against me as he leaned forward. "Ye look like yer worth a fair price."

Reaching for my dagger, I aimed it for his most sensitive spot. "You ever want to feel the pleasures of a lady again, I suggest you remove your hands."

His eyes widened in shock before he stumbled away. "Forget it. Yer too scrawny to be any good anyways."

Winking at him, I returned my blade to my boot and smiled back at the boys. "Divide and conquer?"

They both looked ready to mutiny, but, considering that Kitty was still at my heels, they nodded—albeit reluctantly. I half-way expected someone to yell "No dogs," but good luck to anyone who actually tried to remove him from the premises. Kitty would go wherever Kitty wanted—and right now that happened to be with me.

Colter ambled towards the bartender and Samuel faded into the crowds as I spied out the men I wanted to talk to. A middle-aged captain caught my gaze, and I let a smile widen my lips. Ebony hair, sly eyes, and a healthy amount of scars made a rather ravishing sight. Pirate, to be sure, and here he was, sitting right out in the open, ripe for the picking. Fool or not, I intended to talk to him.

Snaking around the crowds, I made my way to his corner table with a singled-minded purpose. Pulling out the empty chair with my foot, I peered at him. "Seat taken?"

A rugged smile lit his face as he leaned back in his chair and crossed his arms. "Would my saying no really stop you?"

I chuckled and sat down. "Not likely."

"You don't seem the type to want to warm my bed," he murmured, taking a long gulp of his drink.

"You would be so lucky," I quipped, tapping my fingers against the table-top.

He choked slightly and set down his cup with a loud bang. "Oh, I have a feeling this will be a highly interesting conversation."

His voice was too cultured for the typical pirate captain, and I had the strangest feeling I was meeting the precise person I needed. It couldn't be this easy. I hadn't even inquired about Daniel; the rightness of the situation had to be a fluke. Yet, I couldn't shake the feeling, as I stared across the table at the man, that he was going to prove invaluable. "I suppose it depends on your definition of interesting."

Out of the corner of my eye, I saw Colter lean against the counter and take a long drink of something while he not-so-subtly watched me. He was receiving a lot of looks, and I had only so much time before a fight would begin to brew. Saerdothians weren't exactly welcome people, especially when it came to the upper class.

"Friend of yours?" the man asked, nodding towards Colter.

Kitty plopped next to my feet, his back to the pirate and his eyes on the crowd. His presence was comforting, and I silently thanked Isidora for the use of her friend. "You should probably be less concerned with him and more worried about the dog sitting at my feet."

"A pup hardly frightens me; however, a Saerdothian . . . Usually a slave is left outside. Your mother seems to have neglected your training a bit."

The pup would frighten him a lot more when he took a chunk out of him. We both bristled at the word slave, and it took all my restraint to keep from tipping his drink into his lap. As appealing as the idea sounded, though, I didn't think it would produce the results I desired.

He leaned forward, his eyes trailing over my face. "Of course, we both know he isn't your slave, and your momma didn't neglect a thing when it came to your education. A price on your head, and you really come over to join a pirate for a drink?"

I inclined my head appreciatively. "And you really think Titus would pay a pirate for my head? Your head would be rolling right after mine."

He grinned. "Well, at least my last moments would be spent staring at something infinitely beautiful."

Flattery would get him nowhere. Crossing my legs, I watched the men crowding closer to Colter and calculated how many seconds it would take to reach him. Pulling my blades from my boots, I placed them on the table and started counting my dwindling time. "Let's cut through the pleasantries, shall we? You have no intention of turning me in; if you had, you would have called the Imperialist soldiers sitting three tables away long before now."

He threw his cloak over to me, and I caught it with one hand. "Now that we have that settled, why don't you make yourself a little less conspicuous."

Swinging the cloak over my shoulders, I pulled the hood up and breathed easier when it completely enfolded me in its shadows. Luxurious fabric, and not worn at all—he must be a very successful pirate. Exactly the type of person I had needed to locate. He would have contacts and resources that would be immensely helpful.

He eyed my weapons resting on the table. "Can you actually use those things without losing a finger?"

I tipped my head back to peer at him from under the hood. "Care to find out?"

Chuckling, he shook his head. "Not particularly, no."

Voices were beginning to grow louder behind me, and I grimaced. My time had expired.

His eyes sought out the disturbance. "If you manage to get your friend and yourself out alive, would you be so kind as to return my cloak to me?" He winked and grinned devilishly. "Look for the Falcon; I will be waiting."

Nodding sharply, I swiped up my blades and used my chair as a launching point. Racing across the table-tops, I ignored the cursing and falling drinks. About ten men had crowded around Colter, and they were going to regret messing with him.

Skidding off the last table, I landed in front of him, teeth bared. "That is enough!" It figured that, in my haste, my hood had fallen to reveal me.

"It's her—"

"A witch?"

"Savior—"

"One touch will kill—"

The whispers and stunned looks didn't surprise me. Out of the corner of my eye, I watched the tavern-keeper maneuver around the counter, his hands up in surrender. Keeping my focus on the restless soldiers, I didn't pay much attention to the burly man advancing on me.

"We don't want trouble here," the tavern-keeper placated, his eyes also shifting to the soldiers.

I arched my eyebrow and stared at him like he was daft. "That," I said, "is why you shouldn't bother a man trying to have a drink."

The man grimaced. "He's a—" Shame colored his face as his eyes dropped to his toes.

My eyes shifted around the room, trying to guess what man would move against us first. The pirate had disappeared, and Fairchild was nowhere to be seen. Wonderful.

"A Saerdothian?" I supplied, not feeling an ounce sorry for the man. "And your point is?" I asked, pinning him with my gaze. The conversation may be momentarily focused on Colter, but the new problem had become my presence.

And everyone in the room knew it.

Colter's hand touched my back lightly, signaling that the soldiers were moving towards us. I guess stealth had gone out the window. Tullaryn wasn't going to be a friendly place after all, it appeared. I should have known the Imperialists' presence would be thick near the port cities.

Sweat beaded the keeper's forehead. "Please, I want no trouble . . . Just leave."

He may not want trouble, but I doubted the Imperialists shared his feelings. It was astounding, the difference between the people here and the people in Archercrest. Here, they all swept reality and their sorrows under the rug. Titus was going to destroy them all, and yet they were pretending they were perfectly safe.

A small voice spoke up from the doorway. "Most of you will die in servitude. You will die believing it was your only option. Those of you brave enough to hope had better start following her."

I knew that voice, and it brought fear rushing through me. All attention had shifted to the small girl with the innocent face and terrifying words.

"Hedia," I breathed, watching her brown pig-tails bounce as she walked towards me. How in the world had she gotten here?

She edged past the narrow-eyed soldiers and only stopped when she was toe to toe with me. "Wehjaeel sent me," she said, calmly blinking up at me like this was an everyday occurrence.

Well, this wasn't going to turn out good.

Kitty sprang out from under the table and gently snatched the back of her dress. Nodding at him in gratitude, I watched as he growled his way out of the tavern, Hedia swinging from his mouth. The silence was thick enough to choke on, but it was just a precursor to the attack that was about to come.

As expected, the soldiers attacked first. Colter faced the first one, but the other two flew past him. Elbowing one in the mouth, I brought my dagger up and slammed it into the other's heart. He fell with a guttural cry, and it was enough of a distraction to dispatch the other Imperialist. Staring down at the bodies, I heard everyone shift backwards.

Lifting my head, I spoke softly." If any of you wish for a life free of a tyrannical king, meet me at the border during the next gold moon." My eyes burned with fear for them; they were lambs being led to the slaughter, and they didn't even care to *try* to break free. "I don't know what you've heard, or the lies Titus Ephraim has spread. What you need to realize is that he will not rest until our land is ash—and I don't aim to sit idly by and watch that happen."

Colter grabbed my arm and moved me towards the door, his sword gleaming menacingly. He tried to pull me out of the door, but I resisted him. "I will stand for you; so remember that when the reach of Titus floods your city."

CHAPTER XXIV

F airchild was holding Hedia protectively when we finally made our way out of the tavern. Silently, we drifted deeper into the city and holed up in a grimy-looking alley. Kitty took up guard duty as I knelt in front of Hedia. "Hedia, what in the world were you thinking?" I asked, quietly wiping the loose curls away from her eyes.

Her lips puckered determinedly. "I told you: Wehjaeel sent me."

"Do you understand how dangerous it was to follow me? You were supposed to stay with Logan." And so help me, how had Logan not noticed her absence?

She reached up to touch my cheek. "I'm meant to be with you."

No, she was meant to be back in Etherdayle, safe and sound. This was exactly the type of situation I had been hoping to avoid.

"What," Samuel asked, "do we do next?" He was staring at the little girl, and I knew we were all thinking the same thing. Good intentions aside, she had just made our lives that much more difficult.

I needed to find the Falcon, and I couldn't do it with a little girl on my arm. "Kitty and I are going on a little adventure. You boys stay here with Hedia. I'll be back as soon as I can."

Samuel grasped my wrist. "Be careful?"

At least he seemed tired of arguing with me about what I could and could not do. I looked into his eyes and tried to keep the pounding of my heart at bay. I certainly had some distancing to do, and soon. His touch would not be my undoing. "Always."

After kissing Hedia on the forehead, I pulled the hood back over my wild hair. My best feature had just become my biggest giveaway. Go figure. Slinking out of the alley, I meandered my way to the docks. Kitty was tight on my heels, and I knew his massive size was drawing a lot of unwanted attention. I guess it didn't matter, though, because I didn't plan on going anywhere without him. Isidora had gifted me with the gryphon's presence, and I wouldn't take him for granted.

Dusk was beginning to obscure Tullaryn, making it exceedingly difficult to find the Falcon—which, I assumed, was a ship. A pirate, telling me to find him at the Falcon, could only mean his ship, right? Kitty barked and shoved his head against my leg. "What?" I asked, glaring down at him.

He tilted his head to the right, urging me to follow his gaze. Squinting, I stared at what he was pointing out. The Falcon. She was a beautiful ship, painted heavily in golds and navy blues. She looked too majestic to be a pirate vessel; no doubt that was why she was so successful. The ship glinted at me, and I groaned, realizing it was moored offshore. "So, how do you feel about swimming?"

He rolled his eyes and I chuckled softly. "My thoughts exactly."

Hiding in the shadows of the mercantile, I pulled off my cloak and laid it flat. Dumping my boots, socks, one of my daggers, and my bag of keys inside, I rolled it up and tied it off tightly. Walking to the edge of the dock, I stared down into the sapphire depths. The last time I had been in the water wasn't a pleasant experience, and I never wanted to feel the despair of drowning again. Gritting my teeth, I looped my bundle around my back and clenched the hilt of my other dagger in my mouth. Sucking in a shuddering breath, I dived off the dock. Kitty followed, not even a splash accompanying his descent after me. We swam steadily through the ships, clinging to the dark shadows.

My arms and legs were beginning to burn by the time we made it to our desired location. Kitty bumped into me in agitation, and I splashed his muzzle for his impatience. He snapped at me, but I didn't take it personally. I was too busy worrying about how to get us on board. I was a lot of things, but even I knew I couldn't climb the rope with Kitty on my shoulders. Yeah, not quite that talented.

"Stay put," I mumbled as best as I could. Latching onto the rope, I shimmied up and crawled over the side with nary a squeak.

"And here I was beginning to think they managed to kill you after all."

Dropping the dagger into my hand, I swiveled towards the voice. He was leaning against the opposite railing, his eyes appraising my appearance. I immediately began wringing out my clothes. "And here I thought you might make it a little easier to get on board."

His lips curved into a smile. "Where precisely," he asked, "would the fun be in that?"

Scoffing, I nodded my head towards the small skiff tethered to his ship. "Mind lowering that?"

His eyes narrowed. "You brought company?"

I shrugged and pointed over the side. "In a matter of speaking."

In three long-legged strides, he was peering over the side. "Ah, you brought your pup."

My eyes scanned the ship. Where were all his crew-members? "Careful, he holds grudges," I murmured, wriggling on my boots. Once I was all situated, I threw his cloak back at him. "Thanks for the loan. Now, do you mind?"

He hesitated for a brief second, looking back over the side at a very irritated Kitty. "I will probably regret letting that thing on my ship."

With another exasperated look from me, he promptly lowered the skiff and brought up a soaking-wet Kitty. I couldn't contain my laughter when Kitty took great delight in shaking off right in front of the disgruntled pirate.

"Where is your crew?" I inquired, after Kitty had situated himself at my feet. His ears were perked and his eyes roved the ship as I talked.

"How foolish do you think I am?"

My head whipped around to stare at the handsome man. "Pardon me?"

His head fell back as he laughed raucously. "You really think," he howled, "I was going to invite you onto my ship with a bunch of drunken mongrels? They would hit land and begin spouting off about the angel with a halo of blood-red hair who had climbed aboard." His eyes darkened. "No, I'm not quite that foolish."

My fingers tightened ever so slightly on the hilt of my weapon. "Are you telling me you sail with a crew you don't trust?"

His eyes swept over me. "We're pirates, darlin'; of course I don't trust 'em." He gestured for me to follow him. "Now, let's get off deck before we're spotted."

Rolling my eyes, I nudged Kitty off my feet and we followed the pirate reluctantly. He led us across the deck and up a small flight of stairs. Throwing open the double doors to his quarters, he waved me inside, kicking the doors shut behind us.

"What is it about you that the king wishes your death? I mean, look at you . . . you're a tiny little thing." His voice was skeptical as he walked around his desk and sat down with the arrogance of a king sitting on his throne.

His quarters were impeccable. Furnished in rich mahoganies and silk, they looked like the epitome of wealth. I didn't expect the floor-to-ceiling bookshelf or the stacks of parchments next to his bed. There were no rum bottles or half-eaten leftovers. A nice surprise, really.

"Well?"

I didn't bother to hide my amusement. "I don't think my height, gender, or general strength has much to do with anything."

His fingers clasped behind his head as he leaned back in his chair. "That did not answer my question. What is so fearsome about you?"

My smile was cryptic and my gaze unabashed. "He's afraid," I said, "because I can stop him." I may not be certain on *how* to stop him, but of one thing I was sure: I could.

Weaving my fingers behind my back, I leveled my gaze at the map hanging behind him. Not only did it portray the realms, it also depicted the seas and islands beyond.

He leaned forward to rest his chin on a closed fist. "I don't know what it is about you, but I believe you."

Ignoring his intense scrutiny, I strolled over to lounge in one of the chairs facing his desk. I knew exactly what it was about me that stirred him to action. It was the exceedingly dangerous gift that had been placed in me regardless of what I would have preferred. How much easier it would have been to be born an artist.

His smile was cat-like. "My name is Jamieson Daniels. How can I be of assistance to your noble quest?"

Idly, I wondered if it was possible to turn off my gift. Like staunching the flow of water, could I put a stopper in the hope that flowed through my veins? It sounded like a bad idea with even worse consequences. A flutter of a smile brushed my lips. "Is there something about me that screams I need assistance?" His laughter was infectious, and I smiled wider when I caught sight of his dimples. A pirate with dimples—now, who'd have thought?

"Nothing about you, darlin', screams damsel in distress." He settled against the back of his chair, his laughter dying down. "However, you walked into that tavern for a specific reason, and it was no mistake you chose to sit at my table."

I looked down at Kitty, who was eyeing Jamieson with an unusual amount of interest. Fingering the pendant around my neck, I waited for the temperature change that never came. Obviously, it wasn't receiving any dangerous waves from the man, and that was enough to garner my trust for now. Considering my next words carefully, I spoke slowly. "I am in search of someone who was in Tullaryn seven years ago."

Jamieson's mouth gaped the slightest bit before he caught himself and snapped it shut. "I'm a pirate, not a god!" he exclaimed, agitated. "Do you realize how many people pass through Tullaryn *daily?*"

I gently nodded. "His appearance would make an impression. And," I said, "if I'm guessing right, he would have lingered on the docks for several days but never actually boarded a vessel."

His head fell back against the chair in defeat. "And you think I can help you locate this fellow?"

I shrugged. "It's worth a shot, no? Surely someone in your position has a vast network of connections. Or am I mistaken about where you sit on the food chain?"

He sighed, disgusted. "How do you even know this guy is still alive? Or that he didn't decide to actually board a ship and settle in another land?"

I had no assurances to offer him on whether Daniel lived or not. I was working off my gut and pure luck. "Will you help me," I asked, "or do I need to go elsewhere?"

He gave me look of longsuffering. "Tell me about him," he commanded briefly, closing his eyes in resignation.

That description was going to be short, sweet, and to the point. I had scarce information to work off of, and it had better be enough. "He would be close to seven feet tall, bordering on the size of giants. His eyes will be the deepest violet you will ever see in your lifetime, and on his back he will have a tattoo of a phoenix. If you look closely, you should see the start of it behind his left ear." I paused, gauging his reaction. "His name is Daniel Quinn, but I imagine he's not tossing that little piece of truth around."

Another long sigh. "Let me guess. The fact that his last name is Quinn is a massive coincidence?

Crossing my legs, I smiled with false demure. "Nothing that happens is a coincidence."

The flames crackled with restrained power, and I watched them uneasily. Even a small campfire had become a beast waiting to attack, and, the next time they engaged me in battle, I would not lose. Pulling my attention away from the fire, I peered down at Hedia. She was nestled in my arms, sound asleep, and still sucking her thumb.

It was three days ago when I talked to Jamieson Daniels, and I hadn't seen him since. This waiting was more wearying than any physical fight. I just wanted some concrete answers and a direction towards which to move. I knew the task I had asked of him was a nearly impossible one, but I couldn't stop the nervous energy building inside me. I had a week before the golden moon, and I couldn't take on even more people with no place to go. Of course, I didn't expect a massive turnout, either. People didn't yet understand the horrors coming their way. But soon, very soon, they would.

"What makes you think this guy has any chance of finding him?" Samuel asked, settling down next to me. Colter must have gotten up and relieved him of guard duty without me even noticing. "I mean, wouldn't we have just as much luck out there looking ourselves?"

I rocked back and forth slowly as I pulled the blanket tighter around Hedia. She looked so innocent with those brown curls framing her face.

"Ariel?" he called quietly, reaching over to touch my hand.

I wanted to shove his hand away, but that seemed a little too obvious. Clenching my teeth, I reminded myself for the thousandth time not to get attached, that his fingers against my skin meant nothing. *He* meant nothing, and that was the way it must stay. Reluctantly, I tore my eyes away from her and met the ones that twisted up my insides with a delight I didn't want to experience. "He has connections we could only dream of. If anyone has a chance at finding the heir, it will be him."

He looked down at our hands for a couple of agonizing seconds before reluctantly retracting his. "He's a pirate. What good can his connections possibly be? We don't need rum or black-market goods."

"No," I said, trying to keep my voice low. "We need a man who has purposely tried to hide for the past seven years. He isn't going to want to be found." I took a deep, steadying breath. His presence was making my mind fuzzy, and that irritated me more than anything else ever could.

"You truly think that Quinn is still alive?"

He could only ask that question so many times, and I don't know why he continued to interrogate me. My answer always remained the same: "Yes." He drifted into silence, and I took the opportunity to peek at him out of the corner of my eye. His hair was beginning to grow, and I wondered if it bothered him after having it so closely shaved. He was less skittish now, and I wished I could attribute that to my influence—but I highly doubted it. "Where were you born?" I inquired, against my better judgment. I didn't want to fall deeper into the spell he had cast on me, but it seemed too late to avoid the longing that already seized my heart.

He cocked his head towards me but didn't meet my gaze. "I wondered how long it would take you to start badgering me for information."

I swallowed the smile that rose to my lips. So I was that predictable? "Well?"

Draping his arms over his knees, he leaned closer to me. "The mountain province. I was the oldest of three."

Did he miss his family as much as I missed mine? "So you were born in the mountain province and then somehow ended up in the Shade?" He flinched the slightest bit, and I almost regretted raising the subject.

"I've told you before, Ariel. I'm not the good guy." His eyes cut over to me. "Do you really want to go down this path?"

I didn't just want to, I needed to. I wanted to know what made him tick, what made him into the man he was today. I wanted to know every little thing about him, not just what I managed to glean from observance. The realization was frightening, but it didn't stop me. "Knowing who you once were isn't going to change the opinion of the man I know now." But we both knew it would severely impact it. The secrets he held onto so tightly had the power to be crippling, and I was tired of wondering what dark shadows plagued his steps. I could help him face them, if only he would let me.

His face was grim as he turned his attention back to the fire. "We both know that's a lie. Trust me, you don't want to open the floodgates to my past. It would be best if we just left things as they are."

And what was so great about things now? We continued to waltz around the subject like it was some major taboo. I had already decided I wouldn't pursue a relationship with him, and he didn't seem inclined to take anything anywhere. So why couldn't he give me the answers I craved? "Samuel—" His name rolled too easily off my lips.

His eyes were hooded with memories. "Don't push your luck, Wildcat."

But I was so good at it. "Why can't you tell me something about yourself?" I whispered, not understanding why he was so determined to push me away.

Shoving himself to his feet, he glared down at me. "Just who is it you think you are to me? I owe you no explanations, Ariel."

I blinked quickly, discouraging any moisture from appearing. Gritting my teeth, I ripped my attention away from him. "Then why are you still here?" I asked quietly, afraid to look at him. I could lie to myself all I wanted, but I knew the exact reason I had never voiced that question. I was afraid of the answer. Afraid it would shatter my heart and leave me gasping for air. Asking questions was a dangerous business. His breathing was ragged, and I forced my eyes upwards.

"Because I can't seem to get you out of my system," he hissed. "But I swear to you, Ariel Deverell, I will find a way to free myself of whatever hold it is that you have on me."

My hands shook, and I hid the betraying limbs under the blanket. Shuddering, I focused on taking deep breaths and avoiding his eyes. Death had been more peaceful than the agonizing waves of pain that spread through me. This was the problem with getting attached, and I was stupid enough to ignore the warning bells in my head. When I was sure I had control of my voice, I spoke. "Do me a favor then? As soon as you figure out what the issue is, deal with it and get out of my life."

I didn't stop him when he marched away.

In fact, I prayed I would never see the day of his return.

CHAPTER XXV

"If it is at all possible, you are even prettier when you sleep."

The words sank into my mind slowly, but my fingers were already gripping my dagger. Keeping my eyes closed, I tilted my head towards the voice. "Well, that's not creepy in the slightest."

I felt the whisper of a hand drifting closer to my face, and in an instant my blade was at his jugular. "Bad idea, Jamieson." His laughter unglued my eyelids, and I glared at him, hating his smug smile. "Is there a reason you're trying to get your hand cut off?"

Crouched next to me, he rocked back slightly. "Wake up, sleeping beauty. You have work to do." He grinned excitedly. "I found you your boy."

Reality slammed into me in sickening waves. Throwing myself to my feet, I paid no heed to Colter or the three other behemoths flanking him "Where?" Hedia rolled over with a low moan, and I shifted my weight slightly to hide her from view.

He rose to his feet like a cat stretching. A small outskirt town about five miles south from here."

I debated whether to scream in relief or throw my arms around him, thanking him a thousand times. I decided the best thank you was putting away my weapon. "Does he know you were searching him out?"

Jamieson scoffed. "Please, what do you take me for? He's got no idea."

At least something was going in my favor. "I guess you are a somewhat decent pirate," I praised lightly.

A smile warmed his face. "You know where to find me. Just remember, you owe me a favor." His eyes melted as they swept over my face. "And I always collect."

A pirate collecting a favor was the least of my worries. "The town?"

"Hawkings Crest." He leaned into a low bow. "It's been a pleasure, darlin'. I'll be seeing you around."

I waited until the men disappeared from view before sprinting into action. Colter had followed behind the men, making sure they departed. Kitty was prowling around the perimeter, and I tossed a twig at him. "Make yourself useful and go fetch Colter." He growled in protest but immediately padded away after him.

Samuel had ridden out of camp before dawn streaked the sky, and I forced myself not to think of him. He had made his choice, and my only desire was to never set eyes on him again. Rolling up my bedroll, I shoved it into my pack before rousing Hedia. "Time to rise and shine, princess."

Baby blue eyes blinked up at me. "We shouldn't leave yet."

Gently, I pulled her to her feet and wiped the hair away from her eyes. "I'm running out of time. The sooner we get back on the road, the better."

She looked around, noticing the deserted camp. "We should wait for Samuel."

Swallowing thickly, I kicked dirt over the fire. "We would be waiting a lifetime. Samuel isn't coming back."

"Yes he is," she insisted.

Not in the mood to argue with a six-year-old, I ignored her comment. By the time Colter and Kitty returned, the camp was packed up and our mounts were waiting impatiently.

Colter's eyes met mine in silent understanding. "Just us, then?"

Sooner or later I was going to have to explain to him what had happened, but I was glad he wasn't demanding answers just yet. Samuel's departure wasn't something I was going to be able to get over any time soon. Reaching into my pocket, I fingered the handkerchief that I should have thrown into the fire. Nodding curtly, I swung Hedia up into my arms before situating her on top of Aaleyah.

"Ariel—"

"He isn't." Realizing how sharp my voice sounded, I evened out my tone. "He isn't coming back, Hedia."

She sighed loudly but didn't try persuading me again. I'm not sure why she was clinging so hard to the belief that he was returning, but I hoped the phase would pass quickly. I didn't want to make excuses for him or explain why he had abandoned us. If I could scrape every last memory of him out of my head, I would.

It took us less time to get to Hawkings Crest than I expected. It could be that my mind was so consumed in dark thoughts that time slipped away without me noticing. How did one simply forget someone? Was it possible to remove all traces of feelings that had begun to bloom like a weed? Samuel had managed to wiggle his way past my carefully constructed barriers, and I hated him for it.

Hawkings Crest was a fishing-village that bustled with activity. Tucked along the coastline, it was a prime location for the honest fishermen who lived there. A small wooden sign had been nailed to a post, declaring we had reached the border. Staring at the sign in a daze, I rubbed at my head, kneading away the pounding in my temples. I wasn't sure how to approach Quinn, so I was reluctant to ride deeper into the small village.

"Ariel?" Colter shifted closer to me, his voice low. "Are you sure about this?"

I was sure I needed Quinn, yes. I was also sure there was no turning back. What was sending me for a loop was the fact that I had expected Samuel here to help. Not in my wildest dreams did I expect him to just up and walk out. Isidora had told me to stay with him, and I should have known then that her request was impossible. And here was the double-whammy problem with caring for someone: you lose him, and then you also lose yourself to the subsequent hurt and betrayal. My mind was so consumed with him and his mesmerizing eyes, I couldn't make myself think straight.

"Maybe we could try to get into the Hollow Hills without him," Colter proposed.

Shaking myself back to the present, I gave Colter my full attention. "How? I'm to be killed if I step one foot on the premises. We hardly have an army, so there is no way we can forcibly take over. The only peaceful way to reclaim the power from Burns is with Quinn."

His face fell. "He's not going to want to go back."

"No," I agreed, "he's not." Wrapping my arm around Hedia, I lifted her up and passed her over to Colter. "If anything goes wrong—"

"Nothing will go wrong," he snapped, his eyes flaring.

"Right," I muttered. "Because a runaway king is going to be a real peach about the situation when he is told he has to return."

Colter offered a slight smile. "He hasn't got a chance against you."

With Colter's blind faith backing me, I let Aaleyah walk us into town. Keeping my head low and my eyes wide, I nudged her a little faster. My arrival wasn't going unnoticed; within seconds of being spotted, the whispers started up. Men gripped their swords tighter when we trotted by, and I tried offering them comforting smiles, but it didn't work according to plan. Pulling Aaleyah to a stop, I swung off and stroked her neck softly. "At least *you* won't ever leave me, girl," I breathed, hugging her tightly.

Out of the corner of my eye, I saw a small boy try to dart by, and I caught his arm. "Excuse me, but I'm looking for a friend of mine, and I was wondering if you could help me locate him?"

The boy looked like he feared I was going to eat him alive. "I ain't been bad! I swear I haven't picked on my sister or stolen nothin'!"

Great. Now they were using me as a night-time story to scare children into behaving. Sighing, I loosened my grip. "I'm not going to hurt you, I promise. I just need to find my friend. He's tall—"

The boy's face grew pale. "Sure, sure. Anything!"

Restraining my impatience, I nodded soothingly. "Perfect! Now, the man I am looking for is extremely tall, almost bordering on the size of a giant. He has violet eyes—"

"M-merrick. Yer looking for Merrick. Two miles out of town, look for the cottage in the grove." Stuttering, he ripped his arm from my grasp and stumbled away.

After another deep sigh, I looked down at Kitty. "I think it was you he was scared of." Kitty barked his disagreement as I remounted Aaleyah. Was Quinn scared of people? The fishing town was miniscule, and he still chose to live outside its borders?

Just as the boy promised, the cottage was an easy find. Uncharacteristically, I sat still and allowed Kitty to go sniff around a bit. I smiled involuntarily when I caught sight of the vegetable garden and rose bushes.

Kitty whipped around with a howl, but, before I could formulate a thought, a pair of hands were ripping me off Aaleyah. She sidestepped violently, crashing into him, but it didn't budge him an inch. My negligence was about to cost me my head. With a grunt, I tried reaching for my daggers, but the man repaid me by dumping me flat on my back in the dirt. The tip of a sword pressed against my throat, stopping me from any further movement.

"Explain why you are on my land."

Carefully, I lifted my eyes and breathed a sigh of relief when a pair of violet eyes met mine. "Do you greet all visitors like this?"

Daniel Quinn's scowl deepened. "The term visitor implies the person is welcome. Who are you?"

"Well, that is a complicated question," I snapped, not liking that he effectively had me trapped. "Who am I, as in my name? Or who am I, as in what kind of person am I? Or, who am I to you? Your question lacks clarity."

His eyebrows bunched together in irritation. "Now really isn't the time to play jester—" His words sputtered to a stop.

Kitty had a hold on his leg and was issuing a warning growl. Smirking, I used the distraction to knock away his sword and roll to my feet. Blades in hand, I smiled charmingly. "Now, you were saying?"

Mumbling to himself, he lowered his sword. "State your business and then go away."

"I'm afraid," I said, "that it's just not going to be that easy." The man's hands were covered in dirt, and his skin was sun-touched to a golden brown. I had to tilt my head back to meet his eyes, and his glare was off-putting. But none of it mattered because, when I looked at the hermit, all I saw was a king. A king who ran away, but nonetheless, he was my king. Kitty let go of his leg and ambled over to sit at my feet.

"Explain," he ordered.

Well, he hadn't lost his sense of position in life. "You see, I've come an awfully long way to find you, and, if you would be so generous as to give me a few minutes of your time, that would be splendid." I kept my voice light, but I was watching him like a hawk. His fingers kept tightening around the hilt of his sword, and his face was losing that angry red color and being replaced with confusion.

"Whatever you want, I don't have it. So please, just be on your way."

That wasn't likely to happen. Nice didn't seem to be getting me anywhere, so I got straight to the point. Pulling down the corner of my shirt slightly, I briefly showed him the edge of the phoenix marking me. "I can't do that, sire." Inclining my head in respect, I continued talking. "I don't know why you left—and frankly I don't really care. Today is a new day, and you're needed back."

His eyes remained frozen on my shoulder. "I can't go back."

Frustration ate at me. "Your ancestors left you a legacy! They entrusted you with a people to protect, and you're letting those you are meant to lead be destroyed. Your council is burning everything we used to stand for to the ground. You can't just sit here idle and let that happen!"

His lips went taut. "Actually," he said, "I can."

Stepping forward, I swallowed the acid building in my mouth. "You will return with me, and you will take back your rightful position. And once that is accomplished, you will help me hide as many people as we can before the entirety of the realms is slaughtered."

Laughing, he rocked back on his heels. "You've got to be kidding me!"

I was so very far from joking. My expression chiseled in stone, I stared him down. "You are a Quinn—you can't run away from that."

He paced away from me. "I can try."

I'd lost my best friend and watched Samuel tear my heart out. The last thing I was going to do was let another man walk away from me. If I had to hog-tie this monstrous man and throw him over my saddle, I would. "You tried, you failed, and now you're going back."

"I left that place with good reason!" he roared, and Kitty rose to his feet, fur bristling.

"And now you are returning," I answered calmly.

"What are you? A pesky private sent to terrorize me?" he asked, his eyes lighting with fury.

"You see, I was just recently stripped of my position. So I can say, or do, whatever I want to you. You either pack up and leave willingly, or Kitty here will have a go at you. You will return with me. You will take your rightful place. And then you *will* help me." Leashing my anger a little, I glared at him.

"Your hope and determination are annoying," he spat.

I laughed caustically. "Yeah, don't even get me started on what's annoying about you."

A reluctant smile flitted across his lips. "Why do you need me?"

He could trust me; if I wasn't sure I needed him, I wouldn't be here. "Because you *are* the rightful heir, and the only peaceful way to return things to their rightful position is with you. I could go back and take over—and, in doing that, a lot of innocent people would die. You're needed." What did he want me to do, grovel at his feet?

"Do you know what it is like to have to live up to my forefathers? To be as legendary as Algernon himself?" He shook his head violently. "It's like you go through life with this crushing weight on your chest, and you can never fully breathe. I left to rid myself of that feeling. You will never understand that feeling; you are just a soldier who follows orders."

I had never been that good at following orders, actually. "You would be surprised," I said calmly, "at what I would understand." To be sure, I knew exactly what he was describing; it was a feeling worse than suffocation. What I didn't agree with was his running away from a position he was meant to fill.

Squinting against the sun, I breathed in the ocean air. He had chosen a beautiful location to relocate to, and it was easy to see why he enjoyed the outdoors. "You will never know how great you could have been if you never even try." Tucking my daggers away, I stared at him pointedly. "You may never have historical victories like Algernon, but maybe that's not the man you're meant to be. I can promise, if you return with me, you will be known as the king who dared to make a stand. A king who opened his borders to protect thousands of people who have no place else to run."

"The Hollow Hills aren't equipped to handle that number of people," he said, his skepticism grating.

"The dwarves built the Hollow Hills almost the entire length of the realms. Just because we haven't explored past our little corner doesn't mean the space doesn't exist." I knew the Hollow Hills were the key to everything. I just needed access!

He wavered slightly. "You actually believe it's possible to stop Titus? To get people to realize what's going on before it's too late?"

"It takes only one brave person to have the courage to travel an unknown road. And once that happens, hundreds will follow." I paused, considering my next words. "I believe that, if you would be willing to open the Hollow Hills, the people will follow me."

Sheathing his sword, he crossed his arms in defiance. "And why do you think that?"

Breathing in my laughter, I splayed my arms wide. "How do you feel right now?"

"Disgustingly hopeful, and my skin hasn't stopped tingling—" His words gurgled to a halt. "It can't be."

"Please help me," I whispered, my anger dissipating. "Please help me save them." The people had no idea what was coming their way. They were so lost in their idealistic little worlds, they refused to see the signs. Titus would murder them all, and he would do it with a smile. All I want to do is save as many as possible before I confront the man himself.

"I'm not king material." His words were so soft I had to lean forward to hear him. "I wouldn't even know what to do."

He was a giant of a man, all hard-packed muscle and golden-brown hair, a fearsome specimen . . . and yet, here he was, unsure of himself, like a small boy. "If you can just get me back into the Hollow Hills, I can do the rest," I said, reaching out a hand to tentatively touch his arm. "Get me home, and just let me do what I'm supposed to do."

His jaw clenched as he debated. "I will never be an Algernon."

I beamed up at him. "No, you will be someone entirely different, and perhaps even better."

"Why were you thrown out?" he inquired, his eyes narrowing dangerously.

My heart stuttered the smallest bit. "Because I told them they were responsible for every death that happened on their watch. They would not open the Hollow Hills, and instead chose to cling to their pride and secrets. I didn't back down, and General Burns didn't take kindly to that."

His hand closed over mine, and he sighed. "Let's get you home."

I watched as the pale whiteness of the moon was washed in a deep golden hue. The sight always managed to take my breath, even though I got to see it occur every three weeks. Closing my eyes, I lifted my face to the sky. "Wehjaeel, please. Let them see the truth," I whispered.

"Are you ready?" Daniel asked, coming up beside me.

My eyes springing open, I looked over at him. "As ready as I ever will be, sire."

He groaned the tiniest bit. "Please, just Daniel. This sire business—"

I smiled. "You are my king, whether you choose to like it or not. That is who you are. You don't want to be called by your title? Fine." I shifted so I could meet his gaze. "But that doesn't change who you are."

His eyes swept over my face in a disconcerting way. "When this is all said and done, I won't be the one leading the people," he said quietly. "Just you wait and watch. They won't follow me; they'll follow you."

He was wrong, of course, but I didn't argue the point. "We shall see," I murmured noncommittally as I made my way to Aaleyah. Darkness had just fallen, but my nerves were stretched tight. I didn't want to leave empty-handed; surely someone in Tullaryn recognized the truth?

Standing next to Colter and Hedia, I watched the city with a growing sadness. We stood atop a small hill right next to the gates that had yet to be closed for the night. My eyes scoured the open road in disappointment when I didn't see a single soul straggling up the hill. Hedia reached up and took my hand. Clasping her small hand in mine, I knelt next to her.

"They're coming," she whispered, leaning her head against mine.

I glanced down the hill again and still saw no movement. "Hedia—"

Her eyes sharpened. "They will come this night, and they will be just the first to come forward. I promise you, they will come . . . just as Samuel will return."

Tightening my grip on her, I returned to my feet and swallowed past the burn in my throat. Samuel wasn't going to come back. I had seen the look in his eyes when he left, and I knew with a certainty that I would never see those magnetic eyes again. I would never get to depend on his strong shoulders or imagine what it would feel like to lay my head against his chest. Samuel was lost to me, and I wasn't silly enough to believe any differently. In some things you had to admit defeat and gather the strength to move on. I didn't have to like it, and I couldn't rid myself of the pain eating at my heart. But I had to live with it, and I would, too.

"Ariel," Colter called, grabbing my arm in a vice-like grip. "Look!"

Following the trajectory of his pointing finger, I gasped when I saw what he was so desperate to show me. "Can it be?" I breathed, breaking away and moving closer to the gate. A line of people was climbing the hill, and, even when I stood on tip-toe, I couldn't see the end.

Daniel stepped next to me. "I guess hope can be stronger than fear."

Heart pounding, I didn't flinch when he wrapped his hand around mine and brought our joined hands to his lips. Pressing a light kiss to my fingers, he stared down at me. "I will get you into the Hollow Hills and help you in any way I can," he said, letting my hand drop. "But I won't be your king, because I plan on following you to the edges of the earth if necessary."

His words resonated in me and I beamed up at him. "Whatever you say, my king."

The first individual to reach us was an elegant man with silver hair and sad brown eyes. Stopping in front of me, he looked directly into my face. "May our trust not be in vain," he whispered hoarsely, his eyes trailing down the road toward his home city.

Fear pricked my skin, and I prayed silently that I wasn't leading them all astray. So much was resting on my shoulders, and I feared that moment when I stumbled and everything went to pieces. Gripping his hand tightly, I met him with steely eyes and a tight nod. I wasn't going to make promises I knew I couldn't keep, but he had no idea how far I would go to protect them all. My eyes caught on a dull flash of blue halfway down the hill.

"Colter, do a head count so we know what we are looking at here. Hedia, you stay with Aaleyah and Kitty, okay? Kitty—" I didn't need to say more; the gryphon was already pacing circles around Hedia, his eyes alert.

Checking my blades, I leisurely made my way down the road. I greeted people and exchanged handshakes and soothing words when necessary. There were a lot of tears and blatant fear, but the hope was tangible. It had stirred the people of Tullaryn, and it was an impressive turnout. I stopped next to the Imperialist soldier who hadn't bothered to shuck his blue uniform.

Grabbing the young man by the nape of his neck, I threw him out of line and motioned for the others to continue moving towards Colter.

"Not very bright, are you, soldier?" I asked, watching his eyes dip to the elf blade in my hand.

"You said anyone—"

"Pretty sure I wasn't referring to Imperialist soldiers who are going to report right back to their liege of all our activities," I snapped. I felt someone behind me, and my spine went rigid, but I didn't bother to turn around.

"Please," the boy begged, his Adam's apple bobbing in distress. "Please," let me come along."

I wasn't foolish enough to believe we wouldn't have a problem with spies trying to infiltrate our ranks. We would have to come up with a plan of containment. But I hadn't expected the issue to arise so soon. What I couldn't figure out was why the boy wasn't even trying to cover his identity. Could he be that much of a fool? "Look, kid—"

Daniel spoke from behind me, cementing my suspicion that he was the one who had snuck up. "He won't cause any trouble because he's telling the truth—he just wants to come with us."

Shifting slightly, I threw a disgruntled look behind me. "How—"

"We all have our gifts," he answered simply, his voice already bored with the conversation.

His admission opened a whole new range of possibilities if he was genuinely gifted with sensing the truth. How far did his gift extend? Could he just sense the truth, or was it a deeper gift than that?

Sighing heavily, I looked back at the boy and held out my hand. "Your coat, please," I asked quietly, wiggling my fingers when he didn't immediately snap into action. "Let's not start a riot because you're flaunting the king's colors."

Stripping off the jacket, he threw it at me, catching the eyes of people walking by. "Consider me your man! Timmons is the name," he informed me, his words rushed and his eyes teary.

I offered a small smile in response. "Back in line, Timmons."

He bobbed his head in agreement with such eagerness that I thought it was going to fall off. Wheeling around, I stared down Daniel. "I hadn't heard you were gifted."

He shrugged his shoulders nonchalantly. "Wasn't something I wanted publicized."

My eyebrow arched in unbelief. "Anything else I need to be aware of?"

He smiled. "You now know more than the majority of the populace. If I want you to know anything else, I'll tell you when I'm good and ready."

So he wanted it to be that way, did he? "You're going to be a colossal pain, aren't you?"

A boyish grin I didn't think he could possess flashed across his face. "Yes! I plan on pulling your pig-tails, talking back, and just—in general—being a massive nuisance."

Rolling my eyes, I brushed past him. "Let the games begin." Thinking of his latest revelation, I wondered if the reason he had agreed to help was because he had known I was telling the absolute truth. Must be a handy gift.

It took us hours to count everybody and get them ready for travel. "How many?" I asked, tracking down Colter with Hedia close on my heels.

"Five hundred and thirty-two," he whispered, his face washed in awe. "The majority of Tullaryn is coming with us."

I sucked in a sharp, stunned breath. "More are coming than I could have dreamed of," I whispered, looking around with wide eyes.

Wrapping me in his arms, he swung me in a wide circle. "I knew you could do it, kiddo!"

It was a start—a beautiful, magnificent start.

Colter hoisted me up on his shoulders, and the crowd immediately hushed at the sight of me. Joy pricked at my eyes as I stared at all of them. "I know you are all scared, and aren't sure leaving your homes is really the best choice. I know some of you even doubt the mounting danger." I paused, my eyes sweeping over the nodding heads and murmured agreements. "You aren't making a mistake leaving Tullaryn. In fact, you are saving your very lives and securing a future for your children. Follow me, and I swear to protect you until the last drop of my blood has been spilled."

The answering roar was deafening. "DOWN WITH THE KING! DOWN WITH THE KING!"

My protection duty had just transformed into a full-out rebellion. And it was a beautiful, magnificent sight.

The journey back towards Etherdayle was taking twice as long. We were still a good half-day's journey away, and the pace was grinding. I hadn't been able to sleep a second the entire journey, and it was wearing on me. If I wasn't on guard duty, it was yet another person wanting to come up and talk to me. How I missed the luxury of sleep.

Kitty bumped his head against my leg, and I looked up with bleary eyes. "Cyrus?" I breathed, blinking a few times to make sure I wasn't seeing a ghost.

His smile was strained. "You sure you're able to handle guard duty? You are asleep on your feet."

I didn't really appreciate the observation. I knew how horrible I looked, and I knew how exhausted I felt. A pretty picture I didn't make. My focus was on the fact that he was choosing now to show up. It couldn't be a good sign he was here; it never was. "Well, now that we've determined I look like crap . . ." I muttered, casting an envious look at his perfectly pressed attire. Not a speck of dirt or sweat to be seen.

He laughed softly. "I didn't say that. You are actually a lovely sight for sore eyes." He nodded behind me, to the make-shift camp we had set up. "You've been busy."

Dozens of fires and sleeping forms met my eyes. "It's a start."

"I'm proud of you," he said softly. "Never could I have imagined that you would come so far in such a short amount of time."

The words made me soften my defensive stance, but I sensed he had come for a reason much deeper than wanting to tell me he was proud. "Cyrus, why are you here?"

His apple-green eyes turned a deep emerald. "Am I that obvious?"

"You are predictable," I corrected, crossing my arms to guard me against whatever he was about to say. "You don't usually show up just to chat on my progress."

He paced closer to where I stood, his eyes welling up with a sorrow I hoped I never understood. "I had determined I wouldn't interfere with your decisions, that I would just gently guide you when you were at a loss."

"Cyrus?" I whispered, not liking the weary pitch of his voice and his defeated posture.

"I'm going to break that rule, something I told myself I would never do. Your path was to be of your choosing, and your destiny was to be fulfilled without aid of those who would sway you a certain way." His eyes delved into me, and I shuddered at what he was seeing. "I'm going to go against all that I believe in—and heavens above, girl, you'd better listen to what I am about to say."

"What on earth," I asked, "are you talking about?"

"When Samuel gets back, and he will, so stop shaking your head like a ninny. When he gets back, I want you to get one thing through your thick skull." He reached out and grasped my chin, forcing my eyes not to waver from his.

Lead filled my stomach. I knew where this conversation was going, and I hated him for saying that which I already knew.

"There will never be a happy-ever-after for you," he said vehemently. "Never!" Releasing my chin, he stepped back with severe eyes. "You stay close enough to be covered under his protection, but you keep it to that. There can *never* be a relationship between you two. Never. Do you understand me?"

My heart ached as I worked to keep my expression neutral and my breathing stable. "Why?"

"Why is not important," he snapped. "Stay away from Samuel Fairchild and spare both of your hearts what would come to pass."

I wanted to know why it was so important I keep my distance. Of course, it didn't matter, really. I never wanted to talk to him again anyway, and I certainly never expected him to show his face again. But why was Cyrus so bent on separating the two of us? Not that there really was an *us* . . .

"Keep what I said in mind, please," he warned, before disappearing in silver smoke.

It would be impossible *not* to keep it in mind. I wanted to know why I wasn't allowed to be with Samuel Fairchild. More importantly, I wanted to know why I cared that I couldn't be.

CHAPTER XXVI

"Do you have a plan?" Daniel asked, casually riding beside me.

I shrugged. "I always have a plan." Which wasn't really true, but he didn't need to know that now, did he?

He shot me a knowing look. "So, you don't have a plan." It was a statement not a question, and I chuckled on the inside the littlest bit.

Not bothering to look at him, I shrugged again. "I wouldn't say that."

He grinned. "So, what is your plan, then?"

"To reclaim the Hollow Hills," I answered promptly, sounding like a young school-girl.

"How?" he inquired, amusement shining through his words.

"Well," I paused, "I haven't quite figured that part out yet."

His shoulders shook with laughter. "So again, you haven't got a plan."

"As long as you don't let them kill me when we arrive, I figure that will be a good start." I tossed him a teasing grin. "I would very much like to keep my head." Things never happened according to my plans, and I had long ago ceased obsessing over every little detail. My only goal was to get Daniel back into his rightful position, and, once that happened, I expected the chips to start falling where I needed them to.

"Burns really has it out for you?"

I bit my bottom lip, carefully considering my next words. I wasn't sure of the relationship between the two men, and I didn't want to sour things if they were friends. "The Hollow Hills," I said slowly, gauging his reaction, "were not left in the hands they should have been." That seemed a nice enough answer without going into detail of how the arrogant pig wanted my head on a pike.

"So, he isn't going to be happy to be overruled."

"To put it mildly." My eyes met his, and I tried to hide my tumultuous emotions. "It won't be anything short of a fight."

"Everything worth anything always takes a fight." His voice lowered lethally. "No one is going to touch you."

Daniel was a formidable opponent and the true king, but I wasn't sure he was prepared for what was to come. It wasn't that Burns just disliked me for breaking protocol; the man flat-out hated me. If Burns succeeded in having his way, he would demand my death to keep the order from falling into chaos. Daniel had his work cut out for him, and I could only hope he believed in me enough not to back down when challenged.

The sun began to rise just as we crested the last hill to Etherdayle. Pulling on Aaleyah's reins, I nearly strangled her in my haste to make her stop. Lifting myself out of my saddle, I gaped in shock at the scene below me. People were massed around the outskirts of Etherdayle. Hundreds of campfires winked at me as I stared in astonishment.

"I didn't realize you had so many people already gathered," Daniel said, as I sat back down with a thud.

"I didn't," I whispered.

There had to be over a thousand people gathered in the valley. Colter appeared next to me and took one long look at what had stopped our progression. "Word spread faster than I would have thought."

Bracing my hand against my heart, I took a deep breath. "We've got to get them out of the open." A bit dazed, I blinked a few more times just to make sure I wasn't hallucinating. "Unbelievable."

Daniel reached over and tentatively grazed my arm. "I may have been born to be a king, but you were destined to be so much more than that."

We rode down slowly, shock waves still rolling through me. I had expected a gigantic fight on my hands to get people to recognize the truth about Titus. Yet, here they were, flowing in without me having to beg or plead. I would never be able to comprehend it, but I was intensely thankful nonetheless. "I was going to let you rest a day," I started to explain, "but—"

Daniel winked at me. "I don't think we have that much time anymore. Not many people are immune to you."

Hope. It was such an intangible thing and yet immeasurably powerful. You would have to be completely without heart not to crave a better existence than what Titus was offering.

"Ariel?" Looking over, I saw the smile grow even wider on Daniel's face. "You got a plan yet?"

"Yes—because in the last three minutes I was zapped with divine inspiration," I huffed. "And I thought things were going to be complicated with just my five hundred and thirty two."

His roaring laughter was enough to make my shoulders relax the tiniest bit. When we made it to the border, Father Eli was waiting for us with frenzied eyes.

"You actually found him!" He gawked at Daniel's unreadable face.

Of course I did. He should know me better by now—I set out to find him, and I wouldn't have returned without the man. Not answering, I turned to the people who had followed me from Tullaryn. "Find somewhere to sit and make yourselves comfortable. We will be moving shortly." Sighs of relief echoed as they dispersed to get some much-needed rest.

"Ariel—" Eli began, his voice sounding piqued at my obvious attempt to ignore him for the time being.

About ready to turn around and explain to him the whole story of how I found Daniel, I stopped short at the sight of a young woman who took me by surprise. Curious, I peered closer at the waves of ebony hair falling around her shoulders. Reaching back, I grabbed Colter's arm and dragged him next to me. "Colter, is that—" I didn't get to finish my statement; he was already running towards her. "Blessing," I finished with a smile. How had she ended up here? We had told her to stay put until we called for her, and I certainly didn't remember sending anyone for her. Making sure that Hedia was being watched by Eli, I went to join the reunited couple. When I drew near, she threw her arms around me, hugging me tightly.

"Blessing, how did you come to be in Etherdayle?" I asked, warming at her affection.

She pulled back, confusion spilling across her face. "What do you mean?"

I wasn't sure what was complicated about the question, but I repeated myself anyway. "How did you know to come here?" The look dawning in her eyes made my body coil tight.

"Samuel," she said, returning to Colter's side. "Samuel sent us."

"Samuel?" I whispered, feeling something snap in my chest.

"He told us that, by the time we arrived, you would be back—that you had found us a new sanctuary." Her eyes were filling with an understanding I didn't want to see.

"I see." Numbness settled on my limbs as I staggered away. Samuel had sent them to Etherdayle? Why? What was he up to? How in the world had he known I was going to even succeed in finding Daniel? Stumbling, I braced myself against the fence and gasped for air. How did he manage to continue to affect me? I didn't even know where he was! He had made his feelings clear, and here I was, acting like an idiot because he had sent some people my way. Pushing away from the fence, I continued to wander, just needing a brief moment of privacy. I wasn't sure how I ended up at the white pond, but I didn't care as long as I could have some solitude in which to pull myself together.

Samuel had sent them.

Never in my dreams had I expected that answer. When he left, it wasn't on good terms, and now he was trying to help me? If that wasn't a contradiction, I didn't know what was.

Time drifted by in a cloud of hurt and confusion as I tried to work through this unexpected development. Kitty eventually found me and, instead of being obnoxious, laid his head on my leg and let me pet him. Absently fondling his ears, I stared down at him, not even trying to bury the feeling of desolation that ate at me.

Unfortunately, he wasn't the only one to find me.

"It's okay to cry you know. Every once in a while it's probably even good for you."

Tensing, I buried my face in Kitty's silky fur. "Told you I'd come back," I muttered.

Liv settled on the ground, keeping her distance. "Colter sought me out. He said you needed a woman to talk to, not a man, or else he would have marched after you some time ago."

That sounded a lot like Colter—one of the few guys I would consider decent. Men were heart-murderers, and I should have realized that before now. If any of my brothers did this to someone, I would beat the tar out of them. "I'm fine," I mumbled, irritated for wasting so much time in self-pity.

"I know that."

Surprised, I lifted my head to look at her. "What?"

"You are stronger than all of us combined, and filled with so much courage it borders on the reckless. And if I know you at all, and I think I do, I know how you will respond to this latest curve-ball in your life. When faced with the worst pain of all—heartbreak—you will pull yourself together and move on, just like you always do." She stopped, her eyes searching mine. "That doesn't mean I can't be here while you search for that strength that is momentarily eluding you."

I sighed. "I hate men."

Her laugher sprinkled the air with joy. "They aren't all bad; I promise you that. You'll find one who will move heaven and earth for you—just like you deserve."

Samuel wasn't bad; no, he was quite the opposite. He was just . . . unattainable. Unattainable, and shared none of the feelings I wanted him to. My fingers convulsed around his handkerchief.

"Time," she said, scooting closer.

"Time won't do a thing but remind me of what a fool I was." Leaning my head against hers, I sat with her in total silence for a while.

Time wouldn't erase the ache, but it would remind me not to make the same mistake again. If Cyrus and Hedia were right, that meant Samuel was going to show back up. And when he did, I was going to stay far, far away and never feel the throbbing anguish of a love gone wrong.

I found Daniel surrounded by my kids. Cadell caught sight of me first and shot to his feet. "You're back!"

Grinning, I hugged them all, offering a small piece of assurance that everything was going to be okay. When they seemed appeased, I tugged away their new favorite play-mate. I wouldn't have pegged Daniel as a "kids" kind of person, but it was just another thing I was wrong about, I guess.

"You ready for this?" I inquired, pulling on a pair of gloves Liv had found for me.

"Of course I am!" he beamed. "I'm following a lady with a killer plan."

"Ha, ha, ha." My eyes pinned his. They were unusual and beautiful, but nothing compared to Samuel's shocking sapphire ones. "If you have any—"

His hand closed over my mouth with lightening efficiency. "I didn't come all this way to back out now. Now, the better question is, do you have your head on straight?"

I pulled his fingers away with a disgruntled expression. "Yes." Samuel was going to stay locked tight in the back corner of my mind, and hopefully I could avoid that corner for the rest of my life.

Colter ended up climbing the mountain with us, but he stayed outside when we crawled into the mausoleum. It was comforting knowing he was right outside, ready to assist us if things went terribly wrong. I knew Daniel had to know another way inside the Hollow Hills, but I didn't press for answers. I would get them soon enough.

Approaching the dais, Daniel grabbed my forearm. "Everything is going to go all right."

Well, wasn't he the optimistic type? He said that now, but the sick feeling growing in my stomach told me another story. Nodding tightly, I slammed my foot down on the marble but didn't feel the floor shudder in response. "You open the hatch NOW!" I screamed, losing control of my patience. "Or so help me, I will tear this mausoleum down around your heads!"

The floor shifted and we both went flying down. I guess they believed my threat, as well they should. Before I could completely gather my balance, Liam was hoisting me into the air.

"What do you think you are doing?" he cried.

Fear fluttered in my belly when I saw his horror-stricken face, "Liam—"

"He'll kill you!" He shook me wildly, my head snapping back and forth brutally. "This isn't a game, Ariel! He is going to KILL YOU!"

"I didn't come back just to get myself killed!" I snapped, anger building in my chest. Anger at Titus for trying to destroy our realms. Anger at Burns for ripping away those last few things I held dear. Anger at Samuel for snatching the heart out of my chest and then stomping on it. Anger at Liam for screaming at me that which I already knew.

Before this was all over, it was a good bet I was going to die. Again.

"Famous words from a woman who *never* has a plan!" He tossed me around some more, trying to get his point across. "I will not watch you die!"

"Liam!" I screeched, yanking away from him and rubbing at my neck. "I didn't come back to give Burns the satisfaction of killing me."

Daniel wiggled his way between us, and, with one look, Liam immediately fell to the ground. "Sire!"

Daniel tugged him up by the back of his collar. "Knock it off." He truly did hate people bowing at his feet, didn't he? "Has someone already been sent to warn the council?"

Liam nodded his head yes, his face ghostly white. "I wasn't fast enough to stop him."

Daniel nodded in return. "Good. With them all in one place, I won't have to repeat myself a thousand times."

"Sire?"

Daniel looked over at Liam, his regal bearing already reasserting itself. "Yes?"

"Please, don't let him kill her—"

Daniel nodded slowly, making some kind of silent-man promise with Liam. Slapping the back of Liam's head, I moved past him indignantly. "I can take care of myself—you know that, Liam." I didn't bother to mention that this particular situation was going to require Daniel's help.

He grumbled but followed behind us, his eyes darting around uneasily. I didn't blame him. Daniel was a strong presence to get used to. "He isn't going to bite," I mouthed back at him, and laughed when his cheeks tinged red.

The order was going to be shocked to see Daniel. After seven years with no word from him, all believed him to be killed. No one could have expected that he had run away with no intention of ever returning. Perhaps his presence would be just enough to throw them off and give us the leverage we needed.

I expected tension and fear when I stepped out of the tunnel, but my overwhelming joy to be back overshadowed all that. I wasn't going to lie;

I wanted to pay back Burns for every lash he had given me, and we would see how much self-control I had when it came down to it. He had banished me—and deserved to be punished. And yet, here I was, breathing the air and soaking in the very sights he had tried to deny me. I was home again.

They were waiting for us.

The council stood together, their backs rigid and their faces stone hard. The rest of the order was stretched behind them, most looking panic-stricken. Daniel cupped a hand under my elbow and drew me flush against his side. Leaning his head down, he whispered in my ear: "You leave Burns to me."

I met his hot gaze but didn't remark on his demand. I was making no promises when it came to Burn's fate.

It took a chaotic few seconds for people to realize whom I had shown up with, but as soon as they did, they all bowed in reverence. Head lowered in false respect, Burns glided forward, his beady eyes focused on me. "Sire! We believed you to be dead. What a—" he struggled for words, his eyes searing into mine, "wonderful surprise to find you so alive . . . and well."

Nolan started forward but was caught by Spartz. Sending him a strained smile, I hoped he kept a cool head long enough for Daniel to smooth things over.

The only change in Daniel was the tightening of his grip on my elbow. "As you can see, I am far from dead."

It was obvious that Burns was flummoxed by this new development. He probably never expected to have his power wrested away from him. I grinned inwardly. It seemed fitting he lose it just as I had lost my home.

"Sire—" His face turned a mottled red the more he stared at me. "We can talk about your return later. Your companion, however—"

"Just who is it," Daniel interrupted, "you think you are? You were selected to serve on the council for when times like my absence occurred. That time is over. You were only meant as a temporary replacement. Neither the order nor her—and most certainly not me—bows to you. So step aside."

Burns's chest heaved as his fingers clenched into fists. "With all due respect, Sire, you've been gone over seven—"

The pendent around my neck began to scorch my skin, and I knew things were not going to go my way. They couldn't hurt the absentee king, but there was nothing stopping them from killing me.

Daniel's voice dipped lethally low. "You will step out of my way."

"As soon as you hand her over," Burns spat, his finger shaking in my direction. "She was warned what would happen if she ever returned."

"She," Daniel drawled, seemingly bored, "is a Phoenix—more so than you will ever be. Now, are you really daring enough to defy me?"

The rest of the council members joined Burns when the witnesses started to grow restless. We were causing a scene, and the council hated scenes.

General Kai spoke quietly, his eyes evaluating me. "This conversation needs to be taken behind closed doors. We don't need to be seen arguing with the king."

Nolan's anxious eyes landed on mine. He knew what I knew: this would not go the way it was meant to.

"NO! Our rules are not meant to be broken just because Algernon's heir is taken with her pretty face. She is a witch who has bewitched the goodness out of our deserter king!" Burns reached for his sword but was stopped when Daniel lifted him up by his neck.

"I don't think you are understanding the words coming out of my mouth," he hissed, before flinging him to the ground. "I am, and always will be, the last word. And I say no one touches her."

Keeping my movements casual, I resituated my blades for easier reach. My necklace was still on fire; there was no way this fight was over. But I wasn't going down without at least trying to make a stand.

"I want to meet with you all in the chamber so we can talk about our next step," Daniel ordered the council members, pulling me along with him. The crowd parted for the king as he made his way down the incline, and I was so focused on their reactions to him that I didn't pay attention to the screaming soon enough.

Suddenly, I felt myself being torn backwards—and a sword was drawing droplets of blood from my neck. Standing utterly still, my eyes shifted to where my blades were tucked in my boots. Too far to reach. What an idiot. Why hadn't I put at least one in my hand? The necklace had warned me, and still I hadn't paid attention. Daniel's expression was fierce as he whipped around to see who had dared attack me. I didn't have to guess who it was. Daniel's righteous defiance had sent Burns right over the brink, and now here we were.

"I think, perhaps, *Sire*, you should go back to whatever hole it was you crawled out of," Burns snarled, digging his blade deeper into my flesh.

My eyes swinging from Daniel to the horrified spectators behind him, I debated what I could do to free myself from this predicament. "Did you ever consider," I asked, keeping my breaths shallow, "that as soon as you kill me you haven't a hope of escaping alive?"

More blood rained down my neck, and Daniel's face grew white. "Shut up, Ariel," he ordered, his eyes focusing on Burns.

"What do you think you are doing!" Spartz yelled at Burns, his arm around Nolan's neck to keep him from flinging himself to where I stood, trapped.

"She will be the ruin of everything!" Burns cried, his arm shaking around my waist. "She will be the death of us all. If we just leave King Titus alone—"

My brain went into overdrive. For one, he had referred to Titus as an actual king, and for two, he made it sound like he had made a deal to stay out of his way. For what? An agreement that Titus leave the order in peace for as long as it stayed out of his way? Face it: the order was the only force that could truly oppose Titus's reign. "We leave him alone, and then what?" I shouted. People started to push closer, but Daniel held them back with an outstretched arm.

"He promised us clemency!" Burns cried. "It is only because of me that you are all alive!"

I didn't want to know how Titus had found out about the Phoenixes, and I certainly didn't want to know when he had found Burns to make a deal. He may know of our existence, but there was no way he could breach our gates.

Daniel's roar shook the walls. "You FOOL! What have you done to us?"

"You left! Do you hear me? You left us to rot! I only did what needed to be done!" Burns yelled, backpedaling towards the direction of the prison

If he managed to get me to the prison, they were going to have an impossible time getting me out. The area was too defensible; Burns would be able to hold them off for days. Burns wound his fist into my hair, yanking my head backwards. "Don't try anything stupid," he rasped.

Wallace joined his side and protected Burns's back as he continued to drag me away from everyone.

"You can't come back from this!" Nolan yelled, struggling against Spartz to gain his freedom.

"I don't want to! I just want her head for the true king, Titus Ephraim!" His foul breath blew into my ear. "And trust me when I say that the enjoyment of beheading you will last me a thousand lifetimes."

Flinching, I pressed my head back against him as far as I could. Every time he took a jarring step, his blade bit deeper and deeper into me. "My death will be nothing to the one that you are in for."

Both Liam and Daniel were trailing us slowly, but, if they acted, Burns would use it as his excuse to take my head off.

This was why I didn't make plans—they never went the way I wanted them to.

CHAPTER XXVII

t was about the third time that my head was slammed into the ground that I started to get really angry. I felt it building in my chest and wrapping around my windpipe. So help me, I would see Burns suffer for every moment he had spent making me miserable. And I would start by breaking his nose.

As predicted, Burns and Wallace had enclosed us in the prison of Eldor. How Eldor would have loved to see what his beloved creation was being used for. It was the size of three large houses put together and made completely of stone. The door was composed of steel, *and* reinforced. It had been designed to purposely have no windows, which I could now see was a major flaw. Even if you could gain entrance to the building, you had to get up a flight of stairs without getting picked off with an arrow while doing so. Considering there was a perch over the second steel door, your odds of getting shot before you made any real difference were astronomical.

Eldor had made his prison impenetrable, and I hated his guts for it.

I was locked in his ridiculous building with two mad men and no weapons to speak of. My odds weren't looking that great.

"Now who's going to save you, princess?" Burns inquired, smashing my face into the stone once again.

Spitting out blood, I threw my elbow back and was rewarded with his grunt of pain. It was a small thing, but it filled me with an incredible amount of satisfaction. Yanking me up by my hair, he threw me towards the corner of the upstairs room. I bounced off the wall in a rather spectacular fashion and gravity was not my friend. Rolling into a crouch, I glared at him and refused to wipe the blood off my face.

"What are we going to do?" Wallace asked, his eyes frantic.

It was obvious who the weak link was, and I would treat that knowledge carefully. Wallace would be the first to fall, and then I would take my time repaying Burns in full.

"Titus wants her head—" Burns began, impatient with the interruption.

"We kill her, then what? We will never get out of here alive—"

He also wasn't going to get the chance to kill me. Now bald and having lost his once-toned physique, he didn't have a prayer against me. His eyes were bloodshot, and sweat was pouring off him in waves. Wallace may have once been a great warrior, but now he was nothing but a pathetic has-been. He had let himself fall into debauchery, and death would be his reward.

"Shut up!" Burns yelled, his face a mottled purple. "I'll figure something out, just as I always do."

Yes, because Burns had shown himself to be a pillar of wisdom and good intentions. *Not!* "Good luck with that," I called, my eyes searching for anything I could use against them. At this moment I would have been thankful for a dinner knife. Antagonizing them didn't seem like the best choice, but I had to get Wallace to move closer to me. He was holding my blades, and I wanted them back.

Burns leveled a kick at my kidneys, and I curled up to protect myself from the brunt of the blow. "Witch! If it weren't for you, that impudent whelp would have never returned! He would've never dared to take back what is mine!" Roaring, he slammed his boot into me until Wallace lugged him back.

"Careful. She's our only bargaining chip," Wallace wheezed, letting Burns shake himself loose. His eyes flickered to mine, and I reevaluated my previous assessment. He wasn't weak; he just had a knack for knowing how to survive.

"If we don't bring him her head, it is our lives that are forfeit!" Burns yelled, shoving Wallace back a step. "Don't you understand that, you fool?"

Wallace wiped the sweat off his brow and leveled a disgusted look at Burns. "Did you ever think we could use her as our shield during our escape?" A remarkable weasel he was; me as a shield was probably their only way of ever getting out of here alive.

Scooting back against the wall, I watched them carefully. Burns whipped around to stare at me speculatively, and, biting against a wave of nausea, I straightened myself so that I was sitting up. My only saving grace was that they hadn't yet locked me in the chains dangling from the wall, and I would use my limited mobility to my advantage. If I stayed away from the chains—as well as those gloomy-looking cells—I would be in good shape.

I had a fighting chance if I just kept my wits. I could panic when free, but for now I needed every last drop of strength to figure out my way to freedom.

Wallace and Burns moved to the farthest corner, whispering to each other in a flurry of angry gestures and agitated looks. Watching curiously, I studied their movements carefully. What nefarious plans were they hatching now? There was only one exit out of this prison; they may be protected for now, but they wouldn't escape alive.

Not if I had anything to say about it.

Pushing myself to my feet, I held my hand protectively against my ribs. They cried in protest, but what else could I expect? Burns had done his best to splinter them to pieces. Burns's words dribbled to a stop as he watched me rise.

"You think you have a chance of walking out of here alive?" I inquired haughtily.

Burns gave me a malicious glare. "More of a chance than you do."

Yeah, I didn't think so. Rage leapt to life in me, and I had to tramp down the flames that begged for his blood to be spilled. I couldn't be irrational and bloodthirsty. I couldn't be anything like him.

There was a thunderous pounding on the lower door and a growl that sounded oddly familiar. I grinned—Kitty had followed me and gone gryphon. Maybe my chances were a little better than previously thought. If anyone could best Eldor's designs, it would be a temperamental gryphon that I happened to know.

Wallace's eyes rounded in fear as he hoisted himself onto the perch. "What is that!" he yelled.

Burns stared at him in thinly veiled disgust. "Get ahold of yourself—there is no humanly possible way of anyone getting inside."

But how about inhuman? My grin turned feral. "Have you guys ever encountered a gryphon?" I asked in mock innocence. The prison trembled again as Kitty worked on lowering the door.

Burns sliced his sword through the air as he considered his best options. His eyes zoomed over to me, and they promised a long night of suffering. Stalking to where I stood, he grinned maniacally. "I might as well enjoy myself before I die."

A hilt of a knife was sticking out of his left boot, and if I could just get my fingers around it . . . I waited until he was within striking distance before I tackled him. His sword knocked my forearm, but I managed to grab his knife.

"You will die!"

I may die, but it wouldn't be by his hand. Out of the corner of my eye, I saw Wallace sprinting our way. My attack was about to cost me. I quickly jammed my fist into Burns's face a couple of times before Wallace reached us. Hiding the small knife in my hand, I curled up tight to protect my head and chest as much as possible.

Kitty was still pounding on the door, but it was nothing to the blows I was now receiving. Seeing the shocked expression on Burns's face when I punched him had been worth it, though. A deafening crack sounded below, and the men paused in their assault.

"Impossible," Burns breathed, rushing over to the second door. "How did they breach the door?"

The knife was slick in my hand as I lifted my head to level a pitying look at Wallace. "You should have had more faith in me and less fear of Titus," I said before lunging.

My blade plunged into his heart with sickening force. Yanking it out, I ignored the sticky blood on my hands and flung my eyes up to measure Burns. I was wobbly on my feet, and my head was swimming in horrific circles, but I had no plans of dying. Collecting my blades, I inched around Wallace, who was gurgling for air with his last breaths.

An incredulous laugh burst from Burns. "You just don't quit, do you?"

"I never learned the art of when it's best to stay down. I left the rolling over and playing dead to cowards like you," I retorted, my eyes sweeping him for weaknesses.

He smirked. "I can't wait to slice that impudent tongue out of your mouth."

The door behind him rattled as Kitty howled in fury.

His eyes zeroed in on my mouth as he imagined what he would do, and I seized my opportunity. I flung the small blade I had stolen, and it sliced through the air, impaling his hand. Howling, he took the time to rip it out, and that time cost him. I managed to land a round-kick to his head before he gathered his bearings.

The door was straining against Kitty's attack, and I crossed my fingers that he would manage to get in sooner versus later.

Burns swiped his arm around, but I dodged his feeble blow. How long had it been since he was in the field? With a hard right hook, I skidded him back a few feet, right before I drew my blade across his chest. Blood rained as he heaved for air.

"You truly are a witch," he spat, wiping in vain at the blood pouring from him.

I opened my mouth to provide a choice retort to his ridiculous statement, but I was stopped by steel pelting by. Ducking, I covered my eyes from the debris.

Kitty had breached the second door.

Relief swept through me, nearly knocking me to my knees. Kitty barreled through the door first, followed closely by Daniel, Colter, and—Logan? Logan's eyes met mine, and what they betrayed was startling: regret, distress, and an infinite sadness. What had he done? He had an object twirling through his fingers, and my eyes caught on its dull shine. "Logan?" I whispered, begging my humming sense of impending disaster to be wrong.

Shoving his way through the cluster of men, he gripped the terrified Burns. "I'm sorry."

With a guttural cry, I reached for the object before it fell, but Kitty snapped his jaws around my tunic and held me tight. Dense black smoke filled the air, and when it cleared, a scorch mark was all that was left of Logan and Burns.

"What," I asked, "was that?"

Daniel's eyes drifted over the empty space. "Titus has found a way to portal—which was something only the elves were supposed to be gifted with."

"What do you mean?" I questioned, the pitch of my voice rising as I used Kitty to help me stand.

Daniel's eyes pinned mine. "It means this war just got a whole lot more complicated."

Colter wound his way to my side as Liam and Nolan filtered through the door.

Nolan's blank stare met mine. "Logan?"

I had expected a lot of things from Logan, but never would I have predicted he had ties with Titus.

"Where is Logan?" Nolan cried, his eyes falling on the condemning scorch mark. "Where is my son?"

Logan had been so close to reuniting with his father, why would he risk losing that? No amount of power or money would have been able to buy him over. He had spent his entire life wanting to be with his missing dad. Kitty let go of my shirt and snaked in front of me when Nolan rushed towards me.

"Where is he, Ariel?"

"I don't know," I answered, stunned.

"WHERE IS MY SON?" Nolan bellowed, glaring at the gryphon between us.

A mix of emotions overwhelmed me. "Probably the same place my family is. And when I find them . . . " I would find Logan, and he would give me answers.

Like how long he had been planning to betray me.

And the next time I saw Samuel, I would ask him how long he knew the betrayal was coming.

CHAPTER XXVIII

MIDAS

He wasn't happy.

No, no. He didn't look happy.

Scuttling behind his throne, I clutched the teapot to my chest. Bad things happened when he wasn't happy.

"The witch! The portal was meant for the witch!"

I peeked around the throne to see a nice-looking man cowering to my liege. I could tell he was handsome despite the terrified expression on his face.

Poor, poor boy.

Bad things happened to those who displeased.

"I thought—"

I flinched when sire's hand whipped across the boy's face. Oh dear—this was going to be yet another mess to mop up.

"Do you know what it took to get that portal? All I wanted was her head. Now she knows of your treachery," sire fumed as he stomped away.

I bit my lip and ducked my head when sire headed my way.

"What are you doing in here, Lenora?"

I peeked up at him. What had I been doing in here? What, oh what, had I dared enter in here for? He didn't want me when I didn't—clutching the china in my hands, I perked up when I felt its glossy surface. "Tea!" I shouted, beaming up at him.

His eyes drifted over me and I wobbled a step backwards.

"You said you like tea," I whispered.

He pushed me towards the door. "Later, Lenora. Come later and you may bring me tea."

When his dark eyes made sure I was leaving, he went back to the boy.

Poor, poor boy.

CHAPTER XXIX

With Liam and Colter's assistance, I limped my way to the healer. Kitty was pressed so close to me, I continued to almost trip over him. "I liked you better as a dog," I grumbled, scooting him out of the way with my knee.

He chuffed and nipped at my feet with a warning look. Accidentally-on-purpose kicking him, I was pleased with his skin-melting glare. He seemed to get the hint, though, because he started to walk with a wider gap between us. Who knew the thing actually had some affection for me?

Thinking of our upcoming meeting, I switched my attention to my companions. "Hey Colter. When you see her, don't stare."

He gave me an odd look at my random choice of subject. Shrugging, I figured he would understand what I meant when he saw her. Our healer hated the stares, and she had a habit of calling people out when they did. I figured I could save Colter some embarrassment and awkward moments.

As usual, we found her deep in her herb garden—a garden that would never grow. She didn't seem to understand we were underground and missing some essential elements. No sun and no rain meant no product.

Her vibrant teal eyes assessed me the instant we touched the edge of her property. "You look like crap, Ariel," she announced, dusting off her hands.

Colter was doing an admirable job of not staring, but it wasn't exactly an easy task. She was exotically beautiful, and it was hard to not want to look at her for an unnatural period of time. Her teal eyes were just the beginning of her strange appearance. Deep purple hair and flawless porcelain skin met my gaze. Her tribe's tattoos snaked around her arms, twisted around her torso, and ended at her ankles. She had shown me her full tattoo once, and it was a magnificent sight. She was a wild bird stuck in the midst of a bunch of ravens, and her discomfort with scrutiny was obvious.

"Colter, this is Starr Stormer, the most talented healer you will ever have the privilege of meeting," I said.

Keeping his grip on me, he inclined his head respectfully. "A pleasure."

She granted him a small smile and gestured for us to follow her. "Let's get you off your feet."

I couldn't help but look at her in a new light. Knowing she was gifted and not just a talented medicine practitioner was a strange realization. What else had been under my nose the entire year? She directed me to a pile of warm furs, and I sank into the nest thankfully. Kitty landed at my feet, and I watched disinterested as Starr shooed the boys from her home.

"I didn't expect to see you for a good many years," she remarked, poking around on her medicine shelves. "You were the only one who didn't treat me as some kind of freak."

I closed my eyes, enjoying the peace of her home. "You are no different than any of us—and you can quit with the show. I know those bottles are useless."

She snorted. "Haven't changed much, have you?"

"Neither have you," I retorted. "Still gardening?" I inquired, opening one eye to watch her reaction.

Hands on her hips, she stuck her tongue out. "You're impossible."

"Ha! Coming from you—that's special," I quipped, closing my eyes again.

"Your pet is in my way," she complained, leaving off her incessant rattling of the bottles that were probably just filled with water.

"Then have fun moving him." Because I certainly wasn't risking my limbs. I opened my eyes just in time to see her toss me a dirty look. Easing her way past the mammoth at my feet, she trailed her fingers over my battered face.

"What did you do this time?" she inquired, warmness seeping out of her touch.

"I was just trying to make a new friend," I answered, clenching my teeth when she started to repair my ribs.

"I'm guessing your attempt didn't work." She involuntarily gasped when she lifted my shirt. "You look like a herd of agapas ran over you."

If I knew what an agapa was, that statement might actually make some sense. As it was, I had to content myself with knowing she was concerned. She worked in silence for a long while, leaving me alone with my tangled thoughts—which probably wasn't the best idea. What had happened to Logan Gallagher? How had my best friend turned his allegiances to Titus? And why? Why would he do such a thing? I would get answers from him. I would find him, and he would explain to me why he had chosen Titus over me.

And it had better be one really good explanation.

"I hear rumors," Starr began, sitting back on her heels, "that you brought our king back, and over a thousand people with him."

The blood was wiped away, my skin unmarred, and the only evidence anything had occurred was the bitter taste in my mouth. "And?"

"The Phoenixes won't take kindly to the king—not after he left them."

"He is the true king." I replied wearily, not wanting to get into this argument. They could pout and pitch a fit all they wanted, but the facts didn't change. Daniel would always be the true leader of our people.

She rose to her feet and crossed to the fire. "I didn't say they wouldn't obey, but he isn't the one they want to follow."

I sighed. "They don't have a choice. We all make mistakes, and he is returning to fix his." Although he admittedly had a lot of ground to make up.

"You can be so dense at times!" she snapped, her eyes flashing. "There has been a lot of talk circulating. They want you to lead."

I laughed. "Then I guess it's a good thing Daniel desires the same thing."

Her fingers twisted together nervously. "The actions you are taking, are you sure the realms are prepared for this kind of war?"

I pet Kitty behind his obsidian ear and wished he would change back. His tail twitched in mute happiness. "Who is ever prepared for war?" I asked, not expecting an answer. "All I am trying to do is save as many as possible before darkness swallows all that used to be."

"And what happens when hiding ceases to work? Who will be your army?"

My eyes flew to hers. "We worry about securing our people first, and then we raise our army."

Because I knew that beyond the gate was a generation of soldiers just waiting to be needed again.

I opened Starr's door to find the Phoenixes gathered in silence. Starr hid behind me, not wanting an ounce of attention directed her way. Daniel stood near the front of the group, his eyes drinking me in. When he saw I was steady on my feet and clear-gazed, he stepped forward.

Leaning his head down, he whispered, "I'm sorry I didn't protect you like I swore I would."

Craning my head back, I met his regretful gaze. "You did absolutely nothing wrong—the only one to blame for anything is Burns."

"If I were a better man—"

I held up my hand, stopping his flow of words. "You are a great man; you just don't realize that yet."

His eyes searched mine, and I didn't flinch from the scrutiny. "Why do you have such hope that I can amount to anything?" he asked.

"I guess," I replied, "I just have a knack for believing in the seemingly impossible." However, Daniel Quinn's redemption was far from being impossible, and soon he would see what I did.

Turning, he propelled me towards the crowd. "They want you."

They may want me to lead, but that didn't mean they had any true idea of what they were getting into. Regardless, I would lead and, knowing them all as I did, they would follow or die trying. One hundred and eighty-five willing souls stared back at me. When my attention focused on them, they all dipped to their knees and bowed their heads.

Sucking in a sharp breath, I watched in astonishment. I didn't deserve such veneration, and yet here they were . . . *bowing.* "Please get up," I begged, feeling my traitorous cheeks beginning to burn. "Please."

They rose slowly, their faces solemn. "I can't—" Taking a deep breath, I begged my racing heart to calm. "I won't ever be able to thank you enough for giving me such strong support."

Liam stepped forward. "I think I speak for us all when I say we are honored to follow you."

They'd be honored until blood was spilled. Warily, I shifted my weight. "I will lead you until Titus is defeated, and when that day comes, we will once again follow the true king." Hiding my clammy hands behind my back,

I hoped the fine tremble that swept through me wasn't too noticeable. My eyes danced over them. "Everyone deserves a second chance."

Most eyes dropped to the ground after those words. I couldn't help but be humbled by the unanimous support radiating from them. They all truly wanted to follow me. If that wasn't awe-worthy, I didn't know what was.

"I think," Daniel said, allowing his voice to carry, "that we are a couple of generals down."

A collective gasp rose from the crowd. Never—because of my age *or* my gender—would I be considered for such a position. I may be allowed to fight, but that was the extent of my privileges in the hierarchy.

"Daniel," I hissed, wanting to stop him from doing something he would later regret.

"In fact," he continued, ignoring me altogether, "I believe our head general has defected."

"Daniel!"

His eyes swerved to me. "I believe any objections you have to the increasing of your rank are invalid, and the rest I don't care to hear."

And there was that commanding voice of his. Snapping my mouth closed, I debated on the best way to shut him up without publicly humiliating either of us.

"So, since it is in my purview to name my head general, I hereby appoint you, Ariel Callan Deverell. As of this moment, until Titus's defeat, you are in acting command, and all decisions begin and end with what you choose."

The applause was deafening.

That was an unexpected, startling turn of events. I had always dreamed of making general—not to mention the seat of head general—but never in a million years had I really expected that day to come. Daniel had gone off his rocker. Sending a meaningful look his way, I promised myself to talk some sense into him later. However, I had to admit: General Deverell *did* have a certain ring to it . . .

Fallon would be proud. He had told me from the time I was a toddler that I would be a general someday. How right he had turned out to be—and he wasn't even here to witness it.

"General!"

Yeah, wasn't used to that yet. Pivoting around, I glared at Liam. "Liam, so help me—"

He smiled sheepishly and offered me my missing pack. "I found it in Burns's stuff. I figured you would like to have it back."

He had no idea. I beamed at him while greedily grabbing for my long-lost pack. "Thank you!" My fingers dug through an assortment of clothes and other odds and ends until I felt the soft leather of Isidora's map.

Maybe she wouldn't kill me after all. Pulling out the map, I unfolded it with care. I hoped her map hadn't lost its magic; I needed to know the Hollow Hills just a little bit better. On cue, lines began to slink across the page until I was looking at the key to making all my plans succeed. There were more entrances to the hills, just like I had expected—entrances that would allow large groups of people to enter without having to touch foot on Mt. Algernon.

"Ari girl?"

My concentration broken, I looked up. "Yes?"

"Are you going to talk to General Gallagher?"

I didn't want to deal with Nolan at the moment, but I knew I was going to have to eventually. Logan would be a source of contention our relationship wouldn't soon get over. His son had betrayed me, and I wasn't likely to forget that.

"I will," I answered dully. I just wasn't promising when.

"General!"

I was really never going to get used to that. Swinging around, I steadied the young man who almost crashed into me.

"S-sorry, General!" he stuttered, leaning down into a quick bow.

I'm not sure where this bowing stuff was coming from, but it was going to get old really fast. A salute would have more than sufficed. "It's fine," I answered automatically.

"General, King Quinn sent me to fetch you immediately. There is an emergency above."

"Where is he?" I asked, my mind kicking into overdrive. What could be going wrong already? I hadn't been gone that long; surely nothing drastic could be happening that fast? Would I ever get a single second of not having a looming catastrophe over my head?

"The arena."

Just the place I wanted to go back to, where Burns had whipped me into unconsciousness. Nodding curtly, I threw my pack over my shoulder and hastily followed after him. We found Daniel standing with Colter and the other generals in deep conversation. They stopped the instant they saw me, and all but Daniel and Colter bowed.

Daniel winked at me. "General, so glad you've joined us."

"What's going on?" I inquired, noticing that Liam had slipped close to my side. If he thought he was going to be my new bodyguard, reality was soon going to visit him.

"There is a battalion of Imperialists headed into Etherdayle," Daniel started to say, but held up his hand to prevent me from interrupting, "and that isn't the worst part. They are following a group of refugees also headed our way."

"All our people are up there!" I yelled, my mind working frantically to come up with a plan.

"Ariel, the refugees who are coming—" Colter stepped closer and lowered his voice. "Samuel is leading them."

"Samuel," I whispered, my eyes imploring Colter to be lying. He was headed back, and he was in danger. Bowing my head, I forced air into my lungs. I hadn't expected him to return so soon. I had wanted time to distance myself, to bury the pain and forget he had ever existed.

He nodded, his fingers tucking under my chin and raising my head. "You were born to lead; now is not the time to panic, Ariel."

Yanking open my pack, I let it drop to my feet as I pulled out Isidora's map. My eyes scoured the page for the closest entrance. "Liam!"

He stepped forward with a sharp salute. "Yes?"

I handed the map to him and pointed to a tunnel we hadn't yet ventured into. "You see that tunnel? It should lead straight into the Great Library. You take five of your best men, you follow that tunnel, and you get our people down there as quickly as possible." He nodded sharply, grabbed the map, and took off at a run.

"General Spartz, I need you to gather all the Phoenixes and ready them for battle. We need to hold off that battalion." Saluting, he hurried away to do as I ordered.

"General Kai and General Gallagher, you need to stay here and keep our people calm. They are going to be confused and frightened when Liam brings them back. Keep things composed until I return."

"Daniel and Colter, you are with me." Kitty paced next to me as Starr came running up.

"I heard what was going on," she wheezed. "Here!" She had in her hands a long bow, arrows, and a shirt of chain mail that was feather light. "A gift from my ancestors," she whispered, pulling it over my head. "Be careful, my friend."

I leaned forward and hugged her tightly. "Be prepared for incoming wounded," I whispered into her hair. "I have a feeling today will not end the way we want it to."

Signaling her understanding, she took off towards her home. It took less than ten minutes for everyone to congregate and arm themselves for battle. I looked over them all in deep appreciation. "Today came sooner than I would have liked, but nonetheless it is here," I began, my voice carrying across the crowded arena. "Our goal is not to wipe out the battalion; we engage them only as long as it takes to get our people to safety. We hold them off, and when the horn sounds to retreat, you do so immediately. Is that understood?"

Fists hit their hearts in unison. "To the General!"

We made it off the mountain in record time, and the priests already had horses waiting for us. Father Eli stood with Aaleyah, his eyes shadowed. "They are coming."

I put a hand on his arm. "You and your order need to get underground. Titus will slaughter everyone who remains behind."

Eli shook his head in disagreement. "I belong here. Etherdayle is mine to protect."

"Don't argue with me, Father. You are needed to help shepherd our people. That means you get your priests to help guide everyone to the hills in safety." He looked ready to rebel, and my grip tightened. "Don't force me to have you escorted below, Father. Do as I say." Pulling Aaleyah's reins from his grasp, I swung up into the saddle.

"Colter." Instantly he was next to me. "You make sure to look after Samuel when you get Blessing below?"

He thumped his hand against his heart. "As soon as Blessing is safe, I'll get Samuel below."

Etherdayle was in chaos. People were screaming and rushing around in mad haste. I simply didn't have enough soldiers to deal with the number of people gathered. I had to admit that, when the people saw us riding through the city, most calmed down and listened to Liam and his men. I guess we were a comforting sight, proof someone was going to battle for them. I only hoped Liam was going to have enough time to get everyone below and the tunnel resealed.

Speeding through the streets, we were soon out under the arch, and the sight that met me had my heart thundering. At least a hundred people were running our way, and behind them were thousands upon thousands of Imperialist soldiers.

"Wehjaeel help us," I whispered.

I scanned the crowd desperately running towards us, and it was then I saw him.

Samuel.

CHAPTER XXX

My heart clenched as I nudged Aaleyah faster. Dodging the wave of fleeing refugees, I looped around them to cover the backside. The Phoenixes were close behind me, their war calls more terrifying than the red and orange paint covering their faces and arms. I heard Samuel scream my name, but I ignored his urgent calls.

With an arrow at the ready, I let it fly when I saw one of the lead Imperialists. Even before it smashed into his face, I was loading another arrow and shot it seconds before I was in the midst of enemy soldiers. Swinging the bow over my shoulder, I pulled out my blades and slashed any flesh they met. Aaleyah butted her way through the ranks, and soon I was deep in enemy territory without any friendlies in sight. Probably not one of my more shining moments.

Slamming my foot into a soldier's face, I sliced my knife through his neck and tried to move Aaleyah back towards the other Phoenixes. One of the soldiers grabbed for my leg and was rewarded with a hard bite from Kitty. So, I wasn't as alone as I previously thought. I was lost in a sea of blood that I couldn't escape. For every Imperialist I killed, ten more swarmed in to take his place.

I couldn't stop the scream that tore from my throat when a monster of a man ripped me off of Aaleyah. Smashing into the ground, I tried to gulp for air, but everything was spinning in wild circles. Raising my hands over my face, I waited for the fist that never connected. Kitty leapt over my prone form and ripped out the soldier's the throat.

Heaving against the bile in my own throat, I stumbled to my feet. My hands shook as yet another Imperialist advanced. Would they never stop coming? Aaleyah had backed up to protect my backside, and Kitty was pacing in front of me. Forcing myself to concentrate, I wiped the back of my hand against my mouth and eyed the next solider.

I could do this. I would survive.

"ARIEL!"

My head jerked to the left when I heard my name. I expected Daniel or Colter, but it was neither. His eyes scorched a path straight to my heart, and I wanted to hate him for it. "Samuel!" His face was pale with panic, and I had ceased to hear the words he was yelling. I had forgotten how magnetic his presence was; how had I hoped to resist him? What was it about him that drew me in? Would I never be able to free myself from his spell? What would it take to erase the way my heart pounded in response to him?

Kitty's tail knocked into my leg, demanding I return to the present and the encroaching soldiers. Raising my blades, I sneered and then launched into the fray with a coldness that scared me. It shouldn't be this easy to kill. I could tell myself that I was doing it for the greater good—that it was kill or be killed. Yet, no matter how I repeated the words in my head, it didn't ease the knot in my stomach.

Out of the corner of one eye, I watched Samuel fly off his mount and battle his way to my side. Kitty was making the biggest dent in our enemy's ranks; with his teeth and tail, he was taking down five at a time. Aaleyah continued to butt and kick, and it was enough to keep me from being overcome.

"ARIEL!"

Slamming my elbow into a nameless face, I used Kitty as a springboard and landed with an oomph next to Samuel. I didn't know what to say to him, nor did we have time for chit-chat. I momentarily froze, though, lost in his heated gaze. His hand hovered inches from me as he visibly debated what to do.

"You're an idiot," he finally whispered, crushing me to his chest.

I inhaled deeply, savoring his unique scent. How I had missed him! Choking against my desire, I pulled away. "You're a jerk," I mumbled, searching for incoming danger.

His laughter was a breath of fresh air. "At least we are on the same page."

That was the problem. I didn't want to be on his page; I needed to be as far away from him as possible. His eyes cloaked, and I had no chance to respond before his arm swept out and knocked me flat to the ground. He packed a nasty punch. I watched as his sword slammed into the incoming attacker's heart, and I had seconds to roll out of the way as the man fell.

Pitching to my feet, I slashed my way through the enemy lines in a wild frenzy. I fought until my arms burned and my eyes watered. Wiping the sweat and blood from my eyes, I kept pace with Samuel as he decimated any who dared step into our path of carnage. We fought easily next to each other in a deathly dance of slashes and parries. You would think we had rehearsed our movements and had been training together for years. Kitty circled around us, his roars rippling through the masses and spreading terror.

Hours. Minutes. Days. Seconds. I didn't know what time was anymore. My only thought was to hold them off until I heard the horn of Etherdayle. Just keep fighting. If I could only keep putting one step in front of another . . . Samuel's hand reached out to steady me. "Take it easy, Wildcat."

And how, precisely, did I do that? I was drenched in blood, and everywhere I turned was another enemy. I had yet to stumble across any of my own soldiers dead, and I dreaded the moment I did.

His fingers dug into my forearm as he yanked me closer to him. "Don't lose it, not yet," he yelled, shaking me the tiniest bit.

I already felt the nausea rising in my throat. This was just the beginning of the forces Titus would send against us. I thought I had been prepared to handle war, but if this was just a small taste, I wasn't sure I was at all. I could barely hold my daggers, my hands were shaking so badly.

His head lowered as his eyes bored into mine. "Stay with me," he ordered, thrusting his sword into a soldier to the side of us.

Kitty stalked to where we stood and nodded towards an opening in the mass of fighting; I could see Etherdayle in the distance. Hoisting me over a fallen Imperialist, Samuel took off at a run. This was an all-too-familiar feeling, being yanked behind him with death pursuing our steps. Kitty was hot on our trail, and I looked behind to see Aaleyah keeping pace. I'm not sure how Gabriel had done it, but they sure bred insanely intelligent horses.

The horn sounded just as we reached the edge of the ongoing battle. Liam had done it. I would never know how, but he had succeeded. Now to get my soldiers to safety. Phoenixes came flooding my way, and I smiled wearily.

We had done it.

We had faced Titus's might with courage, and we had made a difference.

There were so many citizens crowded in the lower arena that you couldn't breathe, much less move. We had tried to get everyone settled down, but it hadn't been an easy task. I squeezed through throngs of people looking for some familiar faces. I spotted Slade and Rowan first, and smiled in relief when I saw them huddling with Eliza and Marie. "Slade!" He grinned like a young child when he saw me.

"Ariel! You're safe!" He thumped me a couple times on the back, and I pulled the girls into hugs.

"For now. Where is Liv? And the children?" I asked, searching in vain for the young kids who had managed to weasel their way into my heart.

Rowan shifted uneasily. "We lost track of them."

How had they managed to lose track of them? They were all supposed to be together! If Logan had been around, they would have at least stayed together as a group. Of course, Logan wasn't around. He wasn't around because for some reason he had decided to join Titus. Gritting my teeth, I pressed on through the crowds. I needed to know that Liv and my kids were safe. And where in the world was Colter and Blessing? If he hadn't managed to find her in time, I would never forgive myself. A strong hand landed on my shoulder, and I tensed, ready to react with violence if necessary. I was weary to my bones and covered in filth. I craved a warm bath and clothes that weren't stained in blood—blood that served as a reminder of how many I had been forced to kill today.

"Ariel."

Turning slightly, I met Daniel's saddened gaze. "Daniel."

"Don't ever do that to me again," he said, pulling me around to face him. "Don't ever bust your way through enemy ranks with no back-up besides your demented gryphon."

Kitty growled at him, but I pushed his head away from Daniel's leg. I wasn't going to say I was sorry because, truth be told, I wasn't. I had done what needed to be done, and I would never regret that. We had managed to get everyone underground, and the only thing I was afraid to hear were the casualties. General Spartz had started a head count, but I figured it would take a little while for the results to come in. It wasn't exactly easy to locate anyone right now.

"Okay." The promise was hollow and he knew it.

"Have you lost your ever-lovin' mind?"

Oh, I had lost it some time ago, but no need to accentuate the point. "I'm alive," I answered wearily. "I'm in one piece, and next time I won't be so reckless." But I was so good at being reckless. Heading into things with no thought of consequences was a trait of mine that I never had learned to conquer.

He sighed and rubbed his hands over his face. "Why in the world you crashed into my life, I will never understand."

I produced a mirthless smile. "Oh, come on, admit it. The happiest day of your life was when I crashed into your life. You know that, or you wouldn't have made me head general."

"I made you captain of the Phoenixes because you are our best chance at survival, not because of your assumed lack of mortality," he corrected, his impatience still evident.

I didn't have time for this argument right now. "Please, later—"

Gripping my collar, he lifted me on my tip-toes. "We will have this discussion before the night is out," he demanded.

I wasn't lucky enough to avoid it. "Fine," I muttered, loosening his hold.

"Who are you looking for?" he asked, some of his anger dissipating.

Who wasn't I looking for? I remained silent, my jaw working in agitation at his interruption.

Sighing, he rubbed at his eyes. "After you find them, you know you'll need to make a public address?"

"I know." Everyone was terrified; they needed some assurance that everything was going to be all right. I had been going over and over in my head what to say, and I still couldn't quite figure it out. What was there to say, after all? Our world was going up in flames, and we had nothing to stop the spread of destruction?

His gaze went to his feet. "You're a natural leader, you know that? I don't regret putting you into the position I did." He peered down at me, his gaze earnest. "I just wanted you to know that."

"Thank you," I whispered, emotion clogging my throat. Regardless of what he felt about himself, that was high praise from a king.

"You're fearless—I don't think I've ever seen anything like it." His awe was noticeable, and I shifted my feet uncomfortably.

Biting down hard on my lip, I gathered my nerves. "It's not that I'm not afraid, Daniel," I said. "I just don't let that fear stop me from what needs to be done." And it wasn't always easy to shove that fear into a corner.

For example, when I noticed Samuel heading my way, I ducked around Daniel and disappeared into the crowd. I could be absolutely gutless at times, and I felt bad after glancing at Daniel's confused face. I would apologize later, without mentioning the name of the person I'd been avoiding . . .

As I worked my way through the crowd, I didn't manage to find anyone I knew—but Colter found me. The look on his face caused my heart to lurch to my toes. "Blessing?" I whispered.

He shook his head no. "You need to come with me."

If Blessing was unharmed, what would make Colter react the way he was doing now? I followed his lead as he pushed his way to the edge of the arena. "Colter?"

He scooped an arm around my waist and moved me in front of him to face what he so dreaded to show me. The world crumbled away when my eyes zeroed in on the still form Cadell was clutching. "No."

Woodenly, I walked forward and fell to my knees. "NO!" My fingers trembled as they reached forward to touch an ashen Hedia. "NO!" This couldn't be happening. Of all the people to be killed, a child? Hedia had been full of life, and as sassy as they come. Why her? Gulping for air, I didn't protest when Cadell flung himself at me. I held the sobbing boy with one arm as my hand hovered over Hedia.

Trembling, I closed my arms around Cadell, searching for some sense of comfort. His fingers seized my tunic, and it was a reminder I was alive. Tears filled my eyes, but they didn't fall. I wished they would. I wished I could have relief from the wailing inside of me. Liv pulled Cadell over to stand with the other children and herded them away. Dazed, I pulled Hedia into my arms and pressed a kiss against her forehead. The arrow that had been the cause of her death jutted from her heart in a grotesque reminder of what man could do. My fingers closed around the arrow and tore it from her chest. It snapped in my fingers, and I threw it away from me with a ragged scream. I was receiving a lot of sympathetic looks, but it didn't ease the raging in my chest.

"I'm sorry," I gasped. "I'm so sorry." I had failed her, and I didn't know how to come to terms with that. "Come back to us," I pleaded, forcing myself to breathe. "Give her back!"

But Hedia remained motionless, and Wehjaeel remained silent.

Why return me to life and not Hedia? Even at her young age, she had never faltered or lost faith. She had been a pillar of innocence and true courage. And this was how she was rewarded? It didn't make any sense.

Laying her back down, I gently reached over to close her eyes. "Safe travels, my princess."

Liam, Daniel, and Father Ira were at my back when I rose to my feet. Dry-eyed, I stared at them and tried to hide the growing emptiness in my heart. Colter stood with Kitty to the side of him, and I wondered what he would do if I hugged him. Kitty's head drooped as he walked over to lie across my feet.

"General, three Phoenixes are deceased, and two priests. Father Eli is the only one unaccounted for," Liam informed me, his eyes filled with pain.

My head swiveled to Father Ira. "He stayed above, then?"

Ira's eyes dipped. "I could not sway him."

I wondered if the man knew his noble intentions only injured us. He may consider himself a strong individual, but that thought would fly out the door as soon as they set about torturing him. I hoped the Father didn't know much besides the one entrance. I was sure Ira had tried his hardest to talk Eli out of his choice, but it wouldn't have done any good. No, when Eli made up his mind, he was stubborn as a mule. I would get him back—if he stayed alive long enough to give me the chance to retrieve him. "What does it look like above?"

Daniel clasped his hands behind his back. "They've been searching for the tunnel, but there is no way they will be able to breach it. After they get tired of searching, I don't know what they'll do next."

They would work on getting answers out of Eli, that's what. And when that didn't work, they would wait until the rabbit poked his head out of its hole. Etherdayle was going to become rubble, and that thought pricked at me. "Liam, cave in the entrance at the mausoleum—we don't know what all Burns told them," I ordered, my voice sounding hollow in my ears. He saluted and took off at a run. I wasn't sure how I got such a friend. Even the best of soldiers would have questioned that order, but not him. He had complete trust in me, and I wondered if, were I in his position, I could do the same.

Returning my attention to the remaining men, I singled out Father Ira. "Father, we'll do our best to retrieve Father Eli, but I can't send my men out until I know it isn't a suicide mission. He made his choice, and I won't risk lives until I know there is a strong possibility of success."

He looked ready to argue, but instead nodded regretfully.

"Also, make sure none of your other priests decide to play hero. You all stay put, am I clear?" It seemed wrong addressing a priest of Abisai in that manner, but I needed to make sure he or the others didn't do anything stupid. I heard him grit his teeth, and I knew I had pegged his intentions. "Father?"

"Yes, General," he mumbled, his turmoil evident.

Knowing that his reluctant agreement was as good as I was going to get, I switched my attention to Daniel. "We bury our dead tonight. Tomorrow—" I choked the smallest bit, "tomorrow we start our plan on how to avenge them."

I stood on the steps of Caedmon Hall, my head bowed and my hands tucked behind my back. Everyone sat in solemn silence waiting for me to say something spectacular—to comfort them, to assure them this wasn't the end for us. How did you pull words out of yourself when you weren't sure you believed them yourself? I now had close to two thousand people depending on me—and nothing positive to say to them. I couldn't really tell them that, by the end of this, more than likely most of us would be dead.

Daniel had encouraged me to be honest and speak the truth. But what if they weren't prepared for the truth? My fingers curled around the handkerchief from Samuel, and with new resolve I straightened. Lifting my head, I viewed them with a new fire sparking in my chest.

"I've struggled with what I could say to ease your fears." My voice carried through the crowd, and I was pleased it didn't wobble. "I wanted to say something packed with wisdom and assurances. But I haven't any of those words to offer you. I'm not immortal or all-knowing. I have fears and I know loss, and the last thing I want to be told is that it's all for a reason." Most were nodding in agreement, and it gave me the strength to plow on.

"There are no words to make this situation better. There is nothing one can say to erase the fact that we've lost our homes, family members, and friends. The truth is, for a while we will continue to lose that which we care about. I don't have everything figured out, and we are all just going to have to get cozy until we figure out living arrangements. Life for us is not going to get easier. But for now—we are safe. We will get our land back and reclaim our freedom."

A woman stood and pushed her way to the front. "You will stand for us?"

I was a lot of things, but a quitter was not one of them. "Or die trying." I wasn't trying to placate. I meant it when I said death would be the only way to stop me, and I had no intention of letting Titus Ephraim kill me.

"And what about everyone else?" Murmurs swept through the crowd, and I had a feeling this had been a massive topic of discussion. We were but a few; the majority of our people were still in very real danger.

"As many as want to follow me—I will find a way to get them safely down here. Our ancestors started up the hidden road for refugees during the Great War, so I see no reason we can't do the same thing."

Seemingly content with my answers, she sat back down. "I don't like to think of us as helpless refugees or people without a cause. As a Phoenix, I know it's important to have an identity—a purpose." I stopped, taking a deep breath, not sure of how my next words would be received. "Therefore, after some consideration, I've decided we'll be called the Lights of Gabriel—and we will tear Midas down around Titus's ears."

I was momentarily afraid the applause and cheers would bring the mountain down around our heads. One day we were going to be forgotten stories in history, and ancient lyrics in misplaced songs. But for now I was looking at the moments that made legends.

I was looking at the birth of a rebellion.

CHAPTER XXXI

With a sorrowful look, Starr closed her house door, affording me some privacy. I had only a few minutes before the scheduled funerals, and dread pooled in my stomach. Father Ira had agreed to speak, but it wasn't nerves that stretched me taut. No, it was the fact that within the hour Hedia would be forever gone. The ceremony would end, and we would all have to pull ourselves together and find a way to move on. Never forget, but nonetheless march on.

Stepping in front of Starr's mirror, I recoiled at the sight staring back at me. I didn't know her. Fingers shaking, I brushed the waves of hair away from my face. Who was I even looking at? I had started out as a child on this journey, and now I was an overcomer of impossible odds. My adolescent body had melted to reveal solid muscles, and my face had sharpened into the features of the kind of woman I never thought I would become. My eyes were full of a world my mother had hoped I would never experience.

I didn't want to know the person staring back at me.

Flinching, I hastily moved over to the washbasin and scrubbed off as much blood and grime as I could. The bowl filled with muddy water, and it was an ugly reminder of what had occurred. The rag splashed back into the bowl, flinging water in every direction. What was wrong with me?

I pulled on a black tunic and a pair of fitted pants, wishing the color was anything but black. Lacing up my boots, I tucked the keys back into place and pulled the pendent to rest on top of my tunic. Braiding my hair, I didn't regret that now parts of my tattoo were visible. There was no reason to hide who I was. A soft knock on the door, and I was yanked back to earth.

My brief reprieve was over.

Dirt crumbled through my fingers and landed with a deafening thump on the small grave. Kitty sat at my feet while eight children fanned out beside me.

"Do you think she's okay?" Cadell asked quietly.

"She's in Wehjaeel's land now, Cadell," I answered, my eyes on the marker bearing her name. "She's happy and safe." She was a whole lot safer than we were.

"Will we be okay?" Noah asked, his hand reaching up to clasp mine. "Or are we going to Wehjaeel's land, too?"

I ruffled my hand through his hair. "You're not making that trip yet, buddy."

"Do you think Hedia is lonely?"

I met Emily's tear-stained face with a wobbly smile. "No, I don't," I said. "You see, my brother Bryne is in Wehjaeel's land as well, and he will take good care of her."

That seemed to appease their fears. Kneeling, I gathered as many in my arms as I could. "For the next few days I need you to stay close to Liv, okay? You'll get to explore soon, but I need you to stay with her until things start to calm down. Can you guys do that?"

Everyone but Cadell nodded yes. "Cadell?" His bottom lip jutted out, and I was reminded how young he really was.

"I want to be with you."

"For the next few days I'm going to be pretty busy, and I won't be able to be with you guys as often as you'd like." Their terrified hands clutched at me. "I need you all to be brave for me." I took Cadell's hand and pulled him into the huddle. "And I need you to watch out for everyone when I'm not around."

"I want to be a soldier like you!" he cried.

"You are my soldier, buddy, and your post is here protecting your comrades."

His eyes lit up the tiniest bit. "One day I will be as good a soldier as you."

I smiled. "One day you'll be an even better soldier than me." Because he would follow orders a whole lot better than I ever did.

We stayed for a while longer at Hedia's grave before Liv came to retrieve us. She leaned her head against mine as we watched the kids troop out of the small graveyard. I think Hedia would have been honored to be placed with the other deceased Phoenixes.

"Her death wasn't your fault, Ariel," she said, her voice hushed.

"She was just a child, Liv. Who kills children?" Who could shoot a little girl in the heart and not even pause? How brainwashed did you have to be to commit such an atrocity?

"We aren't fighting people like us. Titus has dehumanized those boys until they desire nothing but blood. That's the difference between you and them—you kill in self-defense and for freedom. They kill because they enjoy it."

"How do you go about fighting that kind of brutality? That senseless killing?" I asked, turning to walk with her. I closed the gate behind us and cringed at the finality of the snap.

She was truly gone, and we were all a little poorer for it.

"All I have to say is at least his champion hasn't made an appearance yet. That is one fight I don't want to see you get into."

Small blessings. There was always a small blessing mixed in with the bad. Which was a good thing, because we were going to need a whole lot of those blessings to start adding up. For example, if the champion never showed up, that would be more than okay with me.

Liv spoke up again, interrupting my ponderings. "Samuel's been looking for you. He seems to be getting the notion that you are avoiding him."

"Now, where would he get that idea?" It shouldn't be that hard to figure out that I didn't want to talk to him. It's not like we parted under the best of circumstances. What made him think I ever wanted to hear another word that came out of his mouth?

"You have some people to face, Ariel. Get it done and you'll feel like you can breathe again."

Confronting Samuel wasn't going to lift the weight off my heart. Nothing could fix the longing or hurt that twisted through me every time I looked at him. Those feelings wouldn't soon go away—if they ever did at all. I was going to have to learn to bury them deep because, like it or not, Samuel was an invaluable fighter. And let's face it: I needed all the warriors I could get.

"I no longer know what it's like to breathe without feeling like I'm swallowing glass," I answered truthfully. "I don't know what sleep is, or what life was like before all of this. I live trapped in the moment I found my home on fire, and I don't think I will ever escape it."

"You give so much hope selflessly to others; why can't you believe you have a future beyond this war?" she asked, her face puzzled.

I didn't like to think of a future beyond the moment Titus was vanquished. If I was forced to be honest, I had a feeling this war was going to cost me my life.

And it hurt to dream of what I knew could never be and of the man I could never possess.

The Generals were gathered in Caedmon Hall awaiting my arrival. Nolan didn't meet my gaze, and I resolved to talk to him after the meeting. Daniel walked in behind me and offered me a salute and teasing wink.

"Sorry I'm late, General."

Rolling my eyes at him, I had to bite down on my tongue to keep from sticking it out. We both took a seat, and I nearly laughed at all the expectant faces. What kind of miracle did they expect me to offer? "How is the situation above?" I inquired, keeping my voice brisk and my face expressionless. I wasn't sure how these gentlemen were going to like taking orders from a girl at least two decades younger than themselves.

General Kai, the one I least expected to speak up, nodded at me approvingly. "Our scouts say it appears the Imperialists are setting up some kind of blockade. They haven't found our tunnels yet, but it is probably only a matter of time. Several of their men have started to venture closer to Mount Algernon."

Leaning forward, I clasped my hands together. "Liam informs me that the tunnels are sufficiently blocked; even if they manage to find the entrances, they won't get more than a few centimeters in our direction."

Spartz sighed loudly. "Meanwhile we are trapped, and supplies will not last long with this number of people."

I smiled tightly. "I said two tunnels had been blocked, not all of them. We are far from trapped."

Nolan shifted in his seat, his interest piqued. "What do you mean?"

Pulling Isidora's map from my tunic, I unrolled it and placed it on the table. "I mean, a friend of mine has given us an instrumental weapon of defense."

Kai reached for the map but paused, the tips of his fingers brushing against the soft leather. "May I?"

I nodded and he pulled the map in front of him. "Incredible." He passed it to Spartz, his eyes blazing with excitement.

"This opens a whole new possibility in re-starting the Hidden Road," Spartz exclaimed, his fingers tapping with an energy I had never before seen in him.

"Food? Enough room to put everybody?" Nolan asked, still hesitant about what I was proposing.

"I have already sent Liam and some of his men on an exploration mission. We know the Hollow Hills extend almost the full length of the realms; we've just never bothered to search past our small corner. As soon as we know the territory a bit, we can spread the people out so we aren't so cramped." My fingers tapped against my leg. "We will set up hunting parties for our meat supply, and I've already talked to Starr Stormer about starting a garden in the Shade."

"That is a dangerous place to set up our food source," Daniel interjected, his eyes-brows furrowing in doubt.

"It can be," I agreed. "However, it is unlikely to be discovered by Imperialists, and if we keep to the edge, we shouldn't have many problems with the Shade's unique inhabitants." I had thought through a lot of things, and I was pretty confident of the path we needed to take.

Dwarves had survived down here for centuries; we could do the same if need be.

"So," Daniel asked, "what do our next few steps look like?"

"With Starr and Liam already at work, our immediate issues will be resolved shortly. We need to get the Hidden Road up and running as soon as possible. Which means some of our Phoenixes are going to have to relocate above ground to shuffle people down to us. I am going to select a few to come with me—I have unfinished business above that needs to be taken care of immediately, before it is too late. Our monarchs deserve to be found, and I don't intend to let Titus get to them first."

Nolan's eyes shot to mine. "You are leaving us?"

"My trips will be short; none of us can risk long periods of exposure above. Once I find a monarch, I will personally return with him or her and make sure everything is running fine down here. While I am gone, Daniel will of course be in command." Daniel was our king, and our people needed to start seeing that.

"There will be no speedy end to this, will there?" Spartz asked, already knowing the answer.

I shook my head slowly. "I think we should be prepared to dig in, for this is just the beginning."

"A war is brewing," Kai spoke softly, "one more devastating than the Great War itself. We have no idea of what is yet to come."

Oh, I had an idea. It just wasn't a pretty one. If Titus got ahold of the Shara'han, we would be in more than just a little trouble. "We will defend what is ours," I said, enunciating every syllable with conviction. "And if Titus wants a war—well then, we'll give him one."

"Nolan," I called, preventing him from leaving when everyone else filtered from the room. He hesitated before plopping back into his chair. He wouldn't bother to look at me, and I almost preferred that he just haul off and slap me. "Nolan—"

His heavy sigh echoed through the room. "I don't blame you, Ariel, for the loss of my son. I don't." He looked up at me, his eyes watering. "Even as a child, there was always a darkness in him that I couldn't understand."

My head tilted in confusion. There was something very odd about this conversation.

"When he was of age, the council asked me if I wanted to initiate him, and I said no." He wheezed for air. "I didn't say no to protect him from the uncertainty of this life, I said no to protect us from him."

I cringed at his calloused words. I had known Logan better than he possibly could have, and never before had I sensed this darkness he was now talking about. Logan may be a lot of things, but evil? "I will find him."

Nolan's eyes finally connected with mine. "That is precisely what I am afraid of."

I didn't understand what was going on. I had thought he was angry with me, and then this? "I think you are mistaken about Logan." He had to be, because I refused to admit that Logan was lost to me.

His fingers curled into fists. "And where is he right now, Ariel?" He didn't wait for me to gather an answer. "With the heart of darkness itself."

I was conflicted between wanting to defend Logan or agree wholeheartedly with Nolan's words. "You aren't angry with me, then?"

Nolan stood, walked over, and knelt next to my chair. "No my dear girl. I am afraid for you."

He was a contradiction I'm not sure I would ever understand. "Logan isn't evil, Nolan. Maybe confused—"

Harsh laughter erupted from him. "The Logan you think you knew died long ago, and it rests on my head for not warning you." Rising to his feet, he kissed my forehead. "I will follow you until the end, Ariel Deverell. Remember that."

Kitty squeezed out from under the table after Nolan left. "You going to change back yet?" His tail thwacked against the floor a couple of times before he ambled away. I heard a pop and blinked against the encroaching smoke. Hiding my grin, I stared at the dog that trotted back. He may be almost as big as a bear, but he was a comforting sight. "Now there's my Kitty."

CHAPTER XXXII

With Kitty on my heels, I slipped from sight and began to follow Isidora's map to the surface. There was a tunnel that opened up in the Shade near where she should be. I wasn't going to allow myself a day of rest until I knew the fate of Isidora Emaggen and the other gryphon. A low whine stopped me mid-stride. "Kitty?" He leaned against me, tail drooping. "It's better to know than to constantly wonder," I murmured, stroking his head.

I followed the tunnel for a good five miles, some places so tight I had to hold my breath to squeeze through. I was afraid I was going to have to leave Kitty behind, but he always managed to squeak through with an agitated rumble. We came to a flight of stone steps curling upwards, and we had to climb five flights all the while avoiding the sagging spots. When we reached the top, I was met with a door made of something entirely unfamiliar. It was pure gold and shimmered when I touched it. Dwarf magic? Shrugging, I looked down at my companion. "Here goes nothing."

I kept my hands in front of me as I walked forward. It felt like I was walking on clouds and, before I could blink, I was standing in the Shade. Looking backwards, I stared at a looming Grenifur tree that appeared no different from the trees beside it. "Amazing," I whispered. Dwarves and their creations would never cease to astound me.

Memorizing my surroundings, I allowed Kitty to lead the way to his previous home. I half expected the mansion to have disappeared like a long-forgotten dream, but it was still there. It was even more splendid than I remembered, and my memory of the place didn't do it justice.

Kitty's growl tore through the air, and, with a horrible sense of foreboding, I looked to where he was glaring. "Samuel." He sat on the stairs, his arms casually draped over his legs. He lifted his head, and I wanted to stagger away from his mesmerizing stare.

"I wondered how long it would take you to show up." His voice sounded raspy, and if I was judging correctly, he was exhausted.

He looked endearing and huggable. I shifted, hating myself. He was meaningless. Nothing. A fellow warrior and *nothing* more. "How did you know I would come back here?"

His lips lifted in a brief smile. "You don't leave anything unfinished." He rolled his shoulders and leaned back against the steps behind him. "And since your intent seemed to be to avoid me, I decided I would wait here until you showed up."

What a smug, arrogant, annoying waste of a man! Rolling my eyes, I looked away from him. I had the worst luck in the entire world.

"We need to talk."

"No," I snapped. "No, we absolutely do not. There is nothing to be said, and I'm positive there's nothing I want to hear."

Out of the corner of my eye, I watched him prop his chin on his fist and just stare at me. "I said some things I didn't mean, and I would just like to clear—"

"I think," I said slowly, facing him, "that you made your feelings quite clear. I didn't come to hash things out with you. I came to find Isidora."

"She's not here. There is no sign of her or the other gryphon," he answered simply, undeterred.

I didn't know whether to sigh with relief that I wasn't coming to find corpses, or worry that she had abandoned her post. Licking my lips, I rocked back on my heels and debated if I could outrun him. I may be a coward, but this was one conversation I really didn't want to have. I hadn't even gotten to have a relationship with him, and already I was going to hear the it-isn't-you-it's-me line.

"I'm faster than you, Wildcat," he murmured, his eyes roving over my face.

I hated how he read my mind. In fact, I hated him. Why was it that, of all the people in the realms, it had to be him who truly knew me?

"Ariel, please?"

His voice was imploring, and I made myself stay rooted to the ground. Besides that, it had to be one of the first times I had ever heard him use the word please. Not bothering to agree vocally, I rested my hand on Kitty's head and tried to draw strength from him.

"You aren't making this any easier, Wildcat," he whispered.

"Should I?" I inquired, my gaze sharpening. "Why, precisely, should I make things *easier?*" I was a woman, after all. Since when did we make matters of the heart anything but disasters?

He jerked to his feet, his jaw clenching back words I knew he wanted to scream. "I'm sorry, Ariel. I'm sorry I ever left you, and, more importantly, I'm sorry for what I said." He dragged his fingers through his lengthening hair. "You drive me nuts, you know that? I just can't seem to get enough of you, and I know I shouldn't want you the way I do!"

My body responded as if it had been doused in fire. My mind whirled as it tried to catch up with what he was telling me. "Samuel—"

He ate up the distance between us in a few long-legged strides. His hands landed on my forearms as he brought me toe to toe with him. "You have managed to fill up every inch of me, and brought back to life a heart I thought would never function again. You, Ariel, *you* did that. You will forever be the only one I desire, and the only one I can never have."

Tears filmed my gaze as I blinked up at him. How could words be so wonderful and heartbreaking at the same time?

"I want to come back to you," he whispered, his forehead leaning down to rest against mine.

My heart hitched as our shallow breaths mingled. "Samuel," I whispered in return, all my agony pouring into that one name.

"I want to once again be by your side, protecting you. But I need you to be willing to accept that I can't give you parts of myself—that I can never share my past." His fingers tightened. "I swear; I am only protecting you. Please, let me be by your side," he pleaded, drawing me closer. "At least let me do that."

My eyelids fluttered closed as I fought to gain control of myself. No heart should have to suffer what mine was currently going through. How was it possible to want one person so badly?

"Please," he begged, his thumb reaching up to graze my cheek. "Please, let me at least be by your side."

His other hand reached up to cup my face, and my mind tipped in dizzying circles. Could I accept that? Never having any answers, and day in and day out being forced to be next to someone I so desperately wanted?

Could I stand knowing that I loved a man who I would one day lose?

Tipping my head back, I tried to hide the feelings I knew were blazing out of my eyes. "Promise me you won't leave me until there is no other choice?"

His head bent down to press a soft kiss against the underside of my jaw. His lips drifted to my ear. "I promise you, I won't ever let go."

How would we ever walk away from each other? We stood on a precipice, and I only hoped the wind didn't tip us the wrong way. We had to stay away from each other, and yet we couldn't stand being apart.

We sat on the steps in silence, watching the sun go down. Our shoulders were brushing, but that was the only contact we had. It was best not to get used to any sort of proximity with each other.

"Do you think I can do this?" I asked quietly, petting Kitty.

"I think you have already severely crippled his hold on the realms, and you've only begun," he stated honestly. "He should be terrified of the damage you are about to do to him."

"To Midas then?"

His hand reached over to enfold mine. "To Midas."

Until Next Time—Be Fearless

ACKNOWLEDGMENTS

It would be impossible to fully express my appreciation to all who contributed to this book. The completion of a novel is not a one-person job, and it took a lot of people for it to arrive where it is today. I may have written the words of Ariel's journey, but it was with help that it truly began to shine.

Starting with my parents, for they put up with the most grief! There were nights I disappeared until past midnight because the inspiration struck, and days where I would stare at them blankly as I tried to figure out where my story was going next. They encouraged me when I rocked back and forth in the corner, trying to figure out how I was financially going to accomplish self-publishing. They dealt with my incessant rambling about plot, characters, and places when they had no idea what I was talking about. I love and appreciate you guys; thanks for believing in my dream with me.

As for my faithful readers—Ashley Jakes, Chris Carlson, Chris Depuy, Rebecca Jaquith, and Steve Turner—thank you for all the input and love you put into my story! A special thanks to Jennifer Manson; there isn't another soul like you! You were there for me night and day; you let me whine and complain when I didn't feel like writing another word; and then you would promptly tell me get back to work because you wanted another chapter. You read faithfully, and were enthusiastic. You celebrated, laughed, cried, and ate ice cream through my worst moments. Thanks for being you, and for helping me achieve the unthinkable. Also, Adrienne Manson—you were my steadfast cheerleader and go-getter. If you knew I needed something, you'd make sure it happened. You had faith in me and reviewed title ideas for me for weeks as I tried to find just the perfect one. You sent me pictures to inspire me, and were always ready with a smile. Thank you for being you. I couldn't dream of a better friend.

I want to thank *all* my friends and family members who contributed and cheered me on. I would never have gotten here without you.

And lastly, a special thanks to Chris Nordquist. This story would not be what it is today without you. I will never be able to tell you how blessed I am that you agreed to be my editor. You didn't run for cover when I told you, no matter how hard you tried to convince me otherwise, that I would never understand where all I needed to put commas. You had a true enthusiasm and love for my story, and you wanted it to succeed just as much as I did. You cheered me on and put a lot of love, sweat, and tears into this book. You will never understand how much I appreciate what miracles you worked with my manuscript. I hope this is the first of many projects together—for it has been the start to a wonderful friendship.